John Hart

John Hart was born in 1965 and spends his time in North Carolina and Virginia. He has degrees in French, accounting and law, and worked as a banker, stockbroker and attorney before beginning his writing career. His first three novels, *The King of Lies*, *Down River* and *The Last Child* have all been international bestsellers.

Praise for
THE LAST CHILD

'Just once in a while a thriller comes along that makes you want to run out in the street and proclaim how good it is. John Hart's third novel is one of those. Written with power, precision and an iron grip on character it makes him out as one of the outstanding talents of his generation . . . it grips you by the throat and never lets go'
Daily Mail

'A gripping thriller that will have you on the edge of your seat'
Sun

'John Hart is already much praised, but his third and most complex psychological thriller is a risk which has paid off with that same unshakeable sense of discovery. The risk lay in the rarely attempted feat of writing a convincing child hero for adults. His success injects extra poignancy into an already compelling blend of southern gothic mock-epic, outright horror and dues-paying whodunit. This one stays with you'
Daily Telegraph

'Hart tackles the sensitive subject of child abuse head on and gets the tone right, making for a compelling thriller which will keep you guessing'   *News of the World*

'Hart is still far too young for *The Last Child* to be called a crowning achievement, but the novel's ambition, emotional breadth and maturity make it an early masterpiece in a career that continues to promise great things'
Washington Post

'I absolutely love this man's writing, and by that I mean all aspects of it: plotting, characterization and its lyrical quality . . . John Hart has joined the highest ranks of crime fiction writing. Thank heavens he's a young man so we'll have his novels to enjoy for many years to come'
Deadly Pleasures

ALSO BY JOHN HART

The King of Lies
Down River
The Last Child

IRON HOUSE

JOHN HART

JOHN MURRAY

First published in Great Britain in 2011 by John Murray (Publishers)
An Hachette UK Company

1

A CIP catalogue record for this title is available from the British Library

ISBN 978-1-84854-179-5
Ebook ISBN 978-1-84854-350-8

Printed and bound by Clays Ltd, St Ives plc

John Murray policy is to use papers that are natural, renewable and recyclable products and made from wood grown in sustainable forests. The logging and manufacturing processes are expected to conform to the environmental regulations of the country of origin.

John Murray (Publishers)
338 Euston Road
London NW1 3BH.

www.johnmurray.co.uk

For
Pete Wolverton
and
Matthew Shear

Trees thrashed in the storm, their trunks hard and black and rough as stone, their limbs bent beneath the weight of snow. It was dark out, night. Between the trunks, a boy ran and fell and ran again. Snow melted against the heat of his body, soaked his clothing then froze solid. His world was black and white, except where it was red.

On his hands and under his nails.

Frozen to the blade of a knife no child should own.

For one instant the clouds tore, then darkness came complete and an iron trunk bloodied the boy's nose as he struck a tree and fell again. He pulled himself up and ran through snow that piled to his knees, his waist. Branches caught his hair, tore skin. Light speared out far behind, and the sound of pursuit welled like breath in the forest's throat.

Long howls on the bitter wind . . .

Dogs beyond the ridge . . .

CHAPTER ONE

Michael woke reaching for the gun he no longer kept by the bed. His fingers slid over bare wood, and he sat, instantly awake, his skin slick with sweat and the memory of ice. There was no movement in the apartment, no sounds beyond those of the city. The woman beside him rustled in the warm tangle of their sheets, and her hand found the hard curve of his shoulder. "You okay, sweetheart?"

Weak light filtered through the curtains, the open window, and he kept his body turned so she could not see the boy that lingered in his eyes, the stain of hurt so deep she had yet to find it. "Bad dream, baby." His fingers found the swell of her hip. "Go back to sleep."

"You sure?" The pillow muffled her voice.

"Of course."

"I love you," she said, and was gone.

Michael watched her fade, and then put his feet on the floor. He touched old scars left by frostbite, the dead places on his palms and at the tips of three fingers. He rubbed his hands together, and then tilted them in the light. The palms were broad, the fingers long and tapered.

A pianist's fingers, Elena often said.

Thick and scarred. He would shake his head.

The hands of an artist . . .

She liked to say things like that, the talk of an optimist and dreamer. Michael flexed his fingers, and heard the sound of her words in his head, the lilt of her accent, and for that instant he felt ashamed. Many things had come through the use of his hands, but creation was not one of them. He stood and rolled his shoulders as New York solidified

3

around him: Elena's apartment, the smell of recent rain on hot pavement. He pulled on jeans and glanced at the open window. Night was a dark hand on the city, its skin not yet veined with gray. He looked down on Elena's face and found it pale in the gloom, soft and creased with sleep. She lay unmoving in the bed they shared, her shoulder warm when he laid two fingers on it. Outside, the city grew as dark and still as it ever got, the quiet pause at the bottom of a breath. He moved hair from her face, and at her temple saw the thread of her life, steady and strong. He wanted to touch that pulse, to assure himself of its strength and endurance. An old man was dying, and when he was dead, they would come for Michael; and they would come for her, to make Michael hurt. Elena knew none of this, neither the things of which he was capable nor the danger he'd brought to her door; but Michael would go to hell to keep her safe.

Go to hell.

Come back burning.

That was truth. That was real.

He studied her face in the dim light, the smooth skin and full, parted lips, the black hair that ran in waves to her shoulder then broke like surf. She shifted in her sleep, and Michael felt a moment's bleakness stir, a familiar certainty that it would get worse before it got better. Since he was a boy, violence had trailed him like a scent. Now, it had found her, too. For an instant, he thought again that he should leave her, just take his problems and disappear. He'd tried before, of course, not one time but a hundred. Yet, with each failed attempt, the certainty had only grown stronger.

He could not live without her.

He could make it work.

Michael dragged fingers through his hair, and wondered again how it had come to this place. How had things gone so sour so fast?

Moving to the window, he flicked the curtain enough to see down into the alley. The car was still there, black and low in the far shadows. Distant lamplight starred the windshield so that he could not see past the glass, but he knew at least one of the men who sat inside. His presence was a threat, and it angered Michael beyond words. He'd made his bargain with the old man, and expected the deal to be honored. Words still mattered to Michael.

Promises.

Rules of conduct.

He looked a last time at Elena, then eased two silenced forty-fives from the place he kept them hidden. They were cool to the touch, familiar in his hands. He checked the loads and a frown bent his face as he turned from the woman he loved. He was supposed to be beyond this, supposed to be free. He thought once more of the man in the black car.

Eight days ago they'd been brothers.

Michael was at the door and almost out when Elena said his name. He paused for a moment, then lay the guns down and slipped back into the bedroom. She'd shifted onto her back and one arm was half-raised. "Michael . . ."

The name was a smile on her lips, and he wondered if she was dreaming. She shifted and a warm-bed smell rose in the room. It carried the scent of her skin and of clean hair. It was the smell of home and the future, the promise of a different life. Michael hesitated, then took her hand as she said, "Come back to bed."

He looked into the kitchen, where he'd left the guns next to a can of yellow paint. Her voice had come as a whisper, and he knew that if he left, she would ride the slope back into sleep and not remember. He could slip outside and do the thing he did well. Killing them would likely escalate matters, and others would certainly take their place; but maybe the message would serve its purpose.

And maybe not.

His gaze traveled from Elena to the window. The night outside was just as black, its skin stretched tight. The car was still there, as it had been the night before and the night before that. They would not move against him until the old man died, but they wanted to rattle him. They wanted to push, and every part of Michael wanted to push back. He took a slow breath and thought of the man he desired to be. Elena was here, beside him, and violence had no place in the world they wished to make. But he was a realist first, so that when her fingers flexed on his, his thoughts were not just of hope, but of retribution and deterrence. An old poem rose in his mind.

Two roads diverged in a yellow wood . . .

Michael stood at a crossroad, and it all came down to choice. Go back to bed or pick up the guns. Elena or the alley. The future or the past.

Elena squeezed his hand again. "Love me, baby," she said, and that's what he chose.

Life over death.

The road less traveled.

The New York dawn came scorching hot. The guns were hidden and Elena still slept. Michael sat with his feet on the windowsill and stared down into the empty alleyway. They'd left at around five, backed from the alley and sounded a single blow of their horn as the sightlines collapsed. If their goal had been to wake or scare him, they'd failed miserably. He'd been out of the bed since three and felt great. Michael studied his fingertips, where flecks of yellow paint stained them.

"What are you smiling at, gorgeous?" Her voice surprised him and he turned. Elena sat up in bed, languorous, and pushed long, black hair from her face. The sheet fell to her waist and Michael put his feet on the floor, embarrassed to be caught in a moment of such open joy.

"Just thinking of something," he said.

"Of me?"

"Of course."

"Liar."

She was smiling, skin still creased. Her back arched as she stretched, her small hands fisted white. "You want coffee?" Michael asked.

She fell back against the pillows, made a contented sound, and said, "You are a magnificent creature."

"Give me a minute." In the kitchen, Michael poured warm milk in a mug, then coffee. Half and half, the way she liked it. Café au lait. Very French. When he came back, he found her in one of his shirts, sleeves rolled loosely on her narrow arms. He handed her the coffee. "Good dreams?"

She nodded and a glint sparked in her eyes. "One in particular seemed very real."

"Did it?"

She sank into the bed and made the same contented noise. "One of these days I'm actually going to wake up before you."

Michael sat on the edge of the bed and put a hand on the arch of her foot. "Sure you will, baby." Elena was a late sleeper, and Michael rarely managed more than five hours a night. Her climbing from bed before him was a near impossibility. He watched her sip coffee, and reminded himself to notice the small things about her: the clear polish she preferred on her nails, the length of her legs, the tiny scar on her cheek that was her skin's only imperfection. She had black eyebrows, eyes that were brown but could look like honey in a certain light. She was lithe and strong, a beautiful woman in every respect, but that's not what Michael admired most. Elena took joy in the most insignificant things: how it felt to slip between cool sheets or taste new foods, the moment's anticipation each time she opened the door to step outside. She had faith that each moment would be finer than the last. She believed that people were good, which made her a dash of color in a world blown white.

She sipped again, and Michael saw the exact moment she noticed the paint on his hands. A small crease appeared between her brows. The cup came away from her lips. "Did you paint it already?"

She tried to sound angry but failed, and as he shrugged an answer to the question he could not keep the smile from touching every part of his face. She'd envisioned them painting it together—laughter, spilled paint—but Michael couldn't help it. "Too excited," he said, and thought of the fresh yellow paint on the walls of the tiny room down the hall. They called it a second bedroom, but it was not much larger than a walk-in closet. A high, narrow window was paned with rippled glass. Afternoon light would make the yellow glow like gold.

She put the coffee down and pushed back against the bare wall behind her. Her knees tented the sheet, and she said, "Come back to bed. I'll make you breakfast."

"Too late." Michael rose and went back into the kitchen. He had flowers in a small vase. The fruit was already cut, juice poured. He added fresh pastry and carried in the tray.

"Breakfast in bed?"

Michael hesitated, almost overwhelmed. "Happy Mother's Day," he finally managed.

"It's not . . ." She paused, and then got it.

Yesterday, she'd told him she was pregnant.

Eleven weeks.

They stayed in bed for most of the morning—reading, talking—then Michael walked Elena to work in time to get ready for the lunch crowd. She wore a small black dress that accented her tan skin and dark eyes. In heels, she stood five-seven and moved like a dancer, so elegant that beside her Michael looked angular and rough, out of place in jeans, heavy boots, and a worn T-shirt. But this was how Elena knew him: rough and poor, an interrupted student still hoping for a way back to school.

That was the lie that started everything.

They'd met seven months ago on a corner near NYU. Dressed to blend in and carrying heavy, Michael was on a job and had no business talking to pretty women, but when the wind took her scarf, he caught it on instinct and gave it back with a flourish that surprised him. Even now, he had no idea where it came from, that sudden lightness, but she laughed at the moment, and when he asked, she gave him her name.

Carmen Elena Del Portal.

Call me Elena.

She'd said it with amusement on her lips and a fire in her eyes. He remembered dry fingers and frank appraisal in her glance, an accent that bordered on Spanish. She'd tucked an unruly strand of hair behind her right ear and waited with a reckless smile for Michael to offer his name in return. He almost left, but did not. It was the warmth in her, the utter lack of fear or doubt. So, at two fifteen on a Tuesday, against everything he'd ever been taught, Michael gave her his name.

His real one.

The scarf was silk, and very light to land with such force on two lives. It led to coffee, then more, until emotion came in its wildness, and the coming found him unprepared. Now here he was, in love with a woman who thought she knew him, but did not. Michael was trying to change, but killing was easy. And quitting was hard.

Halfway to work, she took his hand. "Boy or girl?"

"What?" It was the kind of thing normal people asked, and Michael was dumbfounded by the question. He stopped walking, so that people veered around them. She tilted her head.

"Do you hope it's a boy or a girl?"

Her eyes shone with the kind of contentment he'd only read about in books; and looking at her then was like looking at her on the first day they'd met, only more so. The air held the same blue charge, the same sense of light and purpose. When Michael spoke, the words came from the deepest part of him. "Will you marry me?"

She laughed. "Just like that?"

"Yes."

She put a palm on Michael's cheek, and the laughter dwindled. "No, Michael. I won't marry you."

"Because?"

"Because you're asking me for the wrong reasons. And because we have time." She kissed him. "Lots of time."

That's where she was wrong.

Elena worked as the hostess for an expensive restaurant called Chez Pascal. She was beautiful, spoke three languages, and at her request, the owner had hired Michael, eight days ago, to wash dishes. Michael told her that he'd lost his other job, that he needed to fill the days before he found a new one or the student loan finally came through, but there was no other job, no student loan, just two more lies in a sea of thousands. But Michael needed to be there, for while no one would dare touch him while the old man breathed, Elena was under no such protection. They'd kill her for the fun of it.

Two blocks from the restaurant, Michael said, "Have you told your family?"

"That I'm pregnant?"

"Yes."

"No." Emotion colored her voice—sadness and something dark.

Michael knew that Elena had family in Spain, but she rarely spoke of them. She had no photographs, no letters. Someone had called once, but Elena hung up when Michael gave her the phone; the next day, she changed the number. Michael never pushed for answers, not about family or the past. They walked in silence for several minutes. A block later, she took his hand. "Kiss me," she said, and Michael did. When it was done, Elena said, "You're my family."

At the restaurant door, a blue awning offered narrow shade. Michael was slightly in front, so he saw the damage to the door in time to turn Elena before she saw it, too. But even with his back to the door, the image stayed in his mind: splintered wood, shards of white that rose from the mahogany stain. The grouping was head-high and tight, four bullet holes in a three-inch circle, and Michael could see how it went down. A black car at the curb, gun silenced. From Elena's apartment, the drive was less than six minutes, so it probably happened just after five this morning. Empty streets. Nobody around. Small caliber, Michael guessed, something light and accurate. A twenty-two, maybe a twenty-five. He leaned against the door and felt splinters through his shirt, a cold rage behind his eyes. He took Elena's hand and said, "If I asked you to move away from New York, would you do it?"

"My job is here. Our lives . . ."

"If I had to go," he tried again, "would you come with me?"

"This is our home. This is where I want to raise our child . . ." She stopped, and understanding moved in her face. "Lots of people raise babies in the city . . ."

She knew of his distrust for the city, and he looked away because the weight of lies was becoming too much. He could stay here and risk the war that was coming, or he could share the truth and lose her. "Listen," he said, "I'm going to be late today. Tell Paul for me." Paul owned the restaurant. He parked in the alley, and had probably not seen the door.

"You're not coming in?"

"I can't right now."

"I got you this job, Michael." A spark of rare anger.

Michael showed the palm of his hand, and said, "May I have your keys?"

Unhappy, she gave him the set Paul let her use. He opened the restaurant door and held it for her. "Where are you going?" she asked.

Her face was upturned and still angry. Michael wanted to touch her cheek and say that he would kill or die to keep her safe. That he would burn the city down. "I'll be back," he told her. "Just stay in the restaurant."

"You're being very mysterious."

"I have to do something," he replied. "For the baby."

"Really?"

He placed his hand on the plane of her stomach and pictured the many violent ways this day could end. "Really," he said.

And that was truth.

CHAPTER TWO

There comes a time. Michael did not know how long the words had been there, but they ran through his head as he walked, a refrain timed to the sound of his shoes on concrete. He'd tried to do it right and respectful. He'd tried to be nice.

But there comes a time.

Michael hailed a cab and gave the driver an address in Alphabet City. When they arrived, he pushed a fifty through the glass and told the man to wait.

Michael's apartment was a third-floor walk-up with two bedrooms, bars on the windows, and a reinforced steel door. Elena had never been there, and he planned to keep it that way. The second bedroom closet held rifles and handguns, body armor, and stacks of cash. There was a long shelf of knives and edged projectiles, neat coils of shiny wire. Things that might be difficult to explain.

Michael disengaged the alarm and crossed the large living room. Tall windows let in midday light, but he ignored the things it touched: the wall of books, the fine furnishings and original art. He made for the short hall at the back, walked past the room that held his gear and into the bedroom beyond. The bed was large, but clean-lined and spartan, and on the dresser sat the only photograph he owned. Pressed between glass, faded and cracked, the picture was of two boys in a snowy field splotched with mud. Not sure that he would ever see the apartment again, Michael slipped the photograph from its frame and carried it with him to the closet. It was the only thing he owned that really mattered.

At the closet door, Michael stripped out of his clothes and left them in a heap. From a long cedar rack he selected a pair of hand-tooled English shoes, then a custom suit from a row of twenty. The suit was English, too, as were the shirts. He slipped into a cream-colored one and a tie dark enough to mirror the occasion of his visit. The old man appreciated a good suit. He considered it a matter of respect, and so did Michael. He put the photograph in the jacket's inside pocket, then returned to the cab, where he gave the driver another address. They rode north and east to where the river touched the upper fifties. If you were rich and wanted privacy, Sutton Place was a good area to call home. Celebrities and politicians lived there, and no one looked twice at long cars with mirrored glass. The old man owned the entire building in which he planned to die, and while the FBI undoubtedly knew who lived in the five-story town house with a view of the river, none of the neighbors had a clue; that was the point. After a life in the press and in the courts, after three incarcerations, forty-seven years of persecution, and public scorn, the old man wanted to die in peace.

Michael didn't blame him.

He had the cabbie drive by the residence, then stop a full block north, near the defunct Sixtieth Street heliport. The space was a dog run now, and when Michael stepped from the cab he saw well-dressed women chatting while small dogs played. One of the women saw him and said something to her friends, so that all three turned as Michael paid off the cab. Michael nodded, then turned to walk twice past the house, once moving south, then coming back north. A portico drive led to private parking in the back. When he stopped before the door, he stood with his palms up, eyes moving between the security cameras mounted at the corners and above the main door. Someone moved behind a third-floor window. Curtains stirred at the ground level, too.

Eventually, Michael knocked, and after a long minute the door swung open to reveal four men. Two were low-level soldiers whose names Michael had never bothered to learn. In their twenties, they wore dark pants and shirts that shone like silk under their suit jackets. One chewed gum, and both stood with fingers inside their coats, as if Michael needed to be told they carried. Under slicked hair their faces were lean and frightened. They'd heard stories of Michael, of the things he'd done. He was a fighter and a killer, a prince of the street so widely feared he rarely had to kill anymore. His presence alone was sufficient. His name. The threat of his name.

The third man was a stranger, young and calm and lean, but the fourth, Michael knew well.

"Hello, Jimmy."

Jimmy stood an inch taller than Michael, but weighed thirty pounds less, narrow-shouldered and thin to the point of desiccation. Dapper in bottle-green pants and a brushed velvet coat, he was forty-eight years old, balding on top and vain enough to care. Michael knew from long acquaintance that his arms and chest carried more than a dozen scars. Knife wounds. Bite marks. Bullet holes. Eighteen years ago, he'd shown Michael things that would make a grown man faint. Michael was fifteen years old at the time, hard but not cruel; and Jimmy was all about cruel. He was about message and fear, a hard-core, brutal sadist who even now was the most dangerous man Michael had ever known.

"May I come in?" Michael asked.

"I'm thinking."

"Well, think faster."

Jimmy was a complicated man, equal parts appetite, ego, and self-preservation. He respected Michael, but didn't like him. Jimmy was a butcher, Michael a surgeon. The difference caused problems. It was an ego thing. Matters of principle.

Their gazes held for long seconds, then Jimmy said, "Whatever."

He moved back a pace and Michael stepped into the dim interior. The entry hall was massive, with white and black marble floors and a red-carpeted stairway that curved up both sides of the room before meeting on a landing twelve feet higher. A billiards room filled the space to Michael's right, and he could see through into the formal parlor, the small study beyond. He sensed movement deeper in the house, saw food on a long table, other men, other guns, and Michael knew then that they were marking time, waiting in stillness for the old man to die.

"I'd like to see him, Jimmy."

"He can't save you."

"No one's asking."

Jimmy shook his head. "I'm disappointed in you, Michael. All these years, all the things you've been given. Opportunity. Skills. Respect. You were nothing when we found you."

"You don't have the right to feel that way, Jimmy."

"I have every right."

He was angry and barely hiding it. Michael tilted his head to see the men behind him, then looked back at Jimmy. "The opportunity came from the old man, not you; the respect I earned on my own. Some of the skills may have started with you, but that's all it was, a start. I've made my own way since then."

"And yet, I helped choose you."

"For good reasons."

"Are you really so arrogant?"

"Are you?"

The silence held until Jimmy blinked. Michael said, "I want to see him."

"Do you still think you have that right?"

"Step back, Jimmy."

Jimmy shrugged, half-smiling, then moved back and allowed Michael to enter all the way. In the light of the chandelier, Michael saw how wired Jimmy looked, how taut. His dark eyes pulled in light, and there was emptiness there, the same vacuum-behind-glass look Michael had seen so many times. It was the look he got before people died.

"The old man released me, Jimmy. He gave standing orders that I was to be left alone. I'd say I still have the right to see him."

Jimmy blinked, and the look faded. "Tell Stevan that."

Stevan was thirty-six years old, with degrees from Columbia and Harvard, not because he cared about the education, but because he craved respectability in a city that knew his name too well. The old man's only son, he and Michael had been friends once—brothers— but that bridge was burnt to smoke and ruin. Eight days had passed since Michael quit the life. One week and a day. A world of change.

"How is my brother?" Michael masked the rage with sarcasm. Stevan drove a black Audi, and Michael knew for a fact that he kept a twenty-five in the glove compartment.

"How's Stevan?" Jimmy mimicked the question, rolling the words on his tongue as if tasting them. "His brother's a traitor and his father is dying. How do you think he is?"

"I think he's making mistakes."

"I won't let that happen."

"Where was he at five o'clock this morning?"

Jimmy rolled his shoulders, turned his lips down. "Stevan has offered to forgive you, Michael—how many times, now? Three times? Four? All you have to do is repent. Come back to us."

"Things have changed. I want out."

"Then you leave him no choice."

Michael pictured the bullet holes in the door of Chez Pascal. Two double-taps. Head height. "Nothing personal, right?"

"Exactly."

"And the wishes of his father? The man who built this from nothing? Who built you from nothing? What about him?"

"The son is not the father."

A moment's irony touched his eyes. At fifteen, the old man had made Michael Jimmy's student, and in that capacity he became a mirror to Jimmy's vanity, something Jimmy could point to and say, "Look at this instrument I've made." The old man's business had thrived with the two of them on the street, for as effective as Jimmy had been by himself, it was nothing compared to what they'd done together. They'd killed their way from one river to the other, north to south and over into Jersey. Russian mob. Serbians. Italians. It didn't matter. If somebody crossed the old man, they took him down. But after all these years, that's all Michael was to Jimmy, a weapon.

Disposable.

Michael looked from Jimmy to the man he'd never met. He stood three feet behind Jimmy's right shoulder, a spare man in linen pants and a golf shirt tight enough to show straps of lean, hard muscle. "Who's he?" Michael asked.

"Your replacement."

Michael felt a pang that was neither loss nor hurt, but one more broken strand. He looked the man over and noticed small things he'd missed. Fine white scars on both forearms, one finger that lacked a nail. The man stood six feet tall, and looked vaguely Slavic, with wide-spaced eyes and broad planes of cheekbone. Michael shrugged once, and then dismissed him. "I would never turn on people who trust me," he said to Jimmy.

"No? How long have you been with this woman of yours? Three months? A year?"

"What does it matter? It's personal."

"It matters because you only told us about her eight days ago. You kept her a secret, and keeping secrets from us is one step away from spilling ours. It's two sides of the same coin. Secrets. Lack of trust. Priorities."

"I said I would never turn."

"And yet, you made your choice."

"So did the old man. When he let me go."

"Maybe the old man's gone soft."

That was Michael's replacement—a crisp voice with a slight accent—and Michael could not believe the disrespect, here in the man's own house. He held the man's Slavic gaze, then stared hard at Jimmy and waited for him to meet his eyes. "I've seen you kill a man for less," Michael said.

Jimmy picked daintily at the nail of his smallest finger, then said, "Maybe I don't disagree."

"I want to see him." Michael's voice grated. Every man here owed his life to the old man. What they had. Who they were. Honor the old man and the old man honors you. That's the way it was done, old school and proper.

In some ways, Jimmy agreed. "Nobody walks away, Michael. That's how it's always been. The old man was wrong to tell you that you could."

"He's the boss."

"For now."

Michael's heart beat twice as he considered that. "You were in the car last night. With Stevan."

"Pretty night for a drive . . ."

"You bastard."

Jimmy saw the anger and rolled onto the balls of his feet. It had long been a question between them, who could take who. Michael watched

17

the glint come into Jimmy's eyes, the cold and narrow smile. He wanted it, was eager; and Michael knew, then, that there would be no easy out, no graceful exit from a life he no longer desired. For too many people, the matter was personal.

Fingers tightened on holstered weapons and the moment stretched; but before it broke, there was movement on the stairs, a nurse on the landing. In her forties, she looked like a smaller version of Jimmy, but vaguely female. When Jimmy turned and lifted his chin, she said, "He wants to know who's here."

"I'll be right there," Jimmy told her, and cold touched his face when he looked back at Michael. "Stay here." He motioned to the young Slavic man. "Watch him."

"Where's Stevan?" Michael demanded.

Jimmy offered a second slit of a smile, but otherwise ignored the question. He mounted the stairs on light feet, and when he came back down, he said, "He wants to see you." Michael moved for the stairs, but Jimmy stopped him. "Not yet." He twisted a finger like he was stirring tea, so Michael lifted his arms, and let the man pat him down. He checked Michael's legs to the groin, his arms to the wrist. He smoothed fabric over Michael's chest and back, then fingered the collars of his jacket and shirt.

"None of this is necessary," Michael said.

Jimmy's gaze moved from low to high, and the gaze lingered. "I don't know you anymore."

"Maybe you never did."

A hand flapped on his wrist. "Enough. Go. Up."

On the second floor Michael saw a nursing station filled with monitors tinted green. Cables snaked down the stairs and under the table that held the equipment. The nurse sat with her feet flat on the floor, eyes glued to the monitors. In a small room behind her, an iron-haired priest sat in a comfortable chair, eyes slightly closed, fingers crossed in his lap. He wore shined shoes and black clothing with a white collar at the throat. When the nurse looked up, Michael asked, "Are we that close?"

She glanced at Jimmy, who nodded in permission. "We've resuscitated him twice," she said.

"What?" Michael's anger flared. The old man *wanted* to die. Resuscitating him was a cruelty. "Why?" Michael demanded. "Why would you put him through that?"

She glanced at Jimmy. "The son—"

"It's not up to the son! He made his wishes plain. He's ready."

The nurse raised her hands and looked horrified. "I can only—"

Michael cut her off. "How bad is the pain?"

"The morphine can barely touch it."

"Can you give him more?"

"More would kill him."

"Is he lucid?"

"In and out."

Michael stared at the priest, who stared back, terrified. "How long does he have?"

"Hours. Weeks. Father William has been here for five days."

"I want to see him." Without waiting for a response, Michael moved to the next landing and stopped beside broad, double doors. Jimmy leaned a shoulder against the frame and flicked a piece of lint from his velvet jacket. Michael said, "It's wrong, Jimmy. He wants to die."

"It's Stevan's choice. Let it go."

"And if I can't?"

Jimmy shrugged.

"I'm not your enemy," Michael said. "I just want out."

Jimmy examined his other sleeve. "There's only one way out, and you know it. When the old man dies, so do you. Either that or you convince us to trust you again."

"That's two ways."

He shook his head. "One is a way out, one is a way back in. Different animals."

"Convince you, how?"

He blinked a lizard's blink. "Kill the woman."

"Elena's pregnant."

"Listen." Jimmy leaned closer. "I understand you have this misplaced sense of responsibility, but the old man won't live much longer." He gestured, taking in the house, the men below, then lowered his voice. "Stevan can't hold this together. He's weak, sentimental. He doesn't have what we have." He let that sink in, then said, "You can be my number two. I'll give you a percentage, free reign on the street."

Michael shook his head, but Jimmy didn't stop.

"People might challenge me alone, but no one would risk the two of us—"

"I don't want it."

"We all know how the old man feels about you. The street would accept it. The men. We could do this together."

"She's pregnant, Jimmy."

Jimmy's eyes drooped. "That's not my problem."

"I just want out."

"There is no *out*."

"I don't want to kill you."

Jimmy put his hand on the knob. "You think you can?"

He pushed the door wide, grinned.

And Michael went in to see the old man.

CHAPTER THREE

Michael stepped in and Jimmy left him alone with the dying man who'd all but saved his life. A Persian rug stretched to far windows and a coffered ceiling rose fifteen feet above the floor. No lamps burned, and all the curtains but one were drawn, so that pale light ghosted in to touch a chair, the bed, and the wasted man in it. The space was long, narrow, and the gloom made it feel hollow. Michael had spent countless hours in the room—long months as the old man failed— but eight days had passed since his last visit, and change lay like a pall. Airless and overly warm, the room smelled of cancer and pain, of an old man dying.

He crossed the room, steps loud on wood, then soft when he hit the rug. The room looked the same except for a six-foot-tall cross that hung on the wall. It was made of smooth, dark wood and looked very old. Michael had never seen it before, but put it out of his mind as he stopped by the narrow bed and looked down at the only man he'd ever loved. Fluids ran into the old man's veins through needles slipped under his skin. The robe he wore was one Michael had given him eight years ago, and in it he looked as light and weak as a starved child. His head was a death's-head, with bones that were too prominent and veins that showed like thread through wax. Blue-black skin circled his eyes. His lips were drawn back from his teeth, and Michael wondered if the pain, ever-present, had become insidious enough to find him even as he slept.

He stood for long seconds, bereft, then took the man's hand, sat in the chair, and studied the cross on the wall. The old man did not have a religious bone in his body, but his son professed to believe. In spite of his sins, and there were many, Stevan attended mass every week, a conflicted man twined in self-deception. He feared God, yet was too weak to sacrifice the things violence brought, the money and power, the pleasures of pale-faced models and society widows who found his name and good looks too compelling to resist. Stevan loved the notoriety, yet agonized over his father's lack of contrition; it was for this reason, Michael suspected, that the old man had been resuscitated twice. Stevan feared that his father, unrepentant, would go to hell. Michael marveled at the depth of such hypocrisy. Actions had consequence; choice came with cost. The old man knew exactly who he was, and so did Michael.

He lifted a framed photograph from the table near the bed. Taken a decade and half earlier, it showed him with the old man. Michael was sixteen, broad-shouldered but skinny in a suit that could not hide the fact. He leaned against the hood of a car, laughing, the old man's arm around his neck. He was laughing, too. The car against which they leaned had been a birthday present: a 1965 Ford GTO, a classic.

Michael put the photo where the old man could find it, then stood and walked to the wall of books on the north side. The shelves ran the length of the room and held a collection the man had been working on for over thirty years. They shared a love of the classics, and many of the books were first editions, including several by Hemingway, Faulkner, and Fitzgerald. Michael removed *The Old Man and the Sea*, then sat back down.

Through the window, he saw the river and then Queens. The old man had been born there to a prostitute with no interest beyond folding money and the next bottle it could buy. Shut up for years in a basement tenement, he'd been left alone for days at a time, unwashed and half-starved until he was orphaned at age seven. He told Michael once that he'd never known a childhood harder than his until their paths crossed. That fact made them family, he said. Because no one else could understand the loneliness they'd known, the fear. He said it gave them clarity, made them strong. And Stevan hated Michael for that, for having that bond with his father.

But Michael cherished it, not just because he was so otherwise alone in the world, but because the similarities *did* make a difference; because not even Stevan grasped the scope of deprivation that defined his father's early days. He did not know that the scars on the old man's feet came from rat bites in the crib, or that his missing fingers came from frostbite in the days before his mother died. The old man spoke of those things only to Michael, because only Michael could understand. He was the only one who knew the full story, the only person aware that the old man had chosen this room for the view, so that his last earthly sight would be the place from which he'd dragged himself one brutal day at a time. Michael found an undeniable elegance in this. The tenement house that almost killed the man was a river's breadth away, and a lifetime apart.

The sun moved higher and light slipped from the old man's face. So sunken were his eyes that Michael missed the moment they opened. One instant they were hidden, and the next they were simply there, pinched and deep and shot with red. "Stevan?"

"It's Michael."

The frail chest rose and fell in small, desperate pants and Michael saw pain bite deeper. Skin gathered at the corners of the old man's eyes and his brows compressed at the center. "Michael . . ." His mouth worked. Something glinted in the sun that still touched his neck, and Michael realized that he was crying. "Please . . ."

Michael turned his face away from the thing he was being asked to do. For months, now, the old man had begged to die, so eager was the pain. But Stevan had refused. Stevan. His son. So the old man had suffered as Michael watched the illness take him down. Weeks stretched to months, and the old man had begged.

God, how he had begged.

Then, eight days ago, Michael had told him about Elena. He explained that life had become more than the job, that he wanted out, a normal life. And listening, his pain-filled eyes so very intent, the old man had nodded as hard as such a sick man could. He said he understood just how precious life should be. *Precious.* Fingers clawed into Michael's arm. *Short!* And with those words still in the air above his lips, he'd told Michael that he loved him.

Like a son.

His fingers had tightened as he pulled Michael closer.

You understand?

A coughing fit took him then, and when he could speak again, he released Michael to live life as he wished, then asked him to take his own life in return. There was no irony in his request, just hurt; now he was asking again.

"I can't."

Michael's neck bent because the words were insufficient. He'd killed so many times that this should be the simplest of things. A gentle pressure. A few seconds. But he remembered the day the old man found him, cut a dozen times and fighting for his life under a bridge in Spanish Harlem. He said he'd heard of this wild boy who lived with the homeless, and had come to see for himself. He'd wondered if the stories were true.

A sound escaped the old man's lips but there were no words beyond anguish. Michael had come to assure Stevan that he was no threat. Failing that, he'd hoped to find enough strength in the old man to make certain that his orders were followed, even after death. But seeing the agony behind his haunted eyes, what Michael felt was ashamed. He was thinking of himself first, and the old man deserved more. Michael took his hand and looked at the photograph of them leaning on the hood of the car. His arm circled Michael's neck, head tipped back.

They were laughing.

It was the only photograph in existence that showed them together. The old man had been adamant. *Too dangerous to have more,* he'd said. *Too risky.* And for seventeen years the photograph had never left his room. It was a moment trapped in time—pure joy—and Stevan hated what it said about the leanings of his father's heart. Yet, the old man had been unapologetic. Actions and consequence, choice and cost.

Michael looked down on the old man's face. He saw how it had been, and how it was now: the life he'd had and the one he wanted to quit. Torment wracked his features, but through the pain and fear, Michael saw the old man's soul, and it was unchanged.

"Don't be afraid," the dying man whispered.

Michael could barely hear him, so he asked, "Are you sure?"

The old man nodded without words, and Michael's fingers tightened on his hand. "They'll come for me," Michael said. "Stevan. Jimmy. They'll try to kill me."

He needed the old man to know the repercussions of this thing he asked. If Stevan came, Michael would kill him. The truth of this filled the old man's eyes, but it was only when he said "Make a good life" that Michael truly believed he understood. There was such sadness in his eyes, and it had nothing to do with his own death. Whether the old man lived or died, Stevan would come.

And Michael would kill him.

"I knew . . ." His voice failed, and Michael leaned closer. "I knew when I released you . . ."

Michael forced despair from his face. He'd killed so many, and loved so few. "May I have this?" He lifted the photograph that sat by the bed. The old man did not answer, but his fingers moved on the sheet. Michael slipped the photo from its frame, and put it with the other in his pocket. "Elena's pregnant," he said, but it was unclear if the old man had heard. Tears filled his eyes and he was nodding as if to hurry Michael on. Michael kissed him on the forehead, then placed one hand on his chest and the other across his mouth and nose. "Forgive me," he said. And as he shut off the old man's air, their eyes remained locked. Michael made a gentling noise, but the old man never fought, not even at the end. His heart stuttered, then beat a final time, and through his hands, Michael felt a rush of peace so immense it had to be imagination. He straightened as monitors flat-lined, and alarms screamed on the landing below. He closed the dead man's eyes, and heard loud voices, feet on the steps.

The old man was gone.

And they were coming.

Michael moved to the bookshelf, his eyes on the black rectangle that had until a few minutes ago held the old man's copy of Hemingway's classic novella. In the space behind, he found the two nine millimeters he'd put there three months ago. Each one had fifteen in the clip and one in the chamber.

Vision.

Foresight.

Michael's replacement lacked both.

He came through the right-side door with his own gun low and his smile half-cocked. Michael gave him three steps and enough time to see what was going to happen.

Then he shot him in the heart.

By that time two more men were in the room, both armed. Michael recognized the grunts from the foyer. One yelled, *whoa, whoa, whoa* but both were bringing up guns, barrels going long to short. Michael took one step and shot them both in under a second. They dropped and he heard shouts from the stairs. Three men, maybe more. Fear in their voices. Michael said nothing, but crossed the room and stood four feet from the left-hand door, which remained closed. Fear was a cancer for those who were not used to this, so time was on his side, but not by much. He listened for steps on carpet, and when shoes showed through the gap beneath the door, he put two rounds through the wood, center mass.

A body hit the floor, and Michael rounded onto the landing, where he found three more men, two in full retreat down the stairs and another with a gun in his hand and pointed. But it takes more than a trigger finger to shoot a man. When someone is shooting back, it takes the kind of cool that rock stars can only fake. Michael had that cool, and so did Jimmy.

No one else in the house was even close.

Two bullets flew wide of Michael's shoulder, and he tapped the shooter once in the forehead, stepping past before he was even down. The other men pulled up short, one shooting wildly, the other hands up and empty. Michael shot the first and kept both guns trained on the second. He was late-sixties, a street thug from the old days kept around for sentimental reasons. He was a gopher now: ran errands, cooked food. His hands were steady above his head, his face resigned. Michael stopped one step above him and put a barrel so close to his cheek he could feel heat from the metal. "Where's Jimmy?"

"Gone. Ran."

"How long?"

"Just this second."

Michael glanced down at the open door, the hint of city beyond.

He pressed hot metal against the man's cheek. "If you're lying, I'll kill you slow."

"I'm not lying."

"What about the nurse? The priest?"

"Same thing."

"Are they on the payroll?"

The man nodded, which meant they would keep their mouths shut. Michael looked again at the open door. "You have car keys?"

The man pulled a ring from his pants pocket. "The Navigator," he said. "Out back."

"Anyone else in the house?"

He shook his head. The smell of burned powder was everywhere, a gray haze under the chandelier. Michael studied his face and remembered a few conversations they'd had. His name was Donovan. He had grandchildren.

"Tell Stevan I'm out." Donovan nodded, but Michael realized the lie even as he did. The old man was dead at Michael's hand. Blood ran down the walls, the stairs. He was nowhere close to out. Not after this. Michael gestured with the gun. "Go."

Donovan fled, and Michael went back upstairs. He stood by the bed and looked down on the husk of the man he'd killed. He'd been a hard man, but full of kindness for those he loved. Michael remembered a conversation they'd had on the morning of his fourteenth birthday. A year had passed since that day under the bridge, and the old man wanted to know why.

Why was I on the streets?

Yeah. The old man turned his lips, tilted his head. *Smart kid. Good looking. You could have gone to the authorities, anybody. Why take the hard road? Why the streets?*

I had my reasons.

That's all you're going to say?

Humor shone in the old man's eyes, a kind of pride.

Yes, sir.

Whatever you were running from, Michael, it can't touch you now. You know that, right? Not here. Not with me.

I know that.

And you still won't tell me?

I have reasons for that, too.

He'd ruffled the boy's hair, and, laughing, said, *A man should have his reasons.*

And in all this time, Michael had never told him why he'd chosen the hard road. Because the old man was right. A man should have his reasons.

And his secrets.

Michael straightened the old man's arms and smoothed the blanket across his chest. He kissed one still-warm cheek, then the other; when he stood, tears burned hot in his eyes. He lifted Hemingway's novella from the bedside table, then stood for a long while, looking down. "You were good to me," he said, and when he left, he took the book.

He had reasons for that, too.

CHAPTER FOUR

There were people in the world who could kill better than Michael. A rifle shot from a thousand yards was beyond his skill, as were explosives and poisons and mass murder of any kind. He'd come into the business fighting for his life, and that was all about up close and personal. It was about food and shelter and keeping the blood in his veins. Those lessons came fast on the street, and Michael knew as a child that it was better to be vicious than soft, fast than slow. He learned to steal and scheme and wound, and that was his gift, an utter lack of mental weakness. Jimmy had simply taken that gift and magnified it. He'd honed a natural capacity for violence, then taught Michael an economy of movement that he still found satisfying.

Michael thought of Donovan. Old and gray. White stubble on his face. Jimmy would be appalled that Michael let him live, but Jimmy was not Michael's only teacher. There was also the old man, and it was his death that taught Michael how he wished to live. Not once during his slow decline did the old man dwell on money or power or reputation. He lamented that his son lacked depth. He pined for women lost and the daughters he never had. A world too narrowly embraced.

Make a good life . . .

There had never been more than a small chance that Stevan would let Michael quit the life peacefully, either to honor the wishes of his father or to avoid the kind of grief that Michael could lay at his door. But small as the chance may have been, it was gone, now. Michael had killed his father when he would not, and shot dead six of his men. As long as Michael lived, Stevan would look weak, and that made killing

Michael good business. But, it would be personal, too, and *personal* made things unpredictable.

Michael moved fast.

In the security room, he disabled the security cameras, front and back, then removed the zip drives. Stevan would know who'd done this, but Michael's plans left no room for video proof. He wanted out of the life, and he wanted out clean.

Checking his appearance, Michael saw red spatter on the legs of his pants, his shirt, the backs of his hands. Normally, he would never risk a public appearance in anything but spotless condition. He would change and bag the clothes, strip the guns, and dispose of the pieces in any number of quick and efficient ways. Storm drains. Dumpsters. The East River. But the circumstances were not normal. There'd been no planning, no intent to kill the old man or wage war. The entire event had taken eighty seconds, and Michael was on autopilot, moving fast. Stevan was out there somewhere. Jimmy remained alive and Elena was on the street, unprotected.

Outside, Michael fired up the Navigator and blew south. He needed to get out of the city, and Elena had to come, too. Michael felt a moment's guilt as the lies he would tell spooled out like video, but truth would be the matter of another day.

This was about living long enough to tell it.

Halfway to Tribeca, he hit heavy traffic. He called the restaurant from his cell and asked for Elena. "Everything okay?" he asked.

"Paul's angry."

"Am I fired?"

"Do you care?"

"I care about you." Michael tried to make it light, but she did not respond to the silence that followed. She was angry, and Michael understood that. "Listen, I'll be there soon. Don't go anywhere."

"Where would I go?"

"Just don't leave the restaurant."

Michael hung up the phone and tried to bull through the dense stream of cars. He gunned one narrow gap after another, horns blaring, heavy car rocking. Twice, he rode tires onto the curb, and twice it made no difference. Traffic was a snarl of impatient metal. When he got to Tribeca, more than an hour had passed. Sixty-two minutes since he'd killed the old man. Michael double-parked the big SUV across from the restaurant. He checked parked cars and windows on the narrow street. Pedestrians were thick on the sidewalk. Michael slipped one pistol into the glove compartment and tucked the other under his jacket. He figured two minutes to get Elena someplace quiet, another three to get her away from the restaurant. Michael had money. They would fade into the city, and then he would get her out. Someplace with mountains, he thought. Someplace green. He felt the future like it was already there, but the future could be a tricky bitch. His cell phone rang as he killed the engine. He looked at the screen, and it rang four more times before he answered.

He knew the number.

Stevan's number.

He opened it feeling unease and regret and pity. For all his faults, Stevan had loved his father. "Hello, brother."

For long seconds, Michael heard only breath, and he could picture Stevan on the other end of the line, his manicured nails and lean face, dark eyes that were prideful and hurt. Stevan played strong, but deep down, he needed to see himself reflected in the faces of other men; he drew strength from their fear and envy, defined himself by their perception rather than his own. But his father knew better, and preferred Michael's company for that reason. They were stripped down, the both of them, free of illusion and false want. Power, for them, was a tool to secure food, shelter, safety. That's what childhood taught them.

Appearance means nothing.

Stevan never grasped the difference, never understood why Michael shined so brightly in his father's eyes; and when his voice came over the phone, Michael knew that years of jealousy and distrust had finally darkened to something more.

"He made you family, Michael. You had nothing. You were nobody."

"Your father was in pain."

"The choice was not yours to make."

"I loved him. He begged me."

"You think you're the only one he begged? Where do you get the arrogance? He'd have asked the cleaning lady, a stranger, anybody."

"I only did what you should have done a month ago."

"He's burning in hell because of you."

"He died as he wished to die."

"You took him from me."

"It's not like that . . ."

"You're dead, Michael. So is your girlfriend."

"Don't make me your enemy, brother. We can still walk away from this."

"Dead bitch. Dead, motherfucker."

There was no going back, Michael saw. No peace to be made. "Good-bye, Stevan."

"Do you see the restaurant?"

The question was so pointed that Michael felt a blade of fear slip into his heart. He scanned the street again. "Where are you, Stevan?"

"Did you think we wouldn't plan for this? Did you think you could just walk away? Honestly, brother."

He stressed the last word, mocking.

"Stevan . . ."

"This was supposed to be for both of you, but I want you to see it happen."

"Don't—"

"I hear that she's pregnant."

Michael flung down the phone, and wrenched open the door. His feet touched city pavement and he managed seven steps in a dead run before the restaurant exploded. Flame blew through windows and the force lifted him from his feet, flung him against the Navigator. Black smoke roiled in the aftershock, and for a moment there was no sound. The roof flew apart as a secondary explosion slammed outward, then Michael's ears opened, and he heard screaming. Flames poured out in towers of heat and smoke. Cars collided on the street, while, on the sidewalk, people were dead or dying. A man ran blindly, clothing aflame, then collapsed as Michael watched. And the flames roared higher. They licked at neighboring buildings, and Michael found himself on his feet.

Elena . . .

He walked closer, eyes blurred and one hand out to test the heat. It scorched his palm from fifty feet out, and a corner of his mind shut down. He could not bear to see her face, to picture it blistered and burnt and ruined. He let the heat roll over him, sensed the crush of movement on the street, the frenzied motion and the quiet, still dead. Glass shattered in a car too close to the flames. A black Escalade glided around the corner and stopped. Michael cataloged people and faces, the shock and fear, the sound of distant sirens. And even with Elena's death fresh on his mind, he realized what was going down two seconds before it actually happened.

He turned back to the Escalade as the windows slid down. Stevan sat in the front, his face sharp as glass under brown hair parsed with gray. He made a shooting motion with the finger and thumb of his right hand, and from the backseat, an automatic weapon opened fire. Michael dove and rolled as bullets ripped into a car behind him. People screamed and the crowd panicked. Bodies went down, shot and then trampled underfoot. More bullets slammed metal, but the shots flew wide and scattered. Michael rose from cover, pistol in hand. He fired nine rounds in three seconds. His shots pocked metal on the Escalade, shattered glass, and sudden fear blossomed on Stevan's face. He banged the dash, shouted something at the driver, and rubber barked as the big vehicle cut hard right and jumped the curb. Michael sprinted behind it, away from the heat, the screams. He clambered over stalled cars, felt hard pavement slam through his shins. He ran in a dead sprint, and stayed close for a full block, then the road cleared and the big engine gunned. Michael pulled up, and put his last rounds through the back windshield. He doubted they were fatal—too far, too much movement—but he liked the feel of it, the chance he might get lucky.

Either way, Stevan was dead.

Now or later.

Dead.

Michael watched the car disappear, then realized that he was standing on a city street with a drawn weapon in his hand and blood on his clothes. People were staring. Men in suits. Cabbies. A woman in a black dress.

Mouth open.

Staring.

Michael lowered the gun. "Elena?"

She stood in a loose jumble, shocked and confused. A paper bag dangled from her right hand. It was white, crumpled at the top. She looked from the gun to Michael's face. Her skin was pale, fine hair mussed in a sudden breeze. Around her, people began to push back. Several turned and ran. At least one was dialing a cell.

"Michael?"

Every part of him wanted to grab her up and never let go. He wanted to shield her from the aftershock of what had just happened. The fallout. The way he knew her life was about to change. But mostly he wanted to hold her, to pour out his feeling of relief and love. Instead, he grabbed her by the wrist, his fingers hard and unforgiving.

"We have to go," he said.

"You were shooting at that car—"

"We have to go now."

He began to pull her down the street, tucking the gun out of view as several bystanders found their courage and began to shout for help. A frail woman on the far sidewalk pointed and said, "Stop him. Stop that man."

"Michael, what the hell is going on?"

"We have to go."

"You said that." Elena pulled back on her arm, but Michael did not let go. He broke into a half-run, dragging her behind him. "You're hurting me," she said, but he ignored that, too. Sirens were close. Smoke roiled above the roofline ahead, and the streets teemed with terrified people. "Where are we going? Michael . . ." She trailed off as they rounded the corner. In front of them, the restaurant burned more fiercely than ever. "Is that . . . ?"

"It is."

People were down and bleeding, cut by shrapnel and flung glass. Burned. Shot. Many stood dumb and unmoving. Others scrambled in the wreckage, trying to help the wounded. Elena began to cry.

"But Paul—"

"He's dead."

"The others?"

"Dead."

"Oh, God." Elena stumbled when she saw the first charred body, its torso smoking where fabric still burned. They passed a woman whose lower leg had been shattered by a bullet. Michael pulled Elena through the rubble. She stumbled again, and went halfway down before Michael caught her.

"What's happening?" She was in shock, grasping to make sense of what she saw. "Where did you get that suit?"

"Almost there."

A cop car screeched around the corner two blocks away. A fire truck followed. Michael opened the Navigator's door and pushed Elena in.

"Don't touch me." Her eyes were open but glazed, so wide the firelight danced. Michael snapped the seat belt across her waist.

"It's me," he said. "You're okay."

"Don't touch me."

Michael rounded the vehicle and climbed behind the wheel. He cranked the engine and eased forward, tires crunching on glass and shattered brick. Beside him, Elena stared at the ruined street, the blank eyes and the walking wounded. Michael kept one eye on the approaching cop car. He crawled for half a block, then accelerated when the road finally cleared.

Chaos was everywhere.

No one looked at them twice.

He drove two blocks more and the scene fell away. Buildings obscured the flame and black smoke rose to mist. At Hudson Street, Michael turned south, then cut west on Chambers. Elena said nothing. She looked at everything but Michael. "Elena," he said.

"Not yet." She shook her head.

He worked the car south, past Ground Zero and the North Cove Yacht Harbor. At Battery Park City, he pulled to the curb and sat for a long moment. He said her name, but she ignored him. Michael checked traffic around them, then removed one gun from the glove compartment, and the other from under his jacket. Wordlessly, he stripped and wiped the guns; then he pulled two zip drives from a pocket and got out of the car. He felt Elena's eyes on his back as he walked to the water's edge and flung the pieces far into the river. Back in the car, he said, "Are you okay?"

"Did you just throw a gun into the river?"

"Two, actually."

"Two guns."

"Yes."

Elena nodded once, and her fingers crinkled the white paper bag in her lap. It was small, and when she smoothed the wrinkles, Michael saw that it came from a pharmacy two blocks from the restaurant. She lifted the bag, then let it settle. "I was nauseous," she said, and smoothed the bag again. "Morning sickness." She used two fingers to dash liquid from her eyes and Michael knew she was in shock. "I would have been inside the restaurant."

Trembling fingers brushed the plane of her stomach, and Michael could see her thoughts as if they hung in the air between them.

If not for the baby . . .

Her hands came up, and their emptiness was rich in meaning. The car. The fire. The guns. "What's happening, Michael?"

She needed the truth, he knew. For her safety, for so many reasons. But how could he tell her that the child she carried belonged to a liar? That her co-workers died in her place? That she remained a target? How could Michael tell the woman he loved that he'd killed seven people before lunch? She searched his face, frightened, and when he hesitated, her gaze fell to his shirt.

"Elena . . ."

She touched a dark splotch on the white cloth, traced it with a finger. "Is that . . ."

"Listen to me——"

"Is that blood?"

She looked at him then, really looked. She saw similar stains on his pants, on the backs of his hands. "I'm going to be sick." She folded at the waist, her skin the color of old bone. Michael reached out a hand, but she shied, one hand unfastening the seat belt, the other groping for the door. It swung open and she spilled out onto the street, the sunburned grass that stretched to the river. She managed a dozen steps, then sank to her knees. When Michael tried to approach, she said, "Stay away."

He watched her heave over brown grass, and was so distraught that when his phone rang, he barely heard it. He tore it from his pocket and felt the world slow when he saw the number. He almost didn't answer, but then he did. He turned his back on Elena, and, using every ounce of self-control he possessed, said, "You're a dead man, Stevan."

"Your brother's next."

Michael felt heat on his neck, smelled the river. He looked at Elena and the moment seemed to freeze. "I don't have a brother," he said.

"Yes, you do."

The phone went dead. Michael blinked and an image rose.

His brother.

Like a ghost.

CHAPTER FIVE

Cold air filled the abandoned hall. Gray light. Dirt and debris. The boy who ran there was nine years old and thin, a scarecrow in ill-fitting clothes. Tears cut crescents in the grime beneath his eyes, then tracked white to his chin, his neck, the hollow places behind his ears. Windows flashed past as the boy ran, but he ignored the snow outside, the hints of mountain and other children, barely seen. He ran and choked and hated himself for bawling like some girl.

Just run, Julian . . .

Breath like glass in his throat.

Just run . . .

He came to an intersection, and stumbled left down a darker stretch that smelled of rot and mold and frozen earth. Broken glass crunched under his feet, and his lips moved again.

Sticks and stones . . .

He didn't know that he was talking out loud. He felt the rush of blood, the crack of linoleum, dried out and breaking beneath his feet. He dared a look over his shoulder, and his shoe caught on a broken tile, ankle folding like cardboard. He stumbled against a windowsill that tore skin from his arm.

Sticks . . .

Julian sobbed in pain.

Stones . . .

Metal clattered behind him, distant voices. He stopped at the bottom of a rotted-out stairwell. Light spilled from the third floor, a wisp of snow from some broken window. He thought of climbing but was too weak, the injured ankle shooting blades of pain up his leg.

Make me like Michael, he prayed.

Footsteps behind him, his eyes rolling white.

Make me strong.

Another sob escaped his throat and he fled the sound of their steps, the noises they made as they slammed through doors and banged metal pipes on the hard, concrete walls.

Please, God . . .

Julian burst through a door. The bad ankle crumpled and he went down again, pain a gunpowder flash behind his eyes. He smeared a sleeve across his face because it would be worse if they caught him crying.

Ten times worse.

A thousand.

He dragged himself up and rooms tumbled past: glimpses of naked bed frames and broken chairs, closets spilling old hangers and rotted cloth. He spun into another hall, breath still sharp in his throat, not enough air getting in. Behind him, a wolf-cry rose, and then another. He looked for a place to hide, but a cry skipped down the hall behind him: "There he is!"

Julian looked back and saw tall windows lit by falling snow, then dirty faces and hands, bodies lost in dark, rough clothes. They stormed out of the shadows, five boys in a dead run. He screamed this time, and they came faster, older boys, big ones, their cruelty proven a hundred times in a hundred terrible ways. Their feet made snapping sounds in the shotgun hall, and Julian cried as he ran, half-blind and sobbing and ashamed.

They caught him where the building ended. Julian hit a pocket of cold, heavy air, then metal doors and thick chain; when he turned, hands up and open, they slammed him into the door and drove him down. He shook the big chain once before they peeled his fingers loose and flipped him on his back. Then it was laughter and warm spit, the smell of rubber as a shoe crushed his nose and brought the bright, hot blood.

"Don't mark him this time." A faceless voice above dirty jeans. "Not his face."

Julian screamed. "Michael!"

"Your brother's not here to save you, you little freak."

Julian knew the voice. "Hennessey. Wait . . ."

But Hennessey didn't wait. He bent low, copper hair dull in the empty light, his eyes narrow and dark as he curled his fingers into Julian's hair and pushed down, grinding the smaller boy's skull into the concrete, twisting so that his left cheek came next, pressed flat on the filthy floor. "Say it."

His mouth forced hot air into the tunnel of Julian's ear. Julian rolled his eyes, saw the flush in Hennessey's skin, the wisps of pale hair on his lip, the crazy, unforgiving eyes. "No."

Hennessey pushed closer, his lips touching Julian's ear, the whiskers as light and fine as a spider's silk. "Say it."

"Please . . ."

"Hennessey is the king of Iron House." Julian started to cry, but that only made Hennessey push harder. He leaned in until skin tore from Julian's cheek. "Hennessey is the king. Not Michael. Say it. Hennessey is the king of Iron House. Michael is a pussy—"

"No."

"Michael is a pussy. Say it."

"Please . . ."

"What?" Hennessey thumped Julian's head on the floor, then stood. "Please, what?" They loomed over Julian, all five of them. A smile touched Hennessey's lips and the same mad light filled his eyes. "Please what, motherfucker?"

"Please, wait."

But they ignored him. Hennessey laughed once, said, "Boys." And they went to work with their feet. They kicked until Julian stopped moving, then leaned close and told him what they were going to do. Julian curled tight but it was useless. Hands found his legs, his hair. They pulled until cold air knifed his skin, then threw him naked through the window. He landed in a drift of snow, on his back beneath a metal plaque bolted to the stone wall. Snow obscured the letters on the plaque, but he knew the words.

Laughter came from beyond the window, pale faces pressed against the glass, then gone. Julian touched his gushing nose and saw finger-paint snow on his nails. He spit blood into the drift, and when he tried to pull himself up his hand brushed something sharp and hard, an old knife, lost in the snow. He tilted it and saw a wooden handle, half-rotted, and eight inches of rusted metal. He touched the flat edge to his cheek, then squeezed the handle until his fingers ached. "Michael," he wept.

But his brother never came.

Julian looked at the sky, the pinpricks of white.

Snow like tears.

So cold . . .

Falling.

The limousine crept up a mountain road edged with slush and broken asphalt. Road grit feathered the car's paint, a rough film thrown up by tires that had no business on a black-ice road four thousand feet up in the North Carolina mountains. The air outside was cold, the light flat. Nothing else moved on the mountain, no traffic or blown leaves, just a heavy, wet powder that sifted from the low sky. The woman in the backseat never looked at the drop-offs, the vast open spaces where the earth simply vanished. She closed her eyes until the car plunged back under the trees and the vertigo left her, then she stared out at the forest, at the snow that lay between the naked trunks. She lit a cigarette, and the driver's eyes rose in the mirror.

"I'm not smoking again," she said.

His eyes flicked away. "Of course not."

"It's just today."

"Of course." His hair remained military short, but she noticed that it was starting to gray. Creases cut the back of his neck, and against his black jacket, the collar of his shirt shone whiter than the snow. She twisted her wedding ring and pulled smoke into lungs that burned. They'd been an hour out of Charlotte when the first flake fell. The driver had twice suggested they turn back, but she had refused each time. Today is the day, she'd said. Now, here they were, alone on the edge of the world.

The driver watched his passenger for a long second. She had translucent skin and green eyes, golden hair that curled at the tops of her shoulders. She was barely twenty-five years old, young for such wealth and power.

"We're going to be late," she said.

"They'll wait for you."

"Yes." She lit another cigarette. "I suppose they will."

Snow thickened as the car moved over and around the folds of silent rock. Cigarettes appeared, turned to ash, and she thought of why she was here, high in the frozen mountains. She thought of why she had come. "Stop the car." She rocked forward in her seat, pressed a palm into her stomach. The driver hesitated. "Stop the car."

The driver slowed and stopped. She swung the heavy door into the falling snow and stepped out, her expensive shoes ruined by slush and salt. Three steps carried her to the edge of the woods, where she bent at the waist.

"Ma'am? Are you okay?"

Snow beaded her hair, her fine silk blouse; when she finally stood, she smoothed the back of one hand across her cheek. The cold air felt clean on her skin, and the nausea passed. She turned and found her driver standing by the front of the car, one hand on the hot metal. He nodded. "It's a big day," he said, as if he understood.

"Yes."

"I would be nervous, too."

She allowed his misperception to stand.

"Are you ready?" he asked.

She looked at the wet linen sky, the skeleton trees with crooked arms and a million twisted fingers. "It's so still," she said.

"Let me get your door."

"So cold."

It was after four when the limousine began its slow descent. The road wound into a narrow valley, the town at its center a knot of low buildings. Abigail Vane did not claim to know the place, but she knew what it would look like: properties in decline, bars with vinyl stools and people in cracked skin. There would be a gas station at each end of Main Street, a drugstore near the middle. It was a small town, a blink of light on the dark edge of the mountains, and she knew that in a half-day's drive there were a hundred others just like it. North Carolina. Tennessee. Georgia. Small towns, and people who dreamed of other places. The car edged onto Main Street and she watched the bar fronts, the rough men with bent necks. "Soon?" she asked.

"Yes."

The road narrowed on the other side of town, and the driver turned right onto a barely plowed track of old pavement. Crumbled columns stood in the snow, and a river ran fast and black at the far end of a long field. "This is it," the driver said, and she leaned forward.

An institutional building piled up from the valley floor. Made of brick and stone, it rose three stories, with long wings that spread from each side of the main edifice. One wing was completely dark, its windows rowed and blank, some boarded over. From the rest of the structure, light spilled out to touch smaller buildings and an uncompromising yard. Bent figures moved between the buildings. Small figures. Children. A boy stopped and turned, his features lost behind the falling snow. She strained forward, but the driver shook his head. "Too young," he said.

The drive curved around the yard and they stopped where broad steps climbed to a covered porch. The door opened and a man stepped out. Above him, letters scored the concrete.

Iron Mountain Home For Boys
Shelter and Discipline since 1895

She stared at the words until the driver turned in his seat. Lines creased his face, and hard eyes shone under the salted hair. "Are you ready?"

"Give me a minute."

Her heart beat too quickly, a slight flutter in her hands. Thinking he understood, the driver got out of the car and stood by her door. He nodded to the man on the high porch, but neither of them spoke.

After several minutes, Abigail Vane tapped a ring on the window. The door swung open and the driver accepted her hand.

"Ma'am."

"Thank you, Jessup." She stepped out and he released her fingers. She took in the broken concrete steps, the rust on the iron handrail. Her gaze traveled to the high, sloped roofline, then to that portion of the building that lay in ruin. Windows stretched away in triple rows. She saw cracked glass and missing panes, weather-stained boards under nails hammered flat.

"Mrs. Vane." A round-shouldered man scuttled down the steps. His eyes were attractive and very bright, his Adam's apple large. He'd combed sparse hair above neat ears, and his teeth, when he smiled, were small and white. "We are so pleased that you have come. My name is Andrew Flint. Perhaps your assistant spoke of me? After all the correspondence and phone calls, I feel as if I know her."

She took his hand, found it narrow and cool. "Mr. Flint." Her voice remained neutral, the same used at a thousand fund-raisers, a thousand functions. She'd used the same tone when she'd met the last two governors, the President, a hundred different CEOs. She gave his hand a firm squeeze, then relaxed her fingers and waited for him to realize that he, too, should let go.

Flint glanced at the empty limousine. "Your husband?"

She touched a button on her blouse. "The senator is otherwise engaged."

"But we had hoped . . ." Flint forced a smile. "Never mind. You are here, and that, too, is exciting." He made a nervous gesture, hands spread to take in the snow, the gathering dark. "Shall we go inside?"

Halfway up the steps, she turned. False dusk had settled in the yard, and what children remained were indistinct in the gloom. The scene depressed her: so many lost children. But today would be different. For two brothers, she thought, today would be the beginning of something grand. "You received our donation?"

"Yes, Mrs. Vane. Of course." Flint made another bow and dry-washed his hands. "As you can see, we have ways to use it." He gestured and she followed his gaze. Stretching into the storm, the abandoned wing of the orphanage looked like a derelict ship, massive and broken on some unforgiving shore. She saw movement behind one of the windows, a slash of white that flickered twice and was gone.

"Is that wing in use at all?" she asked.

"God, no. The conditions are deplorable."

"I thought I saw someone."

He shook his head. "A bird, perhaps. Or a wild cat. Both seem to find their way inside. It's a very dangerous place. The boys are under strict orders—"

She stopped on the top step. "I'd like to meet them."

Flint's fingers curled around one another, and he fumbled his words when he spoke. "I'm afraid that's not possible."

"The gift was five million dollars. That should make many things possible."

"Yes. I'm aware, of course. But . . ." He hesitated further, craning his neck to peer at the building behind him. He hesitated, as if waiting for someone to save him. "The truth is. We can't seem to find them."

"You've lost two boys?"

"Ah . . . Just for the moment."

"Does this happen often?"

"No. No. Of course not."

"I had hoped to meet them at once."

"I'm sure they'll turn up soon. Boys, you know. Probably off somewhere . . ."

"Off somewhere?" Her eyes sharpened on his.

"You know . . ."

A nervous laugh.

". . . playing."

Michael ran down the deserted hall, eyes cutting left and right, fingers curled into fists. Windows rose above him, tall as doors, but he did not look at the snow outside, his reflection as he ran. Julian had been gone for an hour, and Julian never did that. He stayed in their room on the third floor, stayed on their hall or wherever Michael was near. And when Michael was gone, which happened, Julian stayed with what friends he had. Because Julian wasn't stupid. He knew he was weak. That weakness led to torment.

Abusing Julian was one of Hennessey's favorite games, mainly because he and his friends lacked the courage to mess with Michael directly. They'd tried it once and left with broken fingers and loose teeth. Five on one and Michael cleaned the floor with them, as if it didn't matter how much he was hit or how much he bled. Michael fought with a noise in the back of his throat, like an animal in a cage. He fought like Tarzan would fight. That's why the younger boys looked up to him, why the older ones stayed clear, because Michael, in a corner, became so wild and fierce that some of the older boys thought he might actually be insane. But that's not how it was. There was nothing but time at Iron House. Time to burn. Time to kill. The place was hell, and his brother wore a target on his back. What other choice did Michael have?

"Julian!"

He called his brother's name and it echoed in the frozen space. Michael had come back from kitchen duty and a kid on the hall told him Julian was gone, culled out of the group, then dragged to the empty wing. He said Hennessey was laughing when he pried boards off the sealed door and kicked Julian hard to get him running. There were five of them, the kid said. They gave him a two-minute head start, and then went after him.

That was an hour ago.

So, Michael ran. He called his brother's name, and when the sound came back alone, he called again.

Cold words.

Smoke on his lips.

Flint showed Abigail to a small bedroom on the second floor. "This is our only facility for visitors," he apologized. "You can freshen up. Rest. The boys will turn up soon."

"Thank you, Mr. Flint."

He started to turn, then paused. "May I ask a question?"

"If you must."

"Why these boys?"

"You ask because of their age?"

"And because one is so sickly." Flint's eyes were kind but puzzled. "It's highly unusual."

"And you wonder if I have some special interest."

"My curiosity is only natural."

Abigail stepped to the window and gazed at the snow. "They're ten and nine, yes? Foundlings?"

"Discovered in a creek bed, just across the line in Tennessee, not that far from here, really. Forty miles as the crow flies, twice that with the roads up here. It was late November, very cold, and two hunters heard crying at the backside of a dead-end hollow. The creek was two feet wide, but fast. Julian was partly submerged and both were half frozen. It's a miracle either survived, but especially Julian. He's a weak child—puny, as my grandmother might have said. The hunters carried them out tucked in their shirts. I believe they'd have died otherwise. A few more minutes. Less kind strangers."

"How old were they at the time?"

"We're not sure, exactly. Julian was newborn, a matter of weeks, probably. Michael was older. The doctor put his age at roughly ten months, though he could have been younger. Julian was definitely premature. We're assuming the same mother, so—"

"Premature?"

"By a month at least."

"A month." Abigail felt her vision blur, and enough time passed for Flint to become uncomfortable.

"Mrs. Vane?"

"I was raised in an orphanage, Mr. Flint. It was a small place, poorer even than this. Cold and hard and unforgiving." She turned from the window, and one palm tilted to catch the institutional light. "You can imagine that I have certain sympathies . . ."

"Yes, yes. Of course."

"I was adopted at age ten, and my nine-year-old sister was not." She showed Flint her eyes, and there was no weakness left in them. "She was sickly, too, like Julian, and left behind because of that. I went home with a loving family and four months later my sister contracted pneumonia. She died alone in that horrible place."

"I see."

"Do you?"

"Well, I should like to think—"

47

"I married well, Mr. Flint, and find myself in a position to prevent a similar tragedy. I've been searching for children just like these boys. Older. Unwanted. It won't bring my sister back, but I hope to find some small measure of relief. A new life for the boys, and maybe for myself. Does that satisfy your curiosity?"

"I meant no undue intrusion."

"I want to meet them, Mr. Flint."

"Of course."

"Please find them."

Julian had hiding places for when things got bad. An abandoned well house in the woods, the crawl space under the chapel. He'd once found a crack in the granite where the river spilled to the lower field. The descent in was a headfirst scrape through a narrow slit, but three feet down, the cave opened up and he could stretch out, the rock wet and black twelve inches from his nose. The cave was cold and dark, and he'd come out once covered with leeches; but the worse things became for Julian, the deeper he went. Deep in the world. Deep in his mind.

Michael found him in the subbasement.

The place was a maze of dark and dusty rooms—dozens of them, maybe even a hundred—but over the years, Michael had been down every hall and opened every door. He'd found ranks of cabinets with files more than eighty years old; a hall stacked with bundled newspapers rotted to mush; an old infirmary; moldy closets full of stored books, bandages, and gas masks. He'd found boxes of glass syringes, chairs with leather restraints, and straightjackets stained brown. Some rooms had steel doors; others had manacles bolted to the concrete walls. He'd once entered a room at the southern corner and been driven to the floor by a flood of bats that had found a passage in through a rotted place at the foundation. The ceilings pressed low in the subbasement. Light was sparse.

The first time Julian went missing, Michael found him in the furnace room, curled up in the tight space behind the hot metal, his knees to his chest, back hard against the brick.

He was six years old, beaten bloody.

Three years ago.

Michael ducked under some pipes, then pushed through a stretch of black to where blue light and furnace heat pushed under a warped door. He heard a low voice, his brother singing; when he opened the door, heat drove past him. The furnace filled the room, blue flame in its guts, damp heat pushing out. Julian had squeezed into the narrow place behind the boiler, his back curved, arms around his knees. Shoeless, he rocked in the narrow space, his upper body bare and red and filthy, his hair wet enough to steam.

He did not look up.

"Julian?" Michael squeezed behind the boiler. "You okay?" Julian shook his head, and Michael saw new bruises, fresh abrasions. He put a hand on his brother's shoulder, then sat; for a long time, Julian said nothing. When he did speak, it was in a broken voice.

"Remember when we were little? Old man Dredge?"

Michael had to think about it. "The maintenance man?"

"He slept in that little room down the hall."

Julian tilted his head and Michael remembered. Dredge had a small room with a cot and refrigerator. He kept girlie posters on the wall and booze in the fridge. He was old and bent, and Julian had always been strangely unafraid of him. "What about him?"

"I come down here, you know." Julian said it like Michael had no idea. "He used to help me when I needed it. I'd hide down here and he'd act mean when the older boys came looking. He'd shake that stick he had, talk crazy talk until most boys were too scared to even think about coming down here. He wasn't really mean, but he wanted to help. He was my friend. When things got bad he would tell me stories. He said there were hidden doors down here, magic ones. His eyes would squint up when he talked about them, but he swore they were here. Find the right wall, he'd tell me. When things get bad, find the right wall, tap it just right, and it'll open up."

"Sunlight and silver stairs . . ."

"I told you about that?" Julian asked.

"A door to a better place. I'd forgotten, but, yeah. You told me." Michael pictured the old man, his seamed skin and bloodshot eyes, the smell of booze and cigarettes. He'd disappeared two years ago. Fired,

Michael guessed. Fired for being crazy or dirty or both. "It was just a story, Julian. Just a crazy old man."

"Yeah. Crazy, huh?" Julian laughed, but in a bad way. And when he cupped his hands, Michael saw the abrasions on his knuckles, the smeared blood and split skin.

His brother had been down here tapping walls . . .

"What happened, Julian?"

He shrugged. "They tried to throw me out naked. They tried to throw me out, but I fought." He sniffed wetly. "They got my shoes."

Michael studied his brother and realized that his skin wasn't red from heat, but from cold; and that it wasn't sweat in his brother's hair, but melted snow. Then he realized something else. "Those aren't your pants."

Julian ignored him. "They locked all the doors but the main one. They wanted to make me come in the front, past all the people. They thought that would be funny, but I beat them. I came in where the bats come in. You know? Right, Michael. The bat room."

Michael saw it now. He saw his brother running through the snow, naked and cold, then squirming through a gap of rotted wood and collapsed subfloor, headfirst into all those bats, all that shit. "Those aren't your pants, Julian."

The pants were stiff with crud and far too big on his narrow waist. They looked like something dug from one of the moldy boxes that littered the basement floor, a man's pants, old and stained and frayed at the cuff. Julian's fingers curled on the stiff knees, and his eyes hung open in a face gone suddenly slack. "Why would I wear somebody else's pants?"

The expression was so familiar, the dull eyes that refused to focus, the open mouth and hint of crazy.

The disconnect.

As much as Michael hated to see it, he understood too well why the look took his brother so often. Harassed at every turn, Julian had been disintegrating for months, so twitchy and pale and hollow-eyed that he barely ate or slept; and when sleep did come, it was as tortured as his days, the dreams relentless. The worst moment came two nights ago when Julian rolled out of bed with a whimper in his throat and silver spit on his chin. He crammed himself into a corner and balled tight, same slack mouth, same nightmare eyes. It took long minutes to snap him out of it, and when Michael finally got him back in bed, Julian remained jittery and glazed and afraid. His words broke as he tried to explain.

Things change in the dark. It scares me.

Things change how?

You'll think I'm crazy.

I won't.

Swear?

Jeez, Julian . . .

You know how a candle starts out all clean and smooth and pretty? How it makes sense when you look at it. Like that's how it should look.

Okay.

But then you light it, and it melts and drips and goes ruined and ugly. Well, sometimes it feels like that when the lights go out. Like everything is wrong.

I don't understand.

It's like everything melts off in the dark. Like the dark is the flame and the world is wax.

The world's not a candle, Julian.

But how do you know if you can't see it?

Why are you crying?

How can anybody know?

Just the thought of it made Michael angry. So what if his brother was soft? "Who did this, Julian? Hennessey?"

"And Billy Walker." Julian started crying again, bright, oily tears. He sniffed loudly, smeared dirt with a forearm.

"Who else?" Michael asked.

"Georgie-boy Nichols. Chase Johnson. And that fuck-head in from juvie."

"The one from north Georgia? The big one?"

"Ronnie Saints." Julian nodded.

"Five of them?"

"Yeah."

Michael stood, even angrier. Furnace heat pulled sweat from his skin. "You have to stand up for yourself, Julian. Once you do that, they'll leave you alone."

"But, I'm not like you."

"Just show them you're not scared."

"I'm sorry, Michael."

"Don't say you're sorry . . ."

"Please don't be angry."

"I'm not angry."

"I'm sorry, Michael."

Julian buried his eyes in a forearm, and Michael stared down for a long second. "You have to stop, Julian."

"Stop what?" Big eyes turned up. A heavy swallow in his narrow throat.

"Stop mooning around all the time." Michael hated the words. "Stop singing to yourself and looking lost. Stop running when they chase. Stop flinching—"

"Michael . . ."

"Stop being such a pussy."

Julian looked away. "I don't mean to be. Please don't say that, Michael."

But Michael was tired of the worry, the fights. "Just go to the room, Julian. I'll see you there later."

"Where are you going?"

"To handle this myself." He shouldered the awkward door and left so fast he missed the look of hurt on his brother's face, the diamond tears and determination. He didn't see the way Julian's arms shook when he stood, how he pulled the knife from behind his back and squeezed until his hand was bone.

"Okay, Michael."

His brother was gone.

"Okay."

Julian glared at the knife, then at his skinny arms and birdcage chest. He didn't have muscles like Michael did, not the wide shoulders, or the strong blue veins that showed in his arms. He lacked the sharp eyes, the even teeth and steadiness. He had over-pale skin and

52

lungs that burned when he ran; but the weakness went deeper than that. An uneven place lurked behind the bones of his chest, and part of him hated Michael for not having the same, soft place inside. Sometimes that hatred was a terrible thing, so strong it threatened to show on his face; sometimes it disappeared altogether, thinned so much by love that Julian remembered it like a dream.

Julian stood for a long time, humiliated and ashamed, his eyes shiny wet. His mind rolled with the memories of a thousand small hurts: taunts and abuse, Hennessey's spit on his face, an old man's pants and the taste of bat shit in his mouth. And he thought, too, of the big hurts, the pain and fear and self-loathing. The disappointment in his brother's eyes. That one most of all. Julian smeared snot on his face and wondered how he could love his brother and hate him at the same time. They were both so big.

The love.

The hate.

Julian wanted to be steady on his feet. He wanted people to say hello to him in the hall and to not hurt him just because they could. If he was like Michael, he could have those things, so Julian decided that's what he would be. Like Michael. But when he stepped for the door, the damaged ankle rolled and he went down so fast and hard his face hit concrete with the sound of cracking wood. The knife clattered away, and he curled in the dirt, lonesome and hurt and wanting to be in his brother's skin.

Michael . . .

Julian's head ached like the bone above his eyes had split, like something sharp and hot had been jammed through the crack. He cupped his face and cried, and when his eyes opened he saw the rust-speckled blade on the floor. His fingers found the handle and metal rasped as he rolled onto all fours, head loose at the end of his neck, vision blurred. He heard a strange noise in his throat, and his face twitched as something in his head gave with a glassy snap. He felt different when he stood, dizzy and distant, limbs heavy. He swayed as the world grayed out, and when his vision cleared, he heard the sound of knuckles tapping the wall, hard, bony thumps as a far part of his mind said: *That hurts . . .*

But the pain belonged to some other boy.

Stop being such a pussy, the boy said, and Julian's feet scraped on the blackish floor. His hand found the rail that angled up, and stairs led past the basement kitchen as the air filled with the smells of sugared tea and fatty meat, white bread and fake butter. Julian climbed another flight, then made a left turn that led to the dining hall where, already, boys had begun to gather. He stumbled past the door, then pulled himself up more empty stairs and down a long hall, knife hard against his leg. He passed a few other boys, and some part of Julian knew how bad he looked, filthy and limping and hurt. Boys stared at his bruises and rotting pants, the swollen knot above crazy eyes. They stepped out of his way when they saw the knife, their backs flat on the rough plaster walls. But Julian ignored the way they looked at him, the pity and the jeers and the odd, kind question.

No, said the boy with Julian's voice. *We don't need any help.*

He found Hennessey alone in the first-floor bathroom at the end of the north hall. He stood at the urinal, and turned when the door swung closed, his disbelief twisting into a leer. "Jesus," Hennessey said, then turned his back and flushed. The bathroom smelled of bad aim and disinfectant, the lights white and cold behind metal cages on the ceiling. Julian kept the knife behind his back as Hennessey spit once on the floor and stepped closer, the freckles dark as flung mud on the slope of his nose.

"I'm not scared of you," Julian said.

Hennessey was tall and wide, eyes muddy brown under red hair. Pale fuzz covered the backs of his hands and a single bad tooth marred the right side of his smile. He flicked a gaze over Julian, and shook out another laugh. "Look at you. Girly muscles all bunched up. Got your angry eyes on." He waved fingers, made a circle of his mouth and said, "Ooh."

Julian's head titled, his eyes dark and dull. "I'm not a pussy."

"Yeah." Hennessey shoved hard and pushed past. "You are."

"You take that back."

"Or what?"

Hennessey didn't even turn. He got one hand on the door before the knife went into the side of his neck. It slid in with a crunch, and

Julian stepped back as the big kid went down thrashing, two hands on his throat, eyes rolling and white. One hand rose, wet and stained, fingers spread. He saw blood and confusion changed to terror. "Julian . . ."

For that instant, a terrible satisfaction boiled in the place Julian's fears were normally found, but a deep-down voice cried out that this was wrong. It said call a grown-up. Get help.

Shut up, you pussy.

The words rang in Julian's mind, so strong they rocked him back on his one good foot.

Such hate.

So loud.

Julian fell into a stall door, clattered inside, porcelain cold and hard on his back. He held his head as Hennessey's legs thumped twice and grew still. So much pain behind his eyes, like something had torn. He squeezed harder and the room tilted into something foreign, angles all wrong, gravity that pulled sideways. Julian let go of his head and hauled himself from the stall, wretched and hurt and confused.

"Michael?"

His voice this time, small in his own throat. On the floor, Hennessey sprawled over the tiles, the knife a strange and foreign thing that rose between the fingers on his throat; around him, red liquid spread, and with it an emptiness in Julian's head. He pushed his bloody palms together and blinked as they stuck slightly, then separated with a noise like plastic pulled off meat. He looked at the high, white lights, the mirrors equally bright. The tile floor was black and white, small rectangles with a red tide that rolled along the grout.

"Michael?"

Silence.

"Michael?"

And it was like the third time was magic. The door opened and he was there, his brother, who for all Julian's life had made things right. He was breathing hard, sweaty, and Julian knew that he'd been running. Julian tried to speak, but had cotton in his head and putty in his mouth. He held up his red hands, blinking, and for five long seconds Michael stood still, eyes ranging from Hennessey to his brother, his brother to the hall, up and down, then back inside. He shut the door, stepped wide to clear the body, and Julian almost cried with relief to see him there. He would make it right. He would make it all better.

Michael's hands found Julian's shoulders. His mouth moved and there were words, but Julian couldn't really understand. He blinked and nodded, eyes dropping from Michael's mouth to the twisted legs on the floor. Everything was wrong, sound rushing in his ears, the taste of vomit in his throat. Michael led him to a sink, still talking, and helped Julian wash his hands, his arms. He wet a paper towel, and gentle as a mother, wiped bloody spray from his brother's face. And all the while his eyes were on Julian's. His mouth moved, and when Julian did not respond, he said it again, stronger, slower: "Do you understand?"

Sound from a long tunnel. Julian felt his head move, and Michael said it was okay, then said something again. It made no sense, but Julian heard the words. "I did this." Michael's face was inches from Julian's, and he was tapping his own chest. "I did this. Do you understand?"

Julian leaned forward, mouth open. Michael looked hurriedly at the door, then stooped and tugged the knife from Hennessey's neck. It came with a wet sound and Michael held it so Julian could see. "I did this. Hennessey was hurting you and I did this. When they ask, that's what you say. Okay?" Julian stared. "You can't handle what's coming from this," Michael said. "Julian? Understand? He was hurting you. I came in. I did this."

"You did this . . ." Thick words. Disconnect. Julian felt his head tilt, and his eyelids fell once.

"Yes. Me." Michael looked at the closed door. "Somebody saw you with the knife. People are coming. I have to go. I did this. Say it."

"Hennessey was hurting me." A pause. "You did this."

"Good, Julian. Good."

Then he hugged his brother once, opened the door, and was gone, blood on his fingers, knife in his hand.

Julian looked at Hennessey and saw eyes as dull as spilled milk. He backed away, blinked, and people came. They shouted and moved a lot, large hands on Hennessey's throat, his eyes. An ear to his mouth. Julian saw Flint and other grown-ups. He blinked as they asked questions, blinked again.

He looked at the open door.

And did what Michael said.

Abigail stood at the window of the narrow room, dark sky outside, snow still loose on the wind. Frost rimed the glass and everything was damp and cold: the furniture, her clothing, her skin. She saw movement on the drive, a boy, and could no longer bear the thought of children in this stark and bitter place. A coat flapped as the boy ran, and she wondered why he was outside in the storm, to what place he was running. She closed her eyes, and asked God to watch over these children, to keep them safe; and when her eyelids rose, she saw that night had come in its fullness, black and shuttered and alive with wind.

She looked for the boy, but he was gone.

Cold wind blew and snow came harder. Her fingers settled at her throat as from beyond the glass she heard a lonesome wail.

Sirens in the distance.

Small hearts beating red.

CHAPTER SIX

Michael had seen this moment so many times: in his dreams and imaginings, in those sweat-filled hours when he could not sleep and the air in Elena's apartment seemed to have no breath at all. He'd tried to envision a graceful way to tell her the things he'd done, some means by which to speak of regret and hope and aspiration, but there was no window to his soul that wasn't cracked through or painted black. He was a killer, and could never take that back. What did the rest of it matter? That he had reasons? That he'd never hurt a civilian?

She wouldn't care, and he couldn't blame her.

He stepped closer, certain only that in all his imaginings, the moment of truth had never looked like this: blood on his hands and Elena on her knees in the brown, brittle grass. She looked so small and unhappy, one hand splayed beneath her, the other twisting fabric from her stomach. Michael could not know the thoughts that pushed through her mind, only that they must be slippery and wet and cold. Thoughts of betrayals, he imagined, thoughts of lies and violence done.

He put the phone in his pocket and stepped onto the grass. She was five feet away, but could have been a thousand.

"Are you okay?" Her back was warm in the sun, lean under a dress that felt like silk. She shook her head as low wind stirred and the river smell intensified. Traffic flowed past, and Michael heard sirens far away, the sound of the city. To the north, an ugly smoke rose.

"I don't know you." Her words came without heat, but tasted of ash and things ruined. She pushed herself up, rocked back on her knees, and shrugged off Michael's hand. "I don't know anything about you."

"You know me in every way that matters."

"You were shooting at those men. You just threw guns in the river. Jesus, I can't even say that without sounding absurd."

She kept her head still, but Michael saw that she was ready to break. Her friends were dead, and Michael's answer was a lie they both recognized. He touched his chest and said, "What's in here hasn't changed. I swear to you, that's true." She refused to blink, and a kernel of panic crystallized in Michael's chest. "You're the only thing that matters to me. Everything we've experienced, everything we've shared."

"No."

"I swear on our unborn child."

"Don't."

"What?"

She searched his eyes, and Michael saw in hers the annihilation of faith. "Don't swear on my baby," she said, and they both understood the power of the words she'd chosen.

Michael turned his face to the sky, then looked back down and saw the police car. It rolled past on the street, moving slowly. Behind glass, an officer's face swiveled toward the parked car and the patch of grass where they knelt. "We need to go." Elena followed his gaze, and some part of her understood. "Now," Michael said.

She looked at his face, then at the police car, which had stopped a hundred yards away. If she chose to call out or run, Michael could do nothing to stop her. "I'll need an explanation," she said.

"You'll have it."

"The truth."

"I swear."

Michael touched his chest a second time, and the air between them crackled with charge. Love scored with fear. Dark energy. The knife blade beneath them felt very real, and Michael knew the keen edge of it could slice them apart in the next second. Elena knew it, too, had the same prophetic glimpse; but in the end, she nodded, followed him to the car, and neither doubted it was love alone that gave her legs the strength. On the sidewalk she took in the police car, the far, black smoke. A siren throbbed in the distance as people died and a piece of the city burned. Elena looked once at the father of her unborn child, then got in the car, her features very still, her small hands twisted pink in the womb of her lap.

Michael started the Navigator and accelerated into traffic. The cop was still there, then the road curved and he was gone. Michael turned east, away from the river. "We need to get out of the city," he said.

"Why?"

The word was small.

"I have enemies."

She sank lower in the seat, and Michael checked the mirror, hating truth for being so absolute. Elena wrapped her arms around her knees. At his apartment, he circled the block, then stopped. Elena leaned forward and peered up through the glass. "What is this place?"

"My apartment."

"But you don't have . . ." The words trailed away. "I want to go home," she said.

"You can't."

"Why not?"

"I need you to trust me." Michael opened the door.

"Why are we here?"

"We need money." He studied the street, the neighboring windows. "You should come up."

He walked around the hood and opened her door. A lady passed, walking a small dog. Birds called from trees down the street, and Michael saw that Elena was smoothing her hands across the fabric of her dress, pulling it tight on her thighs, then balling loose folds in her hands. When she descended from the car, he led her onto a small stoop, then inside and to the third floor. Michael checked the apartment before allowing Elena to enter.

"Come in. Please."

She stopped five feet inside the door, eyes restless on this place where Michael had lived.

"It's just a place," he said.

She touched a painting on the wall, a book on the shelf. "You've had this all along?"

"I almost never come here."

"How long?"

Anger flashed in her eyes, the first flicker of heat he'd seen. "Five years," he said. "Maybe six. It doesn't matter."

"How can you say that?"

Michael had no answer. "This will only take a second. Just . . . wait here." He made his way down the hall to the smaller bedroom. In the closet, he stripped off his bloodstained clothing and put on a different suit, new shoes. He chose two handguns from the racked weapons, then pulled a duffel bag from the shelf and opened it on the floor. One of the guns, a Kimber nine millimeter, went into a carry holster and onto his belt, under his jacket; the other, a Smith & Wesson forty-five, went into the bag with five spare magazines. He turned to the cash. On the lowest shelf, next to boxed ammunition, he had $290,000 in banded hundred-dollar bills. He tossed them into the duffel as Elena appeared in the door behind him. She hesitated and Michael let her take it in—the sight of steel, the smell of gun oil, cash, and English leather. "I have more," Michael said.

"More what?" Her eyes were on the rowed guns.

"More money."

"You think I care about money?" The same heat, skin flushed.

"No. I—"

"You think I'll stay for money?"

"That's not what I meant."

Elena touched her stomach. "I'm going to be sick."

"You'll be okay." Michael's voice was colder than he'd planned, but Elena's accusation hurt. He'd mentioned money only so she'd know he could provide for her. Hide her. Keep her safe. He moved for the door, and she followed.

"How much more?" she asked.

"Enough."

"Please tell me there's an explanation for all this." She caught his arm, and he stopped. "I need something."

They were in the hall. It was empty. Elena was on the balls of her feet, a bird ready to fly. "I have a story," he said.

"About?"

"Beginnings. Reasons. Everything."

"And you'll tell me?"

"Yes, but later. Okay?"

"If you promise."

"I do." He turned on his heel, and they moved to the bottom of the stairs. Michael checked the sidewalk, then ducked back inside and hugged her fiercely. Her hair was warm on the bottom of his chin, and he wanted to tell her one more lie: that everything would be fine, that life would go back to normal. "We have to move quickly. Head down. Straight to the car." He pulled her across hot concrete and into the car. She spilled loosely into the seat. From where they were, Michael had two options to get out of the city fast. He could go north to the Holland Tunnel or east to the Brooklyn Bridge. He rounded to the driver's side, got in, and cranked the car. Beside him, Elena sat with her eyes closed. She mouthed silent words, and it took Michael a second to understand the thing she was unwilling to say out loud.

Please, God . . .

She made a hard knot of her fingers.

Make it a good story . . .

Michael drove north through the city, then out through the Holland Tunnel and south on the interstate. Beside him, Elena watched the city fall away. "I've never been out of New York," she said.

"Maybe this will be good, then. A chance to see the country."

"Is that a joke?" she asked.

"A bad one, I guess."

Miles clicked onto the odometer, the silence painful. "You said you have a story."

The sky outside was a summer sky, a lover's sky. They were in Jersey, and her voice could have belonged to a stranger.

"It's about two boys."

"You?"

"And my brother."

"You don't have a brother." Michael waited, and she nodded. "Ah. Another lie."

"I've not seen him since I was ten." Sun pushed heat through the windows. Michael showed her a photograph. Colorless and cracked, it was of two boys on a field of snow and mud. Their pants were too short, the jackets patched. "That's me on the right."

She took the photo and her eyes softened. "So young."

"Yes."

"What's his name?"

"Julian."

She traced Julian's face with a finger, and then touched Michael's. Color moved into her face, the empathy that was one of her best traits. Her accent thickened as it did when she got emotional. "Do you miss him very much?"

Michael nodded, knowing that she would listen, seeing it in her face, the way it softened. "They say you don't remember much before the age of two, but that's not true. I was ten months old when Julian was left naked on the bank of a half-frozen creek. He was a newborn. It was snowing. I was with him."

"Ten months old?"

"Yes."

"And you remember this?"

"Bits and pieces."

"Like what?"

"Black trees and snow on my face."

Elena touched the photograph.

"The silence when Julian stopped screaming."

Elena kept her eyes down as Michael spoke of two boys dumped like trash in the woods, of cold water and the hunters that carried them out, of long years at the orphanage and his brother's deterioration. He spoke of crowded rooms and sickness, of conflict and boredom and the indifference of malnutrition. He explained how strong kids learned to steal and weak ones learned to run; how older kids had the power to hurt. "You can't imagine."

Elena listened carefully as he spoke. She listened for lies and half-truths and the tells that would reveal them. She did this because she was smart and wary and carrying a child that meant more than her own life. But there was honesty in him when he spoke: flashes of anger and regret, a fire banked long in his heart. "Hennessey died on the bathroom floor. I took the knife and I ran."

"To protect your brother?"

"Because I was the oldest."

"You ran and took the blame with you?" Michael said nothing, but Elena knew from his face that the statement was true. "What happened next?"

Michael shrugged. "Julian was adopted."

"And you were not."

He shook his head.

"I don't know what to say."

"It is what it is."

"And once in New York?"

Michael rolled his shoulders. "The city is not a good place for a boy alone."

"What do you mean?"

Michael slipped into the left lane, passed a slow-moving car. His voice did not change when he said, "I killed a man nine days after I got off the bus."

"Why?"

"Because I was small and he was strong. Because the world is cruel. Because he was drunk and insane and wanted to set me on fire for the fun of it."

"Oh, my God."

"He found me asleep near the docks, and doused me with gasoline before I could get to my feet. He had one foot on my chest, trying to get the match lit. I remember his shoes, black, tied with white string; pants so crusted with grime they crunched under my fingers. The first match didn't light. It was damp, I guess. Or he stripped the sulfur. I don't know. God, maybe. The second match was in his hand when I put the knife in his leg. Right in the side, just above his knee. It hit bone and I twisted it until he fell. Then, I put it in his stomach and I ran."

Elena shook her head, no words.

Ten years old . . .

Michael cleared his throat. "There was a lot of that on the street," he said. "Insanity. Random violence. That's the unpredictable stuff.

64

Beyond that, it's easy to spot. People try to own you. They try to control you, put you to work, use you, screw you. Whatever. If a kid on the streets can't go to the authorities, he doesn't have much. I was lucky, I guess."

"How?"

"I was strong, fast, knew how to fight. Iron House gave me that. It made me alert and unforgiving. What I didn't know until I landed on the streets was that I was smart, too. That people would see that, and that I could use it."

"I don't understand."

"One kid on the streets is vulnerable. Two together are better, but still not safe. A dozen, though, or twenty, that's an army. Ten months after stepping off the bus, I had six kids working for me. Six months later, I had another ten, some younger than me, some as old as seventeen, even eighteen. We slept together, ate together. And we did jobs. Smash and grab. Burglary. Tourists were always an easy mark. Eventually, people started to notice."

"Police?"

Michael shook his head. "Gangs, mostly. Some small-time hoods. We weren't getting rich, but there was value there. Electronics, jewelry, cash. Some people figured it'd be easy to come in and take what I'd built. Kids, they figured, would be easy to scare, easy to co-opt. It was an untapped market, a low-risk opportunity. It got violent."

He touched the white line on the side of his neck, and Elena asked, "Not a glass door?"

"Another lie. I'm sorry."

She knew the scars he carried: two on his stomach, three on his ribs, the long one on his neck. They were pale, slightly raised, and she knew the feel of them, cool under her lips.

"We were living under a bridge in Spanish Harlem, maybe seven of us at the time. We'd been there for a few weeks. We moved around, you see? A week in one place, a month in another. I guess we stayed there a day longer than we should have, 'cause some local gangbangers showed up one afternoon. They didn't want a thing other than to beat the crap out of us. There were only four of them, but everybody else ran."

"The other children?"

"Yes."

"What happened?"

"I stayed."

"And?"

Michael shrugged. "They cut me, I cut them back; but it was only a matter of time. Eventually, they got me down. One of them stepped so hard on my wrist it broke bones. They pinned me down. I should have died."

"What happened?"

"Someone came."

Something in the way he said it made Elena think this was the crux of it. A half mile of industrial buildings slid by on greased skids: metal slabs on dark tarmac, chain-link fencing and sodium lights on tall poles. Elena said, "Michael?"

"I'd heard of him but never seen him. He was just a name to me, then, someone to know about, a man to avoid. He was ruthless, people said. A criminal. A killer."

"Mafia?"

"No. Not Italian. Nobody really knew what he was, although some said Polish; others, Romanian. Actually, he was American, born in Queens to a Serbian prostitute. An orphan, I later learned. He was there when the fight started, a long car on the other side of the street. His window was down. He was watching."

"While you fought?"

"They got me down, put a knife here." He touched the line on his neck. It was seven inches long with a jagged twist in the middle. "I was pretty sure they were going to kill me. I was bleeding. They were working themselves up. I saw it in their faces. They were going to do it. Then he was just there."

Michael blinked and relived it: Crooked legs in a navy suit. Dark hair salted white.

"He looked lost," Michael said. "That was my first thought. This man is lost and dumb enough to smile about it. Then I saw how fear came over the men who were beating me. They stepped back, hands up. One of them dropped his knife . . ."

Do you know who I am?

Michael could still feel the steel in the old man's voice, but there was no way to explain it. No one else could fully grasp what the voice meant that day, what it meant now.

You should leave.

"They didn't stay to talk." Michael cleared his throat. "They just ran."

"Michael, you're sweating."

Michael palmed sweat from his forehead. He still saw the old man's face: a narrow jaw and thin eyebrows, eyes as dark and dull as stone. Two men were with him. They stood while the old man squatted at Michael's side. He was in his forties, lean with city-pale skin and narrow, maimed hands. His teeth, on the bottom, were crooked and white.

The others ran. Why didn't you?

I don't know. I just couldn't.

How old are you?

Twelve.

Your name is Michael?

Yes.

I've heard about you.

But Michael was fading. The blue suit rustled as the old man stood. *What do you think, Jimmy?*

I think he's a tough little shit.

Shoes scraped concrete. Light dimmed as Michael bled, and words came down like fog off the river.

That my son was such a boy as this . . .

Michael was sweating heavily, suddenly warm in the car. He felt the old man's face, papery and hot under his hand. He felt brittle ribs and a failing chest, the old man's final, sucking try at breath. "He taught me everything I know," Michael said. "He made me what I am."

"You're pale. Jesus, Michael. You're white as a sheet."

"He gave me a home." Michael's voice faded as the car drifted left. "He gave me a home and I killed him."

Little else was said for the next three hours. Elena asked, but Michael shook his head, spoke in fragments. "He was dying. I loved him."

"And they want to kill you for this?"

"And because I'm with you. They think I'll sell them out. Go to the cops."

"For me?"

"For a normal life."

"Would you do that?"

"No."

Michael pictured the old man nine days ago. Jaundiced and stripped of flesh, he was propped up with a view of the river. Michael took his hand and told him for the first time about Elena: how he felt, why he wanted to quit the life. He apologized for keeping her a secret.

She's special. I don't want this to touch her.

This life?

Yes.

The old man understood. *She loves you?*

I believe that she does.

The old man nodded yellow tears. *She is a gift, Michael, and rare for men like us.*

Men like us?

Men for whom life makes very few gifts.

But how do I tell her?

The truth? You don't.

Never?

Not if you wish to keep her . . .

"Michael?" Elena's voice was worried.

"Just give me a minute." But it took more time than that. There was so much to convey and so little she could understand. He killed a man at ten to save his life, and killed the next to make the old man proud. "There are no innocents," he said, and the words were a memory of childhood.

"What does that mean?"

Michael touched a patch of skin above his eye. "Something someone told me once. It doesn't matter."

"I need to know more. You told me you loved him and that you killed him. You can't leave it at that. You can't leave me with that and nothing else."

"Just give me a minute."

But the right minute never came.

They hit traffic north of Baltimore. One hour stretched to two. The engine droned, and at one point Elena slept. She went deep and hot, dreamed of babies and fire, then woke with a scream trapped behind her teeth.

"You're dreaming," he said.

"How long have I been out?"

"A few hours."

The car was barely moving. Blue lights flashed through the glass, and she saw police cruisers in front of them, ambulances and cars with ripped skin. Shattered glass made stars on the road, and for one instant she wanted to fling herself from the car, to give herself to the police and be done. She pressed a palm against her stomach, heard a last, far cry as if from the babies burning in her dream.

Michael touched her hair.

"Just a dream," he said.

"Am I okay?" She was not sure what she meant.

"I've got you, baby."

It was a thing he said, words she'd heard a thousand times: late after a bad night at work; walking home in the dark or after some other nightmare; days when she was sick or feeling lonesome. He stroked her hair, and like that, the fear was gone. The nightmare faded, and his voice settled like a blanket.

Heavy . . .

"I've got you, baby."

Warm . . .

She woke again in Washington, still blurry and scared and uncertain. Fifteen miles later, Michael said, "You haven't asked me where we're going."

She shook her head. "It doesn't matter."

"Why not?"

"Because nothing is real until tomorrow." Her eyes glittered, and she shifted in her seat. "Today's too big."

They drove a bit farther. Headlights lit one side of Michael's face and left the other side dark. "There are things I've done—"

"Don't."

"It's important."

"Please, don't."

Her grip was strong on his hand, but when Michael looked right he saw that she was struggling, one eye bright as a star in the hard rush of yellow light.

North of Richmond, Michael found a motel that took cash and didn't worry about identification. It was cheap and clean, fifty yards off the interstate. He let Elena into the room, then watched as she pulled off her clothes and crawled between the sheets. The room was dim but for a blade of light between drawn curtains. Her head found a pillow and she rolled onto her back, one arm up. "Come to bed." She pulled back the sheet, and said nothing as Michael withdrew the pistol from his belt and put it on the bedside table. He stripped off his clothes, slipped in next to her, and stretched out on his back. Elena rolled against him, put warm skin on his. She tucked her head into the crook of his shoulder, spread a palm on his chest, and Michael knew that she could feel his heart.

"Elena," he said.

"Sshh. Sleep first."

She pushed closer into his side, slipped a leg across the two of his. Her stomach pressed his hip, her breasts heavy on his ribs. Breath made a hot wind on the side of Michael's throat, and he knew she was pretending that nothing had changed. Her man was just her man. All was right in the world. He let her have it, the gift of a night; and when she slept, Michael rose. He pulled on his pants and shirt, lifted the gun and checked it from long habit. He released the clip and racked the slide. Copper jackets gleamed in the dim light. Brass casings. Oiled steel. He reassembled the weapon, jacked a round into the chamber, and lowered the safety. Outside, the parking lot was still. Michael noted cars and sight lines and exits. Stevan had fifty guns on the payroll and unlimited resources. He also had Jimmy.

Jimmy could be a problem.

Moving a chair to the window, Michael sat and placed the gun on the windowsill. He watched, he waited; an hour before dawn, the cell phone in his pocket vibrated. Michael looked at the number and was unsurprised. His foster brother had always been a talker. "Hello, Stevan."

"Do you know where I am?" The phone was warm on Michael's ear. Stevan sounded low and tired and angry.

"How could I know that?" Michael kept his own voice low, but when he looked at Elena, she was stirring. He opened the door and stepped outside. The air was velvet smooth, the interstate strangely quiet. In the east, the sky hinted at dawn.

"I'm parked outside the city morgue. Do you know why? Because they took my father's body. The cops took him, and now they're cutting him open. That's on you, Michael, that desecration."

"I'm sorry, Stevan. I never wanted that. I just want out."

"If I let you go, I look weak. Then, there's my father. You killed him in his own bed."

"You killed Elena. We're even."

"That would not come close to making us even, the death of a woman. Besides, I know she lived."

"You don't know anything."

"How long do you think you can keep her safe?"

"You touch Elena, and I'll kill you. It's that simple."

"Should I be scared?"

"You'll never find me."

"I don't have to find you."

"Why not?"

"Say hello to your brother."

"I told you, I don't—"

The line went dead. Michael closed the phone, and when he turned he found Elena standing in the open door. She'd wrapped herself in a sheet from the bed. "Was that him?" she asked.

"Stevan? Yes." Michael turned her back into the room and closed the door.

"He really wants me dead?"

She was afraid. He took her chin in his hand and kissed her once on the lips. "I won't let that happen."

"How can you know?"

"You said nothing was real until tomorrow. It's not tomorrow yet." It was a lie they chose to accept, that dawn's fingers were not yet clawing red from the sky, that it could even make a difference. She nodded, eyes closed, and Michael said, "Let's go back to bed."

Michael took the sheet and spread it over the bed. They climbed in, and she pressed against his skin as she had before. "Love me," she said.

"Are you sure?"

The air was black around them, the door bolted shut. She nodded again, lips soft on his, and Michael rolled her onto her back. His fingers found the vellum of her skin, the warm planes and the dusky bits of her. She kissed his neck, his chest. They loved as if the night were their last, and in a way it was, for both felt the morning sun coming, the stark truths of the day that raced to find them.

CHAPTER SEVEN

Michael slept hard and woke to the sound of the television. When he opened his eyes, he saw Elena perched on the end of the bed, wrapped in a blanket. The clock said it was almost noon. She was watching CNN. "They're talking about us." She did not turn, and Michael threw off the covers, scrubbed two hands across his face, and moved to sit beside her. The image on the screen was from the day before: the restaurant, burning. He watched firefighters assault the blaze, then the camera angle cut away, and the reporter was interviewing a man and a woman, both middle-aged and white, both nervous. They described a man who looked like Michael. They spoke of automatic weapons and people screaming, people dead. They described Elena, and it was a very good description.

"Black dress and long legs . . . very pretty . . ."

The wife tugged on her husband's shirt, interrupting.

"She was holding his hand, running. They got in the same car."

At the bottom of the screen, a grainy surveillance photo of a dark Navigator appeared with the caption, POLICE ARE SEARCHING FOR THIS CAR. Below the photo, they gave the license plate number.

Michael rose to check the parking lot. When he came back, the couple had disappeared, replaced by images of smoke-stained firefighters and paramedics bent over bodies. They showed a row of vinyl bags, wounded people that were blank-eyed and in shock. When the reporter began her recap, Michael heard the words "possible terrorist attack" on three occasions.

Elena stood and did not look at Michael. "The police think I'm involved, don't they?"

"I don't—"

"They're looking for me."

Michael nodded sadly. "Yes."

"They think I killed my friends."

"They don't know what to think," Michael said. "They have your description and mine. They have the car and a lot of questions. That's it. That's all. They don't have our names; they know nothing about us."

"Police want to arrest me and your friends want to kill me?"

"I won't let any of that happen."

"I'm going to take a shower." She gestured at the television screen. "There's more. You should watch it." She hesitated at the bathroom door, still refusing to meet his eyes. "I'll be in here for a very long time. Please, don't come in."

She closed the door. The lock dropped and Michael watched the television: "Sources close to the investigation indicate that organized crime may be involved . . ."

The television cut to an image of the old man's town house in Sutton Place. Police cars lined the street. Yellow tape. Barricades. Cops moved in and out of the front door. Body bags rolled on wheeled gurneys and were hoisted into ambulances with dark lights.

". . . the Navigator identified leaving the scene of the explosion has been traced to this address. Initial reports indicate seven bodies were discovered here just minutes before the explosion in Tribeca . . ."

Michael glanced at the bathroom door. His name was not mentioned, though Stevan's was. The cops wanted to talk to him. They showed his picture.

And Jimmy's.

Michael turned off the television and checked the parking lot again. The day was blue and flawless. He called the front desk, got an older man with a smoker's voice. "What's the best place to shop for clothes?" The man gave directions to the local mall. Michael wrote them down, then pulled on the same clothes from yesterday. He tied his shoes, ran fingers through his hair, then wrote a note that read, WENT OUT TO

BUY CLOTHES, ETC. BACK SOON. PLEASE DON'T LEAVE. She wouldn't, he was sure, not after last night. There were too many questions, too much to say.

Outside, the air was hot and tasted of traffic. Michael drove ten minutes into Richmond, then got off the interstate and found the big shopping mall exactly where he'd been told it would be. He parked the car and entered near the food court. Shopping as quickly as he could, he bought three changes of clothes for himself and for Elena. He kept it simple when it came to his own needs: jeans, casual shirts, good shoes. A light jacket with a zipper would hide the gun.

Michael knew Elena's sizes, the kinds of shoes she liked. He spent lavishly and paid cash for everything. Back in the parking lot, he took the plates off the Navigator and switched them with a dark blue pickup parked in the far, back corner. The last store he visited was a drugstore two blocks from the hotel. He bought toothbrushes, shaving gear, whatever he thought they'd need. At the motel, he did a slow drive through the lot and saw nothing that alarmed him. The place was like a million others.

He parked and went inside.

Elena was sitting in one of the chairs, wrapped in a towel. "I couldn't bear to put the same clothes back on," she said. "They felt soiled."

He put the bags on the floor. "You've done nothing wrong."

Elena said, "You should take a shower."

Michael turned the shower on as hot as he could bear it. He lathered and scrubbed and shaved, so that by the time he came out, dressed in new jeans and a blue shirt, he was fresh as he thought he could be. "You look better." Elena's gaze lingered. She wore expensive jeans and brown leather boots with low heels and buckles at mid-calf. She stood, uncomfortable. "Can we walk?"

"There's not much out there."

"I just need to move."

Michael put on the jacket and clipped the nine millimeter back onto his belt. They slipped out of the room, Elena in front. The parking lot had few cars. Large, metal-sided buildings could be seen down a slight incline. Storage. A boat retailer. Used cars. A second motel pushed close to the feeder road that ran parallel to the interstate.

Blank windows stretched in rows, looking out on the same parking lot. Next to the motel was a diner with brushed metal sides and booths behind the glass. On its sign was a giant coffee cup. Elena pushed her hands into the pockets of her jeans. "I feel like I should run."

"Where?"

"Anywhere."

Instead, she walked. She aimed for the back of the lot and seemed content to walk along the verge where scrub trees and chain-link fencing met. They walked in silence until the trees thinned and they could see rooftops across a wide gulley. Elena closed her eyes and lifted her chin as if testing the faint, acrid breeze with her nose. When she opened her eyes, there was a firmness to her mouth, an edge of decision.

He was going to lose her.

"How many people have you killed?"

The question caught Michael off guard. The words were matter-of-fact, but her face twisted, and fear, suddenly, inhabited everything around them; it gave urgency to the limbs that rattled and scraped, voice to the cars that screamed on the interstate, depth to the reflections caught in motel glass. It was fear of the next step, of crossing some uncrossed line and finding oneself trapped on the other side. Michael worried how Elena would react to the words he chose, and knew, too, the thing she feared. "One or a hundred," Michael said, "does it really matter?"

"Of course it matters. What kind of stupid question is that?" She shoved her hands into her pockets, and together they watched a dog by the interstate. It loped along the verge, nose down, tongue lolling over brown, broken teeth. It looked once up the hill, then nosed a diaper that littered the roadside.

"With the exception of the man who raised me," Michael said, "that dog is better than any man I've ever killed."

Elena shivered at the certainty in his voice, the implications. "A man is not a dog."

"A dog is usually better."

"Not always."

"I have good judgment."

The dog pulled its snout from the diaper, and Elena wanted to scream; she wanted to run and vomit and carve great chunks from her heart. "What do we do now?"

"I take you to lunch."

She shook her head. "I'm not hungry."

Michael laid three fingers on her arm, and said, "It's not about the food."

The restaurant was an Italian bistro with white tablecloths and deep booths. Soft leather sighed as they sat. A waiter brought menus and filled their water glasses. "Anything else to drink while you're thinking about your order?"

"Elena?" Michael asked.

"This is too normal." Her hands found the white cloth and she pushed herself from the booth. "Excuse me." She moved past the waiter and disappeared into the ladies' room.

The waiter's face showed his confusion.

Michael said, "I'll have a beer."

When Elena came back, they ate lunch, but it wasn't easy. There was a reticence in her that went beyond the expected.

Back at the motel, Elena shut herself in the bathroom. When she came out, her hair was damp at the edges, the skin of her face pink from cold water and a rough towel. "I've made a decision." She was resolute. "I'm going home."

"You can't."

"I love you, Michael. God help me for that, I do. And I get it, okay? The whole childhood thing, what's happened to you and how you turned into the man you are. It breaks my heart, truthfully, and I could spend a day weeping for the sad, small boys in that photograph you carry. But I have to put the baby first. This baby. Mine." Both hands covered her stomach. "That means I can't be with you. I'm sorry."

"You're not safe in New York. You're not safe here, not without me."

Her chin lifted. "I called Marietta."

"Marietta who lives next door?"

"She has a key. She is sending my passport here by overnight mail. Tomorrow I will go back to Spain."

"You gave Marietta this address?"

"Of course."

"When did you call her?"

"What does it matter? I called her. She is sending the passport and I will leave."

Michael caught her arm. "When?"

"This morning. While you slept."

"What time?"

"Seven thirty, maybe eight. Ow, Michael. You're hurting me."

"Call her." Michael released her arm and pushed his cell phone into her hand. "Do it."

Elena dialed. "She is not answering."

"Try her cell."

Elena redialed and was shunted straight to voice mail. "She always has it with her. She always has it on."

Michael knew this was true. Marietta worked in public relations. Her phone was her life. "Tell me the conversation."

"She was going on about some corporate event—Mercedes, I think. I told her where to find the passport, in the cabinet above the oven. She said she would mail it first thing."

"What else?"

"I heard voices. People on the stairs, maybe. She said she had to go."

"Get your things. We're leaving."

"Why?"

"Marietta's dead."

"What?"

"We have to move."

Michael checked the window. Outside, three men climbed from a dark green van. They were hard-looking men, one Hispanic and two whites. The Hispanic carried a duffel bag, and it was heavy. Michael did not recognize any of them, but knew at a glance what they'd come for. He took in the plates on the van, how their eyes moved, the way they carried themselves. "Too late." He flicked the curtain closed, stepped into the bathroom, and started the shower. When he came out, he left the bathroom door cracked.

"What's going on? What's happening?"

A connecting door joined their room to the one next door. It had a brass deadbolt, but the wood was cheap and thin. Michael shouldered it open, wood cracking at the jamb, bright metal twisting. "Go." Michael tipped his head at the door. Elena moved into the adjoining room, Michael behind her. He forced the damaged door closed, jamming hard to make it fit. At the window, he eased back the curtain. The men were across the lot, twelve feet away. They walked in a row, the center man eyeing the motel door, the two on the sides checking their flanks. "Elena."

She eased up beside him. He wanted her to see, to understand. One of the men slipped a hand under his shirt, and Elena saw the dull show of black steel. "Jesus."

She crossed herself.

Michael nodded toward the door between the rooms. "In ten seconds they'll be in that room. You know how to use this?" He pulled the nine millimeter from the holster at his hip.

"No."

She was truly frightened now. A different kind of fear. "It's easy," Michael told her. "Fifteen rounds. Semiautomatic. Just point and pull the trigger. If anyone comes through that door, you shoot him. Just keep squeezing the trigger. The safety is off."

"What about you?"

He moved her back, against the wall. She had a clear line of fire at the adjoining door. "Anybody," Michael said, then drew the forty-five and crossed back to the window. The men clustered on the sidewalk. The lot behind them was empty. They made a thorough check, then laid down the duffel bag and unzipped it, pulling out a thirty-pound sledge-hammer. One last look around and the weapons came out. They kept them low against their legs, and when the hammer came off the ground they stepped back to make room for the swing. The man was large. He got his weight behind it, and when the hammer hit, the door didn't stand a chance. It blew open with a tortured squeal. He dropped the hammer, and the other two entered first, the third right behind them.

Michael gave them exactly two seconds, then opened the door and stepped outside. The day was just as warm, but felt cool. Wind licked his face, and part of him felt regret. He took five steps down the sidewalk, then rounded into the room behind them, his feet light and soundless, his heart rate unchanged. All three had their weapons up, their focus on the bathroom door and the shower running beyond it. No one looked back. No one heard him. It took Michael two seconds to kill all three men.

Two seconds.

Three bullets.

The shots came so quickly, they sounded like strung firecrackers. Weapon leveled, Michael closed the door and checked the bodies. They were dead, no question: two in the back of the head, one in the side as he'd turned. Two of them had wallets in their back pockets. Michael checked the IDs, then tossed them in one of the shopping bags. He spared a glance at their weapons to confirm his suspicions, then gathered up spent casings and the bags of clothing. He made a last check and walked out of the room.

The men he left on the floor.

At the door to the adjoining room, he knocked. "It's me."

"Come in." Her voice shook.

Michael found her crouched on the floor, weapon up and aimed at the door. "I heard . . ." She began to shake, and Michael took the weapon from her hands. She covered her face. "I thought . . . Oh, God." She smeared her palms across her face, but there were no tears yet.

"We're leaving," Michael said.

"What happened?"

"They were amateurs."

"How do you know?"

"They died easy." Michael was moving quickly, re-holstering the nine millimeter, pushing the shopping bags into Elena's arms. "Someone will have heard the shots."

"They're really dead? You—"

"I should have seen it." Michael shook his head. "The plates threw me."

"What do you mean?"

"The van was here when we came back. I saw it, but it has Maryland plates. I was looking for New York." Michael checked the window. "They're contract players, probably out of Baltimore. I didn't expect that. Wasn't looking for it. I say they're amateurs because they are. The van is parked so that it could be easily blocked in. No one watched their backs. Their weapons were low grade and poorly maintained. Two of them carried ID." He shook his head. "Amateurs. Are you ready?"

"Where are we going?"

"North Carolina."

"Why?"

"To find my brother."

She blinked, still stunned. "You killed them."

Michael opened the door, took her by the hand. "I'm trying to quit."

They got in the car and drove from the lot. Michael made a number of turns and kept an eye on the rearview mirror. "We'll need a new car."

"I'm going to be sick."

"No, you're not."

"I'm going to be sick on you."

Michael worked his way back to the mall. It swarmed with people. There were thousands of cars. He drove up one row of cars and down another. "This will do."

"What?"

He tilted his head at a late-model sedan. "Nondescript. No visible damage." He parked four slots away.

"And we're stealing it?"

Michael grinned. "The window's open. It's like an invitation. You want to come?"

"No."

"I'll be right back."

"Michael . . ." Her face caught the afternoon sun. "Those men you killed . . ."

"Those men were coming to kill us."

"No innocents," Elena said. "Is this what you meant?"

"More or less."

"Marietta was innocent."

"I didn't kill Marietta."

"Would you have?" She held him with the urgency of her question. "If things were reversed and it was you back in New York? Would you kill her to get what you want?"

"I guess it depends."

"On what?"

"On how badly I wanted something." Michael slipped out of the car. In three minutes he was back. "Let's go. Keep your head up. Act normal."

They unloaded their belongings from one car and carried them to the other. Elena stumbled twice but no one noticed. No one said a thing. In the other car and moving, Elena said, "I can't accept your answer. I can't sit here and accept what you said."

Michael drove in silence, Elena tense and miserable beside him. On the interstate, he said, "Some people deserve to die, if not for one sin, then another. When it happens to people like Marietta, it's unfortunate."

"Unfortunate?"

"It's a bigger word than you think."

"She was my friend. She had parents, plans, and ambitions. A boyfriend. Jesus, Michael. She thought he was going to propose."

"I've never killed a civilian." Michael waited until she looked at him. "If you're smart in this business, you never have to."

"And you're smart in the business?" She was angry, now, the fear fading. She wanted to lash out, and Michael understood. He'd felt it himself: survivor's guilt, the first taste of how fast something bad could happen.

"Yes," he said.

"What does that even mean?"

"It means I take precautions to keep the innocents innocent. It means I plan ahead."

Elena laughed a desperate laugh, white splotches in the center of each cheek. "Plan ahead? What plan? Where?"

Michael sighed heavily, then reached into the inside pocket of his jacket. When the hand came out, it held Elena's passport. The edges of it were crisp against his fingertips. He felt the sudden stillness in her, the parting of her lips. "There's a direct flight from Washington. If you really want to go, I'll take you there."

She took the passport and squeezed as slow understanding twisted her features. "Marietta . . ."

Her voice broke, and Michael showed sympathetic eyes. He wanted to say that Marietta died easily, that she died a quick death, but that would be false. Jimmy would want to make sure. So would Stevan. "I'm sorry about your friend," he said.

But Elena did not hear him.

She was drowning in guilt.

Traffic thickened as they neared the outskirts of Washington. Michael passed a station wagon—in it was a family with young kids. They were playing with toy guns, the guns shiny and small, the small faces intent. "Tell me the rest." Elena kept her eyes on the kids. One of them waved, made a face. Elena touched her cheek once, then turned away. She still saw the kid, though: cross-eyed and puff-cheeked, nose pressed white on smeared glass as his sister aimed at his back and pulled the trigger.

"The rest of what?" Michael passed the car.

"The things you haven't told me." Elena's eyes were smudged red. A pearl of blood rose from the crease of a torn hangnail. "Tell me all of it."

"You won't like it."

"I will tell myself that they are only words."

"Baby—"

"Please."

So, Michael spoke of the things he'd done. He described life as he'd lived it: life on the streets, and then as the old man's strong right arm, what it took to do the job and move on. He spoke of other things, too: the one man he could count on, the care he took and the times he'd almost died. He spoke of his love for the old man, and he spoke of her, Elena; how, with her, he wanted more. "A normal life," he said. "Better reasons to live."

By the time he finished, they were parked at Dulles International Airport. The sky above was clear. Jets split the air, impossibly large, and Elena was shaking her head. "It's too much."

"You wanted to hear—"

"I was wrong." She looked at the terminal. People lined the sidewalk. Bags were being unloaded. She shook her head. "I can't save you."

"I'm not asking you to. Just to understand, to let me try."

She fingered the passport, cleared her throat. "I need money."

"I'm more than the things I've done."

"Must I beg?"

She was breaking, and the sight of it killed something in Michael's heart. This was not how it was supposed to be; not the way he wanted it. He gave her cash without looking at the amount. It was a thick sheaf. Thousands. Many thousands. He took a breath, and gave her the business end of things. "Going to Spain may not keep you safe. Stevan has money, connections. He can find you if he wants to."

"And will he wish to?"

An ember of hope kindled in her eyes, but it burned small, brief and cold. She worried with her nails at the raw place on her thumb. The pearl of blood had dried to a small crust. "Love me or not," Michael said, "the safest place is with me."

"Safest but not safe."

"No. Not completely."

Elena nodded at this thing she already knew. She tucked both hands between her thighs, and said, "Do I look scared?"

"You look beautiful."

"I'm terrified."

It showed in her eyes, a quiet but utter panic. She opened the door, and Michael said, "Don't leave me."

"I'm sorry, Michael."

"I can keep you safe. I can make this right."

"How?"

"I don't know, but I can. Please, Elena. I'll never forgive myself if something happens to you."

"And you think something will?"

"Stevan has a vengeful soul. It's personal between us, now. He'll want to make me hurt. Going through you is the best way to do that." Michael's voice was very intent, close to pleading. "The safest place is with me."

"Then come to Spain. We can disappear—"

"Julian is my brother."

His voice cut her off. She stared hard into his eyes, and there was no barrier between them. "So, you would choose between us?"

"It's not like that."

"Isn't it?"

"I can protect you both."

"I'm sorry, Michael."

"He's my brother."

"And this is my baby."

She touched her stomach, got out of the car, and even though he could no longer see her face, Michael knew she was crying. It was in the slope of her shoulders, the tilt of her head. She shoved money in a pocket, found the sidewalk, and hesitated. People jostled her. The sidewalk was crowded with women and children, with men in suits and jeans and sunglasses. Eyes flicked over her and moved on. People stood singly and in knots; horns blared where traffic snarled. Elena took one step, then stopped again. For long seconds, she stood still, shoulders rolled, head turning first left, then right. A man bumped her, and she shied, dropping her passport, then bending to retrieve it. A space opened in front of her, but she did not move. Michael got out of the car and jogged through traffic. He worked his way to a place behind her, and when he was close, he saw that the passport was bent double in her hand. He stepped next to her, and when she flinched, he said, "It's just me."

She kept her eyes on the crowd. A heavyset man pushed past. A punk in dark glasses watched her from beside a concrete column. "I've never been scared of people before."

Michael scanned the crowd. "No one here is a threat."

"How can you know?"

"I just do."

"I don't want to die," she said.

"Come with me."

"I'm scared."

"I've got you, baby."

"Say it again."

"Will you come with me?"

She paused for a long time. "If you say it again."

Michael put his arm around her shoulder. He kissed a warm place on the top of her head.

"I've got you."

CHAPTER EIGHT

The sun came dimly to the skies of Chatham County, so lost behind black clouds that Abigail Vane barely noticed it; it was a faint presence in a heavy sky, a suspicion of orange in the still air, of color hung in the trees. Rain fell straight down, a hiss in the tall grass that was loud enough to deaden most other sounds, hard enough for Abigail to feel on the backs of her hands, the crown of her head. It stung her face as the horse ran, and as the morning stalled, black and loud and cease-less. After two hours, her body was chilled, her fingers so cramped she could barely open them. Her back ached and her legs burned, but she didn't care, didn't feel. She wanted to push. She wanted to ride hard, and let the wind of a fast horse steal the scream from her throat.

At the end of the field, she reined in, horse snorting as it danced sideways and worked the bit in its mouth. Her pants were coated with mud and horse sweat, her feet heavy in the stirrups. A wall of hard-woods loomed in the rain: oak and beech and maple, trees so tall and broad that night remained complete beneath them. She swiped at the hair that clung to her face, and then turned the horse to face back down the length of the field. From one end to the other, they'd worn a track of crushed grass and churned mud, a violent gash in the valley floor. And the horse still wanted to run. He tossed his head, rolled his eyes, and Abigail felt a wildness in him that suited her mood. He was a dangerous animal, seventeen hands tall with a streak of viciousness she'd never seen in a horse.

But he was fast.

Goddamn, was he fast.

She sawed once at the reins, then put her heels in his flank and let him go. His nostrils flared, and his hooves put a thunder in the mud. They reached the end and turned. Ran it again. Her lungs were burning when the Land Rover pushed out of the trees. It was old, with paint scratched through to metal, and Abigail knew who was behind the wheel even before it lurched to a halt. She turned the horse, her hand sliding once along its hot, reeking neck. The animal jerked its head, but she patted it a final time, then walked it to the vehicle, where she found a lean, broad-shouldered man standing at the hood. He was sixty years old, but hard and straight, with large-knuckled hands and the kind of smile you had to look closely to see. But there was no smile this time. He wore khakis and leather boots, a burgundy tie under rain gear the color of moss. Disapproval pinched his features, so that when Abigail leaned from the saddle, she said, "I don't want to hear it, Jessup."

"Hear what?"

"A lecture on safety or propriety or how a woman my age should behave."

"That horse. In this visibility." Jessup Falls pointed at the horse, his voice tight. "You're going to break your damn neck."

"Such language." Her eyes sparkled, but Jessup was immune.

"You're going to break your neck and it will be up to me to carry you out of here."

"Don't be ridiculous."

"I'm not being ridiculous. I'm being angry. Jesus, Abigail. That horse has injured two trainers. He almost killed the last one."

She waved off his concern, and slid from the horse. Rain clattered through leaves and pinged off the truck. "Why are you here, Jessup?"

Jessup's skin had grown ruddy with the years, his hair thin and white, but other than that, he was the same man she'd known for so long: her driver, her bodyguard. Abigail circled the horse, boots squelching in damp soil. She'd aged, too, but more gracefully. Her skin was lined, but looked more like thirty-seven than forty-seven. Her hair had its natural color. She still turned heads.

"Your husband is up," Jessup said. "He's asking for you."

She slowed as her face angled toward the far hill, where hints of the massive house showed: a slate roof and gabled windows, one of the seven tall chimneys.

"Are you okay?" Jessup's voice was softer, his anger spent.

"Why wouldn't I be?"

Jessup cleared his throat, unwilling to state the obvious: the soaking clothes and the mud, the horse lathered yellow at the neck. Abigail was a fine rider, but this was insane. "Julian, for one," Jessup said.

"How is he this morning?" She kept her voice crisp enough to fool anyone else. She leaned close to the horse, one palm on the broad, flat plane of its cheek. She wished she had an apple or a carrot, but the decision to ride had been impulsive. Five in the morning. Rain falling in sheets.

"I don't know."

"Is he worse?"

"I honestly don't know. No one knew where to find you, not your husband or the staff. No one. The first place I checked was the stable."

"Has he said anything?"

"Not that I know."

She stroked the horse as water dripped from her face. It was colder now that she was off the horse; in the dim light, her skin looked blue. "What time is it?"

"A little after seven."

Abigail turned to look more closely at his face. She saw that he was unshaven, and that the skin beneath his eyes was dark enough to seem bruised. An image gathered in her mind: Jessup awake most of the night, sitting unhappily beside an untouched whiskey, pacing dark hours in the small room he kept. His worry for Julian would be real, as would his concern for her, and for a moment, she felt deep affection for the man whose own emotions were so obvious. "I should go," she said.

He shook his head. "Not like that."

"Like what?" She palmed a streak of mud from her face.

"Barely dressed." Jessup smiled awkwardly. "The rain has made your shirt quite transparent."

Abigail looked down and saw that he was right. Jessup retrieved a long, waterproof coat, then stepped forward and draped it over her shoulders. It smelled of canvas, hunting dogs, and burned powder. She reached out an arm to pull the coat tighter, and Jessup caught her deftly by the hand. His eyes settled on the yellow-green marks on her wrist. They were large and finger-shaped. The moment stretched between them, and he said, "When?"

"When, what?" Her chin rose.

"Don't bullshit me, Abigail."

She pulled her hand free. "Whatever you think happened, you're mistaken."

"Did he hit you?"

"God, no. Of course not. I'd never allow it."

"He got drunk and put his hands on you. That's why you're out here."

"No."

"Then why?" Anger sharpened his features.

"I just needed something bigger." She patted the horse again. "Something clean."

"Damn it, Abigail . . ."

She handed him the reins and made it plain that the subject was closed. "Walk him back to the stable for me. Cool him down."

"Talk to me, Abigail."

"I'm more of a doer than a talker."

Jessup's face showed his displeasure. "Just like that?"

She looked up, and let rain strike her face. "You still work for me."

"And the truck?" His neck stiffened, and a wounded look settled in the dark centers of his eyes.

"I'll take the truck."

She walked to the truck without looking back, but felt him there, unhappy and staring.

"This is not right," he said.

"Walk him the long way, Jessup." She opened the door, slid inside. "He worked hard this morning."

The Land Rover Defender was old, purchased as an estate vehicle in the infancy of her marriage. She remembered the day it was delivered; she was twenty-two years old, and still in awe of her husband.

He was two decades her senior, about to run for the Senate and wealthy beyond belief. He could have had any woman in the world, but he chose her over all the others—not just for her beauty, he'd said, but for her elegance and refinement, for the poise she wore like a garment. After long years as a bachelor he needed a face to go with his political life, and she was perfect. When the Defender was delivered, they drove it to the highest point on the estate, a long narrow ridge that looked down on the house and grounds. He'd lifted her skirt, put her on the hood, and she'd thought then that his sweaty hands were the precursors of happiness. But he never looked her in the face as he screwed her; he watched the house and thought of his glory: four thousand acres and a pair of trophy tits. Two months later, he won the Senate seat in a landslide. A year after that, he had his first new girlfriend.

Leaving Jessup with the horse, she drove to the same spot on the same ridge, a slab of granite that had probably been there for a million years. She parked and looked down on the manicured lawns, the stables, and the twin lakes that looked like black glass shot with gray. The grass was colorless in the rain, the forest beyond a hint of dark canopy. Rain muted everything, but the house, rising, looked as tall and massive as it had that day so many years ago. For an instant, Abigail wished she could reach back through time and touch the young woman she'd been, all smooth skin and conviction. She wanted to slap that girl in the face, tell her to pull down her skirt and run like the devil was at her heels. Instead, she pulled out the revolver she kept in the glove compartment. It was heavy in her hand, the metal cool and blued. She looked into the brutish barrel, then at the bullets nestled like eggs in the chambers. She straightened her arm, sighted at the house, and for a moment entertained dark fantasies. Then she put the pistol back where it belonged: in the glove compartment, locked.

She drove down the rough track, gravel clanking on the undercarriage, the shocks worn and loose. Where the forest ended, she turned across a final field, then picked up the main estate road that ran to the stables and the back of the house. She saw Jessup at the stables, then turned for the garage and caught a brief glimpse of the long, impossibly straight drive. At the far end, the gate was a postage stamp of twisted iron.

Abigail drove to the rear door and killed the engine. Inside, she ignored the stares and the hurried movements of the household staff. She turned down a narrow hall, then through the butler's pantry and into the kitchen, where two cooks looked up, too startled say a word as they took in the long, ill-fitting coat, the mud on her feet, and the ruin of her hair. "Where is Mr. Vane?" Abigail asked.

"Ma'am?"

"Mr. Vane? Where is he?"

"He is in the study."

"Has Julian eaten?"

The cooks shared a worried glance. "Mr. Vane says no one is to go into that part of the house."

"That's absurd."

"Mr. Senator says—"

"I don't care what *Mr. Senator* says." Her voice came too loudly, and she calmed herself. No point in scaring anyone. "Fix a tray," she said. "I'll send someone for it."

"Yes, ma'am."

Abigail left the back halls used by the servants and entered the main house, the ceiling soaring above her. She passed window treatments that hung twenty feet to the floor, a dining room table that could seat thirty. She entered the foyer and felt coolness in the air as the ceiling rose forty feet, the stairwell curving around the vast space as it spiraled to the third floor and the vaulted cupola beyond. She climbed the stairs, passing an iron chandelier the size of her bed and portraits of long-dead men who weren't actually related to her husband. At the first landing, she turned for the guest wing, which was long and broad and rich. Six rooms lined the hall, three on each side. More paintings hung on the walls. Antique sideboards gleamed. A man sat in a chair halfway down the hall. He was middle-aged and fit, with black hair and shoes that caught the light when he stood. He was neither a member of the house staff, nor, as far as she could tell, a member of her husband's office. His hands were large under thick wrists and snow-white cuffs.

"Good morning, Mrs. Vane."

His tie was the same navy as the rug, his gaze as flat as the floor on which it lay. Yet, the eyes moved: up and down, light blue and steady. She let him have his look. Stories circulated about her, she knew; and her appearance this morning would no doubt make for another one.

She could not care less.

"Where's Mrs. Hamilton?"

"Sleeping, I assume. The senator deemed her unfit to watch over his son."

"The senator deemed?"

"He dismissed her three hours ago."

She tilted her head, her own face as hard as his, her eyes just as appraising. "Do I know you?"

"Richard Gale. I work for your husband."

"That was not my question."

"We've never met."

"But you know who I am?"

"Of course."

She weighed his appearance even further: wide shoulders and narrow waist, the first hint of creases in the skin of his neck. He stood perfectly still, light on his feet and amused. Abigail recognized the arrogance common to men of a certain physical quality. She'd seen it often in military officers and in field agents prized by the intelligence community. Years ago, she'd found such men exciting, but she'd never been as wise in her youth as she'd imagined herself to be. "Are we going to have a problem?" she asked.

"No, ma'am. You're cleared to go in."

"Cleared?"

"On the senator's list."

She frowned. "What is it, exactly, that you do for my husband?"

"Whatever is required."

"Are you a federal agent?" He blinked once, and kept his mouth shut. "A private contractor," Abigail concluded.

"I work for your husband. That's really all I'm obligated to say."

"Is my son under guard?"

"He's not tried to leave. He's——"

"What?"

Gale shrugged.

"Let's get a few things straight, Mr. Gale. My son is not a prisoner. This is his home. So, if he wishes to leave this room, you may call me or his father, you may follow him if you must; but if you lay a hand on him or try to restrain his movement in any way, I'll make you regret it."

"Senator Vane left strict instructions."

"Senator Vane is not the one of whom you should be frightened."

The humor drained out of his eyes.

She stepped closer.

"The senator has concerns that I do not: appearances, for one, lawsuits and reporters and voters. His worries are larger than his son, so he does foolish things, like make you sit in this hall with a responsibility you cannot possibly handle. But that's not my problem. I'm a mother of one son, that son. Do you understand me?"

"I think so."

"No, Mr. Gale, you don't. If you did, you'd be leaving at a fast walk and praying that I forget your name."

"But, the senator—"

"Don't fuck with my son."

"Yes, ma'am."

"Now, step away from the door."

Abigail brushed past and opened the door that for three days had shut her son off from the world.

Three days of doubt and uncertainty.

Three days of hell.

She crossed the threshold and closed the door. Inside, the dark was a shock to her eyes, a blackness that was nearly complete. Heavy curtains hung over windows that opened to the lakes below. No lamps burned. Warm air pressed her skin as she put her back to the door and dug deep for the courage to force a smile before turning on the lights. She was a mother first, and found the weight of Julian's collapse nearly unbearable. Wounded and unsure, he'd been a delicate child from the first, a boy prone to night terrors and doubt. Yet, she'd worked hard to make him whole, first for months and then years, until fixing the broken parts of Julian had become her resolve and her religion. She'd given all she could: education and activity, love and patience and strength, and in many ways it had worked, for as weak as he was, as scarred and bereft, Julian had always found the will to endure. He'd overcome the trauma of his childhood, the loss of his brother, and the mark of long years at Iron Mountain. He'd become an artist and a poet, a children's author, successful in his own right. To the world at large, he was a man of deep feeling and nuance, but in his heart, Abigail knew, Julian remained little more than a shattered boy, the brittle precipitate of the things he'd endured. It was a secret they kept, dark matter buried deep.

"Julian?"

Her eyes began to adjust. To her right, the bed was dark and flat and empty. Furniture made vague, humped shapes in the room, while from somewhere deeper, a dull, rapping sound made itself heard.

"Julian?"

There were two more thumps, and then the sound stopped. Something moved in a far corner.

"I'm going to turn on a light. You might want to cover your eyes."

She shuffled to the bedside table and clicked on a small lamp, a Tiffany piece whose soft light touched a pale yellow rug and cream-colored baseboards beneath walls papered French blue with gold fleur-de-lis. Shadows gathered under furniture, and she saw Julian, hunched in the corner beyond the bed. His hair was unwashed, his face buried in knees drawn to his chest. His pants were stained with mud and grass, his shirt untucked and greasy at the collar. Clean clothes sat in neat piles, but he refused to touch them. He refused to eat. Refused to drink.

"Good morning, sweetheart." Abigail moved closer, and Julian pushed into the corner. He clenched his arms more tightly, and in the light she saw that gauze wrapped his hands. The fabric extended from his wrists to the tips of his fingers, tightly wrapped except at the edges, where it had begun to tear and fray. Blood soaked through at the knuckles, red stains on white, and on the walls around him—on all the walls—blood discolored the fine, blue paper. Where Julian huddled, the blood was fresh and wet, while farther away it had dried to thin smears of rust-colored ink.

Abigail froze when she saw how wet the bandages were, how stained the walls. This was something terrible and new: damaged hands and bloodstained walls. She asked why, but had no answer; looked for reason and saw only madness. She turned a circle, barbs of fear hooked in the walls of her chest, the strings of her will simply cut. The marks went as high as the ceiling, as low as the floor. The walls were dashed with red and rust and questions she could not bear.

She sank to her knees and put her hands on those of her son. "Julian."

The bandages were warm and wet.

My baby . . .

Ten minutes later, Abigail found her husband in the study, reading the *Washington Post*, half-glasses on his nose, mouth slightly open. Behind him, French doors showcased the formal gardens and the pool house beyond.

Randall Vane looked good under his silver hair. He was sixty-nine, wide-shouldered and tall enough to carry some extra weight. He had a strong nose and green eyes that worked well with the silver hair. Leonine, he'd once been called; it was a word he favored.

Leonine.

Lion-like.

Abigail entered without knocking. She felt nothing physical as she walked, neither her feet nor the smears of blood that her son's bandages had left on her cheeks. She felt the ache of Julian's eyes and the memory of heat in his wounded hands. She stopped at the desk's edge, her fingers pressed white on the wood. "Julian needs a doctor." Her voice shook, and she thought she might be in shock. Randall lowered the paper, took off his glasses. He considered her appearance: the fine nose chiseled white at the nostrils, the large eyes, and the once-plump lips drawn tight. His gaze traveled to the man's coat she wore and the muddy pants beneath it. "It's getting worse," she said.

"Whose coat are you wearing?"

"It's getting worse."

She put the force of her will behind her words, and, hearing that force, Senator Randall Vane leaned back in his chair, folded the newspaper, and dropped it on the desk. The shirt pulled across his broad chest, the swell of his stomach. His face was ruddy, his teeth impossibly white. The cuffs of his shirt were monogrammed with pale, blue thread. "What do you mean?"

"Julian is harming himself."

The senator laced thick fingers and rested them on his stomach. His voice came smoothly. "It started last night. I don't know when."

"Where is Mrs. Hamilton? Julian should be with someone he knows and loves."

"I found Mrs. Hamilton asleep in the hall."

"She helped raise him, Randall. If I'm not there, she is. That was our deal. How could you send her away without bringing me there first?"

"She was sleeping on the job while Julian beat his hands bloody. I sent her to bed and brought in someone I can trust."

"What happened to my son, Randall?"

The senator rocked forward in his chair, big elbows landing on the desk. "He started hitting the walls. What else can I tell you? We don't know why. He just did it. He was already bleeding when I went to check on him. He could have been doing it for hours."

"And you didn't come get me?"

"Come get you where, exactly?" His eyes drove the knife home, and Abigail looked away, angry and ashamed. "You ran out in the middle of our discussion."

"Our argument."

"Argument. Discussion. No matter. You were not to be found and I was left to deal with Julian. We bandaged his hands, sedated him. The injuries are minor. We're watching him."

"He needs a doctor."

"I disagree."

"He hasn't spoken since he came home. We don't know where he's been, what happened to him . . ."

"It's only been a few days. We agreed—"

"We did not."

"We agreed to give him time to come out of this on his own. He's

97

upset about something. Fine. It happens to all of us. There's no point in blowing this out of proportion. It's probably just a girl, some sweet young thing that broke his heart."

"He's injuring himself."

"Doctors keep records, Abigail. And records can be leaked."

"Please don't make this about you."

"He's a political liability."

"He's your son."

It was an old argument, the line drawn when Julian was a boy. He had trouble looking people in the eyes, and rarely shook hands or allowed himself to be touched. Even now, he was painfully shy, so reticent he did poorly with people he did not know well. To complicate matters further, the books he wrote were as dark as could be and still be for children. They dealt with difficult themes: death and betrayal and fear, the pain of childhood's end. Critics often remarked that a distinct godlessness characterized his stories, and because of that, some conservative communities had banned his books, even burned them. The power of his artistry and storytelling, however, was undeniable, so powerful, in fact, that few could read them without being emotionally challenged in some meaningful way. So, while in some circles he was demonized, in others he was celebrated as an artist of the highest order. His own explanation was simple: *The world is cruel and children can be stronger than they know.* Yet, his books, like life, did not always end well. Children died. Parents failed. *Telling children less,* he'd often said, *would be cruelty of a different sort.*

"It's an election year." The senator frowned. "He'll be fine."

"You're blind, Randall."

"Blind? I don't think so."

"Blind and arrogant."

The senator leaned back in his chair, fingers laced above his belt. "Whose coat is that?"

"That's hardly relevant."

"I can have a doctor here by lunch. All you have to do is tell me who owns the coat you're wearing."

Her sigh was an exhausted one. "Why do you even care?"

"Because you said I'm blind."

"Fine. You're not blind."

"I want to hear you say it."

"It belongs to Jessup. Are you happy?"

"Jessup's a good man." He paused. "A bit humble for your tastes."

"The man loaned me his coat."

"Of course."

Abigail pushed the phone across the desk. "You'll call?"

"Of course." The smile was a knowing one.

"You exhaust me, Randall."

"I consider that my job as your husband."

"A doctor," she said. "Soon."

Back in Julian's room, Abigail found that he'd used a stub of pencil to draw the shape of a door on the wall. It was small and childish, nothing like the art of which he was capable. Normally, if Julian were to draw a door, it would look so real one might try to open it and walk through. He could make it look that solid, or he could shape it in a manner so fanciful it could be a door to another universe, the passage to a world of magic and joy, or a black gate yawning wide to collect a host of damaged souls. But that's not what Abigail saw. The lines on this door wavered and diverged, making an irregular shape less than five feet tall. The doorknob was a scrawl, the hinges thick marks of heavy black. Julian knelt in front of the door, still bent. He was beating his knuckles on the drawn door, the bandages not just wet, but torn.

"Baby." She knelt beside him, close enough to feel his heat. The skin under his eyes was bruised, his face so lean the cheeks were sunken. He ignored her, his eyes fevered and empty, his lips chewed raw and dry as chalk. He struck one part of the door, then another, so intent he did not react when she put a hand on his arm. "Baby, please . . ."

His eyes were shockingly drawn, pulled so deeply into their sockets they looked black. His mouth opened and the tip of his tongue pushed against the back of his teeth. When Abigail reached again to touch him, her arm passed before the lamp so a shadow flickered on the wall. Julian flinched when he saw it, and Abigail cringed from the sudden terror in his face. Then, just as quickly, the emotion fled and his face emptied. She watched his lips move in mindless rhythm, and her fingers stopped an inch from his skin. "Baby, please."

"Sunlight . . ."

His voice was the barest whisper.

"Silver stairs . . ."

CHAPTER NINE

The doctor was like so many doctors, quiet and certain and spare. He arrived in the company of an unfamiliar nurse, and when the door clicked shut Julian froze, a new attentiveness to his features, a contemplation that seemed to emanate from some especially still place in his soul.

"Julian, my name is Dr. Cloverdale. I'm a friend of your father's. I'm not going to hurt you. I'm just going to conduct an examination and fix up your hands. Is that okay?" Julian did not respond, and the doctor said, "We're all friends here."

Moving gently, the doctor checked the sound of Julian's heart and lungs. He shone a light in Julian's eyes, and Abigail imagined her son's face turned up in the dark, a small light seen from the bottom of a deep well.

"You're doing fine, Julian. Just fine."

The doctor continued his examination, and when the bandages came off Julian's hands, Abigail stifled a small cry. "It's okay," the doctor said; but it was not. The knuckles were scraped and torn and weeping lymph. The meat was white, and Abigail thought she saw a wet, gray flash of bone. The doctor dressed the hands, and then sedated him. Julian did not react when the needle went into his arm. Abigail turned down the sheets, and together they got Julian into bed. At the door, the doctor spoke in a whisper. "The nurse will clean him up."

In the hall, Abigail put her back against the wall. "His poor hands . . ."

"There's no permanent damage."

"You're certain?"

"Barring further injury, yes." The doctor's face was kind, but serious. "This just happened?"

"Which part?" Abigail felt a hint of panic in her own voice.

"When did this begin? Let's start there."

"Three days ago. He went away—we don't know where—and when he came back, he was like this. I found him in the garage, barefoot and filthy. He wouldn't say a word, wouldn't go to his own room. He came here and locked the door. He wouldn't answer when we tried to talk to him, wouldn't come out. After a day, we brought in the locksmith."

"Does he often disappear like that?"

Abigail shook her head. "No. Never. I mean, he goes places, of course. But not that often, and never without letting someone know."

"Where does he go, when he leaves? Friends? Vacations?"

"No. Not really. I mean, he has friends, of course, but not close ones. People from school, mostly. No one person in particular. He goes to New York to meet with his publishers. He does occasional conferences, public appearances, things like that. Mostly, he stays here. Walks in the woods. Writes his books. He's a very insular young man."

"Comfortable in his own skin."

"That might be pushing it."

"He's rather old to be living at home . . ."

"He has his strengths, Dr. Cloverdale; it's just that he's complicated."

"The senator filled me in on his history. I understand he suffered some abuse as a boy?"

"Yes."

"Was it severe?"

"Yes." She felt her own madness rise. "It was severe."

Cloverdale frowned. "Did he have counseling?"

"With minimal effect. He went through the motions, but still wakes up screaming."

"Screaming?"

"For his brother. They were close."

"Have you ever seen anything like this kind of self-injury?"

"No. It just started last night."

Cloverdale shook his head. "This is not my area. He needs a psychiatrist, I suspect, maybe inpatient treatment at Duke or Chapel Hill. Someone who specializes in emotional trauma . . ."

"Are you suggesting we commit him?"

"Let's not rush to judgment," Cloverdale said. "If we did commit him, he would be placed under observation for several days. We can do the same thing here, no problem. Your husband hired me for the week, so I'm here. Why don't we give it a day or two? I'll keep Julian calm and comfortable. I'll watch him. Sometimes these things resolve themselves."

"Really?"

"Sure." He showed his calm, doctor's smile. "Why not?"

She studied his eyes. "A few days, then."

"Good." The doctor clasped his hands. "Now, let's talk about you."

He made a kind face again, and only then did Abigail realize how distraught she must appear, mud-spattered and wild-eyed. She'd not slept in two nights, barely eaten. She was pale and exhausted, her son's blood dried to a crust on her cheeks. She touched the nest of hair on her head and felt a sudden blankness move into her eyes as she focused on the doctor's chin. "I'm fine," she said.

"If you're worried I'll discuss it with your husband—"

"I'm fine." The stare continued unabated. She knew it, but could not lift her eyes. It was an old feeling, the denial.

"We all need help at times, Mrs. Vane. There's no shame in it."

"Thank you, Doctor. No." She felt her chin rise, and briefly entertained the notion of telling him the truth; but he would dismiss as a misguided boast her claim that he'd never met a stronger person than she. He would make polite noises, and when he saw the senator, he would shake his head and pretend to keep his confidence. But their eyes would meet, and in that touch would be a faint smile shared at the vanity of women. So, she kept the truth as her own. She did not tell the doctor she had seen things that would crush his heart, done things that would break him at the knees.

"I'm fine," she said.

And when he opened his mouth to disagree, she turned and walked away.

CHAPTER TEN

As large as the house was, and as grand, it was not technically Abigail's home. The main residence was in Charlotte, a turn-of-the-century mansion on two acres in Myers Park. This was supposed to be their summer home, but Abigail loathed Charlotte. It was too large, its people too interested in the doings of their senator and his wife. As life unrolled behind her, Abigail found herself drawn more and more to the space and silence of Chatham County. Over the years, her time there grew longer and more certain, until now, she hardly left. She lived there with horses and privacy and her son.

It was almost ideal.

She swept down the long hall to the suite of rooms she'd taken as her own, where she showered, changed, and restored her face to its normal state of near-perfection. In a ten-foot mirror, her reflection was that of an elegant woman in peak physical condition. She turned once, found herself acceptable, and then went to Julian's room on the third floor. It filled the top corner of the north wing, an extravagant space whose windows faced downslope and across the forest canopy. In spring, the view was of rolling green, an inland sea that in the fall became red and yellow and orange, an ocean of fire that died to brown and fell away.

In the door, she stopped, hesitant. The room had ceiling-to-floor bookshelves that held framed photographs and twenty years of reading. A half-dozen easels stood against the far wall, large sketch pads propped open to show the pictures Julian had been working on: a forest scene, a lake in moonlight, characters for a new book he was considering. Shotguns and deer rifles stood, unused, in velvet-lined cases. They were gifts from his father, and from admirers of his father, expensive steel touched with fine dust; but Julian had never killed anything in his life. He was a gentle man, but a man nonetheless, and the room reflected this duality: dark rugs and expensive art, children's books and silent guns. It was a man's room, and a boy's; and standing in the doorway, vision pricked by tears, Abigail saw the day they'd brought Julian home. He'd been so small and frightened, so lost without his brother.

How many boys live here, he'd said.

Just you.

He'd stared at the room for a long time, his dark eyes restless as he'd looked out the window at the forest canopy, the long miles of deep and secret green. His fingers were small on the windowsill, his chin tipped up as he stood on tiptoes to see out.

It's so big.

Do you like it?

He'd thought for a long time, then said: *How will Michael find me here?*

That was the question that made her cry.

Abigail stepped across the threshold. She ran a finger along the spines of books, lifted a photograph, put it down. She was restless, worried in a way she'd never been, so that when she turned and found her husband in the open door, she jumped. She'd not heard a step, and as large as he was, that fact surprised her.

"About what I said." The voice was his penitent one. "I will, of course, put Julian first. I hope you know that." His gaze ran the length of the room, and it was impossible to hide his distaste. As a politician, he was conservative in all things. As a man, he believed in manly pursuits. People like Julian were not his cup of tea, and Abigail always suspected, deep in her heart, that the senator was pleased that Julian, as a son, was only adopted.

Less of an embarrassment that way.

Less of a liability.

Truth was, the senator had never forgiven Abigail for her inability to conceive. He'd wanted one of each, a boy and a girl, both well mannered and sharing their mother's photogenic qualities. Adoption was a hard-fought compromise, and Julian a massive disappointment. In the end, she'd won the argument on one basic premise: adoption—especially of older, unwanted children—would show he was a man of heart and conscience. His polls were lowest in the mountains. He'd thought about it, nodded once. And that was that.

The senator stepped to the nearest easel and began flipping pages, looking first at one drawing and then another. "About Julian," he said. "I was out of line. I'm sorry." He flipped a final page and considered the drawing there: a half-dressed girl with leaves in her hair and eyes like black smoke. "This one's unexpected," he said.

Abigail glanced at the drawing; a beautiful girl, provocatively drawn. "Why?"

He shrugged. "It's so sexual."

"He's a children's author, not a child. He's had girlfriends."

"Has he?"

"Must you be so dismissive?"

The senator flipped pages until the drawing was covered. He studied Abigail's face, his own features sad and utterly convincing. "Give an old man a kiss."

His eyes broke from hers, and she knew the interruption was purposeful. She extended her cheek and he kissed it, his lips dry and cool. Stepping back, he looked into the room. "This place is a mess."

"I'll speak to housekeeping."

"That's my girl."

She watched him go, then began to pick up the room. She made the bed, stacked books, and gathered coffee cups. Finally, she lifted Julian's tuxedo and carried it to the closet. It smelled of cigar smoke and aftershave. She smoothed it once, and in the pocket found a photograph. The girl was a waif: nineteen years old and small enough to be elfin. She stood on a sagging porch, the house behind her barely painted. Wild, blond hair framed a face that would be striking in another context; but she was barefoot and dirty, her eyes large over hollow cheeks, her mouth an angry line as she glared at the camera. She wore faded cutoffs that rose too high on her legs, a tank top that was too thin and tight for the breasts that pushed against it. Her hands were shoved into her pockets hard enough to push the shorts low on her hips and expose the blades of her hipbones, the plane of tight skin between.

She was burned brown by the sun.

The yard was dirt.

Abigail had not seen the girl since she was a child, but she recognized the house. With a sickening feeling, she turned to the easel and flipped pages until she reached the charcoal sketch of the young woman, nude in the woods. She looked at the drawing, then at the photograph. She stepped closer and held them side by side. The drawing was the work of skilled hands, the young woman made even more attractive, her face at home in the forest, eyes slanted and deep, leaves twined into her hair. The sketch showed the curve of her hips and breasts, eyes that were entirely too knowing.

"Oh, no."

Abigail stared hard at the drawing, a twist of nausea in the lowest part of her.

"No, no, no."

She left the room at a near-run, the photograph bent double in her fist. Outside, the rain had died to mist. She found the Land Rover where she'd left it, cranked the engine, then checked the loads in the pistol and pointed the vehicle toward the rear of the estate.

"No, no, no," she said again.

And the forest deepened.

In a lifetime of conflict, machination, and political intrigue, there was one persistent thorn in the side of Abigail's husband. On the back side of his four thousand acres was a sixty-acre inholding, an island of old-growth pine that had been owned by the same family since the 1800s. The tract was rugged and untouched, a series of sharp hills and ravines with a gravel road leading to ten acres of flat ground and a house that had stood since before the Civil War. The land came with an easement across the back of the estate grounds, and in spite of the senator's offers, the lady who owned the land refused to sell. He'd offered five times its value, then ten, and twenty. He'd lost his temper, and then things got complicated.

The woman's name was Caravel Gautreaux, which she claimed was Louisiana French. But who could say? The woman was a liar and insane. There was history between them. Bad things.

The main estate road led off the manicured grounds and onto the working sections of the estate. Pavement gave way to gravel, and the road curved past vineyards and horse paddocks, the organic dairy operation Abigail had built from scratch eight years earlier. She drove beside the wide spill of river, then turned north through the deep woods and out across seven hundred acres of pasture dotted with cattle. When the road dipped back into woods on the far side, the gravel began to thin out, the road to narrow. Trees pressed close enough to scratch paint, and new growth folded under the front bumper as she pushed harder into the forest. This was the wild part of the estate, three thousand acres of game preserves and hunting grounds, vast tracts of old forest never timbered.

She drove until the ground rose then fell away in a gorge with a fast, white stream at the bottom. She dropped into low gear and ground through water that rose to the axles, then up a steep incline, trail bending. The earth here was folded and raw. Granite pushed through thin, black dirt; hardwoods fell away to longleaf pine that still bore scars from the turpentine trade two centuries earlier.

The trail intersected a narrow, gravel road that led to the state highway south of the estate, but Abigail didn't care about the highway; she turned north between two hills, and the banks steepened as she drove, light fading as the road seemed to plunge. Abigail had not been to this place in twenty years, but the same fingers twisted her guts when Caravel's house came into view. It was small and old, a jumble of poor rooms washed with white paint and left to settle on a bare dirt yard littered with rusted cars and animal droppings. Curtains hung from open windows. Goats stood in mud beneath a pecan tree, shaggy horses in an open shed.

Abigail drove into the clearing and saw details she'd forgotten in two decades' worth of trying. To the right, a springhouse gave birth to a trickle of water. Beyond it, a smokehouse stood with its door open, metal hooks hanging on the inside. Abigail stepped out of the car and a damp smell hit her nose, a scent like wet talcum and crushed flowers.

Wind chimes tinkled.

Bits of colored glass on brown string.

Abigail moved past a fire pit full of scattered ash and small bones charred black. On the steps were stones scarred with pentagrams, ma-son jars filled with what looked like urine and rusted nails. Hides were nailed to a frame near the wall, and dried plants hung on the porch.

Abigail stopped as the front door swung wide. Something moved in the murky interior, and a woman stepped out. "Well, isn't this a thing to behold?"

The voice was the same, as was the knowing look in the bright, mocking eyes.

"Hello, Caravel."

"Richness."

Caravel Gautreaux stopped in a spill of light and put a hand on the rail. If Abigail had expected her to be ground down by poverty and hard living, she was disappointed. Caravel's hands were rough, but she still had the kind of shape men would like. Five and a half feet tall and burned brown, she was barefoot and lean in a dress made transparent by time and the sun. White streaked her hair in places, but her lips were full and lush. "You look well," Abigail said.

"Well enough." She lit a cigarette. "How's your husband?"

"He's yours if you want him."

Gautreaux lifted the left corner of her mouth. "I guess I had the best of him already. Have you come to settle our score after all this time?"

Abigail shrugged. "Men will be men."

"Does he still say my name in his sleep?"

"Hardly."

"No, I suppose not." Caravel flicked ash. "What do you want down here, richness?"

"I came to see your daughter."

"Oh." An amused expression rose. "This is about Julian."

Abigail tensed. Until now, her theory had been just that. "What do you know about my son?"

"Only that he has the same taste for Gautreaux women as your husband, that he has the same wisdom in his soul yet chooses to keep such choices from you. It all seems so familiar—the lies and carrying on, candlelight and warm air, the smell of young lovers—"

"You're enjoying this, aren't you?"

"I enjoy many things." Caravel rolled the words off her tongue. "Men and smoke and warm, red meat."

"I want to talk to her."

"The pleasures of your company when you're in disarray . . ."

"Damn it, Caravel."

The smile fell off, and her voice hardened. "Victorine's not here."

"Then I'll come back when she is."

"You don't understand. She's been gone a week. Might not be coming back at all."

"Ah, the girl finally wised up."

"What?"

"Wised up. Moved on."

"The girl is mine," Caravel said.

"Not anymore, it seems."

A weight of anger settled in Caravel's eyes, deep lines at her mouth. "You take that back."

"Just keep your daughter away from my son. You do that and we'll have no problems. Keep her off the estate, away from the house."

Caravel came off the porch, one shoulder lifted and a sudden, crazy light in her eyes. "You've seen her, haven't you?"

Abigail took a step back. "I wouldn't be here if I had."

Caravel pointed a finger. "Where's my baby?"

"I told you—"

"You tell her Momma Gautreaux's not mad anymore. You tell her all's forgiven if she comes home."

"You just stay away from us."

"You'll tell her what I said?"

"First of all, I don't know where your crazy daughter is. I've told you that a few times already. And second, the best thing that child could do is keep far away from you. I'll tell her that if I see her."

Gautreaux flicked her cigarette into the dirt, a sudden, wild hate in her voice. "You come between me and my daughter? You come between?" She came closer, her sanity gone as if a switch had dropped. "That child is mine! You understand? I won't have you and your boy tellin' some kind of lies to drive us apart. I see it, now." She reached out to touch Abigail. "I see it."

"Stay away from me." Abigail stumbled backward.

"Distance makes no never-mind, richness. I can hurt you from a world away."

Abigail reached the truck, got her hand on the door. "Just stay away from my son."

"Two feet away or the whole damn world." Gautreaux sat on the porch step, laughing. "No never-mind at all."

Abigail got in the truck and fired the engine, wheels chewing dust as she turned a tight circle. Her window was down and she saw Gautreaux watching.

"All roads lead back to Momma Gautreaux," she called.

The house swung into the rearview mirror. Trees rose and Abigail heard last words, faint beneath the engine. "You tell my baby girl . . ."

Abigail drove fast.

"Ever' damn road . . ."

Five minutes into the woods, Abigail finally slowed the truck. She was rattled and shaken, her heart running like a small animal as she took deep breaths and confronted the fact that Caravel Gautreaux scared her on some deep, fundamental level. Abigail was forty-seven years old, a rational woman; but evil, she knew, was as real as she. It had the same beating heart, the same blood. Call it sin or corruption, call it whatever you like, but that woman was evil. It was in the lines of her skin and in the history of that place, in the smell of dust and the weakness of men. All Abigail really knew was that she'd panicked at the look in Caravel's eyes. The madness was too familiar, the cold, hard look.

Abigail knew women like that.

Had reason to fear them.

A final shudder rolled under her skin, then she collected herself as she always did. She crushed the weakness and the doubt, drove home to tall, stone walls and mirrors that failed to see so deep. She reminded herself that she was iron on the inside, and harder than any woman alive.

Ten minutes later, she parked the Land Rover. Jessup Falls waited at the back door. "Where have you been?"

She considered the red flush in his face, the tension in his frame. "I went to see Caravel Gautreaux."

"Why? The woman's insane."

"I think Julian's involved with her daughter."

"Victorine Gautreaux is only nineteen."

"So was her mother when she cut a ninety-mile swath through the married men of Chatham County. Age is irrelevant to Gautreaux women. Caravel started when she was fourteen. High school boys. Farm hands. Drifters."

"That's a rumor . . ."

"Anyone with five dollars and an erection."

"I don't like it when you get like this."

Abigail let a breath escape, and with it went much of her tension, the memory of her fear. "Maybe. Perhaps. Tell me what's happened."

"It's that obvious?"

"I've known you a long time, Jessup."

"Walk with me." He turned and Abigail fell in beside him. They moved along the drive, then off and into shaded grass. "There's someone at the gate."

"There's always someone at the gate. This is a senator's house. That's what the gate is for."

"You'll want to see this person."

"For God's sake—"

"He's Julian's brother."

"That's not possible."

Abigail looked into Jessup's eyes; she saw certitude and worry, the steady flow of a deep current.

"It's him."

"It can't be . . ."

The voice was not hers. It was too small, too young.

"Abigail . . ."

She bent as her vision grayed at the edges.

"Abigail . . ."

She bent farther, no breath. She saw a boy in sideways snow: one glimpse as he ran, the night that stole him away. He was so small, so lost. She tried to straighten, but the weight of twenty-three years settled on her neck.

Michael . . .

"Breathe," a voice said.

But she could not.

CHAPTER ELEVEN

An iron gate rose twelve feet in front of the stolen car. It was beautifully made, but functional, four thousand pounds of hand-wrought metal strong enough to stop anything short of a tank. Behind it, a strip of black pavement cut a straight line through velvet grass. Farther in, the house looked impossibly large; a castle behind ten-foot stone walls. Michael leaned against the car and watched traffic on the road. He studied the gates, the guards. Inside the car, Elena said his name.

"You okay?" He ducked low enough to look in through the window. Elena scooted across the seat until she was behind the wheel. She was exhausted, with dark circles under her eyes and hollows worn into her cheeks. The wear showed in her voice and in the times she'd drifted and twitched, a pale, worn soul on endless miles of interstate. Even at the motel last night, she'd curled alone on the other bed, quiet and still, but awake. In the morning, she'd showered in silence, dressed with the barest smile. She could hardly meet Michael's eyes, and when she did, there was a secret place where none had been before.

"Are they going to let us in?"

Michael studied the men who guarded the gate. They were professional and alert, broad, fit men with short hair and impeccable suits. Both carried holstered weapons and were as polite as they were confident. Their communications gear was state-of-the-art. If they were private, they were expensive, and Michael wondered just how good they really were. "If Julian's here, they'll let us in."

"Do you think he believed you?"

"Depends, I guess."

"I don't think he's coming back."

Michael studied the gate, the walls. The guards' attention was unbroken. Security cameras pivoted from high mounts, and one of them was pointed directly at them. "He's coming," Michael said.

"What if they're not here?"

"Senate's out of session. This is their summer home. It feels right."

Elena chewed a fingernail, hair sliding on her neck as she checked the road, the deep, black woods. She felt naked in the car, and Michael understood. But how could he tell her the truth? How could he explain that Stevan and Jimmy would never let it end with a quick, clean shot from the deep woods? How could he look her in the eyes and tell her that when they came—which they would—it would be to make things close and personal?

"I don't like this."

Cars blew past, and in the forest, a bird's wing flashed. Michael peered up the drive as a vehicle appeared in the distance, a bullet of metal that became a Ford Expedition as it drew closer and slowed at the gate. Michael saw the same white-haired man behind the wheel. He got out and spoke to the guards, who remained alert but impassive as the gate swung wide and the man walked out to speak with them. "Mrs. Vane has agreed to see you. You can ride with me."

Michael checked the road, which was empty. The walls stretched for at least a mile in either direction. "I'd prefer to have my own transportation."

"If you want inside the gate, the car stays here." The moment stretched between them. "The weapon stays, too."

Michael raised an eyebrow. "Weapon?"

"Don't insult me, son. The one tucked in the back of your pants. Put it in the car. Lock the car. Get in. Time's wasting."

Michael studied his face, which was sunburned, rugged, and blunt. It looked like the face of an honest man, but looks meant little to Michael. He'd known so many liars, so many frauds. "Do you know my brother?"

The man squinted, and skin puckered around his eyes. "I know Julian like he was my own son."

"Is he here?"

"He is."

Michael looked away first. "Just a second." He slipped into the car, tucked the gun under the seat, and rolled up the windows.

"Are you sure about this?" Elena ran both palms down the length of her thighs.

"We'll be fine."

They climbed from the car and Michael locked it. The driver hitched a thumb and said, "She goes in the back. You sit up front where I can see you."

When they were in, the old man dropped a hand to the left side of his seat, then turned in a hard circle and drove back toward the big house. Michael saw formal gardens and trees so beautifully groomed they were ornamental. In the distance, another guard stood at the front door; two more patrolled the corners. Michael could not see any sign of it, but he suspected there would be electronic measures as well: cameras, motion sensors, infrared.

"Why so much security?" he asked.

"How many billionaires do you know?"

Halfway down the drive, the vehicle turned left on a narrow, gravel lane that disappeared into a stand of oaks. "I thought we were going inside," Michael said.

"Not to the main house. That comes later. Maybe. My name is Jessup Falls."

"This is Elena," Michael said.

Falls's eyes rose to meet hers in the rearview mirror. He kept one hand on the wheel, the other in the hollow place between his seat and the door. "Ma'am."

"You took longer than expected."

Falls looked at Michael, shrugged. "Your arrival was unexpected. Discussions were had."

"Whether to let me in," Michael said.

"I was on Iron Mountain the day you killed the Hennessey boy, so, yes. That was part of the discussion."

"Is that why your left hand is holding a gun?"

Falls shrugged, then pulled the gun from beside the seat and tucked it between his legs. "Old habits," he said.

"Are you in charge of security?"

"Only for Mrs. Vane. The senator has his own people."

They drove for a half mile, first through forest, then along a ridge that offered long views of the house and grounds. When that view dropped away, Falls stopped the car.

"Are we meeting Mrs. Vane here?" Michael asked.

Falls put the transmission in park. His face was all business. "We're on the west side of the estate. We're going to the guesthouse. That way." He pointed. "It's private. No one ever uses it." He pivoted so he could see Elena and Michael at the same time. He stared for long seconds, then frowned and said, "There's no money for you here."

"That's not why we came."

"Then why?"

"To see my brother."

"Just like that? After all this time?" Michael shrugged, and Falls asked, "Why do you carry a gun?"

"Why do you?"

"Where do you live?"

"Nowhere, at the moment."

"What do you do for a living?"

"My last job was washing dishes."

Falls peered through the windshield. The road stretched out. "You're giving me no reason to trust you."

"You're private security, which means you're probably ex-cop. You don't trust me, and you won't. Nothing I say will change that, so let's not waste time. I want to see Julian. You say I need to speak to Mrs. Vane first. Fine. She's agreed to see me. Let's get on with it."

"Fair enough. I need you both to step out of the car."

"Why?"

"Just because I'm unwilling to pat you down on the side of a public road doesn't mean I'm stupid." Outside, in the cool of the woods, Michael let Falls pat him down. The man was thorough and quick. "I apologize," he said to Elena.

"It's okay," Michael told Elena, and watched Falls frisk her, too. He was just as thorough, and unapologetic.

"You can get back in the car."

They climbed in, and when Falls turned, his mouth was an uncompromising line. "There's no statute of limitations on murder in North Carolina." He squinted, looked from Michael to Elena and back. "I want to make sure you're aware of that."

"I don't understand." Elena leaned forward.

"He's talking about what happened at Iron House." Michael let a few seconds slip by, not taking his eyes off Falls. "He's threatening me."

"Advising you."

Michael smiled a thin smile, no light in his eyes. "We both know there's no warrant with my name on it. No indictment. Nothing in the system."

"Yet, the police spent a long time looking for you."

"Twenty-three years ago and half a state away." Michael leaned a bit closer. "No one is looking for me, Mr. Falls; and we both know the deeper truth of why that is."

They measured each other for ten seconds, and Falls broke first. "Just don't push me, young man. I take my job seriously."

"I love my brother," Michael said.

"Then we should have no problem."

The guesthouse was a stone cottage on a low knoll that overlooked the lakes and house. It had iron boot-scrapes by the door, a covered porch, and green shutters with black metal hinges. A lawn swept down to the water, and dense trees crowded against the back.

"Wait here."

They watched Falls step onto the porch, then open the door and disappear. The house was small and looked as if it had been there forever. The roof was heavy slate stained green in the cracks. Blue sky shone in high windows; the low ones were black. A beat-up Land Rover Defender was parked at the entrance. Michael watched for movement inside, saw none. Elena took his arm, worried.

"Is it true, what he said? Can they really arrest you?"

"It won't happen."

"Because of the deeper truth?" Michael squeezed her shoulders, and she said, "What does that even mean?"

"It means the pursuit of justice is rarely perfect or fair."

"Don't be cryptic, Michael."

"It means no one here wanted publicity around Julian's adoption, not with Hennessey dead on a bathroom floor. The media would have eaten it up, so the senator kept it quiet."

"He can do that?"

"He has money, power. It's not like Hennessey had family."

"What an unbelievably cold thing to say."

"It's the world in which we live."

"But why would they even care?" She gestured at the far mansion. "You told Julian to say you did it. He was in the clear."

"Scandal has been known to assume a life of its own, given the chance. Besides, I doubt Julian was entirely convincing. He's never been a good liar. His heart is too close to the surface."

"The police didn't believe him?"

"Let's just say the senator spent a lot of money and political capital to keep them from looking too deeply."

"How do you know all this?"

"I made it my business to find out." She frowned, and Michael nudged her hip. "Trust me, Elena. With all that's happened in the past few days, a decades-old investigation is the last thing you need to worry about."

"Promise me you won't be arrested."

"I promise."

"Good. Thank you." She leaned into him, looked across the lakes. "Is this what you expected?"

She was talking about the estate, everything. "There's more security than I thought, but that's good."

She sighed. "That's not what I meant and you know it."

"Are you all right?"

"I'm just sad."

"Why?"

She stared at the soft grass and the far mansion, then took his arm and leaned her head on his shoulder. "This could have been your life."

Jessup found Abigail on the sofa in the living room. "Is he here?" she asked.

"Outside. Are you sure you're ready for this?"

Abigail looked down. Her hand cupped a small photograph. It was black and white, very old.

"Is that Michael?" Jessup asked.

"From his file at Iron Mountain." She tilted it so he could see. The boy was young, maybe eight. He had wild hair and a smile that looked forced. "It's the only picture of him I've ever seen." She touched the photograph. "I missed him by minutes, Jessup. I missed his entire life because we were slowed by a storm, by a thing as simple as wind and frozen water."

"He killed a fifteen-year-old boy. He put a knife in his throat and left him dead on a bathroom floor. People like that don't change. I've seen it. I know. That storm saved you a lifetime of misery."

"He would have had a reason for what he did."

"Then he should have stayed and explained."

"He was a child, and frightened."

"That's no reason to trust him, now."

"Of course not, Jessup. I'm neither a fool nor a romantic."

"Then why let him into your life at all?"

"Because Julian would."

"He's dangerous, Abigail. I'm telling you this is a mistake."

"He's dangerous, how?"

"He carries a concealed weapon, for one. And I ran his plates. The car is stolen. He said he was a dishwasher. That makes him a liar, too."

"I won't condemn him sight unseen."

"You pay me to protect you."

"I pay you to do what I say. Now, just . . . be still. Okay. Just give me a second's peace." She closed her eyes, and when they opened, she pointed. "Outside?" Jessup nodded without speaking. She crossed to the window, lifted the curtain. "My God," she said. "He looks just like him."

Michael was taller, stronger. He had the kind of quiet confidence that Julian would never know, but there was no doubt they were brothers. They had the same brown hair, same dark, expressive eyes. But where Julian was soft, Michael was hard. Where one was timid, the other was not. Michael leaned against the car, arms crossed, one foot up on the front tire. He saw them and gave a nod.

"You say his car is stolen?"

"Yes."

Abigail watched for a few more seconds. Outside, the girl paced, agitated; but Michael held Abigail's eyes. There was power there, she thought. Knowing and cunning and calm. "Have it searched," she said. "I want to know everything about him. Where he works. What he does. Who he is. Everything."

Jessup opened his cell phone. "What changed your mind?"

"I haven't changed my mind."

"Then, what?"

"You're right about one thing," Abigail said.

"What's that?"

She tilted her head, peered out through black lashes. "The man's no dishwasher."

Michael was thinking of Elena's last words when he became aware of a subtle perfume on the air. He looked up to find a woman as elegant as the perfume she wore. She stepped onto the drive, and the moment was so many things: commonplace and strange and bittersweet. She could have been his mother. She was a stranger, but knew his own brother better than he did. Michael stepped closer, and saw that her skin was parchment pale.

"Have I interrupted?"

"Not at all." Michael kept his own features neutral. "Thank you for seeing us. This is Elena."

She acknowledged Elena with a nod, and when her gaze snapped back to Michael, she looked embarrassed. "I've often asked myself what I would say to you should we meet. It's a normal question on its surface, you see. An everyday concern. Would I be matter-of-fact, as if we were, indeed, strangers? Or would I simply fold at the knees?" She laughed, a small sound. "I'm not the folding kind of person, but I wondered if it would all just be too much?" She looked awkward. "I'm not making sense."

"You make perfect sense," Michael said. "I completely understand."

She curled one finger across her lips, and her eyes brightened. "I was at Iron Mountain the day you ran. I saw you in the snow that night, coat flapping, then gone. I saw that terrible storm take you away."

"That was a long time ago," Michael offered.

Her eyes went from bright to shiny wet. "If I could have found you, I would have."

"It's okay." Michael didn't know why he said it—he owed this woman nothing—but he said it, meant it, and in that moment felt the pluck of ice on his skin, the memory so real the frostbitten spots on his hands tingled. He never thought of that dark, cold run, saw it only in dreams; yet here they were, the both of them. Her eyes were large and green, and she was about to cry. "It's okay," he said again.

But she stepped closer and put her arms around him. "I'm so sorry." For a moment, Michael tensed, but her hair was featherlight on his cheek. Her skin smelled of lavender and that elegant perfume. "You poor thing," she said.

Jessup stepped closer. "Mrs. Vane . . ."

But she ignored him. "You poor boy."

CHAPTER TWELVE

A small part of Julian knew where he was. He understood that he was in one of the guest rooms, that his mother came and went, that there was a doctor. But that knowledge was a flicker in the dark. He didn't know why he was there or what was going on, didn't know the day or the month or the year. Julian barely knew his own name.

He was scattered.

Afraid.

The bed was too small, a jumble of hot sheets that twisted around his legs and made him feel trapped. That was bad, claustrophobic. He kicked off the sheets, but kept his eyes closed so that he saw red through his lids, red and heat and smears of black. He waited for some kind of pattern, the coolness of reason.

But there was no reason.

The blackness moved, and in the red were flashes of bright, sharp metal. Julian rolled onto his side. His hands hurt and something smelled, so, he focused on the black. The black was safe, and the black was cool. Beyond it was heat, and beyond that was something bad.

Julian squeezed into a ball.

The black made an island, and if he stayed on the island nothing could touch him. That was another thing he knew, the island he'd made in his mind. He could go there when things got rough or frightening or hard. The island was safe, and the island was his. Beyond the island was . . .

He shied from the thought of it, looked for something else; but there were strange voices in the hall.

And that was scary, too.

Voices.

Strangers.

Julian thought he might fade, but the door creaked, and when he opened his eyes, he saw feet on the floor and legs that rose. He saw his mother and a woman he did not know. And there was a man, but the man made no sense. It was like looking in a mirror and seeing your own face twisted.

Julian blinked and darkness rose up. The man said something, but Julian didn't want to see anyone. He wanted to be alone in the black, so he closed his eyes, and tried to break a bridge with his mind.

He knew how to do that, break bridges, float away.

Somebody touched his arm, and when he opened his eyes he saw the face that was his, but not. There was comfort there, and warmth, a reason to not feel so lonesome. But the bridge was already breaking. Julian heard his name, but it had no weight to settle. It touched him once and was gone.

Julian wanted it back, the touch of this voice. Some part of him understood what was happening, and that part wanted the man with the familiar face to understand why he was on the island, that something had *happened*. He had the wild, insane thought that the man with the face could make everything better.

So, Julian waited for the man to kneel, and when he was close, Julian said the horrible thing; he screamed as the bridge twisted and cracked and fell.

But the man was fading.

The island was an island. The red was gone, and there was only dark. But Julian, finally, understood.

Michael . . .

His voice echoed.

He was alone in the black.

Michael rocked back on his heels, then stood. His brother's eyes were closed now, but what Michael had seen of them hinted at insanity. They'd been dilated, shot with red and the kind of wild, raw panic he'd not seen since the worst moments of childhood.

"What did he say to you?"

That was Jessup Falls. He stood in the door, an armed guard in the hall behind him. The guard was like the ones at the gate, competent but detached. Professional. Michael gave Falls a single glance, and then shook his head. There'd been a second of awareness when Michael took Julian's shoulders, one instant of clarity and recognition as they leaned close. He'd whispered something so quietly only Michael could hear. The madness had stilled—understanding between brothers— then, somebody pulled the drain and Julian was gone.

"I'm going to have to ask again." Falls started to cross the room, but Abigail stopped him with a hand.

"Please," she said. "He's not spoken for three days. Tell us what he said."

"It was nothing," Michael lied. "Something from childhood. Gibberish." He squatted again and lifted one of his brother's arms and then the other. Julian remained unresponsive, even as Michael pulled up his sleeves, checked the skin for needle tracks.

"There's no sign of intravenous drug use." The doctor pointed. "I checked between his toes, the backs of his legs. All the usual places."

Michael rose. "May I see the other room?"

Dr. Cloverdale shot a glance at Abigail, who nodded. They'd moved Julian out of the bloodstained room, but the walls had yet to be cleaned. Together, they left Julian's room and crossed the hall. The guard stepped back to make room.

"You can see why I hesitated." Abigail stopped in the door, as if unwilling to commit.

Michael studied the room. "When did you move him?"

"Just this morning."

"And this started three days ago?"

Abigail walked him through it again: Julian's absence, how she found him in the garage and how he beat his hands bloody. "Have you ever seen anything like this?"

Michael touched a dark crescent of dried blood, put a palm flat on one of the drawn doors. "Something smaller, maybe. A long time ago." He pictured Julian in the boiler room at Iron House, the glazed eyes and bloody knuckles. He touched the second door. It, too, was scratched through to plaster. "If things got bad, Julian went deep. Basements, caves. If he couldn't get deep enough in the world, he went deep in his mind. It happened a lot when we were young. If something bad happened, he checked out. Minutes. A few hours. Never this long."

"What about the doors?" Abigail gestured at the drawings.

"An old man told him once that there were magic doors hidden in the walls. Doors to better places, a different life. Tap them right and they open up. All Julian had to do was find them."

"His poor hands," Elena said.

Michael stopped by the bed. The sheets had been stripped. "Something bad happened three days ago."

"You can't be sure of that," Falls said.

"I'm sure."

"It's been twenty-three years. He's not the boy he was. You don't know him anymore. You can't."

Michael cataloged the distrust in Jessup Falls's face, the wrinkled skin, and folds of flesh at the corners of his eyes. The man was tense in his bones, and Michael bridled at the doubt. He looked at the blood-smeared walls, and he felt anger spark in the normally frozen place behind his eyes. Julian was his brother, and they'd allowed him to come to this.

Them.

Not Michael.

The old protectiveness rose as if it had never slept. Twenty-three years of suppressed worry, fear and doubt boiled into anger so immediate and hot that part of Michael knew he was off the rails. But he didn't care. He pushed close to Falls and to Abigail Vane. He ignored the guard in the hall, the blunt, square-faced man who rose up on his toes and slipped one hand under his coat to touch the weapon there. "Do you have any idea what my brother endured as a child? The torment and abuse? The callousness and unconcern of people paid to care for his most basic needs?"

"No, I—"

"That's right." His gaze landed on Abigail Vane. "You don't. None of you. Not how he hurt or how often he broke. You don't know what it took to pick him up day after day, to put him back on his feet, to hold him together. You weren't there and you can't imagine. He was beaten, abused, ignored . . ."

Michael saw red as a day from childhood flashed into his mind with such clarity it was physical. Julian was eight and had been missing for an hour when Michael finally found him in the same bathroom where Hennessey would later die with a rusted blade in his neck. It was the screaming that led him there. They had Julian naked on the cold, tile floor, one boy on each arm and leg. Julian was still wet from the shower, thrashing, begging. Hennessey had a knife against Julian's hairless prick, laughing as he threatened to cut it off.

I would like some beanie weenies . . .

No! Please!

Say it motherfucker.

"Julian doesn't like to talk about his childhood." Abigail put herself in front of Michael.

"That's because nightmares are personal."

"We can't possibly understand what you boys went through at that terrible place, but we've tried." Abigail looked down, sad. "This has been so hard."

"Don't talk to me about *hard*, and don't question me on the past or on my brother. You may think you understand, but you can't. No one can."

Michael felt the stillness in the room, the way Elena stared at him. She'd never seen him raise his voice, never seen him angry.

"No one meant any disrespect," Abigail said. "We understand your connection to Julian. We welcome it. Please, don't be angry."

Yet. Michael was. He was angry at the world, and he was angry with himself. Stepping into the hall, he pointed at the guard. "You. What's your name?"

"Richard Gale."

"Are you any good with that?" Michael nodded at the weapon on Gale's belt.

"Michael, what are you doing?"

Abigail came out behind him, worried. She caught his arm, and Michael pulled it free. He studied Richard Gale and liked what he saw. Assurance that bordered on eagerness. An utter lack of fear or doubt as he sized Michael up. "Try me," he said.

And that moment told Michael everything he needed to know. He took Elena's hand, and turned. "We're leaving." He led her down the long hall and onto the sweeping staircase. Behind them, Abigail followed, Jessup Falls two steps behind the hem of her skirt.

"Michael, please . . ."

He was resolute, but she caught him at the front door. "Why are you leaving?"

"I came to make sure my brother was safe. He's safe."

"What do you mean?"

"I've counted six guards since I got here. There's probably more, all of them well armed and professional. The property is gated and walled. Video surveillance. Electronic countermeasures." Michael shook his head. "Julian doesn't need me."

"But he does. You can't just show up and then leave. He needs you. I need you."

Michael stared out beyond the far gate. Jimmy was out there, coming. Elena's hand felt warm and small when he squeezed it. "Other people need me, too," he said.

That thought burned in Michael's mind, and in Elena's, too. She squeezed his hand in return, and he felt her relief in the way she molded against him. He'd done what he needed to do. Julian was safe. Now, they could make a life, build a family. "We have to go," he said.

But Abigail was not finished. "You said he's safe."

"He is."

"From what?"

Their gazes locked, and she was so desperate to know that Michael almost told her the truth. Jimmy. Stevan. The target painted on his back. But what purpose would such disclosure serve? "I have enemies." He kept it simple. "People I thought might choose to hurt me through Julian."

"What kind of enemies?" Falls forced himself into the conversation.

"People that don't want to hurt Julian badly enough to risk security like this." Michael was confident. Julian was bait, nothing more. "The risk leaves when I do."

"That's not good enough," Falls said. "What risks? What threats? If there's a danger out there, I need to know what it is. I want specifics: names, timing, all of it."

But Michael was confident. Stevan had used Julian to flush Michael into the open. "Julian's in no danger. Not here. Not with this security."

"How did you even find us?" Falls demanded. "Adoption records are sealed. Julian's father is a United States senator."

Michael gave him a second, then said, "I've known for a long time how to find my brother."

"How?"

A shrug. "I have resources."

"That give you access to private information on a senator and his family? What kind of resources?"

What could Michael say? How could he explain that he knew Julian's GPA from high school, that he had copies of their tax returns, photographs of the senator with two different prostitutes. Michael remembered his seventeenth birthday. Early in the morning, the sky outside still black. The old man had come to Michael's room with a thick folder in his hand.

A man should know his family. He'd put the file on Michael's bed, offered a sad, knowing smile. *Happy birthday, Michael.*

It was a dark gift, but extensive. Michael later learned that the old man had spent almost five hundred thousand dollars on private investigators and corrupt officials. The old man did nothing in a small way.

So, yes.

Michael knew the senator and his family. He squeezed Elena's hand. "We're leaving now. It's better for us, better for Julian."

"But you saw him!" Abigail was desperate. "You can't just leave."

"I shouldn't have come."

"Why did you?"

She looked desperate, and Michael answered the question in his mind: *Because I had to see the security for myself; because I had to know he was protected.*

128

"He's your brother, Michael. Please."

"I'm sorry."

"What kind of danger?" Falls demanded. "What kind of threat?"

"Nothing you can't handle."

"That's not good enough."

"It'll have to do."

Michael aimed for the far gate and started walking. Abigail took a dozen running steps and cut him off a final time. "Damn it, Michael." She flattened her palm on his chest, and then hesitated. She threw a glance at Falls, the giant house. "Nothing is ever as it seems. Understand? Nothing. I need you to reconsider."

"Why?"

Elena pulled on Michael's hand, and even he was thinking of the places they could go. Europe. South America.

Large cities where they could disappear.

Long stretches of lonely beach.

"The guard in whom you found such comfort." Her words were clipped. "Richard Gale. In the hall outside Julian's room."

"What about him?" Michael asked.

"He's not just there to keep people out."

"Are you saying Julian is a prisoner?"

Michael felt Elena stiffen beside him. Her fingers tightened in a quiet, insistent squeeze, and he thought of what his brother had said in his moment of clarity. Then he considered the clarity, itself—the cleanness of it, the sharp, bright edges surrounded by madness. He allowed his gaze to drift down and left as he studied the long, narrow lake, the things he saw on its shores. When he looked back, Abigail was imploring with her eyes.

"I'm saying it's complicated, and you should stay."

She stood taller, one hand on his arm.

"I'm begging you."

There was a time, once, when Michael could walk away from people who slowed him down. It was the most basic rule of life on the street: survival first. It was the first thing he learned after stepping off the bus in New York: people will lie, and people will kill. That truth was wound so tightly in his core it was part of him; but that was changing. Looking at Elena, he felt the cable loosen in his chest.

"Are you okay?" They were back in the car, following Jessup Falls to the guesthouse.

"We shouldn't be here."

"It's just a day. Just to make sure."

She stared at a far, gray line in the sky. "Clouds are piling up."

"He's my brother."

"And what am I?"

Michael took her hand. She was angry, and he understood. "Look at me, baby."

"No."

"Look at me." She looked, and Michael said, "You're everything else, you understand? You're my life."

At the guest house, Falls waited for them to climb from the car, then rolled down his window. Like Elena, he was unhappy. "It's unlocked," he said. "There's everything you need. Call the house if something comes up."

"All right." Michael stayed near the car. Elena went onto the porch and sat.

"You won't find the gun in your car," Falls said.

"I noticed."

"I'll give it back to you when you leave."

"Do I need to count the money?" Michael dropped his duffel bag on the gravel, and watched Falls stare for long seconds before looking up.

"There're no thieves here, young man. And no fools, either."

"I'll remember that."

Falls thought for a second, then said, "I may just be hired help, but Julian's like a son to me. I watched him grow up. I helped raise him, and have a warm place in my heart for his mother. There's not much I won't do for him."

"Your point?"

"My point is I'm not as forgiving as Mrs. Vane. It's not in my nature and not in my job description. Point is you need to talk to me.

There're things I need to know and I plan to know them. You think on that. I'll expect you to have a different attitude come morning."

"I'll think about it."

"In the meantime." Falls put the big Ford in gear. "Don't come near the main house without permission. Dogs are out after dark, and the guards are for more than show. I can promise you that."

"I think we understand each other."

Falls waited a heartbeat, then took his foot off the brake. Michael watched taillights fade in the dark beneath the trees, and then joined Elena on the porch. She was in a rocking chair, knees drawn up. Michael sat beside her. "Are you hungry?"

"I'm scared."

"Give me a second." He returned to the car and triggered the release of the driver's-side air bag. It was disengaged, hollowed out. Inside was the forty-five, wrapped in newspaper to keep it from rattling. "See, all better."

Yet Elena did not feel better. She went into a back bedroom, pulled the curtains and climbed into bed. "I love you, Michael, and I can handle this. Your brother. This place. I can give you your day, and you can get some answers. Just tell me you know what you're doing."

"I know what I'm doing."

"Swear it on your soul."

He touched his heart. "I swear on my soul."

She pulled his head down and kissed him. "Do you love me?"

"You know I do."

"What if you had to choose? Julian or me? Julian or the baby?"

"That won't happen."

She cupped his face with both hands, stared deep into his eyes. She kissed him hard, then rolled onto her side.

"It just did."

CHAPTER THIRTEEN

Jessup had a room apart from the servant's wing. It had a small living area, a closet, a bath and its own separate entrance. He could have taken a larger room, but he valued the entrance, the privacy of his own door. Abigail knocked on it an hour after Michael was taken to the guesthouse.

"Come in." Jessup opened the door and stepped back as Abigail pushed in. They were on the north side of the mansion, the door recessed at the bottom of three shallow steps that got little sun and smelled of damp concrete. Abigail brushed past him without a word. She had an unrestrained look in her eyes, an animation she normally suppressed. He shut the door, and she paced. She traced a line of books with her fingertip, sat on the bed, then stood.

"I've always liked this room," she said. "Very masculine." She took in the heavy furniture, the paneled walls and small stone fireplace. She picked up a hand-forged fire tool, tilted it so the hammer marks glinted. "It suits you."

"Are you okay?"

She replaced the poker and it clanked hard against the metal stand. "He's settled at the guesthouse?"

"Yes."

"After all these years." Her shoulders rose. "I can't believe he's here."

"It's concerning."

"That's not what I meant."

"We have different concerns."

"Must you always be so paranoid?"

"Must you always be so naive?"

She allowed a smile, touched his arm. "Such strong shoulders to bear the weight of the world . . ."

"You're damn straight."

Abigail let her hand fall away, and the smile went with it. "Have you informed the senator?"

"I've spoken with his security. Senator Vane is still meeting with lawyers."

"What do his people think?"

"They think Michael's a nut-job with an angle. Money, probably. If not that, then another asshole with ideas on abortion rights, gun control, the death penalty. Most threats against your husband revolve around those issues. They're not looking any deeper than that."

"But you are?"

"My interests are more personal."

"Do you think he's a danger?"

"I think we should be all over this guy."

"I need more than your instinct."

"There's more." Jessup moved to a small table in the corner beneath a window. He opened a file and spread out a sheaf of photographs. "These just came off the printer."

"From his car?"

"The search was cursory, but still . . ."

"Who did you use?"

"Alden."

"Alden's good."

Falls spread out a handful of photographs. The car. The license plate. Shots of the interior. "There was one weapon in the vehicle." Jessup sifted out a close-up of a handgun. "Kimber nine millimeter, a high-quality handgun. The serial numbers have been removed. Not filed off, but burned off with acid. Very thorough. Very professional. We also found this." Another photograph slid across the table. It showed an open duffel and bands of green.

"How much?"

"Two hundred and ninety thousand dollars, give or take. The bills are brand-new. Still in the sleeves."

"Do you still think he's after money?"

"Three hundred thousand is not a billion."

"Is that all you found?"

"This was in the bottom of his duffel." Falls slipped a photograph from the file folder and handed it over. The picture was of a book.

"Hemingway? Should I worry?"

"I'm just showing you what we found. The gun. Clothing. Cash. I saved the best two for last." He slid out another picture. It was a close-up of another snapshot, a black and white photo of two small boys on a field of mud and snow. Time had degraded the image so that their features were washed out, their eyes specks of black.

"Oh, my God." Abigail lifted the photo.

"It's the same picture, isn't it?"

"The yard at Iron Mountain." She touched the two boys. Julian had the same photograph on his desk upstairs. It came anonymously one day when Julian was fifteen. No card. Just the photograph. For years, they'd speculated about that picture. Who'd sent it, and why? She'd often found Julian asleep with it in his hands. "You know what this means?"

"It means he's known where to find us for a very long time."

"But why didn't he reach out to us? To Julian?" Abigail could not take her eyes off the photograph. According to Julian, it had been taken less than a month before Michael ran away. "We could have had him back years ago."

"Which brings us back to timing."

Some inflection in his voice made Abigail look up. "There's more, isn't there?"

Falls pulled a final photograph from the folder. He slipped it out facedown, then turned it up and spun it across the table. It was an enlargement of yet another photograph, this one showing a teenage Michael leaning against the hood of a car. An older man had one arm around Michael's neck. They were laughing. "He had this photograph as well. I'd guess he was sixteen when it was taken. Maybe a bit older."

Abigail studied the photograph: Michael and an older man, brownstones with open windows, parked cars, a fire hydrant. "It looks like a city street."

"New York."

"You sound certain."

"I am."

"This could be anywhere, Jessup. A dozen different cities."

"Do you recognize the man with his arm around Michael's shoulder?"

"No."

"Look again."

She tilted the photograph to the light. "Okay. He's vaguely familiar. Maybe. The picture's almost twenty years old."

"He's been in the news for longer than that." Falls dropped a newspaper on the table. It landed hard. "This is yesterday's *New York Times*." She lifted the paper, looked at the headline, the face of an old man found dead in the slaughterhouse of his own home.

"Otto Kaitlin?"

"Possibly the most powerful crime boss in recent memory."

"I know who Otto Kaitlin is. What does he have to do with Michael?"

"It's the same man."

"You're being absurd."

"There's a full spread on page five. What they know of his life. Some old photographs. The similarity is more obvious."

Abigail turned to page five, compared the photos. Michael and the laughing man. The dead mobster tied to forty years of murder, racketeering and extortion. There was a mug shot of Kaitlin as a young man, another of him on the courthouse steps, cuffed and lean in an expensive suit. The similarities were there: the hair and eyes, the confident smile. Otto Kaitlin was an old-school gangster, a gentleman killer tried a half-dozen times and never convicted. He was articulate and photogenic, a killer with easy grace and a Hollywood smile. Books had been based on his career. At least two movies. Abigail felt her way to a chair and sat.

Falls opened a drawer and pulled out a handgun sealed in a plastic bag. "This came from Michael's car."

"You took it?"

"Seven dead in Otto Kaitlin's house. Six of them shot with a nine

135

millimeter. Then, an hour later, the explosion in Tribeca. Another nine dead. A dozen injured. Police are looking for a man and a woman who fled the scene in a car traced back to Kaitlin's house. A man and a woman. The descriptions match."

Abigail shook her head. "What descriptions? A man in his thirties. A woman with dark hair. It could be anybody. A million different people."

"Six people were shot with a nine millimeter."

"You think that's the gun?"

"It could be."

"Could be. Old photos. Listen to you. This may as well be office gossip, the mindless chatter of old ladies."

Falls pointed to the photo of Michael and the laughing man. "We know that's Otto Kaitlin."

"We know nothing of the sort."

Falls pushed the photograph into her hands. "You're in denial. Look at it."

"Okay. There's a similarity, but it's a ridiculous stretch. Michael is Julian's brother. He was almost my son."

"You're being irresponsible." Falls spread his hand on the newsprint photos of Otto Kaitlin. "These are serious people, Abigail. Mobsters. Killers."

"You're overreacting."

"He shows up in a stolen car with a bag of cash and an untraceable weapon. This is not an average man."

"And yet, I believe his reasons."

"That he loves his brother?"

"Yes."

"What if this danger follows him? If he *is* associated with Otto Kaitlin . . ."

"You can protect us." She put a hand on his shoulder. "Big strong man. Ex-cop. Ex-military."

"Don't be flip."

"We spent over a million dollars on security last year." Abigail dropped the photo and put both palms flat on the table. "Julian is my son, and as hard as his life has been, I've never seen him as broken as he is now. His brother has come back to him after twenty-three years, and I think it's happened for a reason. I think he can help. So, do what you need to do your job. Alert the senator's people to a possible threat, but keep your reasons vague. Be cautious. Be smart. But if you scare Michael off, I'll never forgive you." She straightened, voice crisp. "In the meantime, you keep your theories to yourself. I don't want to hear anything about mobsters or mass murder or old photographs."

Falls shook his head, disappointed. "You're making a mistake."

"I don't think so."

"You said it yourself."

"What?"

Falls watched her carefully. "The man's no dishwasher."

CHAPTER FOURTEEN

Some things are best done in the dark, and alone. This is what Michael told himself, and it was almost enough to wash the taste of betrayal from his throat as he slipped from the covers and swung his feet to the floor. The clock read four twenty; in the bed, Elena lay still. Michael watched her as he dressed, and as the gun came silently from the bedside table. It was loaded—full clip, one in the pipe—and he considered how quickly she had become accustomed to its presence. One day it was an unknown; the next it was merely part of the scenery. In a strange, sad way, the thought gave him hope. He would change what he could to make her happy, but knew, deep down, that violence was more than a stain on his soul.

He tucked the gun into his belt, eased open the door and slipped out. Windows were dark in the far mansion, the night very still under high clouds and a slash of moon. Michael was in the drive when Elena called his name. The open doorway framed her perfectly, shadowed face and wild hair, the ghost of her shape beneath a sheet pulled tight. A catch in her voice made his name a desperate sound. "You're leaving?"

"There's something I have to do. I didn't want to wake you."

"It's the middle of the night."

"I won't be gone for long."

Her eyes looked black and damp and slick as glass. "I want to come with you."

She was shaking, and Michael understood. Her world had gone dark, and she was hanging by a thread. "You don't even know where I'm going."

"I don't care. I want to be with you."

"You're safe here."

Crescents cut the swell of her bottom lip: white teeth and dry skin. "What if something happens to you?"

Michael crossed to where she stood. He kissed her cheek. "I guess, you'd better get dressed."

"You won't leave?"

One eye twinkled. "How could I?"

She slipped into the house. A light winked on, burned for a few minutes, then clicked off. When she came out, she wore jeans, dark shoes and a dark shirt. A clip gathered hair at the base of her neck.

"Are you sure you want to do this?"

"I go where you go."

She was determined; as far as answers went, it was a good one. So, Michael told her what Julian had said and where they were going. She thought about it long enough for Michael to doubt the wisdom of telling her. This was about instinct and trust, about *knowing* that something bad had pushed Julian over the edge. His brother's fears were textured and complex, but they were real, and Michael knew every nuance. Elena might claim to understand, but at the end of the day she was just a normal person.

"Why would Julian say that?" she asked. "It doesn't even make sense."

"That's what I hope to find out."

"But you saw him. He's a wreck. It could mean anything or nothing. This could be pointless."

"I know my brother, and there was a second there when we connected. The confusion disappeared and it was Julian. He knew me. Whatever he's dealing with, whatever hideaway he's made for his mind, he wasn't crazy when he said it."

"But I thought Hennessey was dead."

"Trust me, he's dead."

"Then why would Julian say that?"

Michael replayed the moment in his mind, the sweat on Julian's face, the moment his pupils constricted and the madness fell away.

Hennessey is in the boathouse . . .

"All I know is he believed it, and he was scared."

"That's why we stayed, isn't it? Because Julian is scared, because he said this thing that makes no sense."

Michael shook his head. "It's more than that."

"Then, tell me Michael. Why can't we go far away, have this baby, and be safe? Why must we stay in this place?"

"Because he's my brother, and because helping him is what I do. Because when I see him again, he needs to know that I'm still looking out for him. I need to tell him that I checked, that I made sure. You saw him, baby. He needs to know that people care."

Elena stared into the damp, dark night. "Is there even a boathouse on this property?"

"Northeast corner of the largest lake. You can just see it; stone, I think. It's built out over the water, three large doors, wooden decking along one side. There's a trail along the water's edge."

Her eyes locked on the stain of dark water. "Did he say anything else?"

"Yes."

Michael pictured chalky lips, the knotted muscle of Julian's shoulders.

Please, Michael . . .

"He begged me."

Michael knew the smell of death like he knew the scent of Elena's hair. He caught the first whiff when they were still fifty feet out. "Hang on a second."

"What?"

"Just hang on."

He put a hand on her arm and pulled her down in the dark. The smell was elusive, a light drift of tainted air. Beneath their feet, the trail ran thin and soft around the lake's edge, a footpath between black water and a stand of forest that pushed down from a far ridge. Ahead, the boathouse made a dark lump against the curving shore. Michael took another deep breath and caught a stronger scent. "I need you to stay here."

"Forget it."

He squeezed her arm, one hand finding the pistol wedged at the small of his back. "Don't argue with me, Elena. This is serious." He rose to a crouch and checked the trail behind them, the water with its dull, rippled surface. He stared long into the woods as a finger of warm air slipped along the trees and carried more of the scent.

"I'm not staying here, Michael."

"I can't let you come further." She opened her mouth, but Michael spoke over her. "Don't you smell it?"

"No."

"Wait for it."

Another eddy stirred the air, the same warm finger that brushed once against his face, then stalled and came again. It was a flicker, a taste, and when Elena tilted her head, Michael knew that she had it. "What is that?"

"Something dead."

"You mean like an animal?"

"Stay here. Stay quiet."

"You do mean, like an animal? Right?"

Michael said nothing. No way was this a raccoon.

"You can't leave me in the woods."

"We're alone," he said, then immediately questioned his own words. A sound carried across the water, a scrape that could have been stone on stone. He cut his eyes right, where the lake curved into a shallow cove. Distant light touched the water: pale white of the high moon, a few bold stars. On the far shore, pastureland rolled to the water's stony edge, the grass more purple than black.

"Michael, this—"

"Shhh."

Michael listened but heard no other sounds that seemed out of place. The far shore was empty and still, a long spill of shadow and mottled grass. He stared up the trail, and felt the boathouse solidify: the hard edge of roof, the jut of wood decking on the closest side. The structure was low and broad, with stone walls that grew darker as they neared the waterline. The building extended thirty feet into the lake, and Michael could make out three curved doors for the boats, dark squares that were shuttered windows. "Here." He pushed the gun into her hand. "Same as before. Remember? Safety's off. Don't shoot me."

"I don't want a gun."

"I'll be right back."

"Don't you dare leave me."

But the last thing he wanted was for her to see what he suspected he'd find in the boathouse, so he denied her the chance to argue. He turned and loped along the trail, the death-smell growing stronger with every foot he moved. Twenty feet out, the scent was thick enough to catch in the back of his throat. Another ten, and the last doubt vanished. Whatever was dead, it was in the structure or near enough to make no difference. Michael cast a quick glance behind him, but Elena was lost in the dark. He hesitated, knowing she was frightened and confused, but risks were mounting with every step he took—the risk of being caught, the risk of making a mistake—so he built compartments in his mind and pushed Elena from his thoughts as the boathouse rose before him, taller than he'd expected, longer. At its rear edge, the woods fell away, and he saw hints of gravel where a roadbed slit the grass. He paused, and then made for the back corner, stooping as he hit a final stretch of open grass. He reached the structure, and stopped. Beneath his fingers, the stone felt damp and cool.

Edging around the corner, Michael saw an empty parking area that was overgrown with weeds. Beyond it, pastureland rose to forest on a high ridge. The grass was cropped short, but brush-choked swales snaked down slope to the water's edge.

Turning back to the boathouse, Michael stepped onto the decking that ran along the wall and extended over the water. Moss grew on stone, and the wood was soft with rot so that whole place smelled not just of death, but of decay. A shuttered window appeared and Michael touched feathers of paint that flaked under his fingers. Ten feet farther, he came to the door. The smell was stronger here, unmistakable. A heavy lock hung from a broken hasp, the steel twisted, a half-dozen screws bent by whatever force had torn them from the wood. The door itself stood open several inches, a line of black in the gap. Like the shutters, the door's paint was flaked and thin, adding to the pall of neglect that hung over the place.

Michael eased open the door and a wave of heat and stench welled out, so strong it would have gagged another man. He gave his eyes a moment to adjust, and then stepped across the threshold. Inside, it was quiet, but for the sound of water. Michael eased right to avoid being outlined in the door. His hand found a light switch, but he was reluctant to turn it on. The lake itself was so dark that the light would show for miles. Instead, he pulled a match from his pocket and lit it. When it flared, he caught a vague impression of a vast, largely floorless space. Most of it was shadow and darkness, but he saw hints of black water and canoes on racks. Sailboats lay in a jumble against the far wall. A wooden motorboat rested on slings. It was dusty, and half-covered with a tarp; cracks showed in the once-fine varnish. On the back wall was a workbench littered with ropes and sails and dusty tools.

The match burned out.

Michael lit another and stepped gingerly toward the back. On the bench, he'd seen a gooseneck lamp next to a toolbox and a spill of faded, orange life jackets. He bent the neck until the bulb pointed back and down, then threw a filthy rag across the top of it and turned it on. Yellow light burned through the rag, so muffled and low that Michael doubted it would carry. It lit the boathouse, though—and the body. All Michael saw at first were legs. Protruding from behind one of the sailboats, they were thick and swollen, one straight and the other twisted beneath it. Leather work boots covered the feet. Blue jeans. A tooled leather belt.

Michael stepped over a pyramid of varnish cans, then moved around the stern of the boat. It was eighteen feet long, fiberglass. It looked as if the body had been jammed behind it; perhaps it had fallen that way. He saw hints of the body but the shadows were deep, so he dragged the sailboat away, its keel grinding on the wood, ropes shifting, a coil sliding off the hull. Returning to the body, Michael saw a middle-aged man who'd been dead for some time. The torso was distended, the skin mottled and gray. The face had the slackness peculiar to death, the utter loss of humanity that Michael knew too well. One eye showed, milky-pale, and whiskers were stark on the skin of his face. He was four inches over six feet tall, maybe two hundred and sixty-five pounds, a large man, but unfit. Calluses thickened the pads of his hands; the nails were dirty. Beneath the jaw line was a denim shirt stained black with blood. A knife handle protruded from his neck, and it was the knife that made pieces shift and click. It was the knife that made the picture whole.

"Ah, shit."

Michael rocked back on his heels. The blade had not entered the dead man's neck at the precise place and angle of the blade that killed Hennessey, but it was close. Right side. Just below the ear. More than the wound was familiar—there was something about the face, too. Michael felt hair lift on his arms. He studied the face for long seconds, then checked the shirt pocket, the front pockets of the dead man's jeans. Finding nothing, he shifted the body. It moved loosely, so he knew that rigor had come and gone. A few days, he guessed, probably three, based on when Julian showed up a gibbering wreck. The body was cold and loose and Michael's fingers sank into the fat. He grunted once, and the dead man flopped onto his side, one arm striking a second boat, dried blood making a slight tearing sound as the body rolled. Michael used a rag and two fingers to remove the wallet from the man's back pocket. He saw a few bills, some credit cards. The driver's license confirmed what he already suspected. Michael knew the guy, and so did Julian.

Fuck-head from juvie.

Ronnie Saints.

His features had roughened with age, but Michael had a remarkable memory for faces, especially for those he considered enemies. After Hennessey, few kids had done more to wreck Julian's life than Ronnie Saints. At the age of eleven, he'd pulled three years in juvenile detention for beating a neighborhood kid half to death in a fight over a stolen pistol. When he finally got out, his parents were gone, either dead or lost in some hillbilly meth trailer in the mountains of north Georgia. Speculation had lasted a week or two when Ronnie first rolled into Iron House; after that, nobody really cared. He was just another fuck-head in from juvie.

Michael studied the driver's license. Saints was thirty-seven years old and lived in Asheville. Michael memorized his address, then rolled him onto his back. Keeping the rag over his hand, Michael put one finger on the handle of the knife, right at the end. The blade was utilitarian, the handle stained wood with brushed, metal rivets. A fishing knife, maybe. Something similar. He put pressure on his finger, but the blade barely moved. It was jammed in deep, wedged against bone and gristle. Michael took his finger off the knife and checked the body. He saw no other defensive wounds, no signs of struggle. There was spatter, but beyond that there was no blood except where he'd found the body.

When it happened, he thought, it happened hard and fast.

Michael wasted no time thinking about the whys of it; the old patterns rose as if never forgotten. Julian was in trouble, and Michael was going to fix it. It's what brothers did, what family was all about. He stood and thought of the steps he would take in the next three minutes. He laid them out in his head, mechanical and precise. He needed a boat that wouldn't sink, something heavy enough to drop a body and keep it down. The floorboards were heavily grained, and the blood had soaked too deeply to be scrubbed out, but the place was a mess and clearly unused. He could shift boats, spill some varnish.

He found a pair of old gloves on the workbench and slipped them on. The first canoe he checked was wooden and decayed beyond his willingness to trust it. The second was aluminum. He heaved it off a rack and lowered it to the water, where it settled with a splash and loud clunk against the wooden slip. A canoe would be tough for heaving bodies in and out. It was narrow and easy to tip, but also light and fast through the water, quiet. Michael bent low, caught the dead man's boots and dragged him across ten feet of floor. He stopped at the edge. The canoe rocked two feet down; the water beyond was burnished black. From a shelf on the far wall, Michael retrieved a twelve-pound anchor and a coil of heavy line. Bending, he placed the anchor on the dead man's chest and cinched it tight with multiple loops around the torso and waist. It was hard work; the man was heavy and loose. A final loop went around his ankles, and Michael lifted the legs to cinch the knot tight. That's when he saw Elena.

She stood in the door, one hand over her mouth, her face so pale it was translucent. How long she'd been there, Michael couldn't guess, and under the circumstances he didn't care. The sun was rising half a state away. They had forty minutes, maybe less.

"Help me," he said.

She bent at the waist, overcome by the smell. She gagged twice, then said, "I don't understand."

"There's chain there." Michael pointed. "I need it."

Her eyes drifted down and right, settled on a mound of filthy chain in a hollow space beside the door. She looked back at the body as Michael tore the knife from its neck and tossed it, clattering, into the canoe. "Did you . . ."

"Chain. Elena, please."

"Did you kill him?"

Michael dragged the body another six inches, lined it up with the edge of the canoe. "He's been dead for a while."

"What are you doing?"

"Fixing a thing that needs fixing. I really don't have time to explain. Will you give me the chain, please?"

She didn't move. Part of Michael understood her struggle, and part of him was angry. He'd told her to stay put for a reason.

"You knew you'd find this?"

Michael crossed the space between them and scooped up the chain. "The smell's hard to confuse with anything else." He took the gun from her limp hand, tucked it into his belt. "I wish you had listened to me, baby. I'm sorry you have to see this."

She stared at the body, her throat pulsing as she swallowed whatever bitter emotion the sight conjured. "Who is that?"

"It doesn't matter. Now, come here, please. I need you to do something." Michael began to loop chain around the body, looked up, impatient. "You don't have to touch it. Just hold the canoe."

"Hold the canoe," she repeated. "Why?" The question hung in the air between them. Michael found her eyes, and saw the moment she understood. "You're going to sink him in the lake?"

"It's not my mess, Elena, but it has to be cleaned up. It's important. Trust me. The canoe, please."

She shook her head. "This is wrong."

"It's what has to be done."

"We need to call the police. This is . . ." She trailed off. "This is . . ."

"All you have to do is hold the canoe. Baby, please . . ."

"What's wrong with you?"

"There are reasons."

"I'm not going to sink a dead man in the lake."

"I know what I'm doing."

"Please don't tell me that."

"Sun's coming, baby."

She shook her head. "I can't be here."

"Elena . . ."

"No." She stumbled through the door, wood slamming once on the wall outside. For an instant Michael saw the hint of her, a flash of black cloth and skin, then she was gone. He looked once at the empty door, then at the body. For half a second, he debated; then he went after her.

"Elena."

"Stay away from me."

Her feet were loud on the wood, then quiet when she hit grass. She was running, but blind in the dark. Michael caught her by the water's edge, her arm hot and dry between his fingers. He pulled her to a stop. "Settle down. Come on."

She jerked her arm, but he held on. "Let me go, Michael."

"Just listen."

"Let me go or I'll scream." One second stretched to three, then Michael released her arm. For an instant more, there was total silence, then she said, "What the hell are you?"

"I'm just a man."

"I can't be with you."

Her head moved in the dark, and Michael knew she was about to run. She took a step, and he said, "It's not safe, baby. I need you to stay with me."

"No."

"Elena . . ."

"I need to think. I need time. I need . . ."

But she didn't know what she needed; and the sky was growing lighter. Michael reached for her hand, but she stumbled back. "Don't touch me."

"It's still me . . ."

"Don't follow me. Don't call me." She stepped back, and Michael moved forward. "Take one more step and you'll never see me again. I swear!" She threw up a hand, her palm pale in the dark.

Michael froze, said, "Trust me."

"I can't," she said. "I won't."

And there was such disgust in her voice, such fear and loathing that when she turned to run, Michael declined to follow. He watched her fade along the shore—the moment an agony of indecision—then turned slowly for the boathouse. She needed to think, needed time. So, he poured varnish on the bloody floor, dragged a boat across the stain and rolled the body into the canoe. It was heavy like his heart, cold and broken; so, he sank it in the lake, in the deep, black water surrounded by silent woods and purple hills. For an instant, the face shone as it fell, then, Michael was alone with the choice he'd made.

Back at the house, he was unsurprised to find the car gone and Elena with it. He looked at the place it had been, then stood on the porch, tall and still as the night gathered its last breath and a new day crowned. He wanted to call her, but minutes passed and red light spilled across the valley floor. She would understand or not, return or keep running. So, he went inside and took a shower. He put his duffel bag near the sofa, then stretched out and let sleep take him deep and dreamless, so that he woke long hours after the sun had filled the sky to bursting. He opened the door—felt scorching heat—and standing on the porch, saw two things at once.

Elena had not returned.

Cops were dragging the lake.

CHAPTER FIFTEEN

Elena drove with tears in her eyes and a burn the length of her throat. She could still smell the body, the scent so pervasive it was in her hair, her clothes, steeped into the oils of her skin. And images came with the scent: mottled skin and swollen hands, the look on Michael's face, the cool detachment and methodical precision.

There's a chain there . . .

She checked the mirror and scrubbed one arm across her face, a dark laugh building in the hollow courses of her soul. How could she have allowed herself to believe that he was the same man she'd once thought him to be, that he could kill in cold blood, yet be a decent father to the child he'd put inside her?

"Oh, God . . ."

The laughter came then, an expulsion so sharp and tattered she frightened herself. In the mirror, her eyes were not her own. They were glass eyes, stone eyes painted black. Her fingers felt the wheel, but the wheel felt wrong. Everything felt wrong. Elena did not know where she was: some town in North Carolina, a road with four lanes, fast-food joints and cheap motels. There had been countryside and red light fading to orange, a whisper of trees.

I've done no wrong of which to be ashamed.

The thought felt false but she clung to it, one hand moving to the seat beside her. She had clean clothes and her passport, enough money to get back to Spain. She would forget about Michael, and the death she had seen. She would find her father and tell him that she'd been wrong to leave, that life in a small village was life enough. Elena almost wept at the thought, and at the images that came with such clarity: home and family and people that never changed. Her fingers brushed the warmth of her stomach, and where the fear had been she felt resolve. She would go back to her parents, she decided. She would go home and raise from this mistake a small and perfect child that would never know the provenance of its conception.

Elena reached for the mirror and twisted it up and away. She had had enough of painted eyes and emotionality. She was Carmen Elena Del Portal, and she would go home. But first, she had to rid herself of the smell. That meant a shower, a place to change clothes. The thought was so attractive it became an imperative. Her clothes felt heavy and soiled, her very skin corrupt, so that when a roadside motel appeared on an approaching rise, she signaled a right turn and rolled into the parking lot.

For a moment, she sat in silence as emotion took her down. She thought of Michael and felt a soft place in her heart.

"No."

She smeared both hands across her face, shook her head.

"No."

She got out of the car, her eyes red but dry; a bell chimed as she walked inside. The clerk behind the counter was a tall, spare man, whose face was severely lined for a man who otherwise appeared to be in his forties. He had long arms and wide, square palms. He thumbed a key on a plastic fob and his smile lingered as she placed four bills on the smudged counter. "You need anything . . ." He held onto the key two seconds longer than he should have. "You just call the desk."

She sniffed, then palmed the last moisture from the skin beneath her eyes. "Thank you."

"My name is Calvert." He gestured at the low ceiling, the carpet worn through. "This is my place."

"Thank you, Calvert."

"So . . ." Fingers drummed the small, tight bowl of his stomach. "Anything at all."

"Do you have a map?"

He scratched at the crown of his head. "Where are you going?"

"What's the nearest major airport?"

"That'd be Raleigh."

"Then that's where I'm going."

He showed her Raleigh on the map, and then gave her the key to a room down the hall. Elena put the map on the front seat of the car, then unloaded her few belongings and carried them through the lobby and into a small, dark room whose air was damp enough to feel on her skin. She locked the door and pulled off her clothes. The floor of the bathroom was freshly cleaned, the shower curtain white vinyl faded to gray. Collecting small bottles of shampoo and conditioner, the paper-wrapped soap, Elena climbed into the shower and let needles of hot water stitch dull, red marks on the planes of her face.

Calvert was leaning on the counter when the bell above his door chimed twice. He caught a flash of movement and color, just enough to give the sense of a narrow-shouldered, effeminate man in fancy clothes, none of which made him eager to be of help. He disliked rich people and hated queers, so did not immediately look up from the newspaper he was reading. His mind was still flush with thoughts of the hot little Mexican who'd bent low enough to show some bra when he pointed out Raleigh on the map.

The man cleared his throat.

Calvert turned the page and looked up to see a middle-aged man in black velvet pants and a burgundy coat. He wore sunglasses that let you see his eyes, and a big, gold watch that probably cost more than most cars. Calvert allowed his distaste to show when he said, "A little hot for them pants, don't you think?"

"I find that they breathe."

The man smiled, and Calvert realized he was too dumb to know he'd been insulted. He just stood there, calmly, and some reptile part of Calvert's brain recognized that things were not quite right; but this was his place, and the man was wearing velvet pants. Beyond the glass was a road-stained car with New York plates. "Okay, fancy-pants. What do you want?"

"That's clever. Fancy-pants."

"Look, I'm busy here."

"The lady who just came in . . ."

"I don't give out room numbers."

"I'd like you to reconsider."

"And I'd like you to turn around and go back to whatever big city you came from. As you can see . . ." He flicked a yellow nail at the newspaper. "I'm busy."

"You're not being very helpful."

The paper rustled as a page turned. "I suppose not." A long moment passed, and without looking up he said, "Are you still here?"

"Actually, I'd like to show you something."

"Show me what?"

"It's like a trick."

Calvert looked up, and the man in velvet pants lifted his left hand above his shoulder. He made a flourish—fingers rolling open, and then closed.

"You mean, like magic?"

"Sort of. Are you watching?"

"No."

"It's really quite good."

Calvert closed his newspaper. "Okay, sure. I'm watching."

"It happens fast."

Calvert watched the hand. The fingers moved. The hand closed into a fist.

"Here it comes." One finger straightened, then two. "Get ready."

Calvert was still watching the left hand when Jimmy shot him in the heart with a silenced twenty-two. The shot pushed him back a step, and for an instant, his mouth opened; then he fell where he stood. Jimmy walked around the counter, put one more in the skull for good measure then stepped daintily over the mess and looked at the computer screen. Satisfied, he lifted the key to room twelve from the pegboard, then brushed lint from his sleeve.

"Fucking redneck," he said, and walked down the hall to room twelve.

CHAPTER SIXTEEN

Steam clogged Elena's throat, hot water crashing down. She gripped the showerhead and felt metal pitted with corrosion, a tongue of wet curtain that licked her leg and stuck. She washed herself again.

Yet the smell lingered.

The images.

She lathered her hair, digging hard with her fingers, scraping as she saw so many things that had once been good: the yellow paint on Michael's hands, the smile that lit his face when he spoke of the baby. Seven months condensed to a single moment as she saw his hands on her stomach, her breasts, and then on the skin of that corpse. He'd been so . . . proficient. The body didn't bother him. The smell. The very fact that the man was dead.

There's a chain there . . .

It was real, all of it.

Elena pressed a palm on her stomach, and then prayed as she had as a girl, not just for strength or guidance, but for God to reach down and make it right. But there was no easy fix, and deep down, she was ashamed of her need. Her father taught her to be strong, to count on herself, so she pushed the weakness away. She dug deep and found the core of who she was. She felt fear and sorrow, a blinding streak of bright, sharp anger. Michael was a killer, and in that word—*killer*—Elena found the threads of her strength. It seemed a small thing at first, this tangle of poor threads, but she gathered them up, pulled until she felt strong in her soul. She would recover, and the pain that lingered—the memory of his hands on her skin—that, too, would wither and fade. She promised this to herself, swore it; but lies are slippery and quick—that's how they work—and some part of Elena knew she was being faithless. She loved him. There was no other man like him.

But the things he's done . . .

She turned off the water, which died to a trickle as she smoothed hair from her face.

"I'm okay."

It felt wrong the way she said it, so she tried again.

"I *will* be okay."

That was better. That was real.

She opened the curtain with a metallic scrape, and reached for a robe that was no longer where she'd left it. She saw a man, instead—parts of a man, a blur of skin and hair and eyes. They were cold eyes, and blue, a look of amusement over thin lips and pale, fine skin. He stood a foot from the shower, his forehead high and square, hair wispy thin on the crown of his head. The moment was so unreal, so utterly unexpected, that she almost laughed. It was a misunderstanding, some hotel employee at the wrong place at the wrong time. But the look was wrong. He was too calm, too amused. Her robe was in one of his hands, something black and square in the other. It was only when his smile spread that the scream gathered fully in the back of Elena's throat.

"You're not okay," he said.

And, Elena knew who he was.

Her arms came up, but his hand moved in a blur. Something blue flashed, and she heard a crack of energy as fire tore through her ribs. She felt agony, white heat, and then nothing at all.

CHAPTER SEVENTEEN

Control was part of what made Michael so good at his job: choosing the time and place of the things he did, manipulating the elements involved and then acting with calm regard for every possible consequence. Most people in the business were the exact opposite of Michael. They killed in rage and fear or got off on it for their own screwed up reasons. They let emotions run, and those guys rarely lasted. They burned out or got sloppy, became a liability for the organization that paid their freight. More than a handful ended up with a target on their backs, and Michael had taken out a few, himself. The math was simple in Michael's world. Emotions are bad. Control is good. But there was no control now.

Elena was gone.

A wave of dizziness struck, and he sat on the top step. Everything had seemed clear last night, the problem and how to correct it. It's what he did, fix things, handle them. He'd just assumed Elena could handle it, too. She would be patient, let him explain. But, the way she'd looked at him! There'd been such regret in her eyes, such disgust and loathing.

What have I done?

She was gone and it was his fault. She had hours behind the wheel of a car, could be in Virginia or South Carolina, maybe even Georgia or Tennessee.

Jesus, she could be anywhere.

Stevan and Jimmy could be anywhere.

Worry gnawed at Michael, but he forced himself to think it

through. Without law enforcement resources, Vincent and Jimmy would be as blind as Michael. They couldn't subpoena credit card records, couldn't tap into a law enforcement database. It's why they'd threatened Julian in the first place, to force Michael into the open. Once clear of the estate, Elena would be clear of everything. They couldn't track her. She was safe. She would be safe.

Michael told himself that, repeated it. He forced the emotion down, then stepped to the edge of the porch and studied the scene at the boathouse. A handful of police cars were parked there, lights flashing in the clear, bright air as two boats moved on the water. Men called out and heaved draglines.

They would have divers soon, Michael thought, and wondered how long it would take them to find the body. The lake was large, and although he had no certain knowledge, it felt deep. The earth sloped in from both sides, and he could almost see it plunging down to form the lakebed far below. The water looked very black, and even in the sun it seemed to radiate a deep and steady cool.

But that could be wishful thinking.

He watched one of the lines fly out, a thread from this distance. Broad, metal hooks flashed and then sank. The line was hauled back, and hooks came up trailing weed. Michael's gaze drifted right.

About there, he thought.

A second line flew out, and as it arced and dropped, Michael debated whether or not it was Elena who'd called the police. It was certainly possible. Violent death is not the norm, nor is the sight of one's boyfriend wrapping a body in chains to sink it in a lake. But would she call the police? Michael doubted it. If she'd sold him out, Michael would be running, dead or in cuffs. That left one possibility.

Someone else had seen.

He replayed the events in his mind: the silent approach and grass stained purple, a sound from across the lake's narrow end. He felt a slight chill, and not at the thought that he'd been watched. He heard a dead man's voice. He saw the old man's face, and it was as sharp in the eye of his mind as if the man were alive and sharing the same porch.

Don't look for fancy explanations, son. If the cops are here, then your woman told.

Michael blinked, and the image faded. That was the old man who'd raised him, not the dying man who spoke of loves lost and daughters never born. That man had understood that life is change and life is faith, that not everything is simple. He'd released Michael, after all, and to the detriment of his only son.

Nothing simple about that, old man.

And nothing was simple about his own life, either. Was Michael a killer or a father? Could he be both? Could he change for Elena and still be strong enough to protect Julian? Raise a child? Build a life? One part of Michael was cool as he analyzed this. Another felt compartments fold in his chest. He needed to be cold, but Elena was gone; needed strength when emotion made him weak. He could go crazy thinking about this shit.

Michael went inside, ran cold water and splashed it on his face. When the towel came away, he fingered the glossy scar on the side of his neck. It was long and flat and white as pearl. An inch to the right and it would be in the same location as the knife he'd pulled from the dead man's throat the night before.

Where are you, Elena?

He dropped the towel next to the sink, and forced himself to concentrate. Elena would accept him or not—come back to him or not—and worrying about it wouldn't help him figure out the dead man at the bottom of the lake.

Compartments.

Control.

Michael took a deep breath, and pictured Ronnie Saints. Not the feel or the smell of him, but the whys of him. Why was Ronnie Saints here, in Chatham County? What did he want? Why was he dead, and what did Julian know about it? Michael studied his face in the mirror, trying to remember what the face had looked like more than two decades ago. All he could remember was hunger and ragged hair, the feel of rough wool on his skin and shirt cuffs so filthy they were stiff. He closed his eyes and tried again. He wanted to see Ronnie Saints clearly, but this time saw his brother, not tortured and broken and small, but younger than that, his face turned sideways on a pillow. He was maybe five.

Let's pretend we were adopted . . .

Few memories remained of Julian with a smile on his face, and for an instant, Michael found himself unmade. There'd been times when things were good, a moment here, an afternoon there: small, shy flickers of joy. Had those memories simply faded, or had he buried them with all the other remnants of his childhood? For an instant, Michael felt cheapened and untrue.

How much did he need the ice at his core?

How hard did he need to be?

He gripped the sink. What did it matter? The past was gone. This was now. But was it *only* now? That was a good question. First Hennessey and now Ronnie Saints. Two dead boys from Iron House. Twenty-three years between them, and both stabbed in the neck.

What is going on? Michael wondered.

And who called the cops?

Back on the porch, he dialed Elena's number on his cell. He wanted her to answer, but knew, deep down, that she would not.

Too soon.

Too complicated.

Perhaps it was for the best, he thought, a clean break and a safe, easy life far from his. He tried to feel good about that, but the lie burned deep as an image of them gelled in his mind: Elena and the child—a girl, perhaps, a dark-eyed beauty with her mother's skin. They walked through high fields in the mountains of Catalonia, one lean and sad, one far too young to understand the empty place in her life.

Tell me again about my daddy . . .

The sky above them would be painfully blue, and in the wake of Elena's silence, the question would come again. Michael saw it so clearly: a small child, and lies told often enough to taste of truth. Elena would move on, and his daughter would grow without him. Michael felt that future like a hole ripped in the wall of his heart. But, it didn't have to end like that. There were options, always.

He called her phone again.

*   *   *

Twenty minutes later, Abigail Vane arrived in the same beat-up Land Rover Defender. She looked good in linen pants and light makeup. The fear in her was less obvious, a hint of raw, rough panic buried deep. "I thought you might be curious." She gestured at the boathouse, but Michael kept his eyes on the large, flat envelope in her hand.

"A little, maybe."

She showed no signs of obvious distress, but little things gave her away. Sudden color in fingers squeezed white. A tiny swallow before she spoke. Too much glaze on her eyes. "Let's sit." She gestured at rocking chairs, and they sat in the shade of the deep porch. Abigail leaned forward, the envelope shaking slightly in her hands. "The police came early this morning, local detectives with a warrant to search the boathouse and lake."

"Search for what?"

Her gaze steadied. "A body."

Every nerve in her was strung tight, but Michael could play this game in his sleep: cops, death, secrets. "Any particular body?"

"I'm sure I have no idea."

"Did they show you the warrant? Do you know why they're looking?"

"Someone reported a death in the boathouse, a body put into the lake. That's all I know."

"When you say *someone* reported?"

"A confidential informant—that's what the affidavit said. According to a confidential informant someone was killed in the boathouse. A body was sunk in the lake sometime last night. Our lawyers are circling the wagons, but couldn't stop the search."

"Why would you want to stop it?"

Michael was checking for a reaction, and got one. For an instant, she was dumbfounded, her mouth open and wordless. It didn't last. "They checked the boathouse first, and found blood on the floor. A lot of it, apparently, though, someone tried to conceal the fact of it."

"You've seen it?"

"They're calling it a crime scene. It's sealed."

"Why are you here, Mrs. Vane?"

"Call me Abigail."

Michael leaned closer. "What do you want with me, Abigail?"

This was the crux of it; he saw it in every line of her face. She was frightened, but not for herself. She needed something. Desperately.

"Do you love your brother?" she asked. "I don't mean the memory of him or the thought of him. Do you love him like I do? Like he's still a part of you?"

"Julian will always be a part of me."

"But, do you love him? There's a difference between love and the memory of love. The memory of it is warm but basically meaningless. Love means you'll do anything. Burn bridges. Tear down houses. Love makes normal life mean nothing at all. I want to know if that's what you feel."

"Why?"

"Because I want a reason to trust you."

"You're worried he had something to do with this." Michael gestured at the lake.

"Something made him break. You said it yourself."

She shifted her feet, and Michael leaned away, thoughts moving in the back of his mind. He saw the boathouse, abandoned and rotting, the fear in Abigail's eyes. "What do you think happened here?" he asked.

"I would kill to protect your brother. I need to know if you feel as strongly. Not *want* to know. *Need* to know."

Something was happening. A steadiness rose up in her, a moral certainty that went straight through to her soul.

"I love my brother," Michael said.

Abigail closed her eyes, then exhaled deeply as she laced her fingers and tilted at the waist. "What did he say to you? In his room yesterday, what did he whisper? Something disturbing, I think. I was watching your face when it happened, so please don't tell me I'm wrong. I won't believe you."

"I don't know what you mean."

"I'll beg if I have to. I'm not above it."

She was whispering now, a conspirator, and Michael wondered how much of it was an act. It was gently done, this corralling of common interests. He stood, took two steps toward the lake. "If there is a body under that water . . ." He looked back, and found that her face was ivory-still. "Do you really think Julian is capable of that?"

"Yes." Her eyes were bright and hard. "I do."

"Why?"

That was the question, and in spite of her need and talk of love, it unsettled her. They'd gone too far, too fast. She was shutting down. "You came alone this morning," he said. "I'm surprised Jessup Falls allowed it."

"Jessup's a good man, but he thinks you're bad."

"Bad?" Michael lifted an eyebrow.

"New York bad." She ran one hand across the envelope in her lap, and Michael sensed a weightless moment as she took a step and the earth dropped away beneath her. "Otto Kaitlin bad."

"Otto Kaitlin?"

"I think you heard me."

Michael blinked once as Jessup Falls went up a notch in his estimation. In twenty years, not even the police had made such a solid connection. They knew *of* him, but had no photographs or composites, not even his name; they'd seen his work up close, but had conflicting descriptions. He was short, tall, white, black. Michael was a ghost and a rumor; a threat of violence masked by false names and manufactured stories. He was a shadow who took orders from Otto Kaitlin and no one else. Someone to fear. A cipher. That's how it had been designed twenty years ago—Jimmy's idea—and Michael, too, was careful. He'd never been arrested or printed. He had a dozen false identities and they were all rock solid. "Why would Falls think I have something to do with Otto Kaitlin?"

Abigail narrowed her eyes, and Michael sensed the return of her earlier implacability. Whatever fear she harbored, she'd made her decision. "What do you think I am, Michael?" She opened the manila envelope in her lap. "A rich man's wife who spends her days in idle pursuits? A dilettante?" She slipped a photograph from the envelope and handed it over.

Michael tilted it in the light. It was a copy of the only picture in existence that showed him and Otto Kaitlin together: Michael and the old man and the 1965 Ford GTO Kaitlin had given him for his sixteenth birthday. The photo that had been in his duffel bag. Michael studied the photograph, then handed it back. His face betrayed none of the emotions that tugged at him: love and regret at the sight of the old man; anger that his photograph had been copied and was being used against him. "It's only a photograph," he lied.

She slipped it back into the folder. "There's quite a stir in the city right now, talk of terrorism and organized crime. Police are looking for a man and woman."

"New York seems a long way from here."

"Not that far."

Michael shrugged. He had plenty of money. Julian was protected. All he had to do was find Elena and walk. "So what?" he asked. "Falls thinks I'm bad, and you don't?"

"I think I don't care."

"Why not?"

"Because I think a body is going to come out of that water." She leaned forward, her mouth a bitter line. "And I think you know something about it."

CHAPTER EIGHTEEN

When Elena woke, she heard engine noise and the hiss of traffic. She was blind in the dark, her wrists bound behind her back, ankles crossed and tied. Her limbs had gone numb, but she tasted tape on her lips—a bitter, chemical gum—and when she tried to move, her head struck metal in the blackness. Pain shot down her neck, and in the stifling heat, she panicked. Thrashing and rolling, she smashed her knees and elbows, the small bones of her toes and the soft bottoms of her feet. The air was close and thick, a gasoline burn so strong in the back of her throat it made her gag.

It was a nightmare, she told herself, the skin of some horrible dream; but the skin stuck. She was in the trunk of a killer's car.

Killer's car.

Killer.

None of this could be real! The motel. The shower. But she felt the hotel robe on her skin, electrical burns on her side. She tried to stay calm, to think of the baby; but somewhere, the car would stop, and when that happened he would drag her out at the bitter end of some thin, dirt road. She would see a last wedge of sun, and then it would happen. She would die in the mud, and her baby would die inside her.

The thought made her nauseous, but she tried to think clearly. What would Michael do? God, the question was insane. She didn't even know who Michael was. But, she had to think like him. She had to be strong. *Think, Elena!* Her fingers found a can of some sort, then touched nylon strapping and a hank of stiff rope. She tried to gauge distance, but the car slowed and accelerated, turned left and right.

Once there were railroad tracks—a brief clatter as the car angled up, then down—then two more lefts, and the car turned onto gravel. The shocks worked harder, and Elena pictured the empty, dirt road she feared. The trees, when he pulled her out, would be very tall, and their leaves would move as if nothing in the world had changed. She thought, perhaps, that she should pray; but then silence came, and it was sudden. The car slid to a stop and the engine died. She felt for something sharp or hard, but there was nothing. There never had been.

Michael . . .

Elena tried to make herself small, but when the lid rose she saw the same man leaning over her. He wore sunglasses, and there were other men, too, hints of whiskers and unblinking eyes. They ringed the open trunk, and studied her as if she were a fish in the bottom of a bucket. The man she thought was Jimmy said something and two men reached in to pick her up. They caught her by the robe, her arms. She fought, and one of the men laughed as they heaved her up and out, then dropped her as she struggled.

"Jesus," she heard a man say, and thought it was Jimmy.

"She's slippery."

Elena rolled her eyes and saw a small, green house circled by trees and dead grass. The driveway was long and dirt. The car was silver and smelled of burnt oil.

Hands came at her again. Two were brushed with hair; two were lean and tan. "Nice tits," somebody said, and she realized her robe had torn open.

"Just get her in the house."

Hands gripped her again, and when they got her up, she thrashed and fought until they dropped her a second time.

"For God's sake . . ."

"Damn, Jimmy. She's strong."

"This is ridiculous. Step away." Jimmy appeared above her, his face a pale blur under a canopy of high, green leaves that moved exactly as she'd thought they would. He held the stun gun an inch from her eyes and made blue sparks snap and sizzle.

"You remember this."

She felt herself nod.

He lowered the stun gun, and closed her robe where it had opened. "Be a good girl."

She let the same two men lift her off the ground, and did not fight as they hauled her up four stairs and onto the half-rotted porch of what looked like an old farmhouse. A screen door hung in the frame. Green clapboarding peeled under a baking sun, and from the porch she saw a barn in a sprawl of milkweed and brambles. Beside the barn were a half-dozen dusty cars.

"Back bedroom," Jimmy said. She felt a wave of heat as her body broke the plane of the entrance. The room was filled with ancient furniture and brown carpet tracked muddy. She saw hints of other men, guns on a table. "Right side."

They angled her body around an end table and then into a hall with floors that creaked. The room on the right side had a single chair and an iron bed. They dropped her on the bare mattress, and a musty smell rose up to fill her nose. Men crowded the door as a mosquito whined in her ear. She looked, but there were too many to process. She saw eyes here, a belt buckle there. Hands that opened and closed. No one spoke as sweat rolled on her face, and hot air stroked skin where the robe rode up on her hips.

"Out," Jimmy said.

And everyone left.

Jimmy smoothed his sleeves and closed the door. In spite of the heat, his skin looked as fresh as if it was powdered. He checked his shoes for mud, and then dragged the room's single chair across the floor. When he sat, he removed his sunglasses and tucked them into the breast pocket of his jacket. Then, he leaned forward, got his nails under the tape and ripped it off her mouth. She wanted to speak rationally. She wanted to yell and scream, but nothing came out. All she could think was *don't hurt my baby . . .*

"Let's start with what I know." Jimmy pinched a mosquito from the back of his neck, rolled blood between two fingers. "Your name is Carmen Elena Del Portal. You were born in Catalonia twenty-nine years ago and have been in this country for three years. You're pregnant. You worked at what used to be a nice restaurant." He smiled coldly. "You would be considered attractive by men who go for the obvious—meaning, Michael, of course—and yet one breast is slightly smaller than the other, and you have an unfortunate blemish on the inside of your high, right thigh." Elena shrank away. "Did I miss anything?"

"What do you want?"

Jimmy ignored the question. He crossed his legs, made a velvet sound. "Michael told you what he is, didn't he? That's why you left in such a hurry, why you were weeping in the shower of that disgusting motel."

He lit a cigarette with a brass lighter, and then blew gray smoke at the open window. "Do you know who I am?"

Elena's throat hurt when she swallowed. "Jimmy."

"Michael spoke of me?"

"Yes."

"And what did Michael tell you about me? Some overblown horror story? Something blood-soaked and gothic?" Elena grew still, and Jimmy nodded. "Lack of imagination has always been his great shortcoming. No sense of destiny. No sense of greater things."

Elena saw Michael with paint on his hands: his excitement for the baby, the future. He'd always seen family as something greater than its parts. He'd described it for her so many times: how it would be when they were a family, the *significance* of it. "That's not true," she said.

"A small man with small ideas."

"You're wrong about him."

"A little fire. I like it. But it is true. Probably my one great failing in how I raised him. Not enough sense of his own greatness." Jimmy took a final drag, and then flicked the cigarette out the window. "A depressing lack of self-worth."

Elena worked her wrists, felt tape bite deeply.

"I'll tell you a story," Jimmy said. "It's a funny one. Did Michael tell you about the day the old man found him? How he was about to be killed under a bridge in Spanish Harlem and the old man saved him. You know that one? Did he tell you that?"

Elena felt her head move, and Jimmy laughed.

"'Course, he did. It's his favorite story, his own personal mythology. It's like the novels he reads. Dickens, I guess. Maybe *Oliver Twist*."

Jimmy made a flourish with his hands, and Elena knew she'd never forget the sight of the condescending smile that bent his face.

"Now, here's the beauty of it." Jimmy leaned forward. "You ready? Watch this. Otto Kaitlin hired those punks to cut Michael up. It's beautiful, I swear to God. Otto wanted to see for himself if this kid was as tough as everybody said." Jimmy lit another cigarette, leaned back, shrugged. "Turns out, he was."

"Why are you telling me this?"

"Because, in spite of that, Otto Kaitlin didn't make Michael what he is. I did."

"And that matters?"

"Are you serious?" He laughed.

"I want to know why you're telling me."

"I'm telling you, you ditzy bitch, because Michael's not some random killer. He's elegant, like Mozart would be if playing the piano was killing, like da Vinci if the *Mona Lisa* was body count. He's a work of art, a genius, and I made him. Not Otto Kaitlin. Not the street. I gave birth to that boy as sure as whatever whore pushed him out on the filthy sheets of some flophouse bed."

"And you're proud of that?"

"You don't think God is proud of Jesus?"

A pale, still madness smoldered in the dark centers of Jimmy's eyes, but something else burned in there, too, and for a second, it looked familiar. "What do you want with me?"

Jimmy shot his cuffs. "I want you to tell me about Michael. What his plans are. Where he's going."

"Just let me go."

"No, no, no. Too late for that." Jimmy rose, and then sat beside her, his hip narrow and hard against her leg. He dragged a finger along the sweat of her forehead, and then rubbed the dampness against his thumb.

"There's nothing I can tell you," Elena said.

"Of course there is. Where he's staying. What weapons he has. Security issues. People around him. Where he sleeps and when." Jimmy smiled, but it was small. "Little things."

He licked his lips, pale skin flushed, and Elena had an epiphany. She realized what she'd seen in his eyes.

"You're scared of him."

She didn't know where the certainty originated, but it was real. Jimmy's talk of pride and fatherhood was bluster. He was frightened, and now that she'd said it out loud, it was all over him. His posture. His face.

"Don't say that again."

He made the words a threat, but Elena had been electrocuted and taped up, tossed in the back of a trunk and terrorized. This knowledge was the only power she had, and as small as it was, it was seductive. Her mouth opened, and Jimmy's eyes went dead before the words had formed in her mouth. He caught a fistful of her hair and pulled her off the bed, the same deadness on his face as he dragged her across the floor.

"I'm sorry! I'm sorry!"

The words were glass in her mouth as he dragged her into the living room and across the filthy carpet. Men rose and stared. Skin burned off the backs of her hands and then she heard hollow thumps as Jimmy's shoes landed hard on the boards of the porch. Sunshine struck her face, and he dragged her down the stairs and onto the soft, pungent dirt.

"Please . . ."

He hauled her to the back of the car, rolled her with a foot. Someone said, "What's going on, Jimmy?" But Jimmy ignored him. The trunk popped with a small sound and Jimmy leaned in, pulled out a gasoline can and emptied it onto Elena. The smell hit some primal part of her, so that even as her eyes burned and her mouth filled with the bitter taste of it, she tried to crawl away.

"Who's scared, now?"

His voice had an inhuman quality, an indifference that was too studied to be real. When he lowered the gasoline can, she saw nicks in the bright, red plastic, fine stitching in the seams of Jimmy's leather shoes. Elena blinked against the burn in her eyes, saw the lighter in his hand. It was brass. He spun it between his thumb and four fingers, opened it, closed it. Bright metal winked and she saw the charred, black wick inside.

"Don't." She curled around the baby in her stomach.

"Don't what?"

The lighter spun, clicked open.

"Please . . ."

Jimmy looked up, squinted at the high, blue sky. "Hot out today."

Elena began to cry.

CHAPTER NINETEEN

Julian disliked drugs, in general, but when he needed them that changed. When he was scared and cold in the darkness of his mind, he liked everything about the drugs. He liked the intensity of the doctor's face as the needle went into the little bottle, the way light shone through the glass. He liked the sound of a fingernail tapped against the syringe and the sight of the narrow stream shot out into the air. His eyes went very still when the needle came out.

The needle made the voice in his head go quiet.

The needle helped Julian hide.

It started as a burn where the needle slipped in, but the burn was brief and faded to warmth that spread from his arm into his chest, then down his legs and into the metal of his skull. Into the giant, dark space from which the voice descended when the world was too big or Julian too scared, when Julian knew he was being weak.

That's the right word, isn't it?

Julian shied from the sneer. He was frightened of so many things: of his life and of life's expectations, of the threat of failure and how that failure would ripple into other parts of his soul. He was afraid people would see too deep, that twenty years of illusion would simply implode and everyone would know he was a shadow man. But that was a big fear—a lifelong terror—and those fears were not always the worst. There was the fear of minutes and seconds, the fear of a coward's million tiny degradations. The voice saw all that fear. It was why Julian hated the voice, and why he needed it. The voice hurt, but kept him strong. And, Julian needed to be strong.

You need everything I have . . .

It was loud, in spite of the drugs, angry after so many months of absence. Julian tried to remember what had happened to bring the voice back, but his mind wasn't working right.

Something bad . . .

He tried to remember. He imagined fingers squeezed on the gray coils of his brain.

Something bad . . .

He squeezed a little harder.

Worthless . . .

"Stop it."

Palms pressed the sides of Julian's head. When had the voice come back?

He didn't know; it was too much.

We don't need him . . .

The voice was a thin wire this time.

Say it with me . . .

"No."

We don't need Michael . . .

"No."

Say it!

Julian rolled into a ball even as a faint noise stirred in the world outside his mind. It was a familiar noise, a murmur of words that had power of its own, because the voice turned away. It grew high and faint until Julian was alone in the dark. He huddled on an island in the blackness, watched as Michael and his mother came through the door and spoke with the doctor. He saw them stop by the bed, and he heard the questions they asked. He wanted to speak to them, but was unable. They heard what he heard, a voice that sounded like his own, but was not.

The voice was laughing at them.

And the sound was insane.

Michael stopped at the bedside, and felt Abigail slip into the hollow place beside his right arm. Beneath them, Julian lay on his side, his hair matted, his skin like wax. His arms were pale under a

171

summer tan, his fingers curled beneath gauze dotted red at the knuckles. Michael leaned closer as a faint sound slipped past Julian's lips.

"Julian?"

The sound welled into brittle, ugly laughter. Michael straightened. "Why is he laughing?"

"I have no idea," the doctor said. "He's been talking a bit. This is the first laugh I've heard."

"What has he said?"

"The same thing, more or less. I suspect you'll get a taste soon enough."

Michael squatted next to the bed and put his hand on Julian's forehead. "No fever."

"No."

"Then what?" Abigail's voice showed a mother's fear.

The doctor clasped his hands, and titled his head so that soft flesh rounded out beneath his jaw. "Perhaps you can tell me."

"Meaning?"

"Meaning, the senator still won't release his medical records. That makes my job difficult. Frankly, I'm becoming angry. Clearly, there is more I need to know."

"My husband has worries most men do not."

"Medical records are confidential. There is no conceivable way I would betray a patient's trust. The very thought is insulting."

"Yet, mistakes are often made."

"Not in my practice."

Abigail paled at his anger, but did not back down. "His medical records are sealed."

"Sealed?"

"By the courts." She cleared her throat. "As part of a juvenile matter."

"I don't understand."

Abigail was torn, Michael saw. Her eyes flicked from Julian to the doctor, then found Michael's face. Whatever she was afraid to discuss, it was serious; the doctor seemed to understand. "Let me phrase this a different way." Cloverdale stepped closer, his voice calm. "Have you ever heard of chlorpromazine? It's a drug." He waited, eyebrows lifted, but Abigail was frozen, mouth half-open. The doctor nodded, sadly. "How about loxapine or haloperidol? Clozapine?" No reaction. "How about ziprasidone or olanzapine?"

Abigail looked away, and Michael said, "Those drugs are antipsychotics."

"That's right."

"Why are you asking about antipsychotics?"

The doctor pointed at Julian as the laughter came again. "Look at him."

They all looked, and Julian's eyes went wide and black, the laughter suddenly frozen in the cavern of his mouth. "We don't need . . ." Julian spoke in a reedy voice.

"He's been saying this quite a bit," the doctor said.

"Saying what, exactly?"

Julian lifted his chin, eyelids slipping down to half-mast as a wicked smile cut the planes of his face. "We don't need Michael."

Julian's words sucked the air from the room, and just as quickly as the venom had arisen, slackness overcame his face. His eyes rolled white. His breathing deepened and slowed. The doctor shook his head, then found Michael's troubled eyes. Sadness touched the doctor's face as he spoke. "I think Julian may be schizophrenic."

Michael glanced at Abigail, and the moment crystallized as she stared at a spot on the floor, her face so rigid a hard word might shatter it. "I need to talk to him," Michael said. The doctor looked a question at Abigail, and when she hesitated, Michael hardened his voice. "Alone."

The door opened, closed, and people left the room. Michael sat by the bed, and for Julian, it was as if a black cloud, after many years, had slipped from the face of the sun. His brother's hands were strong, and even though lines creased the skin at his eyes, Julian felt the same connection, like they were boys, still, and Michael had the strength to see him through another night of hell. Relief welled so strongly that Julian thought he might cry, and maybe he did, because he heard Michael say, "It's okay."

One of his hands touched the back of Julian's head.

Such worry in his eyes.

"Talk to me, brother. It's just us. You and me. Whatever has happened, I can fix it. I can make it right."

Julian was so happy, then. All the years he'd been alone. All the years he'd wondered about his brother; worried and missed him. Now, Michael was back, and there were so many things to say, so many words they built like a tide in his throat. Eyes bright, Julian nodded and opened his mouth.

"We don't need you."

No . . .

A steel door crashed in Julian's mind, and from far off, he heard the sound of laughter.

His voice.

No!

But Michael was already standing. Julian tried to call out, but could not. He stood on the shore of a falling island, and laughter burned in the blackness that took him down.

CHAPTER TWENTY

The lighter spun at the end of Jimmy's long fingers. It snapped open and closed, bright metal against the pink skin of his palm. Sun beat down as Elena tried to crawl away.

Jimmy said, "Uh-uh."

He put a foot on her neck and pressed her face into the mud. She tried to stop crying, but her hair reeked where it clung to her lips, gasoline on her tongue.

Jimmy lit a cigarette.

"Jimmy . . ." a man's voice broke in.

"What?"

"Stevan's coming."

Elena heard tires on raw dirt, the sound of an engine. Jimmy stood and flicked the cigarette far away before looking down the drive and sighing deeply. "Typical," he said, and slipped the lighter into his pocket.

Elena watched the hand come back empty, and her relief was so intense that when the car rolled to a stop she was as curled and still as a beaten child.

"What's going on, Jimmy?" A door closed. Feet rounded the car and Elena saw an attractive man in a snowy shirt and crisp suit. Dark hair framed a tanned, even face. He wore no tie, and no smile.

Jimmy raised his palms. "It's all good."

Stevan's gaze settled on Elena, and his curiosity descended into stone cold anger. "Is that who I think it is?"

"No reason to get upset."

Elena clenched her stomach, trying to hold still, but she knew she was begging with her eyes. "Please, don't let him burn me." The words croaked from her throat.

Jimmy nudged her with a shoe. "She pissed me off."

"What's she doing here?"

Jimmy shrugged. "She was running, so I followed her. I thought maybe she could tell us something."

Stevan glanced at her once more, grunted. "Well, get her inside. And clean her up, for God's sake. We're not animals."

Stevan disappeared inside, people stepping out of his way. "Do it," Jimmy said, and two men hoisted Elena. They carried her down the same hall, but when they reached the bedroom door, Jimmy said, "Uh-uh. Bathroom." They squeezed into the small bathroom at the end of the hall. It was not much larger than a closet. No window. A small bulb that protruded above the mirror. "Put her in the tub."

They eased her down, and Jimmy cut the tape from her wrists and ankles. She tasted blood, and realized she'd bit down on her tongue. Her hands burned as circulation returned.

"Get me some clothes," Jimmy said to one of the men.

"What clothes?"

"I don't care. Whatever."

The man came back with some rumpled men's clothing and stacked it on the sink. Jimmy turned the shower on, then squatted by the tub and watched her shake in the bottom of it. "I can cut you, burn you, kill you. I've got seven men here who would love to screw you senseless. The only reason they're not is because I don't allow that kind of behavior." He moved hair from her face. "Do we understand each other?"

Elena said nothing.

He stood and looked down. "I'll be right outside if you need anything. Scented soap. A fresh robe."

There was no humor in his voice. He closed the shower curtain, closed the door. Elena was alone and alive, cold in the shower as she spit blood, and watched red water circle the drain. She curled tight, breathing hard and trying to hold onto herself. It wasn't easy. This terrified person shaking in a cold shower was strange to her. She spit more blood, then tugged her robe open and put a palm on her stomach as she pictured the scars on Michael's body, his strong and capable hands. She saw him differently, saw him the same, and for the first time since running she prayed that he would find her, that he would kill Jimmy while she watched. It was a new feeling, this rage that spread out from beneath her palm. It was maternal, fierce, and in the cold wash of her helplessness, it offered the first real taste of hope.

Jimmy found Stevan outside the bathroom door. The hall behind was empty, and the house had a powerful, vacant feel.

"I asked the men to wait outside," Stevan said. "We need to have words, and I don't want them confused. They need to know where we stand, you and me."

"There's no confusion, Stevan. When the bitter end comes, I'll be standing behind you. The men know that."

"That's good, because . . ." His voice trailed away. "Why are you smiling at me like that?"

"Sorry."

"Well, stop it."

"Fine. Done."

Stevan gave a hard stare, then said, "Do you know what my father told me before he died? What warning he gave?"

Jimmy almost laughed. Stevan was using his *entitled* voice, which had come to mean very little since the old man died. Stevan was smart enough, but he was weak and the street knew it. Bookmakers were already taking odds on how long he would last and who would be the triggerman to take him out. The smart money was on "not long." The really smart money was on Jimmy. The only reason he was still breathing was because of certain considerations, sixty-seven million of them at last count. That was the rumored amount of the old man's cash holdings at his death. Not business interests or future cash flows, but cash. Hard dollars in a dozen offshore accounts.

Only Stevan had the account numbers, the passwords.

Otherwise, he'd already be dead.

Stevan lowered his voice and stepped closer. "My father said I should kill you in your sleep, and count myself lucky. He wanted me to do it before he died."

That got Jimmy's attention. "Really?"

"He thought you were crazy."

"Bullshit. We respected each other."

"He respected your skills; there's a difference."

"Fuck off, Stevan. Your father and I worked together for twenty-five years. Since before you had hair on your pecker."

"That doesn't change what he said. He told me you were inherently unbalanced, that the only thing keeping you on an even keel was fear of him and fear of Michael."

"I'm not afraid of Michael."

"He said you would deteriorate with him and Michael gone. He said you would go off the tracks, said you were a risk."

"Your father was in decline." Jimmy kept his sudden fury in careful check. "I understand."

"Look, Jimmy, I'm telling you this because I think he was wrong, because I want you to trust me and because I want us to be a team. You understand? I want this to be the beginning of something new, of you and me."

"Sure, Stevan. 'Course."

"Then what are you doing?"

"Is there a problem?" Jimmy asked.

"We're here to kill Michael right?"

"Yes."

"We lay low, and we kill him for what he did to my father."

"And for being an arrogant, self-righteous——"

"You took his girl, Jimmy. You don't think he'll notice?"

"You're the one who told him we were coming after his brother."

"That was bait. And hypothetical. Now he *knows*!"

Jimmy waved a hand. "That's irrelevant, and eventually to our advantage."

"You may feel good about going head-to-head with Michael, but I don't. He could blow through this house in thirty seconds."

"Your house. Not mine."

"Forty seconds, then. With you standing in the middle of it."

Jimmy's eyes narrowed. "I think it's you who's fearful."

"You take that back."

"No."

Seconds spooled out, and Stevan blinked first. "You can't beat him, Jimmy."

"Really?"

"Yes, really."

"Why don't you just let him walk away, then?" Jimmy could barely hide his disgust. "Just let him go."

"Because he killed my father in his own *damn* bed!"

Jimmy felt his eyes go flat. Stevan didn't want Michael dead because of how the old man died. He wanted Michael dead because of how the old man lived. Because he loved Michael more than he loved his own son. Because he respected Michael more. Because Stevan was a coward, and Michael was not.

Anything else was a lie.

"I have a plan," Stevan said. "Things are in motion. You don't have to worry about Michael until I tell you. You just have to sit and wait."

"I *want* to worry about Michael."

"Don't make this personal, Jimmy. It's not about who's best. It's about killing him and moving on."

"I don't like it."

"Well, it's arranged."

"Just like that?"

"I'll tell you when I need you."

CHAPTER TWENTY-ONE

"Tell me why the records are sealed." Michael struggled to keep his emotions level, but he still felt his brother's skin, hot under his palm and stretched across a curve of bone that felt so much like his own. For the first time since coming to North Carolina, Michael felt the flesh and blood of his brother's dismay. Not the theory of it or the possibility, but the blade of it, the full and unfettered hurt. For the first time in a decade, Michael was truly in danger of losing his cool.

"He didn't mean what he said." Abigail was distraught. They stood in an empty hall one floor down. "He needs you."

"Don't change the subject. You knew those drugs. You've heard the diagnosis before." She opened her mouth in denial, but Michael said, "Courts don't seal medical records without good reason."

"They do if a ranking senator calls in favors."

"That's what happened?"

"Favors. Threats. Whatever it took."

"To cover up what Julian did."

"To protect my son."

"We're talking about the boathouse, aren't we? How long ago was it? Fifteen years? Twenty?"

"What do you know about the boathouse?"

"I know it's been neglected to the point of decay. The parking area is overgrown, the road in disrepair. The deck is rotten, boats ignored. Everything else on the estate is immaculate, but the boathouse is left to rot. So, how long has it been? Fifteen years? Twenty?"

Abigail hesitated, then said, "Eighteen years next month."

"Who did he kill?"

Her head snapped up. "How do you see these things?"

"You said yourself that he was capable, that you expected a body to come out of that water. So, let's quit screwing around. Who did he kill?"

She shook her head. "I can't talk about it here."

"Then where?"

She was breaking. "Anywhere but here."

They ended up in the Land Rover, Michael driving. He followed estate roads at random.

"It happened five years after we brought him home. He was fourteen." Abigail's face was stone, her gaze locked straight ahead. "He's had very few friends in his life—your beautiful, damaged brother—but his very first was a young girl, Christina Carpenter. She was older than he was, seventeen when she died, but very small. A tiny young thing. Very pretty. Her mother ran the stables; her father worked in town. They lived in a small house a few miles down the road. They were good people, and their daughter took an interest in Julian. Nothing physical, of course. They were young and she was a good girl. They were friends." She blinked, and Michael knew she was looking into the past. "Normal teenage friends."

Michael nodded as if he could see it, but in reality he could not imagine having had a normal teenage friend. His childhood had been about violence and hunger and mistrust, the total absence of friends. At that age, he'd been on the street, and the only girl he'd ever met was one who offered to prostitute herself for a ten-dollar bill and half of the canned fruit she saw in the mouth of his open pack. When he said no, she forced a smile and a hollow laugh, then told him she was relieved. She told him she'd never been with a boy, but thought that's what all boys wanted.

A girl's mouth down there . . .

She said it slow and guilty.

I'll put my mouth down there for ten dollars and half that fruit . . .

Michael had said nothing at first. He was cautious because this was how it happened on the street: distract from the front and attack from the rear. But no one was paying any attention.

No one gave a flying shit.

She had a plastic water bottle and grimy skin, clothes that were crusty and smelled bad. She was a young girl at the end of a short, sorry rope; so, Michael let her talk. She was a runaway, she told him, from some town in Pennsylvania whose name meant nothing to him. She'd been in the city for over a week, but wasn't really sure how many days. She'd stepped off a midnight bus, started walking and still had no idea where in the city she was, no notion of Harlem or Queens or Manhattan.

It's all New York, isn't it?

Michael was dumbfounded by her ignorance. But she was alone and cold and hungry, so he gave her some fruit, and then a little more when she shivered and stole small glances at the can. He remembered how she ate it: small pink tongue darting out, pale juice on her chin and a clean spot where she'd rubbed it off. Afterward, she'd sniffed once and told Michael she was pretty without all the dirt, that if she could get cleaned up somewhere, then maybe she could get a job modeling clothes or shoes or hats. That's why she'd come to New York, because all the men back home said she was pretty as a picture.

One man said I was a flower.

Pretty as a pink, pink rose.

Michael never told her different, not even as she pulled grubby fingers through matted hair. He gave her the last of his fruit and said she could stay with him for a while if she wanted. But, she said no. She wanted a place to get clean so she could get on with being a model. "You have to start young," she explained, and Michael watched a blue fly buzz the sweet spot that fruit juice had made on her face. He doubted she was older than he, and doubted, too, her claim that she'd never been with a boy. Michael knew jaded when he saw it—just like he knew bitter and afraid—and imagined that whatever man told her she was a pink, pink rose had done so for his own reasons. But that was life, and this was the street; so, he said they could be friends, and pointed her toward midtown because he thought it would be safest, what with tourists and cops and all the wealth of the world. But she never got that far. She died four blocks away—knifed and left to bleed out in a cardboard box. It was the talk of the street for a day, and then it was

nothing at all. But Michael remembered her name: Jessica, who preferred "Jess," a pink rose in the gray, cold city.

For the first time in his life, Michael felt a twinge of honest jealousy. It would have been nice to have friends, or anything else *normal*.
It would have been nice to have a mother.

"How did he kill her?"

Michael drove out all thoughts of regret or what might have been.
He parked on a hilltop and watched black water, cops in dark suits.

A third boat was on the water.

He saw divers.

"They were on the lake," Abigail said. "They did that a lot: boating,
fishing, swimming. Sometimes, Julian would take a book and read to
her while they floated. He thought that's what you were supposed to
do with a pretty girl in a boat. But he didn't read poetry or a young
love's prose, he read science fiction novels, adventure books, comics.
He never really understood the point of reading to a pretty girl on
still water. I think he saw it in a movie, once, and thought it's what men
should do." Abigail paused. Downhill, water shone between green banks
that rose like knees softly spread. "No one saw it happen. They went out
on Saturday morning. That afternoon, Julian was found walking down
the side of the road, wet to the skin, blood on his hands."

"And the girl?"

"They found Christina's body the next day. Drowned in the lake.
She had contusions on her face, bruising around one wrist. The police
believed that Julian's damaged hands matched the damage done to her
face, but there was never any credible motive, no reason in the world
he would hurt that girl."

"I don't believe he would."

"Harm a girl?"

"Harm a friend."

"The police felt differently. From the first, they believed Julian
killed her. They thought he made a pass and she rejected him. They
say he most likely killed her in a blind rage."

"Did Julian deny it?"

"He was as lost as a newborn child, with no memory of what happened, no idea where he'd been or how he ended up on that roadside.

All I know is he wept at the sight of her body being pulled from the water. He cherished that girl."

She trailed off, and Michael said, "But?"

"But questions were posed, and the implications led to no other possibilities. The bruising and Julian's blackout, the skin under her nails; their history together. Julian was the last person to see her alive."

"Says who?"

"The police, for one."

"Was he charged?"

"Charged, but never tried."

"Favors and threats?"

"Let's just say an alternative disposition was made."

"What kind?"

"Twenty million dollars to the dead girl's family. Another five to establish a charity in the victim's name."

"You bought off her parents."

"We did what we had to do to protect Julian."

"And the senator."

"We did what we had to do. Period."

She was angry, defensive, and Michael didn't blame her. "What about the schizophrenia diagnosis?"

"That came before the charges were dismissed; part of the investigation. A police psychiatrist first, then a court-ordered evaluation. The judge agreed to seal the records."

"But Julian was treated?"

"Medication. Therapy. Eventually, he quit. He said the medicine made him weak. He didn't like people to think he was weak. A leftover from Iron Mountain, I always supposed; a tear in some deep place." For a moment, they were silent; then a cloud blotted the sun and Abigail said, "Look, I've been patient."

"So have I. There are still a lot of things unsaid."

"Please, Michael. I need to know."

"You want to talk about the warrant."

It was not a question. They watched a diver roll backward off a metal skiff. Sun flashed on his faceplate, then he was gone. "I need to hear the truth," she said.

"You trust me?"

"Yes."

Michael started the engine. "Let's get out of here." He turned the Land Rover and started down the sloping track. He waited until the cops disappeared from view, and then told Abigail Vane what she needed to hear. "They'll find a body in your lake."

"Oh, no."

Michael downshifted as the track steepened. Abigail may have been prepared, but Michael couldn't tell it from looking at her. She was pale and shaken.

"How do you know there's a body in my lake?"

"I put it there." She covered her mouth, and Michael said, "Can you handle this?"

"Yes. I'm sorry. Go ahead."

She held still as Michael told her what he'd found in the boathouse, and why he was there in the first place. He told her what Julian had said to him, then gave her the name of the dead man, and explained that he knew Ronnie Saints very well. It took a few minutes.

"Ronnie Saints?" She turned away. "Oh, God."

Michael watched her. She was in shock. "You know the name?"

"Give me a minute." She took several deep breaths, then nodded, eyes closed. "Julian knew him."

Michael nodded, too. "Knew him. Feared him. Hated him."

"Saints was one of the boys that harassed him." Her face was still turned toward the side window. It was not a question.

"Tortured him," Michael said. "Let's call it what it is."

Tortured . . .

The word fell from her lips, and Michael felt his hands tighten on the steering wheel. "After Hennessey, Ronnie Saints was the worst, big and strong and sadistic, a juvenile delinquent from the mountains of north Georgia. He broke Julian's index finger three times. Same one. Every time it healed. The one time Julian tried to defend himself, Ronnie Saints tore his ear so badly part of it had to be stitched back on."

"Were there no adults?"

"Too few and too uncaring. As long as no one died, we were left to ourselves. The place was tribal."

"But Julian could have told——"

"No one rats at Iron House."

Abigail finally turned his way. She drew herself up and said, "I'm glad he's dead."

Michael felt the same way. But there were problems Abigail had not yet considered. "They spent a year together on Iron Mountain, Julian and Ronnie Saints. The cops will figure that out, eventually. It will give them motive, and after the dead girl eighteen years ago, that's all they'll need to go after Julian with everything they have."

"But Christina died so long ago. Julian was just a boy."

"Nobody holds a grudge like a cop. They're already thinking about Julian. I guarantee it."

Abigail pinched the bridge of her nose. Gravel crunched beneath the tires. It was hot inside the vehicle. "Let's back this up. How do the police even know about the body? Who could have called them?"

"Whoever saw me sink it."

"Why aren't you in custody?"

"Maybe it was darker than it felt. Maybe there's some other reason."

Abigail drooped, still shaken. "Do you think Julian killed him?"

"If he did, he had a reason."

"And that makes a difference?"

"Reasons always make a difference."

She kept her eyes on his face. "Have you killed people, Michael? I mean other than the Hennessey boy?"

She said it scared, and Michael did not need to see her face to know what it took to force the words out. She had ideas about him, the kind of theories that make most people squeamish; he understood that. He'd let her see more than he would normally do, but they had this thing they shared, this bond that came close to blood. So, Michael had a choice to make. He could ignore the question or he could tell the same lies he'd told for most of his life. Today, he did something new. "I've killed people," he said.

"And were the reasons good?"

"Some good." He shrugged. "Some maybe not so great."

"But nothing you can't live with?"

"That's right."

She stared out the window, and her voice came faintly. "That must be nice."

They circled the south end of the lake and cut back through the woods toward the guest house. Even before Michael stopped the car, they saw that the door stood wide open.

Michael killed the engine before they got too close.

"Is your girlfriend back?"

Michael didn't answer right away. He studied the open door, the windows, then checked the woods around them, the tree line on both sides of the house. Elena was strong-willed and had good reason to be upset. No way would she be back yet, not after what she'd seen in the boathouse. "Her car's not here."

"But the door's open."

"That's not the kind of thing she would do."

"Wind, maybe?"

"I don't think so."

Michael studied the windows, saw something flicker inside. "Movement," he said.

Abigail looked back at the house, and when Michael shifted in the seat, she saw that he had a gun in his hand. She had no idea where it had come from. One instant his hand was empty; the next, the gun was simply there. She thought of his talk of reasons, then of bodies on the streets of New York. She thought of blood and death and Otto Kaitlin's forty-year reign of violence.

"Stay here," Michael said.

He exited the car, gun low against his leg as he crossed a patch of grass and dirt, then found the bottom step with his foot. Through the door, he saw shadows and light but no other sign of movement. A look back showed Abigail out of the car, one hand on the open door; then he heard movement deep in the house. He eased onto the porch and felt vibration through the floor.

Abigail appeared beside him.

Inside, something hammered on wood, a dull thump repeated twice.

"Right side. In the back." Michael risked a glance inside, and then spread five fingers, making sure Abigail knew to stay behind him. She nodded, and the hammer moved under Michael's thumb as he slipped inside and shadow swallowed him up. Two feet in, he heard a voice from the back bedroom.

"Damn it . . ."

Michael felt Abigail tense behind him, felt her hesitate. A hallway ran to the back of the house, two bedrooms at the end of it. Michael cleared the kitchen, then heard glass shatter, the sound loud in the small house. Whatever the source, it was a lot of glass. Halfway down the hall he realized what was happening, and rounded into the room in time to see a figure drop through the window and disappear.

Rushing forward, he tried to identify the intruder, but forest pushed close against the back of the house, and all he caught was a glimpse of skin and movement as a body pushed through leaves and disappeared.

Without a thought, Michael followed. He landed on the balls of his feet and took off at a run, stretching hard to clear a wooden stool that lay half-hidden in the moss and ferns. He guessed it had been thrown through the window by the person he was chasing, and that person was fast, cutting hard between trees, staying far ahead as the forest thickened around them. In the distance, he heard Abigail calling his name. He ignored her, pushed harder, ran faster; when a trail opened in the woods, he gained enough to see clearly for the first time.

It was a woman. Long legs under short cutoffs. A narrow waist and a gymnast's build. Small muscles flexed under skin burned brown, and she moved as if she could run forever. Michael pushed harder, closed; as if sensing the change, the woman dodged right, off the trail. For long seconds, Michael lost sight of her, but as smooth as she was, as agile in the woods, she couldn't run in silence. So, he followed the sound of her, and when the trees parted in a shallow clearing, he caught up with her, flicked out a foot and knocked one ankle into another so she came down in a tangle.

"Take it easy," he said.

But she scrambled up on all fours, ready to sprint. Michael put a hand on her back and kept her down as he engaged the safety on the gun and pushed into his belt. "I just want to talk to you." She fought, strong, and Michael said, "Come on, now."

"Get off me!"

She tried to push herself up. Michael pressed a forearm across her shoulder blades.

"I said, get off, motherfucker!" She pushed harder. "Damn it! Get the fuck off!"

"Relax, first. No one's going to hurt you."

He eased off the pressure enough to show he was serious, and beneath his arm, she went limp. Michael saw that she was barefoot, and that her skin was bug-bitten and dirty. She wore frayed shorts and a once-white tank top now stained gray. Her hair was dirty blond, full of twigs, and she was young enough for Michael to feel bad about the way he'd brought her down.

She was just a kid.

"Look, I'm sorry, okay. I didn't realize . . ." Michael ran a hand through his hair, frustrated. "Did I hurt you?"

"Are you finished?"

Her voice was as light and girlish as the rest of her.

"Yeah. You bet." Michael lifted his arm, but she stayed still and limp, a small, dirty girl brought down harder than she should have been. "Listen . . ."

Michael leaned forward, and she moved, rolling fast onto her back as one hand came up from beneath her right hip. Michael saw a whisk of silver; then she was scrambling away as pain flashed and a bright red line opened on his chest. He touched it once and his palm came away bloodied. When he looked at the girl, she was crouched five feet away, a straight razor in her hand. "Nobody touches me, 'less I say."

Michael started to rise, and then caught the look on her face, the wide, frightened eyes, and the cherry lips open over bright teeth. She weighed all of ninety pounds, a smooth-limbed girl with a pretty face and blue eyes so wild and bright they almost hurt; but that's not what took the fight out of Michael. It was deeper than that, and familiar. He settled back onto the dirt as she folded the razor and pushed it into the tight crevasse of her pocket.

"Next time," she said, "I cut your pretty-boy face."

Then she spit on the ground and ran, her blue eyes flashing once, her feet as bare and brown as summer dirt.

CHAPTER TWENTY-TWO

There's humiliation and humbleness, and then there's stupidity. Michael was feeling all three. "She was just a girl. Eighteen, maybe nineteen."

"Hold still." Michael sat on the hood of the Land Rover, his shirt a bloody mess on the dirt beneath him. Abigail stood between his knees, a first-aid kit open on the hood beside her. "This is going to hurt."

The cut was shallow but long, a ten-inch diagonal slice that ran from the sixth rib on his right side to a spot just above his heart. Abigail cleaned it with alcohol, then pressed gauze against it and told Michael to hold it there while she unpackaged a dozen butterfly bandages.

"What did she look like?"

"Beautiful but dirty." He closed his eyes to picture her. "Five-two, maybe, and all of ninety pounds. She had tangled hair, shoulder length and kind of blond. Small jaw. Large eyes."

"Blue?"

"Like some kind of stone." Michael lifted the gauze, frowned at the cut then put pressure back on. "She had a mouth like a sailor."

"Let me guess the rest." Abigail kept her eyes on the work she was doing. "Half-naked and wild as a cat in heat."

"You sound like you know her."

"Victorine Gautreaux. I know her mother."

"What's she doing here?" Abigail looked up, lips pursed, and Michael said, "Julian?"

She shrugged. "I'd call it a suspicion, but I'm pretty sure."

"Why was she in the guest house?"

"I think she ran away from home. Maybe she was looking for Julian. Hang on. Give me that."

He handed her more bandages. She pressed on the wound, then switched out gauze and applied more pressure.

"Did she run away for a reason?" Michael asked.

"I don't much care to speculate about the workings of that family, but I do know social services took her away a few times when she was younger—once when she was about seven, then a couple more times when she was twelve or thirteen."

"Why?"

"Various types of abuse and neglect. No medical history, basically illiterate. The kid barely went to school, and when she did she was fighting all the time, wild and unmanageable. She bit some students, and hurt a few pretty seriously. It went to court, but those idiots in county government never had the courage to take her away. Probably scared of her mother." Abigail lifted the gauze, studied the wound, then pushed harder. "Kid never had a chance."

"And you think she's with Julian?"

"You saw how she looks. I doubt Julian had a chance."

"She's pretty, yes. But how would they have met?"

"Walking in the woods. Hell, I don't know."

When the bleeding stopped, she held the lips of the wound together and worked from right to left, sealing it shut with butterfly bandages. Afterward, she put fresh gauze over the wound and taped it in place. "You can get it stitched if you want, but that'll hold it. It won't be a pretty scar, but looking at the rest of you, I don't think that's an issue." She gathered up the bloody shirt, the bandages. "Let's go inside."

Michael put on a fresh shirt, and they checked the house from front to back. Beyond the broken window, nothing looked disturbed. Michael tried one window frame and then the other. "Painted shut."

"That explains the broken glass." Abigail fingered raw wood where shards had been knocked out. "But not why she was here in the first place. Has to be a reason."

They found it on the second pass-through.

"Abigail." Michael called from the back bedroom. When she came in, she found him in the door of the closet. "Check it out." He pointed up, and she slipped in next to him. The closet was basically empty—just a rod and a few wire hangers—but a trapdoor was visible in the corner of the ceiling. Around it, white paint was smeared with fingerprints and grime.

"The house has an attic. I don't think there's anything up there." She looked around. "We need something to stand on."

"I know where to find a stool."

They retrieved the stool from the ferns outside, and put it down in the closet. "Those look like footprints to you?" Michael pointed at the stool, which was scuffed and muddy.

"Could be. Maybe."

"Well, let's take a look."

"After you."

Michael said, "I don't suppose you have a flashlight?"

"Sorry."

"Can't have it all, I guess." He mounted the stool, which wobbled but held his weight. The trapdoor opened, hinged at the back seam. "There's a ladder. Step back." Michael opened the trap all the way and pulled the ladder down as he descended from the stool. The ladder was hinged as well, and when it touched the floor, its angle was almost vertical. "That's better."

He climbed slowly, a vague, black emptiness above him. When his head broke the plane of the attic, he gave his eyes a few seconds to adjust. Enough light penetrated through ventilation cutouts in the eaves for Michael to get a sense of the space, which was low, but floored. The ceiling was sloped and close enough to touch, the air dry and hot.

"See anything?"

"I see a candle." It was just a few feet away, a thick shaft of wax melted onto a saucer. "Hang on." There were matches, too, and he lit one, flame surging, then burning low. He touched the flame to the candlewick and watched light ripple over the floor. He picked up the saucer, and held it high.

"What do you see?"

Michael lifted the candle higher. "You should probably come up here."

"What is it?"

"Hang on. I'll make room."

The pentagram was eight feet wide and looked to have been scratched on the floor with charcoal or the end of a burned stick. It was well drawn, but black and flaky, darker in some places than in others. Around it, another dozen candles were jammed into bottles or melted onto the floor. A giant circle enclosed the pentagram, and in the center of it all lay a pillow and a tangle of rough blankets.

Michael lit more candles, so that light wavered and spread. Outside the circle was a pair of flip-flops, a jug of water and another pair of cutoff jeans. He also saw a bowl, a toothbrush and small tube of lip balm. "Looks like she's been sleeping here." Michael toed the blankets. "Hard to say how long."

"But . . ." Abigail turned a slow circle. "What *is* all this?"

"Something weird. Pentagrams. I don't know."

"There're plenty of people around here who'd be willing to swear her mother's a witch."

"I'm sorry. You said a witch?"

"From a lengthy line of them. It's a long story." Abigail lifted a candle and made her way toward the far corner of the attic. She had to stoop, but it was not far. She peered into dark places where the rafters came down, then turned and looked the length of the room. "What the hell was she doing up here?"

"I have some idea." Michael nudged the blanket again. He bent and came up with a long, rolled strip of foil wrappers. He let the strip unfold from his fingers. "Condoms."

"Great."

He toed the blanket a final time, froze. "And this."

Abigail came closer, and Michael stood. A revolver rested heavily in his palm, blued steel that showed rust on the barrel and a shine on the trigger. "Colt .357." He cracked the cylinder and checked the loads. "One round fired."

Outside, they stood on the porch and gazed down to boats on far water. Michael spread his hands on the railing, and watched for a long time. Both of them shared the same, terrible thoughts. "Big lake," he finally said.

"We built it just after we married." Some memory softened her face. "It was my husband's idea, a great jewel in the middle of the estate. It was supposed to be a sign of change, and of permanence, a metaphor for our new life together."

Lines flew out. Another diver dropped.

"I wish he'd made it bigger," Michael said.

"They'll find it, won't they?"

"Is the lake deep?"

Abigail looked forlorn. "Not deep enough."

CHAPTER TWENTY-THREE

Victorine went to ground like an animal. She'd found the cave years ago. It was old, with stone worn smooth in the entrance, and the bones of small mammals scattered in its deepest parts. She guessed it had been a panther's den, back when panthers still moved in this part of the state; but that was a hundred years ago, at least. Maybe even more.

So, the bones were old.

The cave was old.

She'd found it as a girl, exploring barefoot when her mother took her shoes as punishment for some laxness or crime of omission. Mother was like that, when it came to Victorine—sharp-tongued and cruel enough to punish in meaningful ways. And she used to take it, too, until Julian told her how life could be better. Until he showed her.

She dropped to her belly and slid into the cave. Inside, the ceiling rose up to where a crack in the granite let light filter in. The crack gave ventilation for fires, but it let rain in, too, otherwise she'd sleep there. But sleeping there was no good. She'd done it once for a week—first time she'd run away—and the pneumonia almost killed her. Mother said it was God's punishment for sins delivered to the good woman who'd raised her, but Victorine figured it was the damp and cold and mushroom spores. And that was a lesson she learned, that some were warm at night, and some were cold.

Victorine planned on being warm, but not in her mother's house. Not ever again. For a second her mind turned on images of the man she'd cut. He had to be Julian's brother. His face was close enough to make no difference, but the rest of him was nothing like the same. He was going to follow her, even after she'd cut him. She'd seen it in his eyes, one fast tick of determination that simply faded away. She still had no idea why he didn't come. He was fast enough, strong enough, too, and the cut wasn't that deep. She puzzled on it, and then let it go.

In the back of the cave she drew out an old crate that held a ratty blanket and a few stubs of candle. She made a bed, then lit the candles. The light glinted on protective markings she'd carved long ago in the rock. Her mother proffered herself as a witch, and in nineteen years, Victorine had seen no reason to doubt her word on that. She was mean enough, and she sure had a power over men. So, maybe she was a witch and maybe she wasn't, but Victorine played it safe where her mother was concerned. There was too much history there, too much bad blood.

She stretched out in the cave, the blanket on a sandy spot that took her shape and held it as she looked down the road at what the next day might bring. At the moment, she was warm, but figured on being warmer. So, that's what she did, there among the dark and bones of the old cat's den. She thought of what she wanted, and of Julian Vane. She thought about how he said her life should be, then of the gifts that God had given her, a body straight from heaven and an artist's eye, a mind as sharp and bright as the middle tine on Satan's big, red fork.

She had a plan, but no money. Had a friend, but he was gone.

Where the hell are you, Julian?

CHAPTER TWENTY-FOUR

"The Gautreaux women have a way with men." Abigail was driving, nothing in sight but dirt track and deep woods as they pushed into the back of the estate. "Something in the way they move, in their looks, the way they smell. I can't explain it. You'd have to see it to understand." She shook her head. "It's not natural."

"It sounds personal, the way you talk about it."

Abigail wiped the back of her hand across her cheek. "Caravel Gautreaux had a thing with my husband. It was a long time ago, but it lasted a while. He'd say he was going hunting, but come back empty-handed. It was early in the marriage. A fling, he said. First of many, as it turned out."

She said it without shame, but Michael felt the hurt and understood. It was dangerous business, trusting a person. "Tell me about her."

Abigail gestured broadly: the trees, the forest. "The Gautreaux clan came over from France in the late 1830s, a mother with two grown sons and a daughter no more than thirteen. They originally settled on the shores of Lake Pontchartrain, but were run out of Louisiana eight years later, eventually finding their way to the Carolina coast, then up-river and inland to Chatham County. The daughter, by that time, was twenty-one and pregnant by one of her brothers, though nobody was ever sure which. They made their living as slave traders and thieves; sold liquor to Indians, guns to anybody that could afford them."

"Opportunists."

"They stole when they could, killed when it paid, and the women were known to be worse—not just the mother, but the daughter and the twin girls she bore to whichever brother got her pregnant. They were prostitutes, all of them, healers and spell-casters known to give a man syphilis one day, then charge three dollars the next to cure him. They grew more isolated and dangerous as the county filled up around them. During the Civil War, they took in deserters with the promise of warm food and a dry bed, only to cut their throats, then strip the bodies bare." Abigail favored Michael with a glance. "An old man in town still swears that, as a boy trespassing, he found a shed on their land with more than a hundred muskets stacked inside."

Michael did not have a vivid imagination, but driving on that tongue of black-earth road, he saw how it could have been: a starving man hidden and fed, then nightfall and a hushed approach, the sheen of sweat and firelight as one of the daughters rode his hips on an animal skin bed, her body dirt-smeared and bare, eyes wide as her mother lifted the man's chin from behind and put a blade in the cords of his throat.

"The story had a few different versions," Abigail said, "but I've never doubted its inherent truth. After a century and a half on the same ground, they're a family of snakes born of snakes, a foul brood grown hard on violence, pride and avarice." Abigail made an unpleasant face. "You found Victorine beautiful?"

"Exceptionally."

"Her mother was, too, once upon a time, pretty and earthy and raw. I'd think screwing her would be a lot like screwing a mountain lion. Some men favor that."

"You're too close to this," Michael said. "I should go alone."

"The girl is involved with Julian. I'm going."

"You're making this personal."

"The mother is evil. The girl will be evil, too."

Michael replayed the moment he'd been cut, the few short seconds after surprise and regret turned to feelings that were more complex. She'd been cruel and fast and ready to fight; but she'd been scared, too, and determined not to show it. He could have taken her down, blade or no blade, but in looking at her face, at the narrowed eyes and purpose, he'd seen so much of his own hard years. "That's not what I saw," he finally said.

"What, then?"

"I saw a survivor."

Abigail thought about what he said. "Survivor, killer, slut." She downshifted as the track dropped away and she worked the Land Rover into the stream at the bottom. "We should have burned these people out years ago."

Michael sensed the change when they crossed onto land owned by Caravel Gautreaux. Smooth earth broke where granite shoulders humped up through the soil. Hardwoods disappeared, and pine rose up. Needles made a blanket on the ground. The forest darkened.

"Don't let her touch you."

"Why not?"

"Just don't." Abigail never looked away from the road. Her foot came off the gas, and she said, "Here it is."

The vehicle rolled to a stop, trees stretching off to both sides, bare dirt and blue sky unfolding. Michael saw the old house, the sheds and animals with patchy coats. Then he saw the cop car. Parked in a shady patch across the bare dirt, it was dark and unmarked, but Michael had no doubt what it was. "Police," he said.

"You sure?"

Michael checked the grounds, and saw no one. "Must be inside."

"We should go." She was thinking of him, his history, yet even as she reached for the key the front door opened and a man backed onto the porch, Caravel Gautreaux following.

"I guess we talk to the cops," Michael said.

"You sure?" She was worried.

"Leaving now would look suspicious." He slipped from the Land Rover and took in the details of Caravel Gautreaux. She was taller than her daughter, but did have an earthy quality that was hard to define. She wore a sleeveless shirt, and had deep eyes under black hair salted white. Her shoulders were broad without being masculine, her hands strong-looking. She had magnetism, he thought, something in the slow droop of her eyelids, the earthiness and ready confidence.

"Abigail Vane!" Gautreaux spoke before the cop could, her smile knowing and slow. "You bring me another one of your boys?" She stepped off the porch, and everyone seemed to follow her lead, the four of them meeting in the middle of the yard. From five feet away, her skin seemed to smooth out, becoming more dirty looking than rough. Another step, and her hair, too, had more shine than Michael expected. She looked at Michael and said, "I heard about this one."

"From who?" Abigail asked. "Your daughter?" Gautreaux laughed and Abigail dismissed her. "Michael, this is Detective Jacobsen." She spoke coolly. "Detective Jacobsen and I have known each other for some while."

"Though it has been too long since we spoke." The detective was a few years north of sixty, ruddy and thin. Animosity underlay his words, as did an obvious and easy distrust. "How is Julian, by the way?"

"We've had dealings," Abigail explained to Michael. "From many years back."

The tension was palpable as Jacobsen cataloged Michael from top to bottom. "The similarity is remarkable." He addressed Abigail. "I wasn't aware you had another son."

"She doesn't," Michael said. "I'm Julian's brother, but not her son."

"He was adopted—"

"And I was not. Yes."

The cop nodded. "What are you doing here?" He looked at both of them. "I was under the impression that you and Ms. Gautreaux had a long-running dislike for one another."

"We want to talk to her daughter. It's a personal matter."

"Talk, talk, talk . . ." Gautreaux made it sound like a chicken squawking, and her laughter spiked as Abigail reddened.

"Have you found anything at the lake?" Michael asked.

"Not yet." Jacobsen's gaze hung on Michael's face. Cool and clinical. Dissecting. "Divers are in the water. We're canvassing the area. Beyond that, I can't really discuss it." He hesitated, kept his attention on Michael. "You really do favor your brother. Have you seen him lately?" He turned to Abigail. "Is he in town?"

"You're wasting your time," Abigail said. "Julian has never hurt anyone. He never would."

"And yet, your husband has six lawyers at the house as we speak. Julian is unavailable for questioning. It all feels very familiar."

"Any questions you have about my son can be addressed to our lawyers. We're here to talk to her." Abigail pointed at Gautreaux. "A personal matter. So, if you're finished . . ."

"Finished? No. We're just getting started."

"Started on what? A pointless search based on a dubious informant? Old stains in an empty boathouse? You're overreaching."

"Maybe. Maybe not."

It might have turned into a staring contest, but his radio chirped. "Nineteen. Control."

Jacobsen stepped into the shade. "Control, nineteen. Go ahead." He turned the radio down and moved away until his conversation faded to a bare hum. When he returned, his face was all business. "We'll continue this later."

He moved for the car and Michael asked, "What happened?"

Jacobsen ignored the question. He opened the door, closed it. The engine started and the car turned a tight circle, wheels chewing dirt, then straightening as the big engine gunned.

"Come on." Michael touched Abigail on the shoulder. "Let's go."

"Why?"

"Just get in the truck."

They turned for the Land Rover, but Caravel Gautreaux wasn't finished. "I want my baby girl."

"And I told you—"

"I know what you said, like I know you're a liar."

"You may know my husband, but you don't know the first thing about me."

Gautreaux's lip curled. "I know hard born when I see it." Abigail turned away, but Gautreaux stepped in front of her, head tilted. "I know marrying rich don't make you special."

"Get out of my way, Caravel."

Gautreaux reached out a hand, and laughed coldly when Abigail flinched. "We both know that truth, too." She moved and Abigail twitched again. "Look at you, all puckered up and white as white."

"Abigail?"

"I'm okay, Michael."

"Then let's go."

"Yeah, run on, now. And don't come back here without an invitation."

Michael got Abigail in the truck and closed the door. He looked once at Gautreaux, who jerked her head and said, "Keep walking, big man."

"You should be more careful around people you don't know."

"Trust me," Gautreaux said. "I know her plenty."

"Do you know me?"

He made a gun of his fingers, then pulled the trigger and drove them out. Beside him, Abigail looked as if she was in shock. After long minutes, she finally spoke. "I'm sorry." She sat low in the passenger seat, small color back in her face. "She scares me."

"Why?"

"You wouldn't understand."

They drove farther, the Land Rover bucking as Michael pushed it harder on the rough track.

"Why are you driving so fast?" Abigail asked.

"We need to hurry."

"Why?"

"They found the body."

"How do you know?"

"I just do."

Twenty minutes later they came out of the woods, and Abigail directed him to a place that looked down on the lake. He stopped at a spot where the low ridge dipped, then fell off sharply. They got out of the car, and no trees grew in the place where they stood. They could see everything: the lake, the cops, the cluster of boats on smooth water. They were gathered at the same place on the lake—four boats—while on the shore, every cop stood silent and still. Two divers were already in the water. As Michael watched, another went over the side.

"What are they doing?"

Abigail stepped close to the edge. One more step and she would tumble off. Michael watched activity on the lake. Cops were trying to lower a mesh basket over the side of the largest boat. The basket was the length of a tall man, and had ropes at each of the four corners.

They eased it into the water, a diver at each end. Abigail spoke when it became clear that Michael was not going to answer her.

"They use that to bring up the body?"

"In theory, yes." He watched until the basket sank, taking all three divers with it. "There's only one problem."

"What kind of problem?"

"That's not where I put Ronnie Saints."

CHAPTER TWENTY-FIVE

They waited for the basket to come up, Michael and Abigail. Bubbles rose from the lakebed and broke the surface, but the basket stayed down. "What do we think about this?" Abigail watched his face as if he could provide an answer that made sense.

"I sank Ronnie over there." He gestured with his chin. "Three hundred yards, at least."

"No current in the lake. No way the body could have moved."

"Unless somebody moved it."

Abigail shook her head. "That seems unlikely."

Michael agreed. "The sun was almost up when I put him in. If somebody moved him, they did it in daylight."

"So, where does that leave us?"

"Two choices, I guess. Either they've made a mistake." Both looked at the cops, the boats. "Or there's another body in that lake."

Abigail crossed her arms over her chest. She rolled her shoulders and looked ill. "I don't like this at all."

Michael looked at his watch, the angle of the sun. "We should go."

"Go?"

"If they pull up a body, they'll shut this place down. It will go from a search to a full-blown murder investigation. There'll be interviews, interrogations. They could declare the entire estate a crime scene. Jacobsen's a hard-ass with a reason to be upset. Nothing will get in or out of here without cop approval."

"But my husband—"

"They'll push harder because of who your husband is, and because of what happened last time. It'll be worse. Federal cops may get involved. Media. No way they can keep this quiet." On the lake, men began to pull on ropes. Water churned between the boats, and Michael took her arm. "We have to go."

"Where?"

"They're bringing something up. We don't have much time."

"I want to see." He pulled gently, but she pulled back, stubborn, and her arm came loose from his hand. "I need to see."

He gave her a minute. She rocked where she stood, the edge of the ridge just a few feet away. On the lake, men leaned over the boats' sides. Agitated movement. Loud voices that barely carried. A diver broke the surface, then a second. Between them, the basket hung just below the surface, a hint of silver the shape and size of a coffin.

"It's too far," Michael said. "You won't see detail."

"I can't stand this." The basket rose the last few inches. It was not empty. "Oh, God."

The cops were shouting now, trying to heave the basket out of the water.

"We need to go." Michael got her in the Land Rover and started the engine. The transmission ground as he shifted into first. "We need to be gone by the time they get that body to shore."

"Gone, where?"

"Asheville's five hours away."

"Asheville?"

"We need answers. Whose body is that? Why is it here and what does it have to do with Ronnie Saints? Why did he die? How? And who the hell put the body in your lake? That's a pile of questions, I know, but they must be connected to Ronnie, somehow. His house seems like a good place to start."

"How do you know Ronnie Saints lived in Asheville?"

"I found his driver's license."

"But what could you possibly learn there? He's dead. It's done."

Michael shook his head. "This just feels wrong."

"You mean Julian doing this?"

She gestured at the lake, and Michael tried to come up with a good answer. Julian could kill, he knew. He'd killed Hennessey when they were just boys, and the thought that he could kill Ronnie Saints was not a great stretch to make. He'd killed one Iron House boy, after all. Why not another? But none of this felt right. He and Julian *had* connected, and even though Julian had been in the throes of a mental break, even though he'd known about a body being in the boathouse, the idea still felt off. "I could see him killing Ronnie, maybe. Ronnie shows up, old emotions rise, they fight, it goes bad. I can see it like that. But this second body . . ."

"You don't think he could do that?"

"It's too much. Another body. Hiding it in the lake. Julian acts in the moment."

"May I ask why you sound so certain?"

Michael considered that, wondering how much he could say. That Julian had learned from birth that he should run before he fought? That he was fearful in his soul? That killing Hennessey had been an aberration? That none of this truly fit? "You've read Julian's books?" he asked.

"Of course."

"Bad things happen in his books."

She touched her throat. "Horrible things."

"His characters struggle; they suffer."

"Evil and violence and children." She looked bleak. "Even the pictures are terrifying."

"But the books are about more than that, aren't they? They're about damaged people finding a way to move beyond the things that damaged them. They're about light and hope and sacrifice, love and faith and the fight to do better. No matter how troubling or terrible the story, his characters find doors *through* the violence. They cope and move on." Michael struggled, then said, "You can see in his books the life that Julian chose."

"Helplessness and abuse?"

"No."

"Fragility?"

Her own fragility leaked through, and Michael understood. Julian would always suffer, and it would always be hard to watch. But that's not what Michael saw in his brother's lifework. "His books don't end happily, no. His characters go through hell and end up close to destroyed, but you see good in the people he makes. You see small strength and the power of choice, movement through fear and loathing and self-doubt." Michael shifted gears and the vehicle lurched. "His characters are conflicted and hurt, but that's the magic of what he does. That's the point."

"Magic?"

"Julian writes dark because the light he hopes to convey is so dim it only shows when everything around it is black. You've read it: dark characters and black deeds, pain and struggle and betrayal. But the light is always there. It's in his people, in his endings. His books are subtle, which is why so many school systems and parents want them burned or banned. They think the godlessness is about a lack of God, but that's not the truth of what he writes. God is in the little things, in a last, faint flicker of hope, a small kindness when the world is ash. Julian scrapes beauty from the dirt of ruined worlds and does it in a way that children understand. He shows them more than the surface, how beneath the ugliness and horror, we can choose the hard path and survive. I've always taken comfort in Julian's books, always believed that he found the same path for himself."

"He's unhappy and frightened."

"Maybe the path is longer for some. Maybe he's still walking it."

"And maybe he killed those men."

Michael's fingers tightened on the wheel. "I won't believe that until I know it for a fact, and even then I'll try to find some way to make it disappear."

"Make it disappear?"

Michael was unfazed. "I'll fix it."

"Like you did with Hennessey?"

"I beg your pardon?"

Michael looked right, and earnestness gave weight to her features. "I used to sit by Julian's bed when he first came home." Her smile was knowing and wan. "He still talks in his sleep."

"What exactly are you saying, Abigail?"

"You're the one talking about love and sacrifice and doors through violence. You tell *me* what I'm saying."

"You think Julian killed Hennessey?"

"It doesn't matter to me if he did, but yes. I think maybe so. Mostly, I'm glad you see his books that way. I do, too."

"Really?"

"I think your brother's a genius. He's also the most deep-feeling, thoughtful man I've ever known. Take a left here."

Michael came to a fork in the road, the house to the right, a Y-shaped divergence to the left. He didn't know what to say, but Abigail didn't seem to expect any response. "There are two smaller gates on either side of the perimeter." Her voice was still empty. "No guards. Just keypads."

"Which way to the closest one?"

"Left."

Michael turned right.

"What are you doing?" she asked.

"I want to take Julian with us."

"He won't talk to us," Abigail said.

"Maybe, maybe not. In the end, I don't care."

"Then, why?"

"I don't want him near the cops." Michael saw the house ahead, a slab of gray stone through thinning trees. "I don't want him confessing."

Abigail closed her eyes, and in her mind saw Julian broken in his room. She saw a body in a long wire basket. It was nearing the surface, black water going green, green water fading to clear. The sockets were empty and frayed. Fish had chewed flesh from the bone, and the lips were tattered over clean, white teeth. Something flickered in the open mouth.

"Jesus . . ." It came as a whisper.

"You okay?"

She rubbed her temples. "Headache."

Michael said nothing. He drove fast, and at the mansion Abigail told him to drive around back, where he saw a twelve-car garage. It was made of stone, long and low. Wooden doors gleamed. Abigail pointed to a bay near the end, and when he stopped they got out.

"Come with me."

She disappeared into a side entrance, and Michael followed. Inside, he saw hints of steel and glossy paint, keys on a long row of hooks. Abigail did not waste time. The car she chose was a thing of exceptional beauty. He didn't know much about Mercedes Benz, but guessed that this car was the most expensive one they made.

Abigail handed him the keys. "The Land Rover's terrible on the highway."

"What's the best way to get Julian out?"

"Julian's not going with you. Neither am I."

"You heard my reasons."

"We don't run from our problems in this family. I trust the senator. Whatever his faults, he always does what needs to be done."

"Julian could implicate himself."

"He needs to be in his home, with people he loves. He's not strong enough to go tearing around the state with you."

"If this is about trust—"

"I trust your intent," Abigail said. "I know nothing of your ability to care for Julian."

"So, come with me."

"I'm staying with my son."

Michael looked at his watch. Minutes were ticking past. "Give a cop a body, and he's like a dog with a scent, especially if it's a headline case, which this will be. These cops . . ." Michael paused to give his words weight. "The only thing they smell is Julian. Understand? They missed him last time. This time, they'll come with the weight of the world behind them. They'll eat him for lunch."

"Julian's under a doctor's care. The lawyers say that will buy us time."

"Lawyers can only do so much. We need to find out why Ronnie Saints was here. We need to know who the other body is. If Julian didn't kill these men, we need to know who did. And if he did do it, we need a plan to save him. We can't do any of that without information. We can be in Asheville in five hours. It's a start, Abigail. It's what we have."

"Just take the car and go."

"They'll break him. Do you understand? Julian's mind will not handle a custodial interrogation."

"I'm sorry, Michael. I have to stay with Julian, and my heart says he should stay home, where he feels safe. You'll have to go without me." Abigail pushed a button and the bay door began to rise. They saw pavement, then trees and a hint of sky. Michael saw the cops first.

"Ah, shit." He stepped to the door. Cars were on the lake road, lights flashing as they accelerated for the house. "We'll never get him out."

The police were a quarter mile away, and coming fast. Abigail's cell phone rang. "It's Jessup," she said, then answered, her face still and smooth, her gaze on the police cars. "Hello, Jessup." A pause while she listened. "Yes, I know. I see them coming now." Another pause. "No, I'm in the garage. Yes, Michael is with me. They found something in the lake."

She listened for a long minute, then covered the mouthpiece and whispered to Michael. "Jessup was on-scene when the body came to shore. He says its been in the water for a few weeks; a male, mostly skeletal. Weighted with cement blocks. No identification."

The first police car disappeared around the front of the house.

"They're at the front door," Abigail said, back on the phone. "I'm going in now." She listened for a moment, and then said, "No. I want to be there."

Michael heard Falls's voice this time, tin-like in the quiet of the garage. "That's not wise."

"But I need to be there. I need . . ."

"I don't want you involved with this. It's not smart. You know it. The senator's there, the lawyers. We need to keep emotion out of this, let the professionals handle it."

"But Julian . . ."

She stopped talking. Falls's voice faded to a low thrum, and Abigail seemed to shrink as she listened. Finally, she said, "Okay. Yes. I know you're right. Yes. May I—"

A light died in her face, and she lowered the phone. "He had to go."

"I'm sure he did."

"He's afraid I'll lose it. Emotionally."

"Would you?"

"Normally, no, but it's different with Julian. I get protective. I overreact. It won't help Julian to see that."

"Come with me, then."

Abigail looked momentarily lost, her gaze uncertain as it moved from Michael to the car, the house. "Do you really believe Julian didn't do it?"

"Ronnie died about the same time that Julian had his breakdown, so maybe he had something to do with it. But you say the other body is skeletal. That means weeks have passed, maybe more. How was Julian a week ago?"

"He was fine."

"Two weeks ago?"

"Same thing."

Michael shook his head. "He didn't do it. We need to know more."

"But, Asheville . . . ?"

"Elena's gone. I can't get to Julian. This is what I have: my brother, who needs me." Abigail looked at the house, and Michael said, "You can't help him here."

"Just there and back, right?"

He nodded.

"Okay," she said. "I'll go."

They got in the car, and the road out was silent and smooth. Abigail said little. *Turn here. Straight ahead.* At the perimeter wall, an arched gate opened in equal silence, and Michael pushed down on the gas, the heavy car sliding into light traffic. Michael worked his way west around the edge of town. Fields gave way to subdivisions. Shopping centers marred the roadside. Traffic thickened.

"You want the main highway north." Abigail spoke softly. "A few miles up. That'll take you to Interstate 40. The interstate goes all the way to the mountains."

"Thanks."

"It's how I brought Julian home."

She said it quiet and small, and when Michael looked at her, their eyes met as a very simple idea hung in the air between them. Iron House was not far from Asheville.

An hour, maybe.

A lifetime.

* * *

Fifty minutes later, Michael gunned it onto the interstate, the Mercedes at 110 before the speed even registered. He took his foot off the gas and settled down at nine over the limit. Put the car on cruise.

When he checked his phone, Abigail noticed. "She hasn't called?"

"No." He put the phone in his pocket.

"Did you two have a fight?"

"Something like that."

"She's a pretty girl."

"She's my life."

"Are you married?"

"Not yet." A mile of tarmac slid under the car. "She's pregnant."

Abigail turned her head, and Michael expected to hear something predictable and bland: *Congratulations.*

That's not what he heard.

"If a schizophrenic has a sibling, that sibling has a forty to sixty-five percent chance of being schizophrenic. Did you know that?"

"No."

"Forty to sixty-five. Better than half. It tends to run in the family. Siblings. Children."

She was talking about Elena's pregnancy. Michael tensed.

"Have you ever been diagnosed?"

"No."

"Have you ever felt—"

"I'm not schizophrenic."

She watched hills rise and fall, shook her head. "It's a terrible affliction."

"A violent one?"

"Different people suffer differently."

"How about Julian?"

"Memory loss. Hallucinations. Muddled thinking. It's why he still lives at home. Home is safe. Less chance of stress. Less chance of delusions."

"What kind of delusions?"

"Voices." Her jaw tightened. "The medicine helps."

212

"Does he ever talk about what it feels like?"

"Once, a long time ago. He said the voice hurts, but keeps him strong. He said it props him up, makes him big when he knows he's small. He was drunk that night, distraught. It sounded pitiful, and he knew it. I think he's always regretted telling me. Sometimes I catch him looking at me, and he always looks worried. He asked me once if I love him less."

Michael pictured Hennessey, dead on the bathroom floor. He saw the blade in his throat, squares of black tile etched in red. Julian's disconnect. "What about stereotypical schizophrenia?"

"What do you mean?"

"Like you see in the movies. Multiple personalities."

"That's rare, and overdramatized, a Hollywood inflation that helps no one. The disease is more complicated than that. It has infinite degrees. Julian is confused, but his problems don't rise to that level."

"You're certain of that?"

"I know this disease inside and out."

The senator called when they were an hour from Asheville. Abigail asked a few questions, then listened for a long time. When she hung up the phone, she said, "Media's at the gate. It'll go national soon."

Michael was not surprised. "What else?"

"Julian's okay for now. A superior court judge granted a temporary injunction protecting him from police interrogation until he hears evidence from medical experts. They've bought a day, maybe two. Cloverdale put him back on antipsychotics."

"Is that it?"

"They're still searching the lake."

Asheville nestles into the Blue Ridge Mountains in the western part of North Carolina, a jewel of a city surrounded by places with names like Bat Cave, Black Mountain and Old Fort. There was culture in Asheville, music and art and money; but there was poverty, too, great swaths of it in the deep mountains that stretched out in all directions. North Carolina, Georgia, Tennessee—it didn't matter.

Abigail explained it as they rolled across the city line. "Iron Mountain is forty miles further west, deep in the mountains, three thousand feet higher, close to Tennessee. It's not much more than an hour's drive, but may as well be in a different country."

"A poor part of the state?"

"State lines don't really mean much down here. Lost Creek, Tennessee. Snake Nation, Georgia. Blackstrap Pass. Hells Hollow. It's all mountains. It's all history."

"You've never been back, have you?"

"Iron Mountain?" Abigail shook her head. "No desire to, and no reason. Julian was safe and you were lost." The road dropped off and Asheville flattened out beneath them. "This part of the world has felt wrong to me ever since."

They found Ronnie Saints's house where the Asheville line rubbed against a broad valley at the base of steep mountains. The road was narrow, black and winding. Michael saw small houses with kids' toys on short grass. Pickup trucks sat in driveways, and American flags flew on short poles. Water flowed fast in the streams and hemlocks rose close to a hundred feet.

"This is somehow not what I expected," Abigail said.

"Ronnie Saints was a horror story figure from your son's worst nightmare. No reason to suspect he'd be human."

They turned onto a short street. The houses were yellow and brick and white with green shutters. Ronnie's house was the smallest on the street, old but decent, the paint just beginning to crack. A panel van was parked in the driveway, SAINTS ELECTRIC on the side in white letters.

"Looks like the right place." Michael drove slowly past. He checked the neighbors' houses, the side yards and parked cars. "That's his work truck. He must have a second car. That could mean he's married. No kids' toys, though. Maybe a roommate."

"This feels wrong."

"What do you mean?"

"I don't know." She was agitated, hands closed tight. The truck sat like a barrier in the drive. The house was dark and still. "Deep down, something says this is dangerous." She shook her head. "I can't place it. It's like a vibration."

Michael turned around where the street ended, drove back and parked at the curb. The Mercedes stood out on the narrow street. So far, nobody seemed to care. "Let's do this."

He opened his door, and Abigail said, "Michael . . ."

She looked frightened, pale, and Michael felt a stab of sympathy. "You should probably stay in the car. If the cops in Chatham County find Ronnie and ID the body, they'll have Asheville PD out here first thing. You're recognizable. It would be best if no one here sees you. Could be hard to explain back home, senator's wife rings dead man's doorbell. You see what I'm saying?"

"Are you sure?"

"Just sit tight."

Michael closed the door and she locked it. He looked back once, then the house was coming up, a white bungalow with a wide drive-way, a covered porch and a single car garage. The gutters were clear of debris. A tall tree grew in a patch of grass near the sidewalk. Michael studied the windows. The truck's hood was cold when he touched it. Stepping onto the porch, he looked back once, then rang the doorbell.

Nothing.

He rang it again.

A third time.

Michael stepped left and cupped his hands at the window. No crack in the curtains. He listened for a long minute, then he tried the door.

Locked.

Solid oak.

He found the key under a planter.

Abigail saw him check under the mat and on the lintel above the door. She saw him find the key, watched him open the door and slip inside. Her heart hammered for reasons of its own, her breath so short she wondered if she were having a panic attack, if everything had simply become too much. Bodies. Secrets. A broken son.

What the hell?

Sweat rolled beneath her shirt.

Jesus . . .

She could barely breathe.

Michael felt the lock give. Metal slid over metal and he was inside. He listened for movement, and heard nothing but the rush of air through vents. The room was neat and orderly, with hardwood floors that needed stain, a brick fireplace and furniture that didn't quite match. On the right, an arched opening led through to a dining room with burgundy walls and better furniture on a cream-colored rug. Ahead, another opening led to a small study. He smelled chicken and cigarette smoke that had not yet had time to fade. His hand found the forty-five at the small of his back. He moved farther into the room, saw a table that could seat four, and shelves with cheap crystal and ceramic ducks. He paused in an archway, and the woman spoke even as he rounded into the room, gun up and tracking right.

"I already called the cops."

She had both legs pulled up on the broken-down sofa, an eight-inch butcher knife in her fist. She was small-boned and pale, with pretty features and thick, wavy hair. Twenty years old, maybe, with eyes that were deep and afraid. The knife shook. A cardboard shoebox was clenched under her left armpit.

"Anyone else in here?" Michael kept the gun up.

"Cops are coming," she said, but that was a lie. The weight of her arm had squeezed the shoebox out of shape so the lid gapped. Michael saw bands of cash in the box. Lots of it. She was nowhere near the phone.

"You planning to stick somebody with that knife?"

"Not if I don't have to."

She wore pink, terry cloth shorts, a white T-shirt with the sleeves cut off. Michael leaned back, checked the kitchen. There'd be a bedroom somewhere, maybe two. "I'm not planning to hurt anyone, okay? But if I get surprised, it could happen. So, tell me. Do you have children? Anyone that might decide to walk in unannounced?"

"No children. No surprises."

"You sure of that?" He kept his voice low, and let her see him drop the hammer on the gun.

216

"Yes, sir."

"Okay. I trust you. You trust me. That'll make this go much smoother." He tucked the gun under his belt. She watched it all the way down; the knife in her hand didn't move. "Are you Ronnie's wife?"

"You know Ronnie?" She lifted the knife higher, but Michael could tell it was getting heavy.

"Are you his girlfriend?"

Her arm bent at the elbow. "Fiancée," she said.

"I'm not here for your money."

She looked down, surprised to see that the money was visible. She fumbled the box into her lap, jammed the lid closed. "Do you work for Flint?" She sniffed wetly.

"Andrew Flint who ran the orphanage at Iron Mountain?" She nodded, and Michael tried to get his head around that. He'd not heard Flint's name in over twenty years, and to come across it in Ronnie Saints's house was surreal. Michael had never imagined anyone from Iron House keeping in touch. It was not that kind of place. "Why do you ask about Andrew Flint?"

"Ronnie said if Flint showed up, I should run. That was four days ago. When I saw your fancy car, I figured you were with Flint."

"Do you know where Ronnie is?" Michael asked.

"Not run off on me, is all I know for sure. Not with this still here." She shook the box.

"May I see that?"

Michael nodded at the box of money, and her arm tightened on it. "He'll kill me."

"I won't take it if you tell me what I need to know." Her eyes flicked to the gun. "I promise."

She blinked away sudden tears, and the fight went out of her, knife coming all the way down. "I told him this was too good to be true." She put the knife on a coffee table, then put the box next to it. She picked up a pack of cigarettes, sparked one with a cheap lighter. Michael put the knife on top of the television and moved a chair from the far corner.

"What's your name?"

She blew smoke, rolled her eyes up and left. "Crystal."

Michael lifted the lid from the box. The bills inside were crisp, still in bands of ten thousand each. He began to lift them out, lining them up on the table.

Fifteen bands.

"That's a lot of money," he said.

"He's going to kill me." She stared at the cash, both arms crossed beneath small breasts. Michael saw a pattern of scars on one arm, a dozen perfect circles puckered white. She saw him looking and covered the scars with one hand. Michael caught her eyes and she looked down. He knew cigarette burns when he saw them.

"How long have you been with Ronnie?"

"Since I was in high school." She flicked ash in a white saucer. "He had a job and told me I was special. He was good like that. A man, you know."

Michael riffled the bills. They were nonsequential and, as far as he could tell, real. At the bottom of the box was a scrap of paper. He picked it up. "Ronnie's handwriting?"

"He writes pretty for a man."

The paper held five names written one below the other. "Where's the money from?" Michael asked.

She looked away.

"Crystal . . ."

"It was delivered last week." Her lips left lipstick on the filter. "All official and sealed up, brought first thing in the morning by a fancy man in a shiny car, all yes-ma'am's and no-sir's. Ronnie had to sign for it and everything."

"What's it for?"

"Ronnie says it's not my place to know. Just 'cause we're getting married . . ." Her voice broke. She stubbed out her cigarette, and covered her eyes. "Please don't take it. I just want a baby and a paid-for house. Please, mister. Ronnie'll do terrible things if he comes home and finds that money gone."

"I'm a killer, not a thief." He gave her a second to process that. He wanted her scared enough to tell him what he wanted to know. Wanted her honest with him. "You understand me, Crystal?" He waited until she looked up and met his gaze. "You understand what I'm saying?"

She stared, white-faced and still. Something in his eyes convinced her, because when she nodded the rest of her body was as frozen as a deer in headlights. "Yes, sir."

"Then, I'll ask you again. What's the money for?"

"All I know is he said there'd be more, another delivery, just like that one. Soon as he got back. That's it and that's all."

"What about Andrew Flint?"

"I just know the name, and what Ronnie said. That I should run if the man ever showed up. I should take the money and go to a place we know. I should wait for Ronnie there."

"Do you know where Ronnie went?"

"Back east somewhere. More than that, he wouldn't say."

Michael considered the bands of cash, the scrap of paper in his hand. He held it up for her to see. "Do these names mean anything to you?"

"No, sir."

Michael began stacking the money back inside the box. He smelled ink and paper and Crystal's fear. He put the top on the box, and saw that she had her hands out.

"Mister?"

He put one hand on the box, looked at the names.

Billy Walker
Chase Johnson
George Nichols

They were names from the past, Hennessey's crew from Iron House. Michael saw them like twenty-three years ago was yesterday. Big kids, and mean.

Predators.

Dogs.

Michael looked down at the names written in a dead man's hand, and in looking he felt it all come tearing back, a current so dark and strong it hurt.

"Mister?" She must have seen the change in him, because her voice came smaller. "Mister . . ."

He looked again at Ronnie Saints's list of names. The three boys were listed first, one above the other, and then a line beneath. Under the line were two other names.

"Who is Salina Slaughter?" He watched carefully, but saw no artifice as Crystal shook her head.

"I don't know."

He held up the paper so she could see it. "Ronnie didn't say?"

"No, sir. I saw the list, same as you, but he was in no mind to talk about it. Ronnie's particular like that. I'm not allowed to question."

"But you see things." Michael pushed. "You pay attention."

"Yes, sir."

"What else did you notice?" Michael drew the box of money a little closer.

"Nothing."

"Phone calls?" Her eyes stayed on the box. "People?"

"No."

"Did he speak to any of the men on this list? George Nichols? Billy Walker? Chase Johnson?"

"Chase Johnson. They're friends, still."

"Where does Chase Johnson live?"

"Charlotte, I think."

"What does he do in Charlotte?"

"I'm not sure. I've only met him once."

"Has Ronnie called you since he left?"

She shook her head. "He says cell phones give you brain cancer."

"Who is Salina Slaughter?" Michael lifted the box, put it in his lap. "Tell me that and you can keep the money."

Tears welled up in her eyes, a kind of wild panic at the thought of losing the money. "I just want a baby and a paid-for house."

"Salina . . ."

"I ain't done nothing wrong . . ."

". . . Slaughter."

"She called here once, that's all I know. Right before he left. That's it and that's all."

Michael stood, box of money in his left hand. He believed her. "Do you know where I can find Andrew Flint?" She rolled into herself, nose red and wet, head shaking. Michael looked down for a moment, then placed the box of money on the coffee table. "Buy a house," he said. "Have a baby if you want. But I wouldn't count on Ronnie Saints."

"What do you mean?"

He thought of Ronnie Saints, dead in the lake. His gaze lingered on the circle of puckered white scars. "You can do better."

CHAPTER TWENTY-SIX

There is an awareness born of fear: Elena knew this, now. She saw every mark on the walls, felt the softness of worn denim, the stiff collar of a shirt that hung to her knees. She smelled her skin, and the staleness of the house. Her heart was more than a distant thump.

At the door, she heard voices and a television. Drawing back, she considered the room for the fifteenth time. She wanted a way out. A weapon. She checked the closet, but it was still empty. No hangers or clothing. Even the rod had been removed. In the room itself, there was only the bed and the chair. She checked the bed frame. It was heavy iron.

Maybe one of the legs . . .

She spent ten minutes trying to turn a single bolt with her fingertips, then went back to her corner and sat. She felt heat on her skin when the sun dipped low. The waiting was killing her. The uncertainty.

Damn it . . .

Angry now, she got to her feet and crept back to the door. The television sounds were clearer: a news channel, something about New York and bloodshed and violence. Someone said, "Fuck this." And then glass broke. Arguments. Shouts. Several men raised their voices, then a gunshot so loud that silence, when it came, was total and complete. Emotions were hot in the small, airless house. She felt it like electricity in the air. After a minute, a key scraped in the lock. The door opened and there was Jimmy. "Feeling better?"

He wore different clothes that smelled of gunpowder; carried her purse and a handgun. Behind him, men stood in disarray. Some looked angry, others frightened. In their midst, the television sat dead and still, a perfect hole in the center of its screen. Jimmy stood as if none of that mattered.

"This is bullshit, Jimmy."

The words came from a man down the hall. Big, thick-boned. Angry. Jimmy's arm came up, and although his eyes were still on Elena, the gun sights settled squarely on the man who had spoken.

"Will you hold this?" Jimmy handed her the pocketbook, then walked back down the hall, men parting. "I'm sorry. Did you say something?"

The barrel settled an inch from the man's face. His heavy arms lifted a few inches from his waist. "I didn't say anything, Jimmy."

"Are you quite certain?"

The big man nodded. Jimmy lowered the gun, and turned his back in a show of obvious contempt. In a casual manner, he put one foot against the television and rocked it onto its side, the screen shattering completely as it struck the floor. Then he gathered up a handful of newspapers and stopped in the center of the room. "I don't want to hear any more complaining." He glared around the room. "We leave when I say."

No one met his gaze. Feet shuffled, and someone said, "Sure, Jimmy."

A few others nodded.

Most did not.

He walked back to Elena's room, took the purse and closed the door. "I would like to leave, now," she said.

"I know you would. I'm sorry. Tomorrow, perhaps."

He tossed newspapers on the bed, and Elena saw a flash of headlines. Street warfare. Explosions. Gangsters. She saw photos of dead bodies, cops in assault gear. Jimmy saw her looking and said, "People are fighting over the old man's scraps. A vacuum rushing to be filled." He paused, eyes flat as he hooked a thumb toward the living room. "They think we should be in the city instead of here."

"You don't think so?"

"The scraps are meaningless. Most of Otto Kaitlin's wealth is legitimate, now, and has been for years. Advertising. Modeling agencies. Car dealerships. He actually owned two beauty pageants when he died. Priceless. Can you believe it? Beauty pageants. Otto Kaitlin."

"Why don't you just tell them that?"

"Because they're children."

He sat on the bed, opened her purse and began removing the contents. He placed each item on the bed, a long line of things side by side. A hairbrush and makeup. Passport. Wallet. Keys. Gum. A few loose receipts. "You can tell so much about a woman by what she carries in her purse. Although, in your case, it's more about what you don't carry." He rummaged more deeply in the purse. "No cigarettes or pill bottles. No booze. No mace. No contraception. No address book. No photographs." He straightened the items, touching each. "Such a minimalist."

He removed her cell phone. "But this . . ." He flipped it open, scrolled through the phone log. "Not many calls the past week. A few women, looks like. Michael, mostly. The restaurant." He pursed his lips in what Elena knew immediately to be false surprise. "You have texts from Michael." He flashed the phone in her direction. "Want to see?"

Elena did not rise to the bait.

Jimmy shrugged, then scrolled through the texts. "Call me. Where are you? I'm sorry. Blah blah. Very domestic."

"What do you want?"

"You have four new messages from Michael. I'd like to hear them." He waited. "To do that, I need the password."

"Why do you care?"

"I just do."

He smiled, but she saw the same insanity from before. Whatever his obsession with Michael, whether fear or pride or something deeper, it was complete. She gave him the password, and his mouth opened as he dialed voice mail. "Ah." He held up a hand, and whispered, "There you are . . ."

His voice fell off.

His eyes drifted shut as he listened.

CHAPTER TWENTY-SEVEN

When Michael got back to the car, Abigail looked shaken. "I've been online." She held up her BlackBerry. "Every major outlet has the story."

"Anything solid?"

"Police presence at the estate. A body found. Some of the bigger outlets are running bits about Christina's death eighteen years ago. One has a chopper over the estate. You can see boats on the lake, police cars at the boathouse."

"Has anyone mentioned Julian?"

"Only that he was a suspect last time. But they're showing his picture. They're leaving the implication out there."

"Your friend Jacobsen made that happen. They're trying to force him out, shame him into facing their questions. Typical cops."

"They'll drag him through the mud, won't they?"

"Drag him. Trample him. Cops are all about pressure points." Michael glanced at Ronnie's house, then started the engine. It was a few minutes after five. The sun would be down in three hours. "Let's get out of here."

They rolled off Ronnie Saints's street; neither of them looked back. Abigail sank into her seat and asked, "What did you find out?"

Michael said nothing. He was thinking.

"Michael?"

He turned right, and the road opened up. Another turn and they were out of residential, two lanes gone to four, light industrial dotting the roadside. He was thinking of Julian and Abigail Vane, of the things he'd learned, and of the names on that piece of paper. He didn't know exactly where he was, not on a map, but the sun was setting and he planned to follow it down.

"Iron Mountain is west?"

She nodded, looked at him oddly. "What happened in there, Michael?"

Michael gave her a look that he knew was equally strange. They'd been allies, but things felt different, and Michael had to get his head around that fact. He had to interpret, and decide. So, he kept silent as the car slid from the shadow of a wooded peak into a burst of flat, yellow sun. He put his eyes back on the road as Abigail glanced at the navigational system and cleared her throat.

"We'll go right a few miles up, then straight for ten miles. After that, it gets complicated."

"How?"

"Back roads and deep woods. No major roads go from here to Iron Mountain."

"How long?"

"Forty miles, but it gets bendy. Maybe an hour and a half."

"Okay."

"Are we going to Iron Mountain, Michael? And if we are . . ." She struggled with the very concept. "Can you please tell me, why?"

He considered how much to say, and the order in which to say it. It was no small thing, this collision of past and present, so he spoke with caution. He told her of Ronnie's girlfriend, and of Andrew Flint. He told her about the box of cash, and then about Billy Walker, Chase Johnson and George Nichols. "Hennessey, Ronnie Saints and those three. They're the ones that ruined Julian's life."

"I remember Andrew Flint," she said. "A nervous man to have such responsibility. He seemed in over his head but eager to do better things."

"And the others? Walker? Johnson? Nichols?"

"I know who they are."

Her voice was brittle, unforgiving, and Michael knew she'd heard stories of the things those boys had done. There was too much anger in her voice, too much bitter feeling. Julian had told. He'd painted pictures with his words, and with the ink of his eyes. He'd opened up and let her see the pain, because Julian, Michael knew, was the kind of boy who had to share. His strength was in the goodwill of others, in strong, knowing hands and souls that had not broken so young.

"What are you not telling me?" she asked.

Michael drove as Asheville fell away and the road twisted higher into the mountains.

"Michael?"

"Does the name Salina Slaughter mean anything to you?"

"Salina?" She hesitated, then said, "No."

"Are you certain?"

"It's familiar sounding, but like a name I heard on the radio. I can't place it."

The road bent right then left; lumber trucks hammered past in the opposite direction. He looked for reasons to doubt, for lies or twisted truth, but her posture was relaxed, her eyes clear and unflinching.

"Michael . . ."

"I'm thinking."

The highway twisted, rose.

"About what?"

"Nothing," he said, but that was false.

There were five names on the list.

Abigail Vane's was number five.

P owerful, isn't it?" Abigail looked sideways. "Coming back."
They were at the crest of the last high pass, the valley spread out below and Iron Mountain rising up on the opposite side, a great slab of stone touched with light so soft it did not seem real.

Michael nodded, wordless.

"That's the town of Iron Mountain." Abigail dragged herself taller, pushing her hips back in the seat and clearing her throat as Michael worked the car down the mountain. Last sun was on the valley floor, a long spill of gold that made the river shine. "It's not as pretty as it looks."

"Where's the orphanage?"

"Through the town and four miles out the other side. The mountain hangs over it."

"I remember the mountain," Michael said, then drove them out

227

onto the valley floor. They crossed small streams that would eventually feed the river, passed barbwire fences and bottomland pasture. Michael strained for a sense of connection, but only the mountain made sense. It piled up as they drew close: low, blanketed slopes and then the massive thrust of granite. The valley itself was three thousand feet above sea level; the mountain soared up another two, its face splintered, its crown brushed dark green.

"Are you all right?" Abigail asked.

"I'm fine."

She touched his arm. "Past is past."

"I may have heard something about that."

"And yet we can all use reminding."

She squeezed his arm, then let it go. They passed small houses on low lots, everything poor and dirty. "Not much here," Michael observed.

"The town was built on mining and lumber, but the coal played out." She tilted her head. "Most of that is national forest and can't be logged. The private holdings were timbered out years ago. Sawmills folded when that happened. Trucking firms. A paper company. All gone."

"How do you know all that?"

"I made it my business to know. I wanted you boys, and came prepared. Money. Knowledge." She pointed. "Left here, I think." Michael turned onto Main Street, and her voice dropped to a whisper. "None of this has changed. Twenty-three years and I still remember."

And she did: package stores and open bars, bent people in red, cracked skin. They passed an open diner, a gas station. A few of the storefronts were boarded up. People watched them pass, and the watching made her uncomfortable. "Did you know that Iron House was an asylum before it was an orphanage?"

"What?"

She hugged herself. "For the criminally insane."

Nine minutes later, Michael parked the big Mercedes in front of tall, iron gates. The columns were familiar, a memory of straight, hard fingers rising up through fallen snow. He'd touched one as he ran, knife in his hand, neck craning back.

The gates were new.

So was the chain-link fence.

Michael climbed from the car, Abigail following. The fence was eight feet high and ran off in both directions. Chain hung from the gates, a large, brass lock clanging as Michael shook the gates. Through the bars, Iron House humped up against the foothills, massive and dark.

"Frightful, isn't it?"

He looked down on Abigail, then back at the gothic sprawl of the place he'd once called home. The building jutted up, its brick black with age, its stonework eternal and unchanged. Sunset put yellow stain on the high, slate roof, but below the soffits and the high third floor everything else looked gray and abandoned. The ruined wing stretched across the same ground, but its back was broken now, walls crumbled, small trees pushing through the rubble. The rest of the building didn't look much better. Shattered windows gaped, shards of glass jammed like teeth in the rotted frames. Ivy climbed the broad, front steps, and weeds stood chest-high in the yard. The place radiated a sense of neglect and institutional decay. It looked forgotten and obscene.

"When did it close?"

Abigail shook her head. "I'm not exactly sure. Some years after I brought Julian home."

He stared at the nightmare building, the smaller ones that hunkered down in its shadow. High grass bent in a hiss of wind. The river ran black as oil. "You say this was an asylum?"

"That's why it was built so far from anything important. Why it was built so big and so strong."

Michael struggled with the idea, but looking at the two high turrets and the broad sweep of stairs he remembered some of the things he'd discovered as a child, roaming the subbasement. Small, low rooms with iron rings bolted to the walls. Chairs with rotted leather straps. Strange machines rusted solid.

"It was built right after the Civil War," Abigail said. "Many of the

229

patients were soldiers suffering from posttraumatic stress. Of course, back then the affliction had no name. People wanted to do right by the soldiers, but they wanted to forget, too. The war was hard on this state. A lot of suffering. A lot of pain. The Iron Mountain Asylum was built to hold five hundred patients, but quickly overflowed to four times that many. Then, six. Damaged soldiers. The deranged. Some truly god-awful criminals feeding off the ravages of war. There're books on this place if you care to read them. Stories. Pictures . . ." She shook her head. "Awful things."

"How do you know all this?"

"I read up after Julian came home. I was trying to find some kind of insight. You know how it is when you're grasping."

She closed fingers on empty air, and Michael felt anger boil up. Kids in an asylum . . .

"What else?" he asked.

"There was never much oversight, never enough money; it got really bad near the turn of the century. Patients were naked and filthy, the medical practices barbaric. Bleedings. Ice baths. Muzzles. Overcrowd-ing was terrible, illness systemic. There were deaths." She took a breath, discouraged. "Eventually, there was enough public backlash to get the politicians involved. They closed the asylum after its conditions were deemed inhumane."

"So, they made it into an orphanage."

"A few years later, yes."

"Perfect." Michael eyed the gunmetal sky, the road that ran empty in both directions. "That's just perfect."

"What do we do now?"

Abigail hugged herself, and Michael jerked hard on the gate. Beyond it, the drive ran off, cracked pavement and weeds pushing through. He put his forehead against two of the warm, iron bars. He wanted a plan, a course of action, but in that moment he was more in the past than not. He saw boys in the yard, heard voices like far, faint cries.

"It's not always pretty, is it?" Abigail put her hands on the bars. "Coming back to the place you're from."

Michael shook his head. "I thought we'd find answers here."

"What kind of answers?"

"Andrew Flint, maybe. Something to tie all this together. A direction." He looked at the wreckage beyond the fence. "Somehow, this is not what I expected."

As if sensing his distress, Abigail said, "It's okay, Michael."

But it was not. Michael thought of asylums and prison and the cage of his brother's mind. "If they arrest Julian," he said, "the things that keep him sane will crack. Walls. Pillars. Whatever props him up will fail. He'll go to prison or to another asylum. He won't survive it."

"But the lawyers . . ."

"The lawyers can't save him, Abigail." Michael struck one of the heavy bars with the flat of his hand. "You think Julian's mind will make it to trial? You think he'll survive a year in lockup while the lawyers collect their fees and drag the case out? While Julian's abused in one of the few institutional settings worse than that?" He jabbed a finger at the ruins of Iron House. "I know people who've pulled time— hard men and violent—and even they've come out a shadow. For Julian, it would be like throwing a rape victim in with a pack of sex offenders. Scars are so deep, they wouldn't have to touch him to break him. No. Even if he's acquitted, he won't come back the same. We need to either prove he didn't do it or give the cops another suspect. We need to *understand* so that we can take steps."

"Surely it's not that bad."

"Have you ever seen the inside of a prison?"

Michael put both hands on the bars as rage built and a weight settled on his chest.

Julian, schizophrenic.

Children in an asylum.

He thought of his years on the street—the hunger and cold and fear—then of the man he'd become. He saw bodies and blood on his hands, the ghost of a life bereft as Elena ran in disgust from the truth of what he was. He felt the way she saw him now, and knew things could never go back to the simple way they'd been. She would never look at him the same.

He'd given up two lives, and done it all to keep Julian safe.

"I won't let him go down for this," Michael said. "I can't."

"I understand."

"Do you?"

His eyes searched hers, and he recognized the connection, the shared commitment to doing what must be done. But her cell phone rang before she could answer. She studied the screen, said, "It's Jessup." The phone rang a second time, and she answered it. "Hello, Jessup."

Michael heard a squawk of voice, and watched Abigail move the phone back a few inches. "No," she said, "I'm not ignoring you." She went silent, her face pinking with emotion. "No. It's none of your business where I go, or with whom." She looked at Michael, lowered her shoulders. "No. We're in the mountains. Reception is sporadic. Yes, the mountains. Michael and me. Yes, he's with me. Where are we?" Her eyes tracked up the weed-choked drive, settled on the highest turret. "Iron Mountain."

Falls's voice rose even further, and Abigail lifted a finger to Michael. "Damn it, Jessup . . ."

Michael looked again at Iron House. He found the third-floor corner where he and Julian had shared a room. Two windows looked out on the yard; one of them was broken.

"What?" Her voice was loud and tinged with panic. "How did this happen?" She listened. "When? And where were you? And the senator's man—what's his name? What about him?" She ran a hand through her hair, left it mussed. "Well, somebody screwed up." She found Michael with her eyes, then she turned away, back straight, one arm locked at her side. She spoke for another few minutes, and even when she hung up the phone she kept her back turned, her spine as hard and straight as any of the iron bars that hung between the ancient brick columns.

"What is it?" Michael asked.

She turned. "He's sending the helicopter. It's fast." She nodded to herself. "I can fix this."

"What?"

"Hour and fifteen minutes to get here. Another one-fifteen back. I can fix this."

"Fix what? Abigail?"

"The police found another body in the lake."

"Ronnie?"

"No." She shook her head, voice bleak. "Not Ronnie."

Michael processed, his mind slipping into this new gear with practiced ease. Two bodies, now, with Ronnie Saints still to be found. The discovery would inflame the investigation, the media. They would scour every inch of the lake, and that made it only a matter of time. They would find Ronnie Saints very soon. Once they linked a body to Julian, they would get their warrant and they would bring him in.

Michael looked at the building, at high, broken glass that caught the sky.

Ronnie Saints. Iron House.

The cops would figure it out plenty quick.

He checked his watch.

Abigail's phone rang again.

"Yes." She listened, turned left and stared off as if she could see something far away. She nodded. "We'll find it. Okay. Yes." She hung up. "Jessup," she said. "There's a high school on the eastern edge of town. Shouldn't be hard to find. It has a football field. We'll meet the chopper there."

"Tell me about the body."

She shook her head, swallowed. "Not like Ronnie. It's older. Maybe a month in the water. Clothes have rotted off. Mostly bones." She pulled at her hair. "Oh, God, oh God, oh God . . ."

"Abigail." She was scattered and trying hard to fight through it. "Look at me. What can you fix?"

She looked at everything but his face, and Michael knew what she was thinking. Sun would be down soon. High school. East side of town. She threaded her fingers, twisted them white, and Michael thought maybe he understood that, too.

"Is it Julian?" he asked.

She nodded.

"What about him?"

She blinked once, caught a tear on one finger and then straightened as best she could. "He's gone," she said. "Run away."

CHAPTER TWENTY-EIGHT

The helicopter came in low and fast. It started as a rumble down-valley, then swelled to thunder as it roared across small, painted houses and circled the high school at a thirty-degree bank. The sun was twenty minutes down, purple sky turning black. Michael and Abigail stood beside the heavy Mercedes. Its headlights spilled out onto the football field, and in the bright cone of light they saw brown grass and white hatch marks worn through to nothing. Across the street, people stepped onto porches to watch the helicopter and point at the bright light that stabbed down as it circled. It came in over the east bleachers, swung onto the length of the field and flared at the twenty-yard line. For an instant, it hovered—dead grass flat beneath it—and then it settled as gentle as a kiss.

The rotors slowed, but did not stop.

A door opened.

"This is a surprise."

Michael looked at Abigail. "What?"

She tilted her head at the chopper. Two men climbed down, and walked, bent, beneath the blades. "The senator came, too."

Michael recognized Jessup Falls: tall and rangy, his face unforgiving. Beside him, the senator looked broader, more solid and more sure. His hair was white, his suit impeccable. He moved as if the world owed him a living.

Abigail stepped out to meet them. Michael followed.

"Hello, darling." She raised her voice to be heard. The senator kissed her lightly, then held out a hand to Michael.

"I'm sorry we have to meet like this," he said. "Abigail has told me much, of course, but I would have preferred to do this in a more civilized manner. I'm Randall Vane."

"Senator."

They shook. Jessup Falls did not offer a hand. He held back and looked unhappy as the senator took Abigail's hand and cupped it in the two of his. "When Jessup said you'd left the house, I didn't think you'd gone quite so far."

"It's a long story."

"And a long flight home. You can tell me all about it."

"Any word on Julian?"

"No. Nothing. I'm sorry."

"Do the police know he's gone?"

"Of course not. God. It would be a disaster."

"How did this happen, Randall?"

"He's a grown man, Abigail. He'll be fine."

"I wish you would not be so blasé."

"And I wish you would keep the boy under control." He kept the smile, but his voice cut. "This is not doing me an ounce of good. Christ, the headlines alone . . ."

"You don't think Julian has something to do with those bodies?"

"I don't know what to think, and neither do you. That's the problem with Julian—after all these years, we still don't know what goes through that head of his."

"God, I hate that politician's smile." Abigail stepped past, angry. "It's a miracle anyone buys it. Jessup . . ." She took Jessup's hand. "How did it happen?"

"We took men off to cover the perimeter. A few reporters came over the wall earlier in the day. The crowd was building. Apparently, the doctor left for a few minutes, and Julian simply walked off. He wasn't under lock and key, as you know. I suspect he's on the grounds, still. Too much commotion beyond the wall. It's his pattern. We'll find him."

"Does he know about the bodies? Is he aware of what's happening?"

"Unknown, but possible."

The senator interrupted. "The locals are getting restless." He gestured at a small crowd forming on the roadside. Cars angled on the verge. People had come down off their porches. "If there's nothing that can't wait, we should go. Jessup can drive the car back."

"I'll drive it back," Michael said.

The group pulled up short, and Michael saw Jessup press his hand against the small of Abigail's back. "You're not coming?" She stepped away from the other men, closer to Michael.

"I need to finish this."

He lifted his chin toward the far, black mountain, and she knew he meant the orphanage beneath.

"Andrew Flint?" she asked.

"I still need to find him. It's connected. It has to be."

"It's been decades, Michael. You saw how the orphanage is. Flint could be anywhere."

"It's a starting place. It's something."

Abigail glanced over her shoulder; she looked at the chopper, the men waiting for her. "Come with me," she said. "There are no answers here. Julian needs us."

"Do you remember what you said at the gate? How it's hard going back to the place you're from?"

"Yes."

"I need to see it again. The halls. The rooms. Maybe I'll get lucky with Flint."

"What about Elena? Women get angry. They settle down. What do I tell her if she comes back?"

Michael glanced at the helicopter and felt an unexpected weight of emotion. He wanted on that chopper, and for an instant regretted every decision that had brought him to this place. They could be in Spain, by now, or on a beach in Australia. He felt Elena's hand in his, imagined the small, bright spark she carried. "I'll be back by tomorrow night. If she shows up, tell her that. Tell her I love her and to please wait."

"Are you sure?"

"You should go."

"Michael . . ."

"Go."

"Okay." She nodded in a small way, eyes unsure as the senator took her arm and led her to the helicopter. Falls gave them five seconds, then leaned in close to Michael, his anger unmistakable. "I can't keep her safe if I don't know where she is."

Michael felt armor drop across his eyes. "She's a big girl."

"In a dangerous world, you arrogant, insensitive prick. She's my responsibility, and has been for twenty-five years. Do you get that?"

"I was looking out for her."

"Did it occur to you that there might be risks you don't understand? Skills you don't actually possess?"

"You're going to miss your flight."

Falls glanced back, saw that everyone was in the helicopter. He raised one finger. "Don't take her away from me again."

Michael watched him climb in beside the pilot and strap himself down. Abigail's face was a pale, round blur as she lifted a hand in his direction. Michael waved back, conflicted. He knew what to do, but didn't want to do it; needed Elena, yet was here. Michael told himself to get a grip, to chill out. He could still fix everything: Julian, Elena, the life they'd yet to make. But the comfort was illusory. Everything he loved was far away.

He dropped his hand as the helicopter lifted and turned. Its nose dipped, and it accelerated past the car, red paint flashing once and then gone in the dark.

Michael was alone with the mountain.

He drove back to Main Street and found a parking place between a diner and one of the open bars. Standing on the sidewalk, he checked his phone and willed it to ring. He glanced once at the mountain, a black hulk that blotted out the stars, then turned his back and called information. When the call was answered, he asked if there was an Andrew Flint in or around the town of Iron Mountain. Was told no. Unsurprised, he hung up the phone. Then, knowing that she would not answer, he dialed Elena's cell and left a message.

I can fix this.

I can change.

And he thought that he could. If the circumstances were right. If the world changed, too.

Turning for the diner, Michael walked along the broken sidewalk, then swung in through the glass door. A small bell chimed, and the smell of buttered greens came like a memory. He took in the row of booths along the window, the aged bar with small, round stools, the pies under glass and the thick, pretty woman who offered up a smile from behind the register. "Sit anywhere, sugar."

A few people looked up, but nobody looked twice. Michael said hello to the woman as he passed, then sat in the farthest booth, a red-brick wall behind him, thirty feet of plate glass stretching halfway to his car. He caught a glimpse of a white-shirted man moving in the kitchen.

Suddenly, he was starving.

He studied the menu, a laminated sheet greasy with fingerprints and ketchup smears, then ordered a cheeseburger and a beer. "Want fries with that, sugar?"

She was in her thirties, and happy enough, a genuine twinkle in her eyes as she held her pen ready.

"That'd be great."

"Glass with your beer?"

"Sure."

She wrote that down, and before she could leave, Michael asked, "Do you have a phone book, by any chance?"

"Who you looking for? I know most everybody."

"Do you know Andrew Flint?"

"Sure. 'Course. He lives out at the orphanage."

"I was out there earlier." Michael shook his head. "Nobody lives there."

The waitress smiled and stuck the pen behind a tuft of soft, brown hair. "Have you been out there after dark?" Michael admitted that he had not, and she smiled more broadly. "Then you should trust old Ginger."

She winked and walked off to the kitchen, a slow, proud swing in her hips.

The beer was good. The burger was better. At the register, he asked Ginger, "Is there a hotel in town?"

"Two miles that way." She pointed to the south end of town. "It's not much, but I've caught my ex-husband there enough to know it gets the job done. We close at nine if you'd like me to show you the way."

Michael handed her a five-dollar tip. "Maybe some other time."

"You sure?"

Her fingers brushed his, and they were soft.

"Only that I will curse myself in the morning for missing an opportunity such as this."

He winked, pushed outside; and through the glass he saw her smiling.

The road out to the orphanage was nearly empty. Michael passed a few cars going the opposite way. No headlights behind him. When the tall gates drew near, he slowed and turned, the big car smooth and nearly silent. The dome light engaged when he opened the door, then went off as he stood and waited for his eyes to adjust.

The night was dark this far out, a warm blackness that collected between the mountains. There was no moon. No streetlamps. The stars seemed too high and colorless to offer much light, and even the town, four miles off, seemed to keep its glow dim and low to the ground.

Michael walked to the gate and listened to the night sounds, to crickets and wind and the slide of the river. It took a full two minutes to understand what Ginger had meant when she spoke of coming here after dark. The moment came as Michael took his gaze off the giant black ruin and let it wander the grounds. He saw buildings and dark, a hint of fallen stars where the river went smooth enough to shine. There was nothing, he thought. The place was as black and barren as the far side of the moon. Then his eyes snapped back to one of the small buildings at the rear of the grounds. Thin light shone from a ground-floor window. It was only a sliver, a blue glow through half-drawn curtains, but it was enough.

Michael went over the fence.

He landed lightly, gun in his hand. Under his feet, the drive felt cracked and loose. Small weeds scraped his shoes, and as he walked he felt the past rise up again. He pictured Andrew Flint and contemplated if he were, indeed, an evil man. He was a weak man, yes, incompetent and uncaring. In the end, it didn't matter. Michael knew it like he knew his bones. Evil or weak, Flint had left the prison to be run by the prisoners. He'd turned his back on the smallest, failed in the most basic manner, and Michael felt an anger stir down deep, a tight fist that thumped harder as familiar shapes gathered in the dark, as old hurts rose and memory crowded close.

Ten years of hell.

Of pain and fear and want.

Michael sucked night air deep and let the emotions run as he moved light and fast over ground that he remembered with shocking clarity. He passed trees he knew, leapt a drainage ditch without seeing it. The building piled up beside him, put a taste in his mouth as he pictured Julian weeping in his narrow bed. He slid along the east wall, reached out to touch brick and found it unchanged. There was ruin here, and strength; that should mean something, but did not. He gave himself the time it took to pass the main stairs, then tightened down the valve of resentment, so that when he reached the window with the television glow, he was himself again, cold and keen and eager.

He put his back against the wall, scanned the open ground and saw nothing out of place. The building was two stories tall, redbrick with shutters that had been green when he was a boy. It had been housing then, a collection of rooms for the few staff that chose to make Iron House their home. It had always been off-limits to the boys. One more rule. One more place to avoid.

Not anymore.

Michael looked through the window and saw a small room with poor furniture. A television flickered in the corner. The TV was old and small, sitting on a trunk. There was no one in the room, but through a door Michael saw yellow light from another room. He made a slow circuit of the building. In the back, he found an old car and empty windows. The light came from a room near the front door. Michael found more curtains partly drawn, bare hints of the interior. He saw a coal-burning fireplace and a tattered wingback chair beside it, two books on the mantelpiece, wooden floors and an area rug worn threadbare on one side. He thought about the gun in his hand, then tucked it away.

He knocked on the door, knocked again and then rattled the knob as something scraped inside. He put his ear close to the wood, fingers spread. There was stillness at first, then he heard the ratchet of metal—an unmistakable sound—and jerked back as the door blew apart at chest height.

Light spilled through the hole.

Gun smoke.

Michael heard another round racked into the chamber. He saw fingers of shadow as someone moved toward the door, then rose himself, his back against the brick, forty-five heavy in his palm. He removed the safety, finger inside the trigger guard. He slipped closer to the door: two feet and then one. Breathing sounds came from beyond the hole in the door. Erratic. Forced. Footsteps dragged as the muzzle appeared in the hole. Black metal with a red bead sight, it trembled as it broke the plane of the door. Michael didn't screw around. Moving fast, he grabbed the barrel, pushed it away and yanked hard. The weapon discharged a tongue of fire. Michael heard a small cry, and then it was his: hot metal and a walnut stock. Large bore shotgun. He pulled it through the hole and tossed it down, bringing up his own weapon and sighting on an old man inside who was loose-skinned and white. His hands were up and in front of him as if still holding the shotgun, mouth open. A bathrobe hung to his knees, bare legs beneath and worn, red slippers on his feet.

"Open the door." Michael kept the gun steady. The old man—Andrew Flint—stared, but seemed unable to move. Patchy hair covered the dome of his skull. His cheeks were sunken, his hands liver-spotted and veined. He peered through the hole as if he had no idea what it was. "Please," Michael said, and his voice came cool and calm as Sunday morning. It seemed to have an effect, because Flint put his hand on the dull, brass knob. The door swung open, and Michael stepped inside. When light landed fully on his face, Flint squinted, his lips pulling up.

"Julian Vane?" Something like hope moved his features. A knobby finger rose, and then the recognition died. He shook his head. "No. Not Julian."

"Step backward, please." Michael used the same Sunday morning voice. He knew from experience that it kept people calm, even when they understood, deep down, that Michael had come for a reason. The voice lulled them because it sounded nothing at all like the end of the world. It was too reasoned and too calm; it gave people hope.

Flint backed up until his knees struck a small coffee table. Michael checked the room, saw the cold fireplace, the wingback chair. A bookshelf dominated a wall that had been invisible from outside. On the right, a wide hall ran off into shadow. The television glow came from a room halfway down. "Is there anyone else in the house?" Michael asked.

A head shake. "No."

Michael kept the gun on Flint. "What made you think I was Julian Vane?"

Flint's hands moved, fingers spread, toward the bookshelf. "I have his books. All of them." He took a step toward the shelves. "Here."

"That's enough." Michael stopped him two feet from the books. He could see a row of books, spine out, which bore the name Julian Vane.

"His picture is on the back . . ."

Flint moved another foot, reached out and Michael cocked the forty-five. Flint froze and Michael said, "A dangerous man might have a weapon behind those books."

"No . . ."

"Nevertheless." Michael wagged the muzzle at the chair.

Flint looked at the wingback.

"Sit."

"Please, don't kill me."

Flint collapsed when his knees hit the back of the chair. In the sad, brown robe he looked like nothing more than a bag of old bones. Michael dragged the coffee table so that he could sit across from Flint, three feet between them. He kept the gun on Flint, one eye on the dark, empty hall. "Do you know who I am?"

"The hand of God come for vengeance . . ."

He sounded insane when he said it, the words a bare whisper, his eyes shocked wide and yellow-white. Michael smelled liquor on the man's clothes, his breath. He saw a worn, leather Bible on the floor beside Flint's chair, noticed that the man's nails were chewed to the quick, his hands as horny as alligator skin.

Michael leaned closer into the light. "Do you know me?"

"I . . . don't." He turned his head but kept his eyes on Michael. "No."

242

"But you can guess."

Flint nodded, and light caught in pale, pink crescents at the bottoms of his eyes. "You don't have to do this."

"Do what?"

"Kill me."

"All I want at this moment is for you to say my name."

Flint stared at the muzzle of the gun.

"Say it."

"Michael . . ."

"Why do you think I'm here to kill you?"

"Because everyone else is dead. Because I knew it would come back to me. Because taking that money was a sin. Selling those boys out . . ." His voice broke. Michael released the hammer and shifted the barrel until it was pointed five degrees left of Flint's gut. Flint followed the movement, then said, "I never blamed you for killing that Hennessey boy. He was a rotten child."

"Is that right?"

"So many rotten boys back then." Flint's eyes darted to the open door. "So few like your brother. But this, now . . ." His eyes were pinned to the floor, head shaking sideways. "This now." His gaze came back up, and his soul was tortured. "It's been twenty-three years. Why would you kill those boys now? After all this time . . ."

"I don't know what you're talking about," Michael said.

But Flint's head was still shaking, eyes distant and damp. "Evil and vengeance and God's chary eye . . ."

Michael edged the muzzle back three degrees, and it got Flint's attention. "Why did you blow a hole in your door, Mr. Flint?"

"I put a motion sensor at the gate."

"So, you knew someone was coming. That doesn't tell me why you put a round through your door." Michael waited for Flint to focus. "Did you even look to see who it was?"

"No."

"Then why?"

"Just figured I was next. Been waiting. I was scared."

"Of what?"

"Don't pretend." Flint's voice thickened, his face suddenly hard. "I

243

may be an old man and afraid, but I'm smart enough to know what's what: you, here, with your calm voice and shark eyes, those other boys, gone and so silent they got no choice but to be dead. All that money with no price to pay . . ." He rolled his eyes, sucked in a sudden breath. "I know now what I've done. And I know what you are."

"You don't, actually."

"Well, I don't have the money, if you came to get it back." He dragged an arm across his mouth, looking sly and angry. "It's gone with the rest of it. Damn Indians. Damn Cherokee with their cheap booze and rigged casinos." Flint's eyes flicked left, and Michael saw a bottle of whiskey and a glass down to half a finger. Flint scraped a palm over white whiskers, then tore his eyes away. "It makes sense, now I think on it. You being the one."

"Why is that?"

"You're the only killer come through this place. Killing as a boy, killing as a man." He nodded. "Like rain in springtime."

Michael stood. "You know nothing about me, Mr. Flint." He walked across the room, picked up the liquor bottle and the glass. "And I know less about you. Not your needs or weakness, not those other boys you say are gone and silent." He sat back down and sloshed three inches of brown liquid into the glass. "But you're going to tell me."

"Why should I?"

The pistol barrel tracked right and settled squarely on Andrew Flint's forehead. "There's nothing I won't do for my brother, Mr. Flint. If nothing else, you should remember that."

Flint watched the glass, licked sandpaper lips. "And you won't kill me if I tell?"

Michael kept the gun steady, and handed the glass to Flint. "I don't make promises I can't keep."

"What does that mean?"

"It means I have questions." Flint drained the glass. "And I expect you to have answers."

CHAPTER TWENTY-NINE

Eighty miles east of Iron Mountain, the helicopter raced along at two thousand feet. To the south, the city of Charlotte looked golden and compressed, a setting sun dipped in a giant, black sea. Abigail sat behind the pilot, the senator to her left. Jessup rode up front, his face all angles and lines, with deep shadows in the creases and a hint of pale whiskers. A few times, he looked back, and when he did his face reflected a quiet agony of things unsaid. But because the senator was there, he said nothing beyond the mundane. He consulted the map, spoke to the pilot. Occasionally, he radioed the estate with updates on their position and flight path.

After twenty minutes, Abigail tuned out. The cabin was warm, the noise soothing, even through the headset. She replayed the last few hours with Michael. His face at the gates of Iron House. His determination as they parted. She closed her eyes, and flinched when the senator put a hand on her leg, sat still as he flicked a switch that would isolate their headsets.

"I thought we could use a little privacy."

His features were heavy in the dim light, his eyes wide-set and deep. She smelled the cologne he preferred, something French, and marveled at the strength in his thick fingers. "It's a little late to whisper sweet nothings."

"Do you doubt that I love you?"

"I'm no longer sure."

"Don't confuse the occasional dalliance for anything other than what it is. It's just sex and ego."

"You're a man of appetites."

She said it flatly, but he nodded as if she were preaching. "And honesty where it matters."

"And does honesty still matter with me?"

He squeezed her leg, a dark twinkle in his eye. "You've never been anything but a perfect spouse—elegant and beautiful and poised. I knew the moment I saw you—"

"That I would look good on your arm."

Vane frowned. "That you would be discrete and loyal to your husband. That you would know the value of the things I was building, and the many ways in which you would benefit from those things." He shifted in his seat. "That as beautiful as you were, you would also understand how the game is played. That you were a pragmatist."

"Perhaps I'm not as mercenary as you imagine."

"Perhaps you are more so."

"What are you saying, Randall?"

He showed his cold, politician eyes. "I'm asking if you know anything about these bodies."

"I would never—"

"Let's not pretend you're incapable."

"Of killing a man?"

"Of keeping secrets." The senator glanced at the pilot and at Jessup. They were cut off from the conversation, oblivious. "Of protecting Julian, even if it meant lying to me." Abigail touched her throat, but he was unflinching. "Dead people are turning up on my property, and I'm being crucified in the media. They're calling me obstructionist, elitist and every other thing. It's eighteen years ago all over again, and the election is in three months! I need to know what's happening, Abigail. This is no time for reticence or misplaced loyalty."

"I don't know anything."

The senator frowned. "I don't pretend to know all of you, my dear, and have found you, in fact, as layered as any politician. But I know when you're lying."

"I tire of this game."

"And I marvel at your depths; but I still want to know what's going on." His head moved, and she saw it reflected in the Plexiglas window. "Running back to Iron Mountain with Michael was neither accident, nor idle destination. You do nothing without good cause."

"Nor do you. And this interrogation makes me wonder if there's something you're not telling me." Vane glanced down, and Abigail said, "Oh my God. There *is* something you're not telling me." A pit opened in Abigail's stomach. She thought she understood. "They've identified the bodies, haven't they?"

The senator had connections everywhere: men on the payroll, people who owed favors. He had at least one person in the local police department, and probably more.

Please, God . . .

"George Nichols went missing five weeks ago."

"George Nichols . . ." Abigail repeated the name, appalled and suddenly nauseous.

"He runs a lawn service in Southern Pines." Vane leaned closer. "He has friends, Abigail. Employees. People who reported him missing. The police found his car weeks ago, burned out and abandoned on a deserted lot in the far south of Chatham County, less than twenty miles from the estate. The license plate was removed, but the VIN number was intact. The police traced it as a matter of course, so his name was already on file, the missing persons report. Dental records were faxed in this afternoon, the body confirmed by dinnertime."

Abigail's mouth went dry.

"Does the name mean anything to you?" he asked. "George Nichols. White male. Thirty-seven years old."

She shook her head, unfeeling.

"What about Ronnie Saints?"

"Ronnie who?"

The deadness spread to her arms, her legs. Vane nodded. "They pulled him out of the lake less than an hour ago. He'd not been in the water long. Still had his wallet in his pocket. I suppose that name means nothing."

"Should it?"

The senator leaned back. "I think we both know that's a lie, too. It's been years, but I've heard those names. George Nichols. Ronnie Saints. I can't remember where or the precise context, but I'm certain

247

it had something to do with Julian. Something to do with Iron Mountain." ⸗

Abigail looked away.

"Why did you go back there, Abigail?"

She said nothing, but felt panic well up in her chest. He took her hand, and his touch was surprisingly gentle.

"Can't you see how dangerous this is?" He waited for her to turn. "Can't you trust me?" Her head moved, and the senator looked crushed. "Why not?"

He was pleading with her, begging in a way she'd never seen. There were a dozen lies she could tell, and a handful he might actually believe. In the end, she told none of them. "You've never loved Julian as I have." She lifted her chin. "You've never loved him enough."

Their gaze held for three seconds, then Vane released her hand. His mouth opened, but in the end he simply looked away.

He could tell when she was lying.

And knew enough to see the truth.

Victorine knew something big was going down. Helicopters every-where. Cops and more cops. She'd followed the noise to the edge of the woods and seen them all at the lake. She'd seen the body come out of the water just as the sun went down: a big man, his skin oily white and gnawed-looking; water running out of his mouth. She'd watched for a good, long time, then crept back through the darkening woods. In the cave, she'd lit her candles and eaten the small bit of food that was left.

Then she stretched out and thought about what to do. She had no money, and no car. Her momma was like to kill her and she'd lost the gun she'd stole out of the cupboard. She thought on that, a wicked smile at play on the planes of her face. She pictured her mother's face as their argument got hot, how she'd been so high and mighty and then brought low when Victorine squeezed a round through the roof of her kitchen. That had settled the fight, right there, and it had been so sweet, the look on her mother's face, the fear and full-on shock. But now things were messed up. Julian had put her up in the guest house, all quiet-like and full of promises about how no one ever stayed there.

But then someone stayed there, and now Victorine was in this cave with no food, no money and nowhere to go. That shouldn't have been a problem, but Julian had gone missing, too. How many days, now? Three days? Four? When he'd told her to run away, she'd believed that he would help her. He'd told her so, sworn it, even. They had a plan, a good one, so good she'd done something she'd never done before. She gave a man her trust; and now she had to wonder.

Where the hell was he?

She fell asleep pondering that, woke late in the dark. All of the candles but one had burned out, and the one was barely a stub, its light low and fluttery. Victorine started to rise, but stopped sudden.

Something was wrong.

Low, rustling sounds came from out past the cave's mouth. Something pushing through the scrub. Whispers. Talking.

Victorine picked up a flat rock as big as a carton of cigarettes. If somebody planned to come in this cave, he'd have to do it headfirst.

She blew out the candle, and darkness plunged down. She waited, still and stiller, yet. The sounds were louder, closer, a body dropping down and the sound of something heavy sliding in. She lifted the stone over her head, and then heard Julian's voice. "Please God . . ."

"Julian?"

She lowered the stone.

"Victorine?"

"It's me." She caught his hands and dragged him the rest of the way inside. He was breathing hard and hot, his neck slick with sweat as he wrapped her up with both of his arms.

"I'm sorry," he said. "I'm so sorry."

"Sorry for what?"

"I don't know what's happening. Sorry you're alone. Sorry for being so . . . thick." He let her go and pounded one fist against the side of his head. "Everything's wrong and nothing's right. I can't . . ." He struck himself again. "I just can't . . ."

"Hang on, now. Let me get us some light."

Victorine disentangled herself and groped around for the matches. Finding them, she lit the last candle, Julian's face damp and washed out in the bright, sudden flare. "Damn, Julian." She smoothed sweat and dirt off his face. Small streaks of blood from where brambles had caught his skin. "You look like hell."

He pulled his knees up, and put his head against her chest. "I just don't . . ."

"Don't what?"

"I can't stop seeing . . ."

He clawed at her shirt, drove his face hard against her breasts.

"Seeing what?"

"A dead man on the floor. Red spray and the sound of something heavy dropping. I see my brother and my mother, bits of Iron Mountain, bits of stuff long gone. Old faces. Voices. Nothing makes sense." He pulled harder. "I forgot about you, V. I'm sorry for that, but my head's not on right. Everything's messed up."

"Slow down, Julian. Just tell me what happened."

"I don't know. Sometimes I feel like I can see it, and then it just goes. It goes and I'm deep in the black. Water all around. People laughing. Memories. Faces. It's never been this bad."

He pulled at his hair, pushed one heel on the cave floor.

"Just breathe, now." She hugged him tighter, knowing he was a struggling kind of man, but never having seen him like this. The man she knew was more boy than not, a quiet soul with a store of patience for a lonesome girl brought up rough. He knew what it meant to be stepped on, knew how long, black hours piled up in the night, and how even the sun could rise too pale. But now she was starting to think maybe she should have listened to her momma after all, her momma who said there was no God in heaven and no man worthy of faith, no truth beyond flesh, family and folding money, no decent place in the world for women named Gautreaux. "It's all good, Julian." She said it like she meant it. "Victorine's here, now."

"I need you to do something for me."

"What?"

He told her.

"Your mother?" He nodded, and Victorine pictured lily hands and white skin, servants and bankers and beds that were feather soft. She thought of her own hard years, of beatings and loneliness and a crazy mother who whored herself out to any man with fifty dollars and a truck strong enough to force its way up the road that led to her bed. "I know how to handle your mother."

Light flickered, and a moment passed.

"Do you know why I love you?" he asked.

She rocked him, silent, and he asked again.

"You know why?"

"I know," she said.

And, she did. It wasn't her looks or her brains or her fine, hard body. Julian loved her for one reason.

"You're so strong," he said.

And that was it.

The helicopter circled the far side of the estate and came in where the reporters couldn't see it. Treetops thrashed as it slowed, then an opening appeared below the skids and Abigail saw the hard, sharp edge of the helipad. It was lit. Cars in the darkness beyond. When the pilot made his final adjustment and the skids scraped concrete, Abigail unfastened her harness.

Her anger had grown as dark, broken countryside flicked past outside her window. She knew it was unfair and fed largely by fear, but the smell of her husband made her furious. His self-interest. His calculation. Outside, blades ripped the air into vicious downdrafts; engine noise like a rockslide. Abigail was at the first car when a hand landed on her shoulder. She spun and found her husband.

"Think about what I said."

He had to yell, white hair aflutter on his large head.

Abigail raised her voice to match. "No. You think about what *I* said."

He looked at the long, black car. Two members of his private security stood waiting. Beside the car, the Land Rover looked worn and old in a way that seemed to insult him. "I assume you'd prefer to ride with Jessup." He said it with wounded pride and a need to hurt.

"We have things to discuss," Abigail said.

"Will I see you in the morning, then?"

The leer spread on his face, and Abigail's anger kicked up a notch. She strove to be civil with her husband, but was only so strong. "I've never cheated on you. Whatever you choose to believe, I would never do that."

"Please . . ."

"We're different that way."

"I've told you before that we can all use distractions, but, don't insult my intelligence. Screw him all you want, but be honest about it."

She shook her head. "I chose a long time ago the kind of person I wished to be."

"You're absurd, sometimes. Do you know that?"

She wanted a clever retort but had nothing, so what came out was simple and plain. "Were you ever a moral man?"

"Morality is a relative concept. You, of all people, should know that." He settled into the car, and when his window came down, he said, "Tomorrow morning, first thing. I need an answer to my question."

Jessup materialized beside her as the senator's window slid up and the car eased into motion.

"You okay?"

"In the car."

They got in and the doors closed as the helicopter engine finally died. The silence was shocking, Jessup's voice equally so. "What the hell's going on, Abigail? You leave without telling me, take off with a man you barely know, a dangerous man, a goddamn gangster . . ."

But she had thoughts only for Julian, and waved him off angrily. "You've checked local motels? The friends we know of?"

"Of course."

"The grounds?"

"All four thousand acres? No. Of course not."

"He's with Victorine Gautreaux—"

"We don't know that."

"Don't bullshit me, Jessup. It's the only explanation. That little bitch has got her claws in him. We need to search Caravel's place."

"Already done."

"She allowed it?"

"For a five thousand dollar cash payment. We checked every inch. She sat on the porch the whole time, counting her money and laughing at us. Julian was not there. Victorine, either. By the time we left, the police were there."

"Police?"

"Jacobsen and some other detective. I don't know what they wanted."

Abigail shook her head. "Ronnie Saints. George Nichols." She felt herself staring. The windshield was a blur; outside was a blur.

"Don't even go there, Abigail."

"I'm frightened, Jessup."

"There's nothing here we can't handle."

Abigail scrubbed her face with both hands, then said, "I know who those dead men are. Ronnie Saints. George Nichols. Dear God, help me, I know who they are. But I don't understand what's happening."

"You don't have to. Okay. Just take a breath. I'll take care of this."

"I don't think you can."

"Just start from the beginning. Tell me everything."

She explained where she and Michael had gone and what they learned. "The list was at Ronnie Saints's house. George Nichols's name was on the list. So were Billy Walker and Chase Johnson."

"That's why you were at Iron House?"

"To talk to Andrew Flint. Michael thought he might know something."

"But you didn't see Flint?"

"No." She bit the edge of a finger, thinking about the lake. "There's a third body they've not yet identified, the second one out of the water, the one that was all bones." The finger came away from her mouth. "What if it's Billy Walker or Chase Johnson? It can't be coincidence. Oh God, Jessup, what if there's another body in that lake? What if they're all dead? What is happening here?"

"Julian did not kill those men." Jessup was firm. "You have to believe that. No matter what, he *needs* you to believe that."

"You really love him, don't you?"

"Of course."

"But why, Jessup? Even the senator struggles and fails."

"I love him because you do."

Abigail touched his cheek. "Thank you for that, Jessup. Thank you so very much." Jessup leaned into her touch and she said, "Does the name Salina Slaughter mean anything to you?"

He drew his face back. "Why would you ask that?"

"The name was on the list."

Jessup shook his head. "No."

"You're certain."

"Yes. But, look. I have a question of my own."

"Okay."

"How do you feel about Michael?"

"It's complicated. Why?"

"The senator has been asking about him. He's mentioned him to the cops. His men are digging for background. They want to know everything. Who he is. Where he's from. Everything. They want to track him. They want to find his girlfriend. They're building a file."

"I don't understand."

"I think your husband is looking for a scapegoat."

She saw it, then, how it could play. "Someone to blame for the murders."

"It's how the senator thinks. Michael is an outsider."

She sat up straighter. "You haven't told my husband what we know, have you? You haven't told him about Otto Kaitlin, about the things you found in Michael's car—the cash, the photos, the gun? Jesus. You didn't give him Michael's gun."

"Not yet, no."

"Not yet. What are you saying?"

He shrugged, unmoved. "I'm saying it might not be a bad idea."

CHAPTER THIRTY

Jimmy was waiting on the front porch when Stevan finally decided to show up. It was late, most of the men either racked out or playing cards. A subtle anger filled the house, a whiff of mutiny. There was no air-conditioning. The only television had a hole, dead center. But it was more than that. Every man inside was an earner. They didn't have Stevan's millions or Jimmy's plans. They had their turf, their hard-won, blood-soaked piece of the American dream, and Stevan was screwing that up—and for what? They should have killed Michael days ago. They should have never let him out of the city. Now, they felt cut off and exposed.

Jimmy understood.

He didn't care, but he understood. Every man needs a reason to feel proud, just like he needs a dollar in his pocket. None of that was a problem for Jimmy, of course. His wants had evolved beyond the simple matter of fear, respect and opportunity. They'd grown, yet become simpler. He wanted Michael dead, so people would know for certain who was best between them; and he wanted sixty-seven million dollars. It was a very specific number. He thought about it as he stood.

Maybe an estate in California . . .

Something with a vineyard . . .

Headlights swept across the house as Stevan parked the car, and Jimmy touched the weapon in his belt. He met Stevan at the top step. "Where have you been?"

"Are you channeling the ghost of my father?"

"Your father would beat you first and ask questions second. He would never drag his people down here in the first place. He would have killed a traitor at the first sign of treason. He'd have never given his men reason to doubt."

"Jesus, Jimmy. Nice to see you, too."

"That was not a polite greeting. Cops are all over the estate. The men are pissed, and Michael is still alive. You're fucking this up."

"I'm too tired for this, Jimmy."

Stevan looked stressed, tie loose enough for coarse hairs to show at his collar, eyes drawn into their sockets. He pushed past, but Jimmy stopped him two feet from the door. "Your people need to be led."

"That's the right phrase, isn't it?" He squared up on Jimmy. "*My* people."

He reached for the door, but Jimmy stopped him again. "I want to call Michael. I want to get this done."

"We've had this discussion. I have a plan. It's set."

"Will you finally tell me what this genius plan is?"

"Look, Jimmy, my father may have trusted you to run parts of his business—I get that—but we're not even close to that point, you and me."

"This is bullshit."

Stevan touched his chest, and spoke as if to a child. "Brains," he said, then pointed at Jimmy. "Muscle. Brains. Muscle." Hand moving. "You get how this works?"

"What about the girl?"

An eyebrow came up. "Is she still alive?"

"What do you want me to do with her?"

"It's your mess." Stevan opened the door. "You clean it up."

The door clicked shut, and Jimmy thought of things unspoken. He thought of Michael and the girl, of how Stevan was a fraction of the man his father had been. He thought about sixty-seven million dollars, and about the things he'd found in the dark, silent barn: the chains and metal hooks, the old stone wheel and the many tools it could sharpen. He pictured Stevan spread-eagled and weeping blood, then wondered how long the little bastard would last, how many hours he might scream before giving up the account numbers and access codes.

Sixty-seven million dollars.

A dusty barn and a world of silent woods.

Jimmy took a deep breath, and smelled all the places he could bury a man.

CHAPTER THIRTY-ONE

"So, that's it?" Michael leaned forward. Flint was talked dry, the bottle down to fumes. A few things made sense, now. Not all things, but some. It's the funny thing about liquor and fear—they can break most men, given time and careful application.

And then there were men like Flint.

He was an edgy drunk, the kind that got cold and sharp the more he drank. Michael could see the gears turning, the mechanical precision oiled by the cheap, brown booze. Flint was smart enough to stick mostly to the truth, but he told small, careful lies. Michael didn't know yet what they were, but he knew they were out there, and he knew they were keys to something bigger. Drunk or not, a man does not lie lightly when a forty-five is pointed at his face. "You have another bottle?" Michael asked.

"In the kitchen. I don't want any more."

That was a lie. Flint was quiet and determined with a bottle, the kind of drinker who stoked low, warm fires, and knew how to keep them banked. Michael knew drinkers like that, hard men and weak, quiet, hungry souls who wouldn't quit drinking until they passed out or the booze was gone.

"Kitchen, huh?" Michael half-turned where he sat, the coffee table smooth and warm under him. He pointed at a closed cabinet under the bookshelf. "The way you've been staring at that cabinet, I thought maybe you had some closer than that."

"I haven't been staring."

Michael smiled because it was the first lie poorly told. Flint had looked at three things since he sat down: Michael's face, the forty-five and that cabinet. "How about I take a look?"

Michael stood, and Flint actually lurched in his seat. "Don't!"

"Don't what?"

"Please . . ." Michael kept an eye on Flint as he opened the cabinet. There was only one thing in it. He pulled out the box and sat back down. Flint's mouth hung open, a world of pain in his eyes. "Please."

Michael lifted the lid and saw cash. Lots of it. He shook the box. The bills were loose, and he stirred them with the barrel. All hundreds. Maybe eighty thousand dollars. He put the box by his side. "This is what's left?"

"All of it. I swear. Please don't take it."

"Tell me again about the man who brought it."

They'd been over this twice. Michael wanted to hear it again.

"It was just a delivery," Flint said. "A package wrapped in plastic. A young man. I had to sign for it."

"Not the same man from before?" Flint shook his head, and Michael considered the things he'd learned. A man claiming to be an attorney had approached Flint seven weeks ago. He wore an expensive suit, carried a briefcase and presented a card from a legitimate firm. North of middle-aged, stern and uncompromising, this man spoke of a client whose name he could not reveal. The client had a proposition. He wanted something very simple, the current addresses of four men who had once been boys at Iron House. Chase Johnson. Billy Walker. George Nichols. Ronnie Saints. Andrew Flint had a memory, access to records. The client would pay well.

Michael lifted a handful of bills and let them fall. "How much did he offer?"

"Fifty thousand for each address. I gave him three."

"Which three?"

Flint closed his eyes and swallowed. "Ronnie Saints. George Nichols. Chase Johnson."

"Why not Billy Walker?"

"I couldn't find him, okay. Just those three. Just them. Please. Can you just go, now?"

Michael lifted the box, shifted it. "It's a lot of money."

"Take it."

That got Michael's attention. He reevaluated. Flint was no longer hostile or despairing; he was borderline frantic. "Take it?" Michael asked.

"Yes." Flint waved his fingers. "It's yours."

Michael waited.

Flint said, "Look, I've answered your questions."

Michael said nothing, and in the silence, Flint glanced down the hall. Since Michael had walked through the door, Flint had not looked down that hall. Not once. Not for any reason.

Then Michael heard it, too: a faint shuffling sound. He came to his feet, gun leveled. And in an astonishing display of speed and coordination, Flint threw himself toward the hall, screaming "No" even as he spread his arms. He faced Michael, pale and drunk and shaking. "Don't. Please."

He was trying to block the hallway. His robe gapped open to show the bones of his narrow breastplate, the few white hairs that remained.

"Who's back there?"

The gun was steady in Michael's hand. The footsteps solidified behind Flint, strange, halting sounds and the scrape of fabric. "He's just a boy," Flint said.

But it was no boy coming down the hall. The man was every bit of six feet tall, with thick legs and broad, heavy hands. He walked in a shuffle, one foot dragging slightly. Michael saw jeans and bare feet and a shock of black hair. He was in partial shadow, blue glow on his face as he passed the television room, eyes down and angled left.

Flint tried to make himself larger. "Please."

"That's far enough." Michael thumbed the hammer.

"Don't shoot!" Something broke in Flint's voice. He was on the verge of tears, cheeks an unhealthy pink. "I'm begging you."

Michael hesitated, and the man behind Flint said, "Hi." Just like a kid would. He scrubbed at his face, then stepped into the light even as Flint tried to shield him. The sight of the gun had no effect. Nor did Michael's presence. The man moved Flint aside as if he were a curtain, and Michael saw that one of his eyes drooped beneath an obvious depression in the curve of his skull. "I'm thirsty." There were long scars on his forehead, old stitches that ran into the hairline. "Can I come out yet?"

Flint flashed a glance at Michael, then put a hand on the man's shoulder. "Sure, you can." Small defiance, now. "No one's going to hurt you."

"Okay."

"Say hello to the nice man."

The man shifted from one foot to the other. He looked shy and embarrassed, then lifted one hand in a furtive, boyish way. "Hello, nice man."

And Michael recognized him.

"Hello, Billy."

Billy Walker smiled at the sound of his name. "Do we have any milk?"

"Sure we do," Flint said.

"Chocolate?"

Worry deepened the lines on Flint's face, but he kept his voice warm as he smiled lightly and smoothed the hair on Billy's head. "Let's go see."

What happened to him?" Billy was visible at a table through an open door. He was eating sugared cereal, milk on his chin as he rocked in his seat and stared at the glass of chocolate milk. Flint was broken, now, the lies all told and done. He had nothing left, and Michael knew it.

"He got into an argument with Ronnie Saints." Flint dug a knuckle into his right eye, and then sighed deeply as he poured another glass of bourbon. "This was about a year after you ran away. The argument got ugly, and Billy went headfirst down some concrete stairs."

"Ronnie pushed him?"

"He denied it, of course." The glass went up and came down empty. "Didn't really matter in the end. Doctors spent six hours picking pieces of skull out of Billy's brain, and he's been like this ever since."

"But why is he here? Why with you?"

Flint smiled a melancholy smile. "No one was going to adopt a sixteen-year-old boy with half his skull smashed in. But it's funny, life. The concrete edge that put that dent in his head seems to have

261

driven the rottenness right out of him, just took all that blackness and baked it in the sun." Flint shrugged. "He was different, after, gentle and sweet and unassuming. Even after he turned eighteen, I couldn't bear to see him loose in the world, so, I let him stay. He'd do odd jobs. Picking up sticks, sweeping. It was okay for a while. Billy. The orphanage. Then they opened the casinos." A bright edge came into Flint's eyes, and he sniffed loudly. "And I lost everything."

"Are you speaking of the money Abigail Vane donated?"

"Five million dollars and I blew it. Gambling. Bad investments." Flint was too guilty to be apologetic. "I thought I could make things better, double down, you know. But I failed everybody. All those boys. Myself. I ruined everything."

"And when the orphanage closed?"

"There's salvage value here. Copper gutters and pipes. Slate roof." Flint rolled his shoulders. "A company up north bought the property and kept me on as caretaker until they could break it up. That should have been years ago, but they keep putting it off. Not that I'm complaining. They pay me a little. We have a place to live."

Michael looked for more lies, but found none. "You've kept Billy with you this whole time."

"Yes."

"Why?"

Flint lifted eyes that shone with bright, clear love. "Because in sixty years of screwing up, caring for that boy is the one thing I've done right."

Twenty minutes later, Flint put Billy Walker back to bed. When he came out, Michael said, "I'll help you do something with the door."

They patched it with plywood and ten-penny nails. Outside, with the moon rising low and fat, Michael said, "You really think they're dead, don't you? All of them."

"They've all gone missing."

"Why were you checking on them?"

"I got a bad feeling after I gave up the addresses. I was hoping I was wrong."

"Did you talk to any of them?" Michael asked.

"Just Ronnie Saints, but he was paranoid and confused. Thought I was after his money or some such thing. I warned him other boys had gone missing, but he told me to mind my own damn business. Said he knew what he was doing. Two days later he was gone, too."

Michael nodded, unsurprised. Even as a kid, Saints had been paranoid. "Any of them have families?"

"They were never going to be the family types, if you follow."

Michael closed the door, pounded a fist on the patch. He thought of Ronnie Saints's girlfriend, who wanted a baby and a paid-for house. "Maybe you should leave. Take Billy and find some other place. A new start."

Flint was nodding when he said, "I just need one big win."

Michael said nothing. Drunks and gamblers rarely changed. He picked up the shotgun and emptied it of shells. When he finished, Flint was staring.

"You really didn't kill them?"

Michael studied the ruins that spread out in the dark. "I haven't thought of those boys in twenty years."

"Maybe they're not dead," Flint said.

"Maybe."

Flint picked up the bottle of bourbon, swayed. "I did the best I could, you know."

Michael tightened his jaw, but Flint was oblivious.

"When you were here," Flint went on, "I never meant for bad things to happen. I hope to God you'll believe me when I say that. It was just hard. So many boys, and so few of us." He sniffed wetly, truth in his voice. "I know it was bad."

Michael stared hard at Flint, mind turning as he sifted his own emotions and came up cool and unfazed. It was done; he was over it. He didn't tell Flint the truth, though, did not explain that he'd come over the fence more or less inclined to kill the man. Strange that it was Billy Walker who'd saved him. Stranger still that Michael felt such compassion.

"It's good what you're doing for Billy."

That was all Michael had, simple words and the gift of his life.

Flint cleared his throat. "I'm going to bed. Sofa's yours, if you want it."

Michael considered the offer. He wanted to see Iron House in the light of day. He wanted to walk its halls, to see the places of childhood. Maybe, he'd find unexpected insight, some sort of fresh understanding; or perhaps in the high-ceilinged halls his rage would find cause for resurrection. "There's a hotel in town," Michael said.

"The Volonte. It's decent."

A hotel sounded good: a shower and four hours of blackness; but Michael didn't trust Flint yet, and the locals cops would love a shot at closing the Hennessey file from all those years back. A simple phone call would do it. Cops at his hotel door. A hard rush in the predawn stillness. That would be the height of irony, if with all the blood on Michael's hands he went to prison for the one murder he didn't commit. "The sofa's good. Thanks. I'd like to bring my car inside the gate, though."

Flint fished a ring of keys from the pocket of his robe. "The brass one opens the lock."

"I'll leave early."

"Early or not." Flint shrugged. "I sleep late."

Michael gestured at the orphanage. "I'd like to have a look first."

"Really?" Flint leaned left. "You want to go inside?"

It was more of a need than a want, to touch the place where he'd been made. Abigail had said it best: it was powerful, coming back. "Not now," Michael said. "In the morning."

"Okay. Sure. I guess you know your way around." He pointed at the key ring. "The big silver one opens the front door. Just leave the keys on the kitchen counter."

"I'll leave your gun, too."

Flint swayed again, creases like map lines in his skin. "I feel like there's more to say."

Michael shook his head. "Enough is enough."

"Just good-bye, then." Flint put out his hand, and after two long seconds, Michael took it.

"Good-bye, Mr. Flint."

Flint released his hand and turned. He stumbled on the bottom step but got himself inside without falling. Michael saw a light go on three windows down, the silhouette of a frail, thin man tipping back

264

a bottle. In another minute, the light went out, and Michael put Flint out of his mind. He walked to the gate and moved his car down the long, broken drive. Then he dug out his phone and called Abigail. "Hi. It's me. No, I'm okay. Any sign of Julian?"

"No."

"How about Elena?"

"Nothing, Michael. I'm sorry."

"It's okay," Michael said, but it was not. Faint, high stars spread out, and the night air was cool. A wisp of cloud crossed the rising moon as he tried to force Elena from his thoughts. He needed to know she was okay. "Listen." He scrubbed at his eyes. "I have a question."

"Anything."

"Does Julian have money?"

"What do you mean?"

"Does he have access to large sums of cash?"

"Oh, Michael." She almost laughed. "Do you have any idea how many books your brother sells?"

"A lot, I guess."

"Millions. Many millions. Why do you ask?"

Michael squeezed his eyes shut. "It's nothing."

"Are you sure?"

"Yes. It's not important."

"Will I see you tomorrow?" Abigail asked.

"I'll leave early."

A silence spread between them, dark and difficult until Abigail broke it. "Listen, be careful when you come back. Okay?"

"Is anything wrong?"

"Just . . . be careful."

"Abigail . . ."

"I'm very tired."

Michael felt it through the phone, a well of worry and fatigue. "Good night, Abigail."

"Good night, Michael."

CHAPTER THIRTY-TWO

Jimmy gave Stevan ten minutes to play mighty ruler and disappear into his room, then he went back inside and stopped in the entry to the living room. The place was disgusting: pizza boxes and cigarettes, clothes worn for days without washing. Jimmy saw bare feet and socks stained black on the bottom. Fingers scratched at hairy skin. A man dug in his ear with a pen cap.

Animals.

"Hey, Jimmy. What's up?"

That was Clint Robins, the only man in the room who was not a total embarrassment. He was lean and quick, an exceptional thinker in a crew of dullards. He was playing solitaire and winning. Jimmy lifted his chin. "Stevan in his room?"

"Yeah."

"How about the girl."

Robins smiled. "She's a honey."

"That was not my question."

"I know, Jimmy. Just messing with you. She's locked down."

"Did you give her dinner?"

"It's like Stevan said." He winked at the man sitting beside him. "We're not animals."

Jimmy frowned, and another man leaned forward. He sat on the sofa. His name was Sean. His had Irish parents, and some of that accent remained. "When are we doing this, Jimmy?" The room stilled, and suddenly everyone was listening. Sean lowered his voice in dramatic fashion, hooking his thumb toward the room Stevan had taken as his own. "Rich-and-perfect won't say."

Several of the men nodded, and it was a sign of dwindling respect that Stevan was mocked so freely. Jimmy took stock of the room. He saw seven men, all frustrated and ripe with scorn. Guns lay scattered about. Handguns, mostly, a few pump-action twelves. Nothing fully automatic. That was good.

"This will be over soon," Jimmy said.

"You sure about that?" Sean asked.

The room remained dead silent, and Jimmy allowed himself a smile. "Ninety-nine percent sure."

"When will you be a hundred?" Robins asked.

"Soon."

"Better be."

Jimmy felt cold steel snap shut behind his eyes. That disrespect had been directed at him. Veiled. Not enough to call the man out for, but it didn't matter. "Five minutes," Jimmy said.

Robins laid his final card.

Elena heard the knob turn, and opened her eyes in time to see Jimmy come inside. It was eerie, the way he moved. Like his joints were oiled. She swung her legs off the bed, and a chain rattled. Jimmy nodded toward the handcuffs that locked one arm to the bed. "Sorry about that," he said. "It's dark out. Can't have you running off." He nudged her plate with his foot. A fast-food burger, congealed and untouched. "Not hungry?"

Elena flicked hair from her face. "What do you want?"

"An answer to a question."

"What question?"

Jimmy tilted his head. "Does Michael love you?"

"What?"

"Not generic love, mind you. The real thing."

"I . . ."

"He implied as much, you see. But I've known him a long time, and I've never seen him love anything but himself and Otto Kaitlin. If he

267

loves you half as much as his own reflection, then maybe I'll trade you for him. That's where my business is, really. With Michael. You can go home. Have a life." He paused. "Have your baby."

Her hand moved involuntarily to her stomach. The man was smiling, but his eyes were too cold for the question to be random. He would use her to hurt Michael. It was the only thing that made sense. "I used to think so," she said. "But no. He doesn't love me like that."

"Are you telling me the truth?"

She pictured the good in Michael, all the things she loved. He would lie for her, kill for her. A day ago, the thought ruined her. "Yes," she said. "That's the truth."

"You're a pretty woman." Jimmy laughed. "But a poor liar."

"We fought. It's over. He doesn't love me."

"A pretty woman." Jimmy turned, and Elena jerked on the cuffs. "Telling poor, pretty lies."

It's not a lie!"

The woman's voice followed him down the hall.

"It's not a lie!"

He heard the bed rattle and scrape, and smiled in the black place behind his eyes. She'd chosen Michael over the baby, and that told him everything he needed to know. They loved each other, which meant that whatever plan Stevan had, Jimmy didn't need it. He stepped back into the living room. "Robins."

Clint Robins looked up. "Jimmy."

"We need to talk."

"Are we at a hundred percent?"

"Ninety-nine point five. Come with me."

Jimmy slipped back into the hall, and felt Robins behind him. He turned deeper into the house and made his way up a flight of steep, narrow stairs to a room with angled ceilings and small, square windows. In the corner of the room, an old desk showed water stains and the scars of hard use. Its surface was littered with yellowed papers and plastic pens that had dried out years ago.

"Pull up a chair."

Jimmy pointed to a chair across the room, then sat at the desk and fiddled with pens while Robins pulled the chair closer. Four pens: three blue ones and a pink one. He lined them up as Robins sat. They were in similar chairs. Carved wooden seats. Ladder backs. The room smelled of mold and dust and mouse shit. Robins said, "What do you want to talk about?"

"Getting to a hundred percent." Jimmy selected the pink pen, and spun it between his fingers. It had no cap, and some kind of grunge on the point. "There's a certain frustration with Stevan, and I understand that. What I want you to tell me is this: If Stevan were gone, would the men follow me?"

"If he was gone . . ."

"Retired. Missing. Dead."

Both men knew only one of those words mattered. "Look, Jimmy—"

"I know the men are scared of me, but would they follow me? Would they trust me?"

"If Stevan . . . retired?"

"Exactly."

Robins shrugged. "Stevan has the money. The companies are in his name. The real estate. The old man is dead, but the Kaitlin name still carries weight on the street."

Jimmy nodded. "That matters, of course."

"And most of the guys are comfortable with him. He may not be his father, but they know where he stands. He's steady."

"And with me, they worry."

"Truthfully?"

Jimmy smiled. "We're friends. You can speak plain."

"You're edgy." Robins showed his palms. "Unpredictable."

"And how about you, Clint? Where would you stand?"

"Look, Jimmy, I don't feel great about this conversation."

"I guess that's your answer, then."

"Kind of."

Jimmy offered a thin smile. "Hey, I asked for the truth and you gave it to me."

"Still friends?" Nervous.

Jimmy held out his hand. "Just keep it between us."

"Of course. Obviously." Robins took his hand—relieved—and was still holding it when Jimmy slammed the pen into his eye socket. He drove it deep, made a bright pink pupil in the ruined eye. The body went limp, one leg twitching as Jimmy lowered him to the floor. Blood was minimal. Little sound. Jimmy wiped his hands on the dead man's shirt. "Now, we're at a hundred percent."

He stepped to the bed and dragged a hard case from underneath. He put it on the bed, opened it. Inside was an array of weapons, none of them indiscriminate. No Uzis. Nothing fully automatic. He selected a nine millimeter and released the clip so bright casings and copper jackets shone. When Michael shot his way out of Otto's house, he'd killed six men with only seven bullets. That story was already on the streets.

Six armed men, seven bullets. A legend in its infancy.

Michael, Michael, Michael . . .

Jimmy thumbed out every bullet in the clip, then reloaded seven and racked one into the chamber. With Robins dead, there were seven men in the house. Seven men, seven bullets. 'Course, he wasn't going to kill Stevan just yet.

But still . . .

Jimmy lifted a second weapon from the foam padding. It was one of his favorites, a twenty-two automatic that was light, accurate and held an awful lot of bullets. He tucked that one against the small of his back.

Vain as he was, he wasn't stupid.

Closing the case, he slipped it back under the bed. In the mirror, he looked ready enough to wink at himself, so that's what he did: a slow wink over a happy grin.

Sixty-seven million dollars.

Finality.

Change.

He went down the stairs on light feet, rounded into the living room without slowing down. Part of him knew it would never meet the challenge Michael had overcome, but most of him didn't care. So the men were half-drunk and not expecting it, so they blinked like cattle when the gun came up in Jimmy's hand. So what? The gun felt light as a feather. Reflexes sharp as a blade, vision perfect.

Two men were standing when Jimmy came into the room. They went down first; both shot center mass and lifted off their feet. Two more were seated, one trying to stand. Jimmy took head shots for all of them, rounds snapping off as he pivoted and dropped to a crouch.

Five down. Where was the sixth?

There.

Kitchen door, gun coming out of his belt.

Jimmy shot him through the mouth before the barrel cleared leather. Then there was silence and smoke in the air, a taste like matches in the back of Jimmy's throat. He checked the room, no movement.

Six bullets. Six dead.

Eight seconds, max.

He had one bullet left, and there was Stevan. He stood in the door, eyes so pink and glassy they did not look real. His hand came up as Jimmy straightened. "You . . ."

"I know. It was something, wasn't it?"

"Something?"

Jimmy shook his head as he stepped wide to clear a patch of bloody carpet. "Yeah. Did you see how fast that was? Michael couldn't do it that fast."

"You killed them."

"Obviously."

They were only feet apart, now, Stevan's shock wearing off. Color spiked in his cheeks as he found his anger. "What the hell, Jimmy?" He stopped and drew up taller. "You're fucking done. I don't even know what to say, you insane bastard, you dumb, stupid shit."

"You still don't get it."

"Get what?"

Jimmy put his last bullet in Stevan's knee.

CHAPTER THIRTY-THREE

There was near-perfect silence in Elena's room, stillness as every muscle strained against the iron bar on the headboard. Her feet pressed the wall, widely spread and white from the pressure. The cuff cut cruelly into her wrist. It bruised bone, tore skin, but she pulled harder, sweat popping on her face, her free hand on the chain, fingers slippery-wet, three nails already broken. The other manacle scraped up the length of the iron bar, peeling white paint as it moved. Elena dug deeper, and it hurt as if the bones in her narrow wrist were burning.

She pulled harder, misery in her back, now, legs shaking as she built a sheltered place in her mind, a tall, square room with soft floors and cotton sheets that touched her skin like feathers. A cool fountain gurgled in the corner. There was music, and Michael waiting beyond a closed door. She tried to feel it, thick stone walls and a breeze on her face. For long moments, the vision held, then the sound of gunshots brought it crashing down.

They were loud and close, concussions she actually felt. She sat up on the bed, handcuffs forgotten.

What was happening?

She had no idea. Everything felt compressed after the noise, the stillness absolute.

Then voices. Another gunshot.

And screaming.

God, the screaming . . .

Elena held herself still, and knew she'd never been so scared. Not when Jimmy took her from her hotel room. Not when he doused her with gasoline. This was so sudden and absolute, a handful of seconds and screaming like she'd never heard, a horrible, animal sound that went on and on and on. She watched the door, knowing that it would open and she would be the next to scream and die. She knew it, felt it as sure as anything.

But it didn't happen.

The screaming faded and she heard a door slam, then the noise was outside. Elena got off the bed and moved for the window.

Cuffs.

Damn!

She gripped the iron frame and pulled the bed across the floor. At the window, she had a view of the yard and the barn on the other side of it. A low moon hung over the trees, and in its light she saw Jimmy dragging a man across the dirt. She couldn't tell who it was, but thought maybe it was Stevan. Jimmy had him by the foot. The barn rose above them, and its shadow obscured them until Jimmy opened the door and light spilled out. Then she saw them clearly: Stevan on the ground, clutching his leg; Jimmy in the open door. He had a baling hook in his right hand. She could see it clearly—dark metal, a vicious point—and remembered them from childhood, from long days on her grandfather's farm.

Stevan had his hands up, now. Voice lower.

Begging.

"Oh, God!"

The words escaped her throat, and she felt her stomach lurch as Jimmy swung the hook in a fast, looping curve that drove the point through the palm of Stevan's hand and jerked the arm tight. For a second, the image froze—arm extended, hook rising from a palm stained black—then Stevan screamed again, feet drumming dirt as Jimmy dragged him into the barn.

For a moment more, light spilled out on the yard, then the door closed and Elena found herself alone in the still, hot air of the silent house. For long seconds, she was paralyzed as the scene flashed again in her mind. She saw the glint of steel, then yellow light and crazy shadows as the taste of fear rose like acid on her tongue and her ribs ached from the hard, sharp stutter in her chest.

"Michael . . ."

His name fell soft from her lips.

"Please . . ."

But Michael couldn't save her. That was real; that was fact. She felt horror and panic, the ache in her arm as she stared around the room and found nothing there. If she was going to escape, she realized, she would have to do it on her own. Not later or tomorrow, but now, while Jimmy was busy. Because she knew one thing with certainty: he'd left her alive for a reason. And whatever that reason might be, it would not be good for her.

So she attacked the bed. She didn't care about noise, pain or saving some last reserve of will. This was about survival, about whatever time she had left. She tore at the metal frame. She ripped off the mattress, then lifted one end of the bed and slammed it down over and over. She drove it against the wall, kicked hard metal and leaned on the cuffs until her arm was slick and torn and red. It lasted for a long time, until she was exhausted, worn and shaking weak. But she never gave up, never cried.

Not until Jimmy came.

It was dawn. His clothes were dripping wet, and even his hair was spiked red. Bits of Stevan spattered his arms, the backs of his hands, but it was the calm that scared her most. He walked through the door as any man might at the end of working day. Breath exhaled in a light puff; small shake of the head. As if to say, *You wouldn't believe the day I had.* Elena pressed into the corner. He stepped into the room, lit a cigarette.

"That man . . ." He took a drag, shook his head and pushed out smoke. "Tougher than I thought."

The lighter snapped shut, and Jimmy shoved his hand into a pocket, kept it there. Elena went totally still, eyes on the cigarette, the stained fingers.

"Still . . ." Jimmy looked pensive, but content. "Lots of time, you know."

"Is he . . ."

Her voice cracked, and Jimmy picked up the thought.

"Is he dead? No."

He was still too calm. Too matter-of-fact. Elena waited for the bad thing that was coming. "Why are you here?"

A shrug. "Thought I'd make coffee."

"Please, let me go."

"Maybe some breakfast."

"What do you want with me?"

She was losing it; she was going to lose it.

Jimmy took a final drag, then pulled his hand from his pocket and dropped a bloody ear on the floor.

"Nothing yet," he said.

And Elena lost it.

CHAPTER THIRTY-FOUR

Abigail rode hard in the cool dawn: same horse she always rode, same muddy track through the low field by the river. The animal was a well-spring of strength and purpose, a touchstone when nothing else made sense—and right now, nothing made sense. Not Julian's collapse and disappearance; not the bodies in the lake or the things Jessup said when he tried to make it right.

"Hah!"

She drove her heels into the horse's flank, and the animal did what it was meant to do. Mud flew, and the reins snapped once in white lather before they found their stride.

It was all coming apart.

Everything.

She reached the end and turned, ran it again as her thoughts burned and the sun rolled close enough to ignite the sky. This was the day, she thought. Another body would surface or Julian would be found and arrested. Michael would find Andrew Flint or learn some terrible thing.

She reached the end of the field and was startled when Victorine Gautreaux stepped out of the trees. Abigail reined hard, horse side-stepping. "Damn, child, you're going to get somebody killed." The girl said nothing. "What are you doing here?"

Victorine rolled lean shoulders. "Looking for you."

"How'd you know I'd be here?"

"You're here often."

"You watch me ride?"

"I like your horse."

Abigail looked from the girl to the far house. They were alone. "What do you want?"

"Julian says there's medicine—"

"What do you know about my son?"

"I know he came to me instead of you."

There it was, the challenge that made Abigail despise Gautreaux women. "Is he okay?"

"He tells me there's medicine to help get his head on right. He says you'd know what it was and that I was to collect it."

Abigail peered down at this ragged child with perfect skin, small breasts and blades for hipbones. She was pretty enough, but pretty only went so far. "Are you sleeping with him?"

"Nobody touches me 'less I say."

"We found condoms."

"I'm not saying we haven't talked about it, neither." She shrugged. "Julian's nice and all, but still . . ."

"Then why do you care?"

"He's helping me."

"With what?"

"With running away."

Abigail could find no argument there. Running away from Caravel Gautreaux made more sense than most things. Her voice softened. "Are you telling me Julian sees some reason beyond the obvious to help you?"

She lifted her chin. "Coming from nothing don't make me nothing."

Abigail studied the girl more closely. She talked tough, and stood straight, but there was fear there, too. The stare didn't hold as long as it could have. "I want my son back," Abigail said.

"And he wants to get his head straight first. He's scared."

"Of what?"

"Will you give me the medicine?"

The horse moved back a step, and Abigail put a hand on its neck. "You're out in these woods a lot."

"I'm not doing nothing. I just like the woods."

"Do you know anything about the bodies they're finding?"

She shook her head, but it looked like a lie.

277

"Don't lie to me," Abigail said.

"I don't want to talk about it."

"Julian says he'll help you, fine. I'll help you, too. Money. A place to live. I'll set you up, little girl. I'll change your life."

Defiance dwindled to shiftiness. "You lie."

"We have a billion dollars and change. Try me."

The stare held between them, and it was Victorine Gautreaux who broke first. "All I know is what Julian told me."

"And what did he tell you?"

"You won't like it."

"Tell me anyway."

"He told me it was you."

"What?"

"He told me it was you who killed them boys."

CHAPTER THIRTY-FIVE

The second time Jimmy came for Elena, he was breathing heavily. She heard the front door slam, then fast, hard steps. When her door opened, it struck the wall and framed him perfectly: shoulders square and locked, jaw so tight muscles showed under the skin. The calm was gone, and in its place Elena saw anger so clear and bright it was unmistakable.

"Stubborn son of a bitch . . ."

Muttering.

"Goddamn selfish . . ."

Then he seemed to remember that he was not alone. His gaze settled on Elena, and he forced a smile. "Ah, still with me. Good."

Elena tensed, and the chain drew tight.

"I'd like you to call Michael," Jimmy said. "I'll give you directions. He can come collect you."

She dragged herself up from the floor. "No."

"No?" Jimmy was too surprised to be angry. He laughed, a small, conflicted sound. Then he got angry. "Is that what you said? No?"

"I'm not going to help you."

"I'm not required to ask, you know." A dangerous glint came into his eyes. "I can put the phone to your bland, female face and I can make you scream. But as I'm tired . . ." He offered a wholly unconvincing smile. "I'd rather not do that."

Elena understood, then, and in spite of her fear, she stood taller. "You want Michael to come, unsuspecting. You want me to set him up."

"That's not——"

"You're frightened."

Her chin came up, and Jimmy grew very still. "Do you believe in free choice?" he asked. "I do. It's an important concept, a right that far too many people take for granted. They follow the herd; do the expected thing. Even Michael is guilty. He plays the good son, the good lover, the good man. It's disgusting because it's not who he is. He's like me. Same thing."

"Michael's nothing like you."

"If he told you different, he's a liar."

"I won't help you."

"Ah, ah. You don't know what the choice is, yet." Jimmy took a small key from his coat pocket. He stepped closer and Elena moved back until her cuffs snapped tight. The bed slid a few inches before Jimmy put a hand on the rail and halted it. "See . . ." He leaned close. "Words are easy." He unlocked the cuff from the bed rail. "Choice is hard."

"What are you doing?"

He yanked on the cuff and pulled her toward the door. "Making you a gift."

Elena stumbled through the house, tripped and went down in a room of dead men. Jimmy jerked her hard, dragged her through bodies that were cold and stiff. She wanted to vomit but never had the chance, for as lean as Jimmy was, he was strong, too, and dragged her fast enough for rocks and dirt to tear skin off her back. Her arm twisted as if it might break, but that hurt was nothing compared to the thoughts that squirmed in her mind. He was taking her to Stevan, to the barn that rose hard-edged and dark against the pale, pink sky. From inside, she heard a sound that touched her in a terrible, intimate way. It was the sound of a shattered man weeping, wet and shameless and utterly broken. That's where Jimmy took her, off the hard dirt and through a two-foot gap in the big doors. She saw high, dusty beams, shadows and weak, yellow light. She saw tools on nails, smelled oil and old straw.

And she saw Stevan.

"This is your choice." Jimmy hauled her up, one hand in her hair, the other on the cuffs. He bent the arm behind her back, forced her up onto her toes and drove her forward. Stevan was naked and spread on his back across the hood of a rusted tractor. Rope led from his wrists to the rear axles of the tractor, where they were twisted tight. Baling hooks had been driven through the meat of his calves and tied down, one to an engine block, the other to a hundred-pound sack of fertilizer. He was stretched tight, his back bent, calves weeping blood. His body was a patchwork of open wounds.

But that was not the worst of it.

Not even close.

Elena turned away, but Jimmy jerked her straight. "No, no, no. Choice must be informed, and you haven't really looked—"

"I have. Oh, God."

"Looked but not seen."

Jimmy moved her closer, and one of Stevan's eyes rolled to follow her. The other eye didn't move, couldn't. The socket was a bloody hole, the eye just gone. A mirror hung above Stevan's face, angled so he could witness the damage with his remaining eye.

"See?" Jimmy flicked a fingernail against the smooth, polished surface. "He can watch himself."

"You're insane."

"No. There's method here."

His hand tightened in her hair and he moved her head, forced her to look the full length of the tortured man. "The eye should have done the trick. But like I told you earlier, he's tougher than I thought."

"Why are you doing this?" Elena was weak, choking.

"Money."

"I don't have it . . ."

The words croaked from Stevan's throat, and Jimmy slapped one of the open wounds hard enough to make Stevan scream.

"I'm not talking to you," Jimmy said.

The screaming went on, but Jimmy ignored it and spoke louder as he forced her to look at Stevan's face. "I decided to take one side at a time. Left eye, left hand. You see?"

Elena nodded. Where the eye had been carved out, so, too, had the ear been removed. Strips of skin had been cut from his face, and four of his fingers had been snipped off, leaving only the thumb. Jimmy saw her looking, and said, "Thumb's up." He put a hand on Stevan's bloody leg, leaned close so the one eye settled on him. "Thumb's up, right?"

He laughed, and Stevan sobbed.

"I'll probably do the eyebrow next," Jimmy said. "Then maybe the scalp. Still on the left side. Do you see the method? The reason?"

"No."

"He's always been a two-faced, spoiled little shit. Now, everyone can see it."

Elena tore her eyes away; she looked down at straw on the floor, then at the collection of sharpened tools. She saw chisels and wire brushes and shears and pliers. Sharp blades, serrated blades. Terrible tools, and bloody. They rested on a small, rickety table. Neatly ordered, largest to smallest. "Why are you doing this?"

"Otto Kaitlin died with sixty-seven million dollars in offshore accounts. I thought pretty-boy here could help me get it. I'm starting to think I was wrong." Jimmy let go of Elena's hair and lifted a chisel. Its edge gleamed silver, and he studied it. "See, Stevan claims he could never find the account numbers and passwords. We all assumed Otto gave them up before he died, but Stevan says that's not true."

Moving calmly and without apparent thought, Jimmy pinched an area of skin on Stevan's left side and slipped the sharpened chisel between skin and rib. It went in smooth and matter-of-fact, and Jimmy left it there, handle-out, even as the screaming ramped up. Jimmy gave him a second, then said, "Stevan thinks Michael has the numbers."

"Michael doesn't have sixty-seven million dollars."

"I don't know." Jimmy wiggled the handle until a sucking noise escaped. "The old man loved him. I can see it happening that way. Which brings us back to the matter of choice."

Elena understood. "You need Michael alive."

"I knew there was a reason he liked you." Jimmy lifted another chisel, this one smaller. He bent over Stevan, pinching one area of skin then another as Stevan begged and his one eye rolled. "Killing Michael would be easy. Taking him alive . . ." He slipped the chisel in. "That's another story."

Stevan began to convulse.

Jimmy looked at Elena, who stood unmoving. "I want you to bring Michael here. A simple phone call, and then I let you go."

She shook her head, so grimly fascinated by Stevan on the tractor she could not look away. Her gaze settled on the largest chisel. Blood welled from the pale mouth it made. The handle was molded rubber, blue like the sky.

"You can help me. You can make this easy. Or we can make room here in the barn. You're a woman, and weak." He waved a hand at Stevan. "Most of this will be unnecessary, but still . . ."

He reached for another tool on the table. His eyes dropped for one second, and Elena yanked the chisel from Stevan's chest.

Jimmy turned back.

And she stabbed him with it.

CHAPTER THIRTY-SIX

The front room of Flint's house was pitch dark and silent, yet Michael tossed and turned, unable to sleep. He stared up for long hours, worrying first for Elena, then agonizing over Julian. Had Abigail found him? Was he alone and frightened, or still lost somewhere in the dark halls of his schizophrenia? It killed Michael that the people most important to him were not only gone, but beyond his reach. He wanted to find them, gather them up; several times he rose to leave. But Iron House waited beyond the glass, and questions still demanded answers. Somebody was tracking down boys from his childhood, somebody with money and a grudge, with the means to lure them east, kill them and sink them in the senator's lake. Ronnie Saints was dead, as was George Nichols. Billy Walker was accounted for, but Chase Johnson was missing. Where was he, and how did he fit? Why were they back in Julian's life at all?

Michael shifted on the rough couch. He pictured them as the boys he'd known, then saw them older and stronger, still as predatory. What would they want from his brother? Money? Payback? Something else? Possibilities raced through Michael's head, so that when sleep finally took him down they were waiting in his dreams, tall slat-eyed men that chased a figure down long halls under high ceilings. They moved like wolves, fast and sure, then laughed cruelly as they dragged Julian down and went to work with metal pipes and steel shank boots. Michael tried to stop them, but his feet were nailed to the floor; he opened his mouth, but it was full of sand. They laughed in chorus as Julian begged; then Julian was Elena, pregnant and curled on the same brittle floor. Her belly was swollen, one hand out as she met Michael's eyes, then screamed his name as they kicked her bloody.

Michael bolted up in darkness, the pistol grip rough and warm as he swept the empty room. It was unfamiliar, hot; sweat stung his eyes as he choked on Elena's name. He checked the corners, the empty doors, then remembered where he was. The gun came down. He leaned back on the sofa, and palmed sweat from his face. This was Iron Mountain, Flint's house. The cushions were damp with sweat and deep beneath him. It was a dream.

"Damn."

The gun clattered against a bottle when he put it back on the table. Michael rolled his back, ran his hands through his hair and then checked his phone. Nothing. He dialed Elena and got voice mail. "Where are you, baby? I really need you. Call me."

He hung up reluctantly, then stood. The house was airless and overly warm, the dream still thick enough to linger. He got off the sofa, did some quick push-ups to clear his head and then pulled on his shoes. His body felt loose and ready, his mind sharp as he checked the yard and the drive. He felt an urgency to move, yet at dawn stood on the broad, flat steps of Iron House where he watched the sun rise like a red crown burning. It inched high enough to make shoulders of the mountains, and in that instant, eyes narrowed against the light, Michael realized that Elena was right to be angry. He should have never touched that body. He should have taken her hand, led her from the boathouse and never looked back.

Yet, what choice did he have? He and Julian were brothers, forged in the same cold winters of this place. But she was family, too, the mother of his child, the woman he loved. And wasn't it right that she know the truth about him? That she, too, be allowed a choice? Damn, he could go crazy thinking about this; but there, on the steps of Iron House, what he really felt was his own flush of anger. Michael had never begrudged his life, never complained about the hand God dealt him. He did the job and moved on, but that was no longer good enough. He wanted more. He wanted Elena home and his brother whole. He wanted payment for injustice done, wanted his childhood back, and Julian's, too, wanted to lash out, but would not. Flint would live, and

Billy Walker, too. That was Michael's decision, a bittersweet choice. But it was right that a red sun rose, that he should see the color of blood, and remember the things that made him.

He took a last look at the yard, the mountain and the climbing sun, then opened the door, stepped inside and was home. The ceiling soared above a broken floor, and he saw wooden furniture sheeted in dust, jigsaw puzzles of broken glass. His skin tingled, and he told himself again:

Just a place.

A long hall took him to a switchback staircase that led to the third floor. Light was brighter there, wire mesh in the windows lighting up like the edge of a razor. The room he'd shared with Julian was at the far corner. He pushed the door with two fingers and stepped into a space that seemed smaller than it should have been. The bunk bed was still there: one on top, Julian's on the bottom. His finger left a line in the dust on the side of the bed, then he stood at the window and looked at the face of Iron Mountain, weathered and cracked and unchanged. He searched for emotion, but found his anger gone. Inside, he was a stone, and thought that maybe he'd buried this, after all.

But that felt like a lie. His hollowness was too hollow, the echo too persistent. He took a deep breath and sat on the edge of Julian's bed. It felt the same, a thin mattress with rough ticking. Even the pillow remained, and when he lifted it he saw words scratched into the wood behind it.

Make me like Michael
Make me strong

Michael stood abruptly. This was not just a place. It was the hard, jagged mouth of the world that vomited them out. Julian ruined, and Michael . . .

What?

He knew the face of every man he'd ever killed, not as they'd been when dead, but in the last moment of life, their features twisted in fear or disbelief or anger, and he knew a few like Otto Kaitlin, tired men ready to die. They ordered themselves in his mind, a line of faces stretching back, yet he felt no guilt or doubt. Was he so certain of his rightness? Or had this place scored a crease in the rough, dark diamond of his soul? He knew only a few things to be absolute truth. He loved Elena and their unborn child. He loved Julian. It seemed a small collection, but felt like the world, like the kind of gift he would kill to protect. Maybe that's what Iron House had given him, that clarity. Maybe that was its purpose.

He walked down the stairs and decided that it was.

But there was no peace in him for having come back to this place, no warmth or understanding. Yet, *acceptance* might be a decent word. The building was in ruins. Flint was a drunk and a gambler, Billy reduced to innocence. None of this was a good thing of itself, but it reinforced what Michael had believed since childhood, that life is hard, and it pays to be strong. But as he got in his car and left that place, as the gate came up ahead, he wondered for the first time what his life might have been had he let Julian take the fall for Hennessey's death. What kind of man would Michael have become had he been the one to go home with Abigail Vane?

Probably the same, he decided. *But with less killing.*

He followed a strip of road back into town, and stopped at the first gas station he found. It was small, with two weathered pumps under a plastic shelter that made the same V shape as a bird in flight. The day was fresh on him and there were decisions to make. Elena was still beyond his reach, but Julian was not. He could return to Chatham County and help Abigail look for him, or he could try to figure out what was going on.

He pulled the Mercedes next to a pump, got out of the car and thought about names as he filled the tank. Where was Chase Johnson? Who was Salina Slaughter, and why was Abigail Vane's name on the list?

There had to be a connection.

The pump clicked off as the tank filled. Michael replaced the gas cap and concentrated on Chase Johnson. He and Ronnie were still friends; they spoke from time to time. Maybe Chase was dead in the lake. Maybe he was in hiding, and knew what was going on. Whatever the case, Ronnie's girlfriend said he lived in Charlotte, and Charlotte was not far away.

Michael debated as he walked inside to pay, wondering if it would be possible to track Chase down. He could go back to Ronnie's house, squeeze the girlfriend a little bit. She had to know something more.

The door dragged as he opened it, the sound like shoes on pavement. He noticed little things as he entered, a doll-shaped woman buying candy, a curve of mirror high in the corner. A weathered man stood behind the register, and nodded as Michael walked up to pay for the gas. "Morning."

Michael took in the stained, creased cap, the worn shirt and the hearing aid in the man's right ear. "Good morning."

"Pump number four." He lifted black-rimmed glasses, squinted at something behind the counter. "Thirty-seven dollars."

Michael put two twenties on the glass, saw postcards slipped beneath it. Grand Canyon. San Diego. The Flatiron building in New York City. That one made him smile.

"Here you go, son. Three dollars."

Michael took the change and came to a decision. "Do you sell maps?"

"Of?"

"Charlotte. The state in general."

"Right there behind you." He pointed past a shelf of oilcans and antifreeze to a wire rack feathered with neatly folded maps. "North Carolina's near the top, Tennessee and Georgia and a few others down by the bottom."

"Thanks." Michael walked over, noticing as he did a topographical map pinned to the wall above the rack. It was large and pale green, with wavy lines that showed folds in the earth.

Michael stopped two feet away, an odd tug in his chest when he saw how small Iron Mountain looked in the middle of all that green. The map covered the very western part of North Carolina, bits of Tennessee and Georgia. Mountain country with small towns and narrow valleys, lakes and rivers and large tracts of national forest. Iron Mountain showed an elevation of 5,165 feet, the town at its base a small splotch of yellow. He found the river, which in his mind was broad and black. It fed the valley from the north, and Michael saw how it stretched and branched, how smaller streams fed it as it bent west, toward Tennessee. He put his finger on it, traced it to the state line, where it ran along the base of another mountain. There was small writing there, and Michael stared, a kinetic charge building. He did not believe in coincidence.

Not big ones like this.

The mountain had a name, Slaughter Mountain, and it was thirty miles from Iron House.

Iron Mountain.

Slaughter Mountain.

Heat gathered in Michael's skin.

Slaughter Mountain.

Salina Slaughter.

It had to mean something, but what? He heard the door scrape and glanced in time to see the petite woman leave with a bag of candy. There were no other customers. The old man came around the counter, feet shuffling. "What are you looking at so fixedly?"

"Fixedly?"

He smelled of cut grass and tobacco. "You're staring holes in my wall."

"Do you know anything about Slaughter Mountain?"

He shrugged. "Hill people."

"Meaning?"

He pulled out a pipe and started packing it. "Meaning they sleep with their mommas and eat their dead." He lit the pipe, sucked hard and blew a sweet cloud. "'Course, the Slaughters were a thing back in the day. Timber. Coal. Gold, maybe. There was a grand old lady back when I was a young man. I think she's dead, now. That seems right."

"Does the name Salina Slaughter mean anything to you?"

"Can't say it does."

Michael deflated, but the man continued, unaware.

"I think her name was Serena."

That got his attention. "Serena Slaughter?"

"Money. Politicians. Parties. Word is they raped that mountain bare."

"You have a map of that area?" Michael asked. "It looks pretty isolated."

"You going up there?"

"Maybe."

"I'd carry a gun," he said, and slapped a map on Michael's palm.

CHAPTER THIRTY-SEVEN

Elena made no sound when the chisel sank into Jimmy. It struck him as he turned, missed his chest and sliced into the soft place beneath his left arm. She felt metal scrape bone, and stumbled back as Jimmy howled and snatched at her clothing. His fingers missed by inches. Elena pivoted and brought up her arm so that the loose cuff snapped out and cracked against the bridge of Jimmy's nose. He screamed louder, bent convulsively as blood jetted and his fingers settled on the sky blue handle that jutted out of his side.

Elena didn't wait around. She bolted through the door, into damp grass and the cool air of a brand-new day. She felt that air on her cheeks, very cold, and knew that she was crying, that strange sounds filled her ears and that they were coming from her. She looked at the cars, and doubted they would lead to an easy escape. Keys were on surfaces in the house, in the pockets of dead men, and she had no time for that. Jimmy was hurt, but not dead. She looked at the woods, which were deep and dark, then remembered the guns she'd seen scattered in the house, some on tables, other spilled from loose hands. Instinct screamed for the woods, for shadows and cover, a million places to hide.

For an instant she was torn, then ran for the house, the guns, and got one foot on the steps when she heard Jimmy scream as a shot crashed out. She looked back. He'd fallen to one knee, but was coming up.

The gun, too, was coming up.

"Ahhh . . ."

He yelled, and lurched as a second shot snapped out and struck the house. Blood was in his eyes, the skin split between them. He smeared a sleeve across his face, and Elena doubted he would miss a third time. She leapt off the stairs and sprinted for the forest. It was all she had, woods and dark and hope.

Ninety seconds in, she knew she was in trouble. Leaves layered the forest floor, but the ground beneath was stony hard. At a dead run, she kicked an unseen rock, and felt toes break.

She went down, hurt.

And Jimmy was coming.

She saw him at the wood's edge, smooth and fast and whisper-quiet. He moved as if all his rage was channeled to that single purpose. He ducked limbs and slipped between trunks as if he'd been born in the woods. He flowed, face streaked red, and called out when he saw her.

"Right side first, I think."

Elena dragged herself up, ran on broken toes. The pain was exquisite, but fear made a fist around her heart, its fingernails long and black and chisel-sharp.

Please, God . . .

She found a gulley and tumbled in; splashed through puddles as roots touched her face, and damp air clogged her throat. She staggered as muddy walls rose up. For long, sweet seconds she thought she'd lost him, but the walls dropped off after fifty yards. Jimmy ran parallel, and his face was a hunter's face.

"Little girl . . ."

He was mocking her. She turned away, ran faster as the world blackened at its edges. There was only the run and the breath in her lungs. Trees pressed in, branches like hooks. She stumbled and rolled, popped back up. Ran. A ditch appeared; she leapt it.

And that was all it took.

She landed in a hole obscured by rotting leaves, and her ankle broke with the sound of cracking plastic. Pitching forward, she went down for keeps, crippled, hurt and frozen to her core. The leaves smelled of decay, and she curled in the desperate hope that she might sink into them and disappear. It didn't happen. Metal scraped, and a whiff of bitter smoke filled her nose.

"That's a shame."

The voice was behind her and god-awful, terribly close. She saw a stream of thin, blue smoke that gathered as it slowed. She turned her head. Jimmy stood just a few feet away, one hand on his bloody side, the other holding a cigarette between two fingers locked straight. Red smears made a mask around his eyes, but he carried it like war paint, and the effect was terrifying, the blood and calm, the velvet jacket and cigarette smoke.

Elena looked down, and saw the twisted mess of her ankle. The skin was white where bone pushed against it; everywhere else it was dark and starting to swell. She rolled onto her back, and it twisted as she moved.

Screams and tears.

A handful of hard, black seconds.

When her vision cleared, Jimmy was squatting by her side. "Let me help you."

"Don't touch it . . ."

He pinned her leg with his knee.

"No. Don't. Please . . ."

The foot had twisted sideways. He held her down and pulled it straight. When her senses returned, pain led the way, then memory. Jimmy sat cross-legged in the dirt, her injured leg in his lap, toes pointing the way they should. She saw bluish whiskers on his face, the ruin of her ankle.

And she saw her cell phone.

"We're going to call Michael now."

Sunlight licked his eyes and made them look like glass. He laid a hand on the curve of her knee, and looked down his nose, mouth slightly open as he dialed. "I hope we get reception . . ."

Talking to himself. Holding the phone higher.

"I won't set him up for you."

She had to force the words; thought she was in shock.

"You don't have to say anything you don't want to. Ah. There we go." Elena heard a faint trill from the phone. Jimmy pushed it against her face.

"I won't do it."

"Shhh. It's okay. Just say hello."

"Oh, God. Just—"

"There he is," Jimmy whispered.

Elena heard it, too.

His voice, so clear and close she almost broke.

"Michael . . ." The phone was hard against her ear, the forest very still. "Michael, listen . . ."

Jimmy grabbed her foot, twisted.

And Elena screamed a forever scream.

CHAPTER THIRTY-EIGHT

Michael hit the parking lot at a fast walk. He'd been around long enough to know the feel of things coming together. Pieces were shifting in his mind, working for the fit. He didn't have the picture yet, but believed now that it would come. He had this thing about Slaughter Mountain.

Call it a conviction.

He unlocked the Mercedes, fired it up and blew out of the parking lot, map open on the seat beside him.

Slaughter Mountain. Salina Slaughter.

The words tumbled over each other in his head. There was history at Slaughter Mountain, money, politicians, connective tissue. If Michael was to save Julian, he needed to know more about the makeup of that tissue. Was it linked to Iron House? The boys from Iron House? Could it be connected to the senator? Michael heard the old man from the gas station.

Money. Politicians. Parties.

He reached the edge of town.

Word is they raped that mountain bare.

Michael wondered at the origin of Randall Vane's money. Could that be the connection? He was chewing on that question when the phone went off in his pocket. He dug it out, looked at the screen and then cut the wheel right, tamping hard on the brakes as the car hammered rough pavement and slewed to a stop on the edge of the road. The world was empty around him; hope a warm glow as the weight of her absence lifted.

"Elena?"

"Michael . . ."

"Thank God, baby—"

"Michael, listen . . ."

Something was off in her voice, something bad. He looked down the long snake of twisted road, and Elena started screaming.

"Elena!"

He pushed the phone against his ear.

"Elena!"

The screaming went on for a long time. He bore it because he had no choice, and because he knew how the game would play. Jimmy wanted something. Or Stevan. They wanted him dead, and this was their play, so Michael gripped the phone and died inside as Elena's voice rose and broke and finally failed. He listened to the sobs, so pale with rage and hurt that when Jimmy came on the line, Michael looked as if God himself had turned him to stone.

"I suppose you know what I want?"

"Your life?" Michael said it coldly. "You can't have it."

Jimmy laughed, but said, "No, no. Too late for humor."

"You shouldn't have done that, Jimmy. You shouldn't have made this personal."

"Oh, Michael. Still acting as if the old man were alive to cover your ass."

"You know how this will end."

"Of course, I do. That's why I called you. It's why I've been entertaining your friend."

"I want to talk to her."

"And you will. Right after you bring me sixty-seven million dollars."

There it was. Michael was not surprised. Rumors of the old man's money ran long and deep. "Let me talk to Stevan." Jimmy laughed, and Michael understood. "Stevan is dead."

Elena screamed again, louder, longer. When it was over, Jimmy said, "This is not a discussion. I want the numbers. Either you have them or you don't."

"I have them. Don't do that again."

"Where are you?"

Michael looked at the empty street, the high pink stone of a distant mountain. "Five hours away."

Elena screamed.

"I'm in the mountains! I swear it! Five hours. I swear, Jimmy. I can be there in five hours. I have what you want. A few hours. Don't hurt her again. Please."

"You really love her, don't you?"

"I'm begging you."

Jimmy was silent for a moment. Michael squeezed the phone until his hand ached. Finally, Jimmy said, "I'll give you four. Call when you hit town. I'll tell you how to find me."

"Four hours is not enough time—"

"Four hours, and don't be late. This phone's running low on juice."

"I'd like to talk to her."

"Sixty-seven million, Michael."

"Jimmy . . ."

"You'd better have it."

CHAPTER THIRTY-NINE

Abigail took coffee on the rear terrace. An awning shaded her from the low sun, but light glinted off the lake. She was clean, dressed in attire she deemed appropriately somber. Cops had been on the lake since dawn, and as far as she knew, another body could come up any minute. That's how uncertain life had become, how tenuous the bonds of normalcy.

She sipped as she watched, said nothing as the senator dropped into a seat beside her. "If they find another one," he said, disgusted, "I'll kill someone myself."

She looked at the boat and saw thin, black lines come in over the side. Water trailed from metal hooks, and as they flew out again, someone in the boat turned her way, looked up the hill and shaded his eyes. It was Jacobsen, she thought. He had that stiff, officious air.

Vane poured coffee. "Three bodies and the whole damn world watching. There'll be subpoenas soon, warrants for the house. They'll want Julian in custody, I suspect. Interrogation, at the very least. It's a goddamn disaster."

He added cream, and she said, "I won't let you take Michael down."

"What?"

Her skin was washed of color, her eyes clear even though she'd been up all night, thinking. "You'll drag him down for no good reason. You'll ruin him for your own cause."

"That's absurd."

"I know how you work, Randall. I've seen you do it before."

He smiled, but convinced no one. "It would be nothing sinister,

297

Abigail, just public relations, just politics. Smoke and mirrors. It wouldn't stick."

"I won't let you do it."

"You couldn't stop me if your life depended on it."

"Is that some kind of threat?"

"Of course not."

"Well, keep those offensive comments to yourself, Randall. I know how the world works."

He frowned, changed the subject. "You were seen with Victorine Gautreaux this morning. You brought her to the house."

"I gave her Julian's medicine."

"Why?"

Abigail watched boats move for the shore. "Because he's delusional. Because he needs it."

"I mean, why did you let her go? Do you even know where Julian is?"

"In the woods, I suspect."

"He needs to be controlled."

"Until his head is clear, I'd prefer him anywhere but here. He's hallucinating."

"But you hate that family."

"I hate Caravel. There's a difference. The daughter surprised me."

"Meaning?"

"I was impressed."

"How could the white trash daughter of a white trash whore possibly impress you? What could she have possibly said?"

"She wants a better life. Julian is helping her."

"I bet he is."

"Must you be so juvenile? She's an artist. Carves bone, apparently. Something her grandmother taught her. She must be exceptional at it."

"Because Julian wants to bang her?"

"Because for all Julian's faults," Abigail finally raised her voice, "he is a man of exquisite taste. If he says she has talent, she does. He sent her work to New York. He got her a showing at one of the finer galleries. His publisher wants to do a book."

"About bones?"

"About a disappearing art form. About an illiterate child who does this exceptional thing."

"Artists. Writers. Jesus. How did my life come to this?" The senator stood. "If you need me, I'll be with the lawyers. They're bloodsuckers, but at least I understand them."

He got halfway to the door before Abigail stopped him. "What I said about Michael . . ." She waited for him to look back. "I meant it. If you try to hurt him, I'll take it personally."

The senator smiled thinly. "You would choose him over me?"

"Don't force the choice."

"Sometimes, Abigail, it's you who I don't understand."

"Perhaps it's best that way."

"And perhaps not."

The senator left; she finished her coffee.

Two hours later, they came for Julian.

Michael heard about it on the radio. He was doing 110 on the interstate, eyes wide for state troopers, weapon cocked on the seat beside him. He'd never killed a cop or a civilian, but knew Jimmy well enough to know that four hours meant four hours.

The needle touched 120.

He checked the rearview mirror again, turned up the radio.

". . . sources close to the investigation indicate an arrest warrant has been issued for Julian Vane, the internationally best-selling children's author and adopted son of Senator Randall Vane. Authorities have converged on the sprawling estate . . ."

They had few details, but the story was sensational. Celebrity. Politics. Multiple bodies. When it was over, he called Abigail. "How's Julian?"

"Michael? Where are you?"

He heard voices in the background, a low, vital hum. "Is he arrested?"

"No, but they're looking for him, and its only a matter of time. He can't hide forever, and if he runs, God alone knows what'll happen. I'm coming apart, Michael. Randall says the warrant is trumped up, but it won't matter. If they arrest him, they'll break him. You said it yourself. He can't handle it."

"I'm on the road—"

"Don't come here!"

Michael hesitated as hairs stood up on his arm. "What's wrong?"

"Just . . . don't."

Michael thought for long seconds. "I need my gun," he finally said.

"What?"

He pictured Elena, broken in some dark hole; Jimmy with an unknown number of men, and a full day to prepare. Michael had the forty-five, and that was it. "The nine millimeter you took from my car. I need it. I don't have time to find another one."

"What's going on, Michael? Please don't tell me you're in trouble, too."

"Can you get it?"

"Yes, of course. But—"

"Where can we meet?"

Abigail descended shallow, mossy steps and knocked on Jessup's door. She knocked again, then opened the door and stepped into the low, spare room. Dim light filtered through covered windows. A teakettle whistled on a small stove in the kitchen alcove. "Jessup?" She lifted the kettle from the heat. It was light, most of the water boiled away. The whistle died, and she turned off the stove. "Jessup?"

The bedroom door stood ajar. Inside, she saw Jessup. He wore a crisp, white shirt, buttoned at the cuffs, black pants, a black tie and shoes that had been recently shined. He sat on the edge of a narrow bed that was tightly made. His back was rigid and straight, head bent so that his neck creased at the collar.

"Do you remember when you gave this to me?"

He kept his head down, but lifted a hand so she could see the small cross that swung from a platinum chain. She'd given it to him for Christmas on their fifth year together. They'd become very close, and he'd told her one cold night that he believed in hell. Not the vague concept of it, but the physical place: a lake of fire and remembrance. There'd been weight on his shoulders when he said it, tears in his eyes and sweet, dark whiskey on his breath. He was one of the strongest men she knew, and he was breaking. She'd always imagined some terrible thing that haunted him: the barbarism of war, a breach of faith or some poor woman broken to the marrow. But he would never talk about it.

"I remember."

She stepped closer, rounding the end of the bed. His eyes were sunken, cheeks drawn. The nine millimeter lay on the bed beside his leg.

He let the cross swing. "Did you know then that we would spend our lives together?"

"How could I have known such a thing? I was barely into my twenties."

She stared at the gun. Jessup shook his head. "Yet, here we are, twenty years later."

"And you have been the most perfect friend."

He laughed, but the laugh was broken.

Abigail hesitated. "Is that Michael's gun?"

His hand moved unerringly to the gun, and Abigail was reminded that Jessup Falls was a dangerous man. That was the reason her husband hired him. Ex-special forces. Ex-cop. Her driver and bodyguard.

"Yes."

His voice remained empty, and Abigail thought of screaming kettles and boiled-off water. She wondered how long he'd been sitting in the dark, a cross in his hands and a gun by his side. For that instant, Abigail felt as if she knew nothing of this man at all, but when he looked up, his gaze was familiar and fresh and raw. "I thought for a long time that you loved me . . ."

"Jessup, we've discussed this."

"You're married, I know." He smiled, and was suddenly the same old Jessup. "It's just that I'm torn." He met her eyes, then lifted the gun. "Do I do what you want me to do? Or do I do what's right?" He put the gun down. "What I *know* is right."

"You're speaking of Michael."

"He's dangerous."

Abigail saw it, then. She understood what he wanted to do, and why he was so torn. "You want to give the gun to the senator."

"To his people," Jessup said. "The gun. The photographs. Everything we know about him and Otto Kaitlin."

"You can't do that."

"His arrest would take the pressure off everybody. The cops would have a warm body and the media would have its story. A year from now, this would all be a fading memory. Our lives would go on."

"And what of the truth?"

"No one wants that."

"Maybe I do."

"Then call it a sacrifice for the greater good."

Abigail sat beside him, the gun between them. "Such a sacrifice would be my decision."

"And yet, you don't always make the right choice."

She put her hand on the gun; his hand settled on hers.

"You are a good and decent man, Jessup, but you've never told me no, and this is not the time to start."

His hand tightened. "They've pulled three bodies from the lake, Abigail. How long before they link them to you?"

She smiled, but it was tired. "I didn't kill anyone, Jessup."

"But you brought them here. You tracked them down; you paid them. The cops will figure that out."

"What I did, I did for Julian. No one here had ill intent."

He shook his head. "There will be witnesses somewhere. A paper trail. A girlfriend. Someone at the law firm you hired. Something will lead the cops here, to you."

"I didn't kill those men, and neither did Julian. That's all that matters."

"You should let me do this, Abigail."

"I can't."

"Why not?"

"Because Michael matters."

"I don't understand."

"And I don't expect you to." He peered down, his deep eyes filled with strong emotion. She stared back until he lifted his hand. Then she kissed his cheek and stood with the gun. "It's been a good twenty-five years, Jessup."

"It's been grand."

"As for what might have been . . ."

He swallowed hard, and let two fingers brush her leg. "In another life," he said.

She pressed a palm to his face, felt her own eyes soften.

"In another life."

Michael met Abigail at eleven o'clock in a drugstore parking lot on the far edge of town. The building was tired, with a flat roof and lime-white streaks that ran from the mortar. An empty lot stretched away to the left, and another ran out behind the building, both of them overgrown and littered. Traffic was sparse. Michael approved of the choice. Few people around. Good sight lines. Easy to find.

He parked in back.

Abigail came in the beat-up Land Rover. Damp mud coated the wheels and splattered paint as high as the mirrors. She swung out, dressed in high boots and crisp khaki pants. A green vest hung over a white shirt that clung damply. She saw him looking at the truck. "Reporters," she said.

He understood. The rear of the estate was un-walled, protected only by three thousand acres of woods. She'd gone off-road to slip out unseen. He looked at his watch. "Thank you for doing this."

"Tell me what's happening." Michael hesitated, and she spoke bluntly. "You want a gun. I brought it. Now, tell me why."

They stood at the rear of the Land Rover. Her gaze was unflinching and he was out of time, so he told her about the phone call, the screams, the threat and the white-knuckle drive he'd just made.

"Are you sure it was Elena?"

She'd accepted every word he'd said. No hand wringing. No judgment. Her head was tilted up, jaw set.

"I'm sure, yes."

"And this Jimmy person will do what he says? He'll kill her?"

"Without hesitation."

"And kill you, too, when he gets the account numbers."

Michael shrugged. "He'll try, yes."

"Who's more dangerous?"

"I am." No hesitation.

"But he has Elena." Michael nodded. "And you don't know if he has other men with him. Other guns. Going in there alone is not very smart."

"I have no choice."

"Do you really have sixty-seven million dollars?"

"More like eighty." Michael opened the trunk and pulled the Hemingway from his duffel bag. He ran his hand over the cover, smiled. "This was Otto's favorite book. He'd read it so many times he could quote entire passages. Toward the end, when he was failing, I would read it to him. It was a thing we shared, a love of the classics." Michael opened the book and showed her the inscription.

> *For Michael, who is more like me than any other . . .*
> *For Michael, who is my son . . .*
> *Think well of an old man . . .*
> *Make a good life . . .*

The writing was spidery and thin, a dying man's scrawl. "He wrote that eight days before he died. It was the day I told him I wanted out of the life."

"I don't understand."

Michael opened the book to the middle and riffled the pages. Numbers blurred past. Pages and pages in the same loose hand. "Twenty-nine different offshore accounts. Different countries. Different banks. He never wrote the numbers down; kept them all in his head. Then he did this. For me."

"A generous man."

"I loved him."

Michael closed the book, touched it to his forehead, then put it in the car. Abigail went silent for a long minute. "He'll kill you, Michael. You know that. He'll kill the girl. He'll kill you."

An ironic smile touched Michael's lips. "It's not in my nature to call the police."

"Perhaps my husband's men. They're professional, highly trained." She thought about it, then said, "It's not an option. They're looking for a scapegoat and you're tops on the list."

Michael saw it. "They'll implicate me to protect Julian."

"Julian. Me. The senator."

"It's a good plan. You should let them do it."

"That's not how I am."

Michael held out his hand, asking for the gun. "I need to do this, now. It's not far. They're waiting."

"I could go with you."

Michael lowered his hand. "To what end?"

"To buy your life as well."

"I don't understand."

"I'll offer him another ten."

"Ten million dollars?"

"Or twenty. It doesn't matter."

"Why?"

"Because you're Julian's brother."

"That's not good enough."

She shrugged, unmoved. "Because I chose a long time ago the person I wished to be. Because ten million dollars is pocket change."

"And that's it? That's the only reason?"

"What else could there be?"

Michael stared down at her for long seconds. His face was naked, as rare emotion stirred; but, for once, he didn't fight it. He let it move him, let it show. "Do you know what fantasy all orphans share? Strong, weak, young, old. Do you know the thing they have in common?"

Abigail's head moved, but she kept her jaw clenched tight. Cicadas called from the scrub, and sweat rolled on her cheek as the bright sun beat down.

"Why did you come for us?" Michael asked.

"I wanted children, but couldn't bear them. The senator and I agreed—"

"Why Julian? Why me?"

"I don't understand."

"We were too old to be cute, or easy, too long in the system to be anything but damaged goods. So, why did you want us?"

"I had my reasons."

"Personal reasons?" A touch of anger showed on Michael's face.

"Yes."

"And now? You don't need this. You barely know me."

Abigail tried to stand tall, but a weight was pushing down. She looked at the scrub, the high blue sky. "I chose a long time ago the person I wished to be."

"And what person is that?"

"The kind that's brave enough to do the right thing. Always. No matter what."

A thing remained unspoken, something large. He saw it in the line of her jaw, the way she drew her shoulders back. It was a big decision she'd made, and a hard life to live. Something caused her to make that choice, and Michael thought he knew what it was. "Are you my mother?"

Abigail's mouth opened, eyes wide and green above it.

"That's the fantasy," Michael went on doggedly. "That your mother will come back for you. It's what we all dreamed, day and night: that it was a giant mistake, that we'd been misplaced, and the error might be fixed. The math works. I'm thirty-three, you're not yet fifty. You'd have been young, but kids make mistakes. No one would blame you for walking away. I wouldn't. I would understand."

Abigail felt momentarily overwhelmed. She looked up at this tall, strong man, this rawboned killer with his beautiful face and his wide, naked eyes. She felt so many things, but first among them was the disappointment she was about to deliver. "No, Michael." She touched his arm. "I'm not your mother." He looked away, nodded. "But I am Julian's."

He nodded again, blinked twice, and the emotion was gone. "You should stay here," he said.

"Everybody has a price, Michael. Jimmy will have one, too."

"How can you know that?"

"I'm a senator's wife."

She was right about Jimmy. He would do anything for that kind of money: kill his own mother, put personal vendettas aside. He would take the money and come back for Michael later. No question. No doubt. "Do you propose to write him a check?"

Her mouth tilted. "Do you still have that bag of cash?"

"Yes."

"All we have to do is give him a taste." She let the words sink in. "Human nature will do the rest."

"I can't guarantee your safety. You understand? This man is not like other men. There's no balance in him, no limits."

"If you don't take me, Elena will die and so will you. It's a setup, Michael. It's why he called you in the first place."

"Then I'll take the cash. I'll arrange it."

"The cash is just the start. We'll need to settle on the price, then it'll take a wire transfer that only I can authorize. I have to be there. It's not optional."

Michael looked away, torn. "It's not your fight."

"I lost you once."

He shook his head. "I was a child. You were there for a reason."

"I'm a big girl, Michael. I want to do this."

He studied her face, which had become very familiar. "Someone is liable to die," he said.

"Then let's make damn sure it's Jimmy."

CHAPTER FORTY

Abigail's false confidence melted off as she turned for the Land Rover. She felt disconnected, the sky too blue, the metal too hot when she put her fingers on the truck. She swallowed away a bitter taste, and realized she was afraid—not a little bit, not in theory, but truly frightened. She drove the feeling down, disgusted with herself, then slipped inside to retrieve Michael's nine millimeter from under the seat. It was heavy and warm, the metal smooth as butter. For an instant she saw Jessup's face, and wondered what he would think if she failed to come back. Would he think she'd left after all these years? Or would he know that something bad had happened? Would he feel anger or grief? Seek revenge if her body were found?

She studied Michael through dirty glass, then opened the glove compartment and took out Jessup's gun. It was old with a nicked, wooden grip and a shine on the hammer. It was a nasty, ugly little weapon. Words stamped in the metal said COLT COBRA .38 SPECIAL. She fumbled open the cylinder, saw it was loaded, closed it. She took a deep breath, then slipped the gun into her waistband, covered it with the vest and joined Michael at the Mercedes' trunk. The duffel bag was open inside, the cash visible. She handed Michael the nine millimeter, watched as he ejected the clip and worked the action. "You ready?"

"I think so."

"You need to know so."

She felt the thirty-eight, smooth and hard against her skin. "I know so," she said.

He handed her the cash.

* * *

The road Michael followed took them around the south edge of town. Abigail sat beside him, the duffel bag heavy enough to drive metal against the bone of her hip. The taste was back in her mouth; pressure behind her eyes. She tried to blink it away.

"Are you okay?"

His voice sounded distant. She licked her lips, nodded. "Just warm."

"You don't have to do this," he said.

"Just drive, please."

"You sure?"

She touched her thudding chest, felt vibration at the back of her skull. "Just let me think."

Michael found the turnoff exactly where Jimmy said it would be. A narrow, dirt drive three miles past the Exxon station. It was on the left, a gash in the trees next to a mailbox with blue reflectors.

He nosed in and stopped the car.

Took out his phone.

"What are we doing?"

Abigail didn't look great. She was flushed and sweaty, her breath shallow. "The only way this works is if the guns don't come out." Michael spoke softly; he wanted her calm. "Jimmy's good and he talks a big game, but he's scared of me deep down. He's got something to prove here, something that matters in ways you and I can't fully appreciate. That makes him even more unpredictable." Michael held up the phone. "I'm going to let him know we're coming in."

She flicked a glance down the long stretch of dirt road. Her eyes lingered on the forest wall, the places light cut in. "Are you sure that's smart?"

"All I can do is go in there, hands open, and hope for the best. He either likes your idea or he doesn't. He makes a mistake or not. Maybe he's alone; maybe he's got ten guys in there." He gave her time because he thought she needed it. "I have two fine weapons and can use them better than most, but this will probably not end well."

She looked skittish, got control. "How good are you?"

He showed steady eyes. "It doesn't really matter."

"Because he has Elena."

Michael saw no need to answer.

He dialed the phone.

It was hot in the barn, and Elena hurt in ways she'd never imagined possible. Her foot. Her bones. Her soul. The wire at her throat cut deep, and breath came at a price. She looked for Jimmy, could not see him. She tasted gun oil and blood. Her mouth ached; she could not move. For long minutes, she wondered if she'd made the right choice. She thought of the baby, and of Michael's dark eyes. She wept and thought of dying.

Behind her, a phone rang.

Jimmy answered, and there was a smile in his voice when he spoke. "Michael, my friend. Where are you?"

"I'm at the end of the drive."

"Well, come on down. Someone here's very eager to see you. Wait. Here. Say hello." Michael heard muffled noises, then a muted scream. "Sorry." Jimmy had the same smile in his voice. "She can't talk right now. She has something large in her mouth."

"I'm doing what you asked—"

"Well, you're late!"

The smile was gone. Tight anger in his voice. Impatience. Michael forced himself to stay calm. "I've brought someone with me."

"That wasn't our deal."

"It's a better deal. More money. No trouble."

"How much more money?"

"Another ten."

"Million?"

"Plus what Otto had offshore. It's a lot of money, Jimmy. Let me come down. We'll work out the details."

"Who's with you?"

Michael told him.

"Ah, the good senator's wife. I've seen her picture. Pretty lady. What does she hope to buy with her extra ten?"

"The lives of everyone involved."

Silence for a full minute, then, "Why does she care about you?"

"She just does."

"Anyone else with you?"

"No."

"All right, Michael. We'll talk about it. I'm in the barn with your lady-friend. No windows; one door in. So, let's make this nice and simple. You both come in. I tell you what to do. I want your hands where I can see them."

"I want to talk to Elena—"

The phone went dead.

Elena heard the phone click shut. Jimmy was right behind her; had been right behind her the whole time. How long? She'd not seen him in over an hour. He'd been behind her and dead silent.

Then the pain!

God . . .

Such terrible pain. She fought to control herself, felt breath on her ear, fingers where the wire cut into her throat. Her eyes settled on Stevan, spread on the tractor. She had no idea if he was dead or alive. No movement or sound.

Black flies buzzed the open wounds.

"Sorry about that."

Jimmy's voice was intimate; his mouth so close that if he stretched his lips he could kiss the shell of her ear. She sobbed around the metal lodged in her throat, choking, barely able to breathe. Wires cut her skin in a dozen places. His hand slid down her shoulder, traced the edge of her breast, then ran down her arm to the finger he'd just broken. He touched it lightly, and her whole body locked in anticipation. But he didn't hurt her further; he took her palm in his hand and gently squeezed.

"Don't go anywhere."

He stepped where she could see him.

"Michael's coming."

A killer's calm descended on Michael, and he knew the feeling like an old friend. The way time slowed, the clarity of his perceptions.

His thoughts ordered themselves, as muscles loosened and possibility stretched out like lines on a graph.

"There it is."

Light swelled where the drive emptied from the forest. Trees fell off and the land opened. Michael saw an old house at the edge of uncut fields. He saw vehicles. And he saw the barn.

"So many cars." Abigail hunched forward, her hands white on the bag of money. "He's not alone."

Michael checked windows in the house, saw blackness behind empty glass. He considered the tree line, the high, brown scrub. There was deep shadow and lots of cover. Anyone with a decent rifle could take them out. He stopped the car. Everything around them was perfectly still.

"Jesus, Michael. We're sitting ducks."

"He wants his money. We control it. Try to remember that."

"Okay." She nodded, swallowed. "Where are we going?"

"There."

The barn was like any barn, rough and angular on a patch of dirt and weed. The wood was weathered and unpainted, the roof rusted metal. On its peak, a fox-shaped weathervane leaned at a drunken angle. There was an opening in the loft, but other than that, it looked as if Jimmy was right.

One way in.

One way out.

"Don't do anything unless I say." Michael opened his door. "Understand?" She reached for the door handle, fumbled it. "Abigail?"

"I can take care of myself."

And then they were out, in the yard, with the barn tall above them. Michael had a gun in the front of his belt, and one at the back. Rounds chambered. Safeties off. He looked once more at the empty clearing, then lifted the book from the dash and walked for the barn door. Three feet from the place it gapped, he called out. "Jimmy. It's Michael." He waited, but got no answer. "Abigail Vane is with me. We're coming in."

He put a foot through the gap and nudged the door, which scraped on dirt and old straw. He went in, hands first, Abigail close on his back.

"Slowly."

That was Jimmy, deep and to the left. Out of sight.

"Slowly," Michael said.

He eased around the door, came five feet into the barn and stopped, Abigail hard against him. The place was brighter than he expected, well lit by at least a dozen lanterns. He heard Abigail take in a shocked breath, but felt his own calm flow as he catalogued the barn in a few clear, brutal seconds. He saw Stevan first, but wasted no time breaking down the extent of his injuries. He was dead or not. No matter. He glimpsed Elena, but forced himself to move away from that, come back later. He located Jimmy in a shadowed place, partially concealed by a heavy post. One arm was out, gun in hand.

That was not the hand that Michael feared . . .

"Can I assume we understand each other?"

Jimmy's voice sounded surprisingly deep in the high, vast space. Michael watched the hand that held a small, wooden dowel that was maybe ten inches long. The dowel was tied to a length of baling twine. The twine ran through an eyehook embedded in the post, then to another hook in a second post, then to a third, and then to . . .

Elena.

She was wired to the barn's central support structure, a thirty-inch beam that soared to the roofline. The wires that held her were twisted razor tight, so they cut into her forehead, her neck and limbs. Her arms were pulled back so fiercely that her shoulder bones jutted. Blood from her throat made a sharp V at the collar of her shirt. She stood on one foot, and Michael saw lacerations and several toes bent sideways. The other leg was broken at the ankle, bent at the knee and wired high on the post so the foot dangled at a tortured angle. Michael had no idea how long she'd been forced to stand like that, but he'd suffered enough broken bones to imagine the hurt. Yet, the pain was nothing compared to the fear he saw in her eyes. They nailed him where he stood; they begged and said so many things.

"It's okay, baby."

But it wasn't.

A double-barreled shotgun wedged her jaw open; it was jammed deep in her mouth and secured with bright, silver tape that twisted

313

thickly around the barrel, her head and jaw. Michael saw teeth smeared red, a glimpse of crushed lips. She was sucking hard through her nostrils: panicked, in shock. Her skin had blued out. Tears gathered in her lashes.

The shotgun hung from nylon straps.

Twine ran from the trigger to the dowel in Jimmy's hand.

"Are we clear on the stakes?" Jimmy said.

Michael took his eyes off Elena; felt his cold center expand. What was the trigger pull on a Remington twelve gauge? Three and half pounds? Less? He looked at Stevan, spread on the tractor. Most of his face was gone, fingers clipped off and lying in the dirt. Hours of work, there. Lots of screaming, lots of noise. Jimmy had hung a mirror so that Stevan could watch the work on his face. That meant Jimmy had felt free to take his time, enjoy himself. Michael guessed that whoever else had come south with Stevan was dead now, too. Jimmy wouldn't run the risk, not with Stevan alive. "I think we understand each other."

"Weapons on the ground, please." Michael removed both guns, placed them on the ground. "Kick them away." Michael did as he was told. "Lift the shirt." Michael did it. "Pant legs." Michael did that, too. "What's with the book?"

Michael lifted it. "It's Otto's." Jimmy hesitated, hand tight on the dowel. "The numbers you want are inside."

"All of them? Accounts. Passwords. Routing numbers?"

"Everything you need."

Michael watched Jimmy's mind churn. He wanted to hold the book, check the numbers, but his hands were literally full. He gestured with the gun. "If the woman would step out where I can see her better . . ."

"It's okay," Michael said. "Just do as he asks. Nice and slow."

Abigail stepped sideways, duffel bag at her side.

Jimmy cocked his head. "That doesn't look like ten million dollars."

"It's just a start," she said. "I can get the rest."

"How fast?"

"I just need a computer."

"Bring it closer."

Abigail glanced at Michael, who nodded. She walked closer, and when Jimmy told her to stop, she did.

"Drop it there."

The bag landed in soft, dry dirt.

Jimmy took his hand off the dowel and stepped out of the shadows. His shirt was bloodstained under the left armpit, his nose swollen and split. Other than that, his eyes had the same cold, crazy light Michael had seen so many times. The man was a narcissist and a psychopath, an unpredictable, deadly son of a bitch. He pulled a second pistol from his belt, kept one trained on Michael and pointed the other at Abigail's face. "Open it."

She looked scared, uncertain.

"Get on your knees and open it."

Abigail felt the lump of steel at her waist. Something sharp dug into her skin, but all she cared about was the gun in her face. It had a giant, black muzzle, a circle with a silver sheen on its edge and a center that was dark and deep and smelled of burned powder. It moved, and her eyes followed it as they would a snake. Left and right, small circles. She felt the same vibration at the back of her skull. Headache. Dizziness.

"Open it!"

Jimmy thumbed back the hammer, leaned in so the muzzle was inches from her right eye. Abigail stared into it. She swayed once, then told her knees to bend. They were stiff; they fought. But once they bent, they broke fast. Her legs failed, and she hit the dirt, hard.

Hair swung over her face.

The thirty-eight fell out of her pants.

Before Abigail could move or blink or utter a word, Jimmy kicked her in the head, sent her sprawling in the dust. He kept a gun on Michael. "Uh-uh." Michael forced himself to stillness. Jimmy kicked Abigail in the ribs, drove her on her side, where she rolled halfway to the wall. He took quick strides; kicked her again. She came off the ground and hit a wall covered with tools. A shovel fell, the handle cracking her on the head. Metal rattled and scraped. A sledgehammer toppled on its side. A jar of nails spilled with the sound of dull, metal chimes. Jimmy waited, but Abigail didn't move. She slumped, on all fours. Her head hung loosely, eyes swimming. He tapped her on the head with the barrel of his gun. "Stay there, you crazy bitch." He looked at Michael. "Can you believe that? Jeez. People."

Michael risked a glance at Elena, then back at Jimmy. "I didn't know she had that."

"You think?" Sarcastic. Biting. "I didn't train you to trust a woman with a gun. Jesus. Give them anything more dangerous than a salad fork, and they're liable to ruin somebody's day." He tucked one of the pistols back into his belt. "Now, where was I?" He looked at the bag of cash. "Ah."

Jimmy stooped for the bag. Michael surveyed the room. His pistols were seven feet away, which may as well be the moon, fast as Jimmy was. A collection of knives and other edged instruments sat on a table by Stevan, but again, too far. He looked at Abigail. She was breathing, eyes open, but barely. Near her were axes and scythes and sickles. He'd never get his hands on them.

Across the room, Elena was crying.

Jimmy lifted the duffel, and kicked the thirty-eight into the far corner of the barn. A smile lit his face. Account numbers were great and all, but there was something about cash—and he could see large, green bundles of it. "You never cared enough about money." He stood with the bag, waved the pistol. "That was always your problem, Michael. Priorities. The scale of your ambition. I could never get you to see past Otto Kaitlin, to see the things you could be."

"We had the same job, Jimmy, did the same things."

"But I was never content. That's the difference between big men and small. You'd have been Otto's whipping boy for the rest of your life."

"Otto was a great man."

"Otto fed you scraps." He shook his head, disgusted. "But you took it, didn't you? You were all about family this and family that. Otto never loved you like you think he did."

"And yet he left his money to me."

"But it's not all about money, is it? It's about being more. About seeing and taking and making the world *feel* you. That's where my true disappointment lies." He stabbed the gun at Michael. "We could have run the city, you and me, done things Otto never dreamed in all his years. Jesus, Michael. I'd have made you a fucking prince."

"With you as king?"

"Who's more your father than me? Otto may have found you, but I made you." He gestured at Elena. "She understands. She gets it. That's why this is such a disappointment. You used to care about family."

"Family? Are you serious?"

"It's not too late. You can have the girl. We can still do great things."

"Don't screw with me, Jimmy. I know you better than that."

"Well, okay. She'd have to die. But you and me . . ." He grinned. "No one would stand against us."

"I just want us all to walk out of here alive."

"That's your answer?" His voice hardened. "That's your sole ambition?"

"Take the money, Jimmy."

"You really think that's all I care about, don't you?" He stepped toward Stevan, spread on the tractor. "You're the one who made this personal. You're the one who left. And for what? A woman?"

"It's a lot of money." Michael spread his fingers. "Just let us go."

"You never change, do you? Always in control."

"Just like you taught me."

"Always chilly." Jimmy kept the gun trained on Michael as he heaved the bag up and dropped it squarely on Stevan's bloody stomach. "This guy, though . . ." Jimmy patted Stevan's ruined face, smiled. "Finally good for something."

He looked back at the cash, and Stevan—tortured, skinless and half-dead—turned his head and sank perfect, white teeth into the meat of Jimmy's hand.

Abigail watched it all as if she was falling down a smooth, dark shaft. She saw Jimmy's back arch, and then his scream grew faint as light constricted.

Her fingers closed on something sharp.

Pain behind her eyes.

* * *

Michael moved as Jimmy howled, as Jimmy's gun came around to meet the curve of Stevan's skull. A shot crashed out and Jimmy's hand came free, a ragged chunk missing between the thumb and first finger. Another step and Michael dove for the forty-five, right hand on the grip, shoulder rolling to take the fall. He felt dust in his teeth, movement as he came up on one knee and slid in the dirt. Jimmy fired first, two rounds that should not have missed, but did. Michael snapped off a shot, hit Jimmy high in the chest. Staggered him. But Jimmy's finger was still on the trigger, still pulling as shots crashed through the barn, and Michael took one in the leg. The shot knocked him down, pain enough to star his vision, but not nearly enough to take him out. Michael fired half-blind, buying seconds. He got a hand down, steadied himself as Jimmy lunged left, going for the dowel that hung four feet away. Maybe he knew he was done; maybe he thought he'd use it to get Michael under control. Michael fired again, took a piece out of Jimmy's neck. He stumbled, hand out and grasping. Michael fired another round, hit an inch right of the spine. It drove Jimmy forward, all but dead on his feet. But his hand was out and close.

Inches.

Spread fingers coming down.

Michael moved for a head shot, but knew he'd be too late. Three and half pounds of pressure. Jimmy's fingers almost there.

Then Abigail Vane came out of nowhere, small and fast and lightning sure. Michael hadn't even seen her get up, but there she was, a crescent of rusty metal in her hand—a twenty-inch sickle that rose in a blurred, brown arc and took Jimmy's hand off at the wrist. The stump of his arm hit the dowel, made it swing.

Michael put the next one in his skull.

CHAPTER FORTY-ONE

Abigail drove them out. She looked small behind the wheel of the Mercedes, shoulders rolled, head tucked down as if to dodge a blow. In the back, fingers twined, wet and slick. Blood pooled in the seats as Michael cradled Elena and fought the pain in his leg. They kept their heads down, and no one spoke until Abigail pulled into the lot of a dump motel two towns over. She found an empty spot under the limbs of a tree. Traffic flickered beyond a chain-link fence. "You alive back there?"

"We're still here."

"Stay in the car."

She didn't look at them as she got out.

Air blew warm from the vents. A coppery smell. Gun smoke and clean leather. Michael kissed Elena's hair, and her hand tightened on his arm. She was in shock, he thought, her skin cold to the touch, lips dusted blue. He gentled bits of tape from her skin, her hair. An acorn hit the roof, and she jerked in his arms. "It's okay, baby."

There was silence and breath and dark eyes staring.

"You keep saying that."

It came as a whisper, her first words since he'd carried her out. Michael kissed her forehead, and when she turned her cheek into his chest, she said, "You came for me."

"Of course I did."

"You came . . ."

Her fingers twisted into the fabric of his shirt. Her voice fell off, and Michael smeared tears from his face with the back of his hand.

.When Abigail returned, she said, "I got you a room in the back."

"We need a doctor."

"Is it bad?"

Michael ground his teeth. "Pretty bad."

She moved the car, opened the room and got them out when no one was around. They were a pitiful sight, all broken and cut and gunshot. Michael's leg worked, but barely. No bones broken, no arteries hit.

Elena cried out when he put her on the bed.

Michael got her water, while Abigail brought things in from the car. She put a first-aid kit on the table. "From the trunk," she said, then laid out Michael's pistols and Jessup's thirty-eight. She brought in the duffel bag, which held the Hemingway and the cash. She looked at Elena, at the sodden cloth tied around Michael's leg. "I should hurry."

Michael caught her at the door. His face was ashen, the pain a devil in his leg. "I need to thank you." She stammered something, and for the first time since it went down, Michael really looked at her face. She was shell-shocked, her eyes bruised-looking and scared.

She shook her head, seemed for the first time to be doubt-filled and old. "Don't—"

"I would have lost her without you." He took her hand, felt bones that were light and small. "Do you understand what that means to me?"

"I mean it, Michael. Don't."

"Look at me, Abigail."

"I don't remember."

That stopped him. "What do you mean?"

Her eyes darted to Elena, the guns, the door: everywhere but Michael's face. "I remember being kicked and being hurt." She touched her temple, which was wine-dark and swollen. "I remember the feel of sharp metal in my fingers."

"The sickle—"

"I remember rage, and I remember driving."

Michael took her head gently in his hands and tilted it so light touched on the place she'd been kicked. Jimmy had struck her in the right temple. The swelling was considerable, skin dark and stretched. "Painful?"

"Extremely."

"Is your vision blurred?"

"No."

"Nausea?"

"No."

"Can you drive?"

"I feel okay to drive."

He released her, but put one hand on the door. "You saved Elena's life," he said. "That means you saved mine. Things like that matter to me. I won't forget it."

"That's funny."

"What?"

She managed a decent smile. "It seems I already have."

The mood lightened as much as it could, but Michael kept his hand on the door. "Listen, I know a thing or two about situations like this. Don't let people see blood in the car. Don't tell anyone what happened."

"I won't."

"Not Jessup or the senator."

"Okay."

"Doctors are required by law to report gunshot wounds—"

"I'm not an idiot."

He grimaced, desperate to lie down. "I'll take care of Elena, and then I'll take care of the bodies. Don't go back there. Okay? It has to be done right. This can still come back on us."

"I understand."

He took his hand off the door, swayed a little and caught himself. "Abigail . . ."

She reached for the handle, looked up.

"You did good."

Michael collapsed on the bed and felt the world gray out. When color returned, he dug Tylenol from the first-aid kit, got three down Elena's throat and then swallowed three himself. His eyes moved to her ankle. It was mottled and swollen, still at a painful angle. "I need to look at your foot."

She stared at the ceiling, lungs filling shallow and fast. "It hurts."

"I don't know how long the doctor will be . . ."

"Just do it."

She was crying when she said it, head turned against the pillow. He lifted her leg, touched the foot gently; she screamed so loudly he had to smother the sound with his palm. Her face was hard and hot. She fought him. When she finally settled, he removed his hand.

"I'm sorry." She was crying. "I'm sorry . . ."

"Shhh . . ."

"It hurts, it hurts . . ."

"Okay. I'm sorry." He lowered her leg gently. Tending to the ankle would require massive painkillers, so he draped it with a towel and left it alone. Same thing with the broken toes, the finger. The rest of her injuries were superficial lacerations, and he handled them as if she were an injured child.

She took his hand once, held it to her chest and squeezed tightly. "I've never been so happy to see you as when you came through that barn door." Her eyes were filling up again. "I thought I was going to die. I thought the baby . . ."

Her voice broke.

"Do you want to talk about it?"

"Not now."

"I'm sorry," he said.

"But you came." She squeezed harder.

"That's not enough, I know."

"It is for now," she said.

And that was all the talking they did. There was too much, and it was too fresh. The doctor came two hours later, and both, by that time, had reached whole new levels of agony. Cloverdale put his medical bag on the bed, frowned. Michael said, "Do her first."

He examined her foot, and then lifted the sopping bandage on Michael's leg. "Your injury is more severe."

"Ladies first."

"Are you serious?"

"Yes."

Cloverdale waited for the punch line, then shrugged and got to work with a swab and needle. When the leg was numbed and Elena barely there, Cloverdale lifted the towel and got to work. "I'll set this as best I can, but it'll be a temporary fix. There's tendon damage. Nerve damage, probably. Bones that need to be pinned. She'll need surgery soon. Wait too long and she'll never walk right."

"Can she go a few days?"

"No longer than that."

"Just get her so she can travel."

The doctor did Michael next. He sewed up damaged vessels, sutured muscle and skin. When he finished, everything looked fine under a bandage that had not yet stained. "You're a very lucky man. An inch to the right and the bullet would have shattered the bone." Cloverdale pulled an orange pill bottle from his bag. "The pain will get worse before it gets better. These are very strong. Don't kill yourself with them."

He held out the bottle and Michael caught his wrist. "No one can know about this."

The doctor looked at Michael's hand until the fingers let go. "Mrs. Vane has already stressed that point."

"I fear she's not stressed it enough."

Cloverdale frowned and packed instruments into his bag. When he turned around, Michael was holding twenty thousand dollars in cash. "Not the senator. Not anybody." Michael held out the money. "This is for you."

Cloverdale looked at Abigail, who shrugged. He shrugged, too, and took the money.

"That's the carrot." Michael waited for the doctor to meet his eyes. "Don't make me bring the stick."

"Are you serious?"

Michael let some killer show. "Don't ask me that question again."

The doctor left with an angry step. Elena was out, her breath a light rattle. Michael wanted to join her, needed blackness and stillness and drugs in his veins. But he couldn't do it yet.

"I need one more thing," he said to Abigail.

"What?"

He told her.

"Are you sure?"

"Just do it, please."

When Abigail came back, she had the key to another room. "Is this really necessary?" She gestured at Elena. "Look at her. Jesus, look at yourself."

Michael swung his legs off the bed, hissed in pain. "Where's the room?"

"Across the way." She gestured through the window. The motel was U-shaped, the parking lot in the center. "Number twenty-seven."

Michael stood. "Help me get her up."

Elena endured it, half-conscious. It took five minutes, and by the time they had her in the other room, Michael's bandage was soaked through.

"Cloverdale won't tell anybody," Abigail said. Michael gave her a look. "Even if he did, it would just be the senator. My husband may be amoral and self-serving, but he's neither stupid nor shortsighted. I'm implicated in this. I'm involved." Michael stretched out beside Elena; Abigail lifted his leg. "Jesus. Look what you've done to yourself."

"I've been shot before."

"Let me at least change the bandage." Michael nodded, and she changed the pads, the gauze. She threw the bloody mess in the trash. "Can I put a pillow under it?"

"Sure. Why not?"

"Why are you smiling?"

"I've never been fussed over before."

"Not even once?"

"Not ever."

That touched something in Abigail. "Let me get you some water."

She came back with a glass, and Michael said, "What I need is a car."

"I have the Land Rover . . ." She hooked a thumb at the lot.

"I can't drive a stick shift with this leg."

"I'll bring another. How do you want to handle it?"

324

"Just leave the keys at the desk." He was exhausted, voice fading as his body finally crashed. He reached for the pill bottle, but Abigail beat him to it.

"Let me."

She shook out two pills and watched him swallow them down. The bed creaked as she sat beside him.

"How's Julian?" he asked.

"Still hiding."

"Cops?"

"Looking for him with a frenzy. His face is all over the news. They're talking about roadblocks and dogs. They've got search warrants, helicopters. Sheriff's deputies are coming in from other counties to help search the grounds. The senator has lawyers, but they're helpless. It can't last much longer."

Michael needed to worry about Julian, to think of names and connections.

Iron House . . .

Slaughter Mountain . . .

He closed his eyes, drifted, and then snapped awake. "The guns—"

"Beside you." He saw them on the table. "It's okay," she said. "Everything's done that can be done."

"We need to find him. We need to understand—"

"I know we do. I know. But, tomorrow."

Michael felt warmth and weight. Pills or blood loss or both. "I've only trusted one person who knew the truth about me."

"Otto Kaitlin?"

"Yes."

"Well . . ." She folded her hands, stood.

"Thank you, Abigail."

He closed his eyes and was gone.

"You're welcome, Michael."

The clock read 4:00 when he woke: red numbers that glowed in the dark. Demon eyes. A double barrel, fired and hot. Michael blinked, and the clock rolled to 4:01. His throat was dry, but pain stood at a respectful distance. He checked Elena, who made a hump in the

325

dark; then, he checked the guns. The forty-five was down to two rounds; the nine millimeter had a full clip. The thirty-eight was gone.

Michael went to the window, where he studied the lot and the cars in it. A late-model Range Rover angled in near their door, and he guessed that Abigail had been true to her word. Everything else matched the motel—old and tired and dirty—but the Rover's paint was clean enough to catch starlight. He looked at the sky, at the white moon and high, clear flecks of gold, and was confused about what to feel. Men were dead: Stevan, who'd once been like a brother, and Jimmy who, for good or ill, had helped make Michael the man he was. He didn't regret that they were gone, but it was strange to be so alone in that world.

Otto was dead.

Stevan. Jimmy.

Then the enormity of that settled on Michael. No one was looking for him or had reason to want him dead. In one fell swoop, his life had been made free of violence and baseness and fear. Elena slept eight feet away, and they had eighty million dollars to start a new life. They could disappear in safety. Have the baby. Be together. Michael took a deep breath, and felt his chest loosen.

No one was looking for him . . .

As illusions went, it was a good one.

The van rolled up two minutes later. It entered the lot slowly, lights off, windows black; Michael knew at a glance it meant trouble. It was the darkness of it, the slow, predatory roll. It eased onto the asphalt and stopped on a silver spray of broken glass. For long seconds nothing happened, then it rolled deeper into the lot, pulled toward the center, then backed to a stop near the first room Michael had occupied. The door slid wide and men spilled out as smooth and quiet as blown smoke. They moved professionally: hand signals and short-barreled, automatic weapons, black clothes and body armor. But they weren't cops.

No badges or insignia.

License plate covered.

They took position on either side of the door, the center man with a two-handled battering ram. In two seconds they were in: a violent entry and a spill of silent black. In another twenty seconds they were out. They displayed no disappointment or anything else unprofessional. Three of them got back in the van, while the fourth dragged the damaged door closed. He walked to the passenger side, looked once around the dim lot then climbed inside and said something to the driver. As the van began to move, he looked in Michael's direction.

Then the van moved past.

They left as slowly as they'd come, and did not turn on headlights until all four tires were on the road. Taillights faded, died; Michael watched the empty road. After five minutes, he lowered the hammer on the nine millimeter and climbed back into bed. They would need to leave soon, but Elena still slept, and her body was warm on his. He pushed closer and thought of the man he'd seen, a flicker of face in the high, thin light. Michael had met him once, outside Julian's room.

Richard Gale.

The senator's man.

CHAPTER FORTY-TWO

Michael gave it forty minutes, then woke Elena in the dark. She was groggy, confused. "Where am I?"

"You're with me, sweetheart. You're safe."

"I don't remember—"

"Shh. Take it easy. Take it slow."

She tried to move, and the pain hit her. "Oh, God. Oh, my God . . ." She curled up in the bed, and Michael knew it was more than pain that found her. "I thought maybe it was a dream."

"Just take a minute. Here." He shook painkillers out of the bottle and helped her get them down. She choked a little, and he dabbed water off her chin.

"What day is it?" she asked.

"Friday."

"Everything feels off. It feels wrong."

"Hang on a second."

Michael stood and cracked the curtains so that dim light filtered in. He limped back to the bed, and Elena said, "You're hurt. God, I forgot that, too."

"You were in shock. It's normal."

"Are you okay?"

"I'm fine."

"Really?"

"It hurts. I've had worse."

"And you really have, haven't you? That's not just an expression." She stared at him for a long time, but when he sat on the bed, her eyes dipped so he saw lashes against her skin. "I've never seen anybody move like that. When you went for the gun, when you shot . . . when you shot . . ."

"Let's not talk about it right now. It's a new day. It's behind us."

"Okay."

"Are you hungry?"

She looked embarrassed when she said, "I have to go to the bathroom."

"Let me help you."

"Michael, I'm not comfortable . . ." Her head moved.

"It's still me, baby."

He flashed a grin, and for that moment he looked the same, felt the same. He had the same dimple in his right cheek, the same twinkle. "I don't think I can walk."

"Here."

"Don't . . ."

"It's okay."

Michael lifted her from the bed, carried her to the bathroom and helped her. When she was finished, he got her back to the bed. She was drawn and shaky, so Michael held a warm, wet towel to her face. He cleaned tape gum from her skin, bits of dried blood and dirt.

"I thought I was going to die."

"Elena, don't."

"I thought the baby would die with me. I thought we'd be dumped in the woods and lost forever. Just gone. My parents would never know. The baby would . . . the baby . . ." She wiped at her eyes, and looked stronger. "I've never felt anything like I did when you came into that barn. I can't even describe it. It wasn't relief or happiness or anything like that. I didn't think you could save us. He was waiting for you, and ready, he was so crazy, so goddamned confident . . ."

"Baby . . ."

"I was so scared, but I saw you and I thought at least we'd die together."

"But it didn't happen like that. It's over."

"It doesn't feel over."

"I promise you it is."

"Can I be alone, Michael?"

"Sure, baby."

"Just for a minute."

He walked outside and looked at the sky, watched a line of pink thin out and fade. Ten minutes later she called his name, and he went back inside. "You okay?" he asked.

"Yes."

Her hair was damp from the towel, face rubbed clean. "Abigail left a car." Michael nodded at the window. "I found these inside." He held out clothes and crutches, then helped her dress and got her into the car. She wanted to be up front, so he slid the seat back and tilted it as low as it would go. "There." He tucked a blanket around her. "Almost like you're still in bed."

He smiled to make it a joke, but she didn't smile back. "Where are we going?"

"Someplace safe. We'll get you to a doctor, get that foot fixed. You'll be fine. You'll see. I'll take care of you. We'll get everything fixed." He was babbling, and knew it.

He was losing her.

"I want to go home," she said.

"Spain could work. We'll get tickets in Raleigh."

"I want to go home alone." His smile faded, but she did not release his arm. "I'm not saying good-bye. I'm saying I need to think. There's so much. There's what's happened, the baby. There's us."

"Of course."

"Michael—"

"No. It's okay." Filters snapped across his eyes. "A lot has happened. Bad stuff. Questions. I don't blame you. Going alone is smart. It's reasonable."

"You don't have to be so businesslike."

"Actually, I do." He closed her door gently, then circled to the driver's side. "The Raleigh airport's not far. We have cash. The doctor says you can travel. Where's your passport?"

"Oh, God." She looked stricken. "He took it."

"Jimmy?"

"Yes."

"It's okay." He started the car. "I've got this."

Everything looked different in the early light. Fog blanketed the fields, so thick the house almost disappeared. The barn looked broken.

"I don't want to be here," Elena said.

"I'll be in and out." Michael handed her the nine millimeter. "You remember how to use this?"

She took it without question.

"I'll check the barn first, then the house."

"He had my cell phone, too."

"I'll get it."

He opened the door and Elena said, "Michael."

"Yes?"

"I know you're not like him." She meant Jimmy. "That's not why I'm leaving."

"Why, then?"

"It's just . . ." She sniffed, shook her hair back.

"Hey, forever is a long time. We'll figure it out."

"You don't understand." She shook her head. "I wanted to kill him myself. I wanted to make him hurt and beg and die. Don't you see? I hated myself for not being strong enough to do it. Hated my weakness."

"There're different kinds of strength."

"I don't know who I am anymore."

"Well, I do. You're Carmen Elena Del Portal, and you're the most beautiful person alive."

"Do you really believe that?"

"It's one of the few things I know for fact."

He closed the door, smiled through glass.

She hugged herself and watched him go.

The barn was darker, but the same. Same smells and sights; same dead bodies. Michael stepped inside, angry with himself. Even shot and dealing with Elena, he'd been sharp enough to collect weapons and shell casings. The cell phone had slipped his mind.

Stupid . . .

The phone was in her name, and could have dragged her into the fallout. If cops had found it first . . .

Stupid, stupid . . .

But he'd been emotional. Elena, hurt. Dead men who had once been family. This time, he was doubly careful. He checked Jimmy's corpse from top to bottom; found her cell phone in his pocket, but no passport. He looked once at Stevan—felt mild disappointment—then kicked dirt in Jimmy's face.

Motherfucker.

He kicked more dirt.

Sorry, sadistic, disloyal, greedy motherfucker . . .

The living room was a slaughterhouse. Even with the door standing wide, the dank, copper reek was unmistakable. Michael stepped carefully, emotionally disengaged as he cataloged faces of men he'd known for most of his life. They were soldiers and earners, hard men who'd died hard.

He found Elena's passport on a battered desk in a room under the eaves; slipped it into a pocket. He found another body there, too, and the hardware case Jimmy preferred. There were half a dozen handguns in padded foam. Knives. Wire. An ice pick. The weapons would be clean and untraceable, but taking one felt wrong, somehow. Not *stealing* wrong, but *dirty* wrong. The man was burning in hell.

Let the bastard burn.

Michael left the weapons untouched. Downstairs, he checked the other rooms for anything that could connect Elena to this place. He tried to see the scene from a cop's eyes, and shook his head at the thought. He should dispose of the bodies, burn the buildings. Because there was another truth about murder this complete: the cops would never let it go. They would dig and worry and scrape; they would track down every angle, every possible lead. And who knew where that might take them? Every one of these bodies could be traced back to Otto Kaitlin. That would tie them to the killings in New York: the dead soldiers at Otto's house, the civilians in the street. How many bodies? Michael tried to count, lost track because he had no idea how many civilians had actually died. And there was a chance, however slim, that it could all lead back to him. He could not allow that. Not now. Not when he was this close.

He considered logistics, timing, the things he would need. He nodded to himself, convinced. Three hours, he thought, maybe four. He would take Elena to the airport, then come back here to dispose of the bodies and burn it all. It made sense. He was satisfied.

Then he found the file.

It was a simple manila folder, four inches thick and bound up with rubber bands. It rested at an angle on a bedside table in a back bedroom. This was Stevan's room, Michael realized. Fine suits hung in the closet; Italian shoes and pocket squares made of silk. Michael sat on the bed, opened the file.

And everything shifted.

He didn't see all the pieces, but certain things made sense: why Stevan was here and what he'd planned, why he'd threatened Julian in the first place. Michael flipped through photographs and affidavits and financial records. Some of this material he'd seen a long time ago. But this file was more complete, more damaging; its presence here changed things. There were implications to its presence. Possibilities.

Michael closed the file and slipped on the rubber bands. Between the porch and the car he decided that nothing would burn, not the house and not the bodies. The cops wanted to play? He'd play. The media wanted a story? Fine.

The file changed everything.

Back at the car he climbed in, slammed the door and sat for long seconds. Elena gave him a strange look, but his mind was still on the implications of what he'd found. He saw a path to walk, and was looking for dangers.

"You all right?"

"What? Yes. I'm sorry."

"Did something happen? You look rattled."

"Rattled? No. Just thinking."

"About?"

He considered telling her, but this was not her problem. It affected him and Julian. He'd get her on a plane, then deal with it. "Nothing, baby." He jammed the file in the crack next to the driver's seat and smiled as he pulled Elena's passport from his pocket. "Now, don't lose it this time."

"Are you making fun of me?" She took the passport.

"Just lightening the mood."

She looked at the house and the barn, the mist that hung in the trees. "You're kidding, right?"

He winked, then took the gun from her hand. "Let's get out of here."

He found the interstate as the sun rose and mist burned, as Elena swallowed more pills and tunneled deeper into the blanket. "Lightening the mood," she said once, and laughed a little. After that, it was an odd drive, and difficult. She was close, yet far. He was losing her, but knew deep down that she should go, at least for a while. Things were getting complicated. After a while, she said, "How much further?"

"Thirty minutes. Maybe forty."

She nodded loosely, and he knew the pills were taking her down. He lifted his phone from the center console. "Do you want to call about flights?"

"I called while you were in the barn. There's one this afternoon."

He pictured her in the fog, gun in one hand and a phone in the other. The image was clear, and hurt because it came so easily. "Did you call your father?"

"I don't really want to talk about it. Is that okay?"

That was hard for Michael, because the scene had played out in his head so many times: flying to Spain to meet Elena's father. Doing it right and proper. Asking for her hand in marriage so that their family would be built on tradition and truth. Now, she would go home pregnant, alone, and the chance would never come again. "Of course," he said; and it was one more lie between them, one more bitter nail in the wall of his heart.

The senator called as they hit the outskirts of Raleigh. "Michael. Hi. It's Senator Vane. Am I calling too early?"

"Not at all, Senator." Michael glanced at the file beside his leg, and felt anger rise like a welt. "What can I do for you?"

"Abigail says you're back in town. I want you to join us for brunch. I thought maybe we could talk about Julian. Things are getting complicated, and we three, I believe, are the boy's best hope. We can put our heads together, plan our best course of action. Are you free around eleven?"

Michael looked at the road, and could see for miles. He thought of the file, and could see even farther. "I can't join you today, Senator."

"Oh."

Genuine surprise sounded in his voice, and Michael smiled. The senator was like Stevan had been. Both spoiled. Both used to getting their way. "Perhaps tomorrow."

"If you're certain you can't make it today . . ." He left it hanging.

"Tomorrow, Senator. I'll call when I'm back in town."

"Oh, you're traveling?"

"I'll call tomorrow. Thanks for the invitation."

Michael disconnected, then dialed Abigail, who answered on the second ring. "It's Michael."

"Are you okay? What's wrong? How's Elena?"

"She's fine. I'm fine."

"Sorry. I'm jumpy today. I didn't sleep at all. Randall kept asking how I got hurt. He wouldn't let it drop. Jessup got involved. It was a mess. Then there's the mind, the tricks it plays. Images, you know."

Michael did. Death had that power.

"Listen," he said. "Do you have plans for brunch today?"

"What? No." She was confused. "Brunch?"

"Never mind. Doesn't matter."

"Are you at the motel?"

"I'm taking Elena someplace safe."

"That's good, smart." She did not ask where, and Michael was glad. "You're coming back though, right?"

There was small panic in her voice, and he knew she was thinking about the bodies. "I don't leave jobs unfinished, Abigail. I can promise you that."

She exhaled audibly. "It's been a hard night in a life of hard nights. I didn't mean anything negative."

"I have something to do, and it might keep me away until late tonight or early tomorrow. I'll call you, though. And you call me if Julian turns up."

"You know I will."

"One more question," Michael said. "It's personal."

"You've earned the right to do personal."

"It's very personal."

"Oh, for God's sake . . ."

"Do you love your husband?"

"That's a very odd question."

"I don't mean in a small way, Abigail. I mean the big way. Does he matter to you?"

She was quiet for long seconds. "Can you tell me why you're asking this question?"

"No, but it's important. I won't repeat your answer."

"I'm forty-seven years old, Michael. I don't like riddles."

"I need to know if you love the senator."

"No." Silence spooled out as the world flicked past. "I love someone else."

They reached the Raleigh-Durham International Airport at ten minutes after nine. Traffic was heavy, the sidewalks crowded. Michael found a car-length of curbside near the American Airlines departure gate, and parked. Elena sat upright, both hands in her lap, neck rigid. Michael leaned forward and looked past her at the crowd. "I'm going to find a skycap." He flagged a porter just inside the door, gave him a hundred dollars and asked for a wheelchair. "The silver Range Rover." He pointed. "Just outside."

"Give me a few minutes to get the chair."

"Another hundred if you'll bring two cups of coffee, one black, one café au lait. And some fresh pastry, please."

The skycap hurried off, and Michael pushed through the crowd. He dug money from the bag in back of the car, then opened Elena's door and dropped into a crouch, one leg stiff and straight. She didn't

336

want to look at him. Creases cut the corners of her eyes. Her foot was heavily wrapped, her lips swollen. Michael folded the currency into a thick wad, took her hand and cupped the money against it. "This is thirty thousand dollars—"

"I don't need that much."

"You don't know what you need. Take it. I'd give you more, but it would be bulky and obvious." He opened the glove compartment and found a large envelope, the owner's manual inside. He pulled out the manual. "Here." He handed her the envelope, and scanned the sidewalk as she stuffed the bills inside. "Listen." He put a hand on her undamaged leg. "Everyone with a reason to want you hurt is dead. Jimmy. Stevan. No one is looking for you." He ducked his head and lifted his eyebrows. "All of that is behind you, now."

"I still taste metal." She paused, breaking. "I feel it in my mouth."

"Don't—"

"I thought I was dead, Michael. I close my eyes and see his fingers going for that stick. I see you shooting, but he never stops." She touched bruised lips. "I still taste metal."

His hand tightened. "It's done. It's over."

"I'll miss you."

"Then don't go."

But she was already shaking her head. "I want to be home, to be with my father. After all this, I need something pure."

"My love for you is pure."

"I believe your feelings are."

"But not me."

"Can you blame me, Michael?"

He looked away, shook his head.

"Then give me time."

"How much?"

"Weeks, months. I don't know. But I'll call you."

"To say what?"

"To say good-bye, or to tell you where I am. One or the other. Nothing in-between."

Michael studied the lines of her face and felt something like panic. He didn't even know where she'd been raised—she would never talk

337

about it. He knew only that it was a village in the mountains of Catalonia. Once she left, she was gone.

But what choice did he have?

He gestured for the chair, then helped Elena into it. He handed the crutches to the skycap.

"Any luggage?"

"No." Michael peeled a thousand dollars off a sheaf in his pocket. "Whatever she wants." He handed the money over. "As long as she wants it. You understand?"

"Yes, sir. Absolutely."

"Give us a minute."

"Yes, sir."

Michael took his coffee and put it on the car. He handed a cup to Elena, then a small paper bag. "I know how you like pastry."

She looked at the bag, thought of yellow paint and breakfast in bed. She thought of unborn children and promises never kept.

"You were right, you know."

"About what?" she asked.

"I should have taken you out of there. None of this would have happened."

"Julian must be very special for you to love him so much. You're right to help him."

"But *you're* my family."

"And he's your brother. It's okay, Michael. I get it."

Michael blinked several times, cleared his throat. "What are you going to do?"

"Be with family. Heal. Try to process this. How about you?"

Michael thought of Slaughter Mountain, a list of names and the contents of a four-inch file. He thought of all the cops looking for his brother, the unique fragility of Julian's mind. "I'm going to find some answers," he said. "Dig Julian out of this mess. Finish what I started."

"Is that all? Save a man's life, solve some murders." She offered a smile. "Little things."

"Are you making fun of me?"

"Maybe a little."

"Do it again."

338

Her smile faded. "I need to go."

"Reconsider."

"I need to go now."

"Listen, baby. I know you think I'm . . . impure." His hands found the arms of the chair and he leaned close. "But I'm more than the things I've done. I hope you find your way to that truth."

"Michael . . ."

He leaned closer and kissed both cheeks. She put a hand on her stomach, felt it move.

"Have a good flight," he said.

And then turned away.

CHAPTER FORTY-THREE

Abigail was perched on the edge of her bed when her husband walked in, restless and tired and rough. White stubble covered his cheeks; his eyes were bloody red and he smelled of last night's liquor. "You look disturbingly fresh."

"Thank you." Abigail stood and smoothed crisp white cotton.

"Jesus. You're too dumb to know sarcasm when you see it."

"That's your fear talking."

"Fear?"

"Your world is falling apart, isn't it?"

"It's your world, too."

Abigail shrugged. "Win the next election. Lose it. I've never much cared for your politics or your reputation."

"Just my money."

She lifted her chin. "I think we've been frank for years about what we expect from each other. Yes, I like your money. What of it?"

"You're still the grasping little tramp I found all those years ago."

"I was never a tramp."

"No. You're right. A tramp would know how to screw worth a shit."

"You're drunk."

"And Nero played his fiddle. What of it?"

"Nothing." She forced a smile. "I'm leaving. I hope you have a nice morning."

She turned, and he put thick fingers on her arm. "Let's not pretend that you don't have your dirty little secrets."

"Let me go, Randall."

"Your own dark little world." She tried to pull free, but he tightened his grip, swayed. "Where were you yesterday, my loyal wife? Huh? Where's the Mercedes? Where'd you get that eggplant on the side of your face?"

"That's enough."

"Where's Michael? Oh, that got your attention. Look at you now." He waved the same heavy fingers. "That got you."

"What do you know about Michael?"

"I know he got shot. I know you paid off *my* doctor. With *my* money. What? You didn't think he'd tell me?"

"I thought you'd be smart enough to trust me to do what's right. I thought if nothing else that we had that part figured out. No one has done more to protect the integrity of this family than I."

"Michael is not family."

"I'm leaving."

"I want to know what's going on."

"Nothing."

She stepped for the door, but he moved with shocking speed for such a large man. He threw out an arm, drove the door shut. "I want to know what the *hell* is going on!"

"I'm not going to speak with you when you're like this."

He made a claw with one hand. "There are things happening . . ."

"I know."

"Things you can't possibly understand or appreciate . . ."

"I know plenty."

"You don't know anything." He pushed closer, towered above her. "Where's Julian? What do these dead men have to do with him? I know there's a connection. The names are familiar."

Abigail eyed the door, then sighed deeply. "Can you calm down enough to have a discussion? Can you be reasonable?"

He took her arm again, and squeezed enough to make it hurt. "Tell me what you know."

"You're hurting me."

"Good."

"Damn it, Randall."

He released her arm, and she rubbed the sore spot. "They were at Iron House with Julian. Okay? They were at Iron House."

"How can you know that? They haven't even identified the third body yet."

"Chase Johnson. It's Chase Johnson. Has to be."

"Another Iron House boy?"

"Yes."

"What are they doing dead in my lake?"

"I don't know. I just . . ."

"Just what?"

"I brought them here, okay? I paid them to come here. I found them and I paid them."

"Paid them, why?"

"To apologize to Julian. He's never gotten over the things that happened in that awful place. I thought if they apologized, he could get some kind of closure. He could finally put it all behind him. He's thirty-two years old, too old to live under that kind of weight."

"You brought them here without asking me."

"Yes."

"To my house."

"Randall . . ."

"You brought them to my house and Julian killed them." It was not a question. His skin was loose, mouth a thin line. "You brought them here and that daft, bastard son of yours killed them."

"And what if he did?" It was Abigail's turn to be angry. "They deserved it." The senator raised a hand as if to strike her, but Abigail stepped even closer, chin up, eyes bright. "I fucking dare you."

He lowered his hand. "Sometimes, my dear, the past seems to come out in you."

"What past?"

"Little glimpses of what you were before I met you."

"Take that back."

He smiled a hard smile. "Bits of white trash . . ." He shook his head, threw her words back at her. *"I fucking dare you."* He straightened his jacket. "Who raised you?"

Something dark moved in Abigail's eyes. "Fuck you."

"There it is again."

"Mock me again, Randall, and I'll make you regret it."

"What are you going to do? Leave me?" She looked away, and his voice chilled. "That's right. You like it here, don't you. You like the power, the money. You like all of it. Little whore."

Abigail brought her knee up, drove it between his legs. The senator staggered, hands on his knees, face red and slick. "Bitch. Fucking . . . bitch . . ."

"I warned you."

"God . . . damn it . . ."

Abigail straightened, smoothed the same, white cotton. "You're pathetic."

She put a hand on the door, walked out into the long, lush hall.

"You're no saint," he called.

She closed the door, but could still hear him.

"You're no goddamn, lily-white saint!"

CHAPTER FORTY-FOUR

Jessup stood in front of a small mirror in the bathroom of his quarters. He'd woken at six, taken a long, troubled walk in the woods, then made coffee in the same pot he'd had for fourteen years. He showered while it perked, shaved with great care and dressed himself in a white shirt and the crisp khaki pants he favored. In the mirror, his face was lean and lined, the deep tan of summer making his teeth and hair seem whiter than they actually were. He was trying to put a Windsor knot in a paisley tie, but his hands were shaking.

He took a deep breath; started over.

Abigail was lying to him. Not little lies, but big ones. First, she'd taken the gun, then she'd disappeared only to come back bloodstained and injured. She wouldn't tell him where she'd been or what had happened. He didn't know what upset him more—the thought that she was in danger, or the fact that she had not included him in whatever that danger was. The woman was his life.

Didn't she know that?

Didn't she care?

He finished the knot, cinched it tight and thought the worry showed in his eyes. They were blue and clear and too old to be looking out from the mirror with such hurt. But he could not change the man that sixty years had made him out to be, and didn't want to, either.

He pulled a chain to turn off the light, then left the bathroom and walked into the tight, narrow living area where he'd lived so much of his life. He'd been here for two decades and knew every inch: the stone fireplace, the walls of books, the corner where he liked to lean

344

the walking sticks Abigail had given him over the years. He sat on the sofa and looked at the boots he'd taken off after his walk. They were old and leather, built to protect the lower leg from briars and shale and snakebite. They stood in the same corner, and from sole to top were slicked with clinging, black mud. He'd seen the same mud on Abigail's pants and shoes when she'd finally come home last night. The same damn mud, black as pitch and reeking of rot. Only one place on the estate had mud like that. So, he'd gone walking. He'd gone looking for something, and found it.

But what did it mean?

He sat for a long time, staring at those boots. He thought of many things, and only stirred when the knock came on his door. Then he rose quickly, because only Abigail came here. Because he knew the way she knocked. "Nice of you to think of me." He stepped back and let her in. "I thought I would have to track you down." The anger boiled up unexpectedly, the worry and fear, a sense of betrayal so profound he missed things he might otherwise have noticed.

"Jessup, I—"

"Save it." He kept himself rigid. "I found the car."

"What?"

"You ditched it in the bog at the south end of the estate. You ditched it and you walked back. You lied to me."

"What if I did?"

"There's blood all over it."

Her stance hardened. "To hell with the car."

He noticed the difference, then. The fierce, hot eyes and elevated color. The rapid breath. The sense that she was not her normal self. She swayed minutely as she stood, then stepped closer, sweat like dew on her skin, the smell of lavender and honey.

Something was off.

The eyes, he thought, but more than the wide, dark pits at their centers, more than the glassy sheen. It was like a different soul lived behind them, a dangerous, different soul.

"Kiss me," she said.

"What?"

"Kiss me. Do me." She touched his arm, and he stepped back.

"You're not yourself."

"No, I'm not. Life is a cruel joke, and I'm not myself."

She pressed so close he felt the heat of her skin, the touch of her fingers on his belt. He saw the fine pores on the slope of her nose, the black hunger that drove her. "Stop." The word came hard.

"I thought this is what you wanted." She touched his buckle. "All these years . . ."

He lifted her hands from his waist. "Not like this."

"Like what?"

He felt his features stiffen. "Please don't do this to me."

"Don't you want me?"

"I want you to get out."

"Jessup, please . . ."

He jerked open the door, voice breaking. "Stop torturing me and get the hell out."

CHAPTER FORTY-FIVE

Slaughter Mountain was as far off the main roads as you could get and still be reached by anything that looked remotely like pavement. More like rubble, Michael thought, slamming through a rut that held a foot of muddy water.

But he was close; he felt it.

Close to answers.

Close to *something*.

The dead boys were connected to Iron House. So were Julian, the senator and the senator's wife. Salina Slaughter's name was on the same list as Abigail Vane, the dead men he'd known as boys, and Slaughter Mountain was no more than thirty miles from Iron House. In a world this large, that was damn close. There had to be a connection.

But what?

The road dropped low, then bottomed out where a single-lane bridge spanned a fifty-foot gulley. It was early afternoon, but dim in the draw. Michael had not seen a car or a person since he'd actually found a gas station clerk who knew how to get to Slaughter Mountain. That was thirty minutes ago. Before that, Michael had already stopped three times with no luck. It wasn't that people were unkind or unwilling, but that road signs seemed nonexistent and directions were hard if you didn't know the dead pine at the edge of Miller's Field or the bridge where that fool tourist kid fell in the ditch and broke his ass bone.

Michael rolled over the bridge and looked downslope. Through a break in the tree cover he could see flashes of the river, which ran fast and white. He eased forward, studying the left side of the road until he found a secondary road that cut through the trees as it rose up. It was narrow and overgrown, limbs pushing in far enough to make it dark as a tunnel. Michael turned, then stopped and got out. The sign was hidden by scrub, but exactly where the clerk had said it would be. Michael pulled off brambles and vines, saw the slab of granite that looked like a tombstone.

Slaughter Mountain
1898

He drove to the top of the mountain and found it ruined. Two-thirds of it had been carved away—blasted and split and hollowed out. He saw pit mines and dross piles, metal equipment that was broken and rusted and spent. The wreckage stretched for two miles.

Ruins of a mansion perched on a far knoll.

Michael followed the road as it curved around the mine site. Stone was gray and shattered and pooled with water that caught reflections of the high, blue sky. He passed conveyors, shelled-out trucks and old, wooden structures fallen into decay. Mountains rolled off to the horizon, hazy blue, and Michael wondered how tall this mountain had been before the Slaughters stripped it down to nothing. He looked west, into Tennessee, east to Iron Mountain, then drove into more trees and up to the high glade and the rubble that dominated it.

One of the wings still stood, but barely. The rest of the structure had burned some time long ago. Grass grew around blackened timbers and mounds of chiseled stone; bits of glass winked in the sun. Four chimneys clawed up from the debris, but two more had collapsed. The house had been massive, once. Now it was as ruined as the mountain.

An old pickup truck was parked near the closest corner, its red paint faded to the color of clay, rust on the hood and knobby tires worn smooth in the center. Michael stopped next to the truck, opened the door and got out. A small bent figure was pushing a wheelbarrow down a path cleared through the wreckage. Michael waited until the man was close. "Need any help with that?"

The man started, and the wheelbarrow tipped. He tried to correct it, but his arms were thin and his load was heavy. The wheelbarrow toppled over. Bricks spilled out. The old man looked frightened, then angry. There was no way to put a number on the years he'd seen. He could be eighty-five or a hundred and ten. His face was a mask of lines and puckered skin, his body wiry and bent. He wore poor clothes and leather boots scuffed white. "Damn, son."

"Sorry about that."

The man squinted, one hand in his pocket like it might hold a knife. "I ain't stealing nothing. Nobody owns this no more."

Michael noticed that the truck bed was full of brick that looked hand-formed, and was probably worth something on the salvage market. He shrugged. "Take all of it for all I care."

The old man looked him up and down. "You some kind of tourist?"

Michael shook his head. "Let me help you."

He stepped onto the path, righted the wheelbarrow and started replacing the bricks that had fallen out. The man watched, then bent and began shifting bricks, his gnarled hands shaky but deft. "Sorry about that, I guess."

"What?"

He pointed at the Range Rover. "Most rich people are assholes. Figured you'd be the same."

"I work with my hands. You going to sell this brick?"

"Building a barbecue pit."

"Really?"

"Might do some entertaining."

Michael smiled, not sure if the man was pulling his chain. "This the Slaughter place?" he asked.

"What's left of it."

"What happened?"

"Burned. Thirty years, maybe."

Michael picked up the last brick, then took the handles and started rolling the wheelbarrow toward the truck. "Any Slaughters left around these parts?"

"Don't think so."

"You sure?"

"Been here all my life. Reckon I'd know."

They reached the truck and Michael set the wheelbarrow down. He picked up the first brick, dropped it in the truck bed. "Any idea where the family went?"

"Hell, I suppose."

"All of them?"

"Far as I know, there was just the lady."

"Serena Slaughter?"

"Meanest cocksucker ever wrote a check or broke a man's back for working. Rich as God a'mighty, but nasty to her bones. She died in the fire, and I hope she died screaming."

He pulled a bandanna from his pocket and honked his nose. Michael stared off at mountains that rolled blue and soft to the east. "Did you know her?"

"Most people around here did. Worked for her, anyways."

"What can you tell me?"

"You already done shifting brick?"

Michael smiled again, then tossed more brick and watched the man use the same bandanna to mop his face. "Did you know her personally?"

"Never cared to."

"Who owns the mountain now?"

"Couldn't say."

Michael put the last brick in the truck. "Does the name Salina Slaughter mean anything?"

"Nope. Catch that side, will you?"

Michael gripped the side of the wheelbarrow and they heaved it into the truck, wedged it upside down among the pile of brick. "Anybody around here that might be able to tell me more? Did she have friends—"

"Son, that's like asking does a rattlesnake have friends, or if a rock gives two shits about the dirt it's sitting on." Michael's disappointment must have shown. The man narrowed one eye and said, "Means something to you, does it?"

"I'm looking for answers, yes."

"You squeamish?" The same glint caught in his eye, part humor and the rest mischief.

"Not at all," Michael said.

"Then you'll be wanting to follow me."

"Why?"

"Because there's a nasty old woman who might be able to help you, and because you'd not find her in a million years if I weren't to show you how."

Michael followed the old man around the truck, watched him get in and slam the door. "Who is she?"

The man put an elbow through the open window, fired up the truck. "Far as I'm concerned," he said, "she's the crazy bitch what burned this place down."

The old man was right. Michael would have never found his way to the place he was led. They went down the mountain, left and then right a half-mile past the draw. There was no sign or pavement or indication of any kind that making that right turn was a smart move. They followed a mud track that fell away and then split twice to end up in a narrow gorge divided by a two-foot trickle of water. Trees had been cleared for the most part—stumps jutting up—but there were enough trees left to put shadows on the ground and keep the whole place from sliding off the mountain. Michael guessed there were about thirty structures in the gorge, a few of them painted, but most of them not. He saw a few trailers that had been somehow dragged down the track, but most of the buildings were poor, unpainted shacks on cinder-block foundations. There were covered porches and oil tanks, ruined cars and dead appliances. Mud was the rule, but flowerpots made a splash of color here and there. Even though it was hot, smoke rose from chimneys. Michael noticed that there were no power lines snaking down from the road above.

The old man stopped by the largest structure, which had been painted white once. The windows were broken out, roof caved in. "You ever heard the term, 'company store'?" He walked around to Michael's window, pointed at the building. "There she sits."

Michael climbed out of the Rover. "I don't understand."

The old man took a round can from his back pocket, pinched a half-inch of tobacco and stuffed it under his bottom lip. "Slaughters built all of this back in the day. Wrote mortgages so we could own our own place, then paid us with a mix of cash and store credit. Half the folks here either worked for them or watched their parents get old and broke doing it."

"Half of them?"

"Rest are hippies and homeless and Mexicans. Lady you want is at the end of that track, last one back, where the water falls off." He pointed at a sloppy, wet scar through the trees. "House used to be yellow. Sits on the creek's edge, with a big, flat boulder for a front yard. Kind of pretty once upon a time."

Michael stared off down the track. "You're not coming?"

"That's my house, right there." He pointed at an unpainted shack fifty yards off. A half-built barbecue pit dominated the patch of dirt off the front porch.

"Your pit looks good."

The man shrugged. "Been telling the wife I'd do it for twenty years." He winked. "Figure building it's the best shot I got of dying in peace. You go on down, now. Her name's Arabella Jax. She hears better than she sees, and has shot more than one dog what wandered onto her porch. So, let her hear you coming. Just don't tell her I'm the one who sent you." He squelched back toward his truck, but Michael had a few more questions.

"Why do you think she knows anything about Serena Slaughter?"

"Not sure she does, but everybody down here worked in the quarry or the mines. She's the only one left who worked in the house."

"Doing what?"

"Dishes. Laundry. Rubbing the old lady's feet. Hell, I don't know."

"Why do you think she's the one that burned the house?"

"They had some kind of falling out." The man swung into his truck, spoke through the passenger window. "Mostly, she's the only one down here mean enough to do it." He put the truck in gear, lifted a hand. "Hang on to your wallet," he said, and drove off laughing.

Michael watched his tires sling mud, then catch. He stepped back to his own vehicle and felt eyes watching him, caught movement in shady places behind open windows. It would be a short walk, he thought, but doubted the Rover would survive his absence. So, he drove.

The track went between two houses, then bent toward the creek and followed it deeper into the gorge. Michael had seen a lot of poverty in his time, but never as entrenched as this. This place had been here for a long time, and it had always been poor. No power. No phone. Trees chopped down for firewood.

The yellow house sat far back from the rest, and he saw how it could have looked once upon a time. The creek slid past the front of it, touched the side of a giant, flat boulder as it formed a wide, deep pool and then dropped off in a whisper of spray. There was a view down-gulley, and the river itself glinted far down in the green.

But that's where the prettiness ended. Most of the gutters had fallen down years ago and lay rusted in the dirt. Those that remained were clogged and sprouting saplings two feet tall. A blue tarp covered part of the roof, and tarpaper showed where windowsills had rotted off the sides. Boards were missing in the porch. What paint remained was deep in the grain.

Michael turned off the car and got out.

A sickly smell wafted from an open window.

"Arabella Jax?"

He stayed well back from the porch. Didn't have to wait long.

"Who wants to know?"

A smoker's voice, and strong enough.

"I'd like to ask you some questions."

"About what?"

"May I come up?"

He thought she was near a window. Right side. He couldn't see her, though. Just a hint of furniture and mustard-yellow curtain.

"I don't talk for nothing," she said. "You got money?"

"Yes."

"Then don't let grass grow under your feet."

Michael stepped carefully onto the porch. The door was open, a torn screen hanging off-kilter. The smell was stronger this close, fetid and thick as oil. "I'm coming inside," he said.

"Don't need a goddamn play-by-play. I see your hand on the door."

The screen door stuck, then swung wide enough to knock against the house. The room beyond was dim and low. Michael caught a glimpse of worn carpet and ancient furniture. Arabella Jax sat in chair by the window. She wore a housecoat that had once been white, but now looked like dirty dishwater. Gray hair clung to her skull; her face was collapsed and sallow, sockets pushing against the skin around her eyes. She had one leg up on a lime green ottoman, and it was the leg that smelled. From the foot to the knee, it was swollen and purple. Two toes were missing, and open sores showed where the skin had broken down.

Diabetes, Michael guessed. Bad, too.

She acted as if unaware of the smell or sight. An ancient shotgun lay across her lap: double barreled with big, scrolled hammers. "Come closer," she ordered.

Michael did as she asked, and she leaned forward. "Pretty one, aren't you?" She leaned back, held out a hand. "Money first."

"How much?"

"All of it." He didn't argue. He had three hundred dollars in his pocket, and handed it over. She thumbed it professionally, then shook an unfiltered cigarette from a rumpled pack and struck a match against the table. Smoke gathered in her open mouth. "Now, tell me sweetness . . ." She narrowed her eyes. "What can I tell you that's worth three hundred American dollars?"

Michael thought of the many ways he could approach this. He could finesse, give the backstory, tell lies. In the end, he said what was most on his mind. "What can you tell me about Salina Slaughter?"

She froze, smoke around her face. "Salina Slaughter?"

"Yes."

"Salina . . ." Her hands went white on the gun. "Motherfucker."

She got a thumb on one of the big hammers, cocked it as the barrel came up and her bad leg thumped once on the floor. There was fear in her face, and anger, too. But fast as she was, she was not that fast. Michael kicked the ottoman aside, stepped forward and snatched the gun out of her hands. She pressed back in the chair, hands up and teeth bared. "God damn it," she said. "No-good motherfuckin' jumped-up city-boy . . ."

Michael pointed the gun at her, let the hammer stay up and cocked. She stopped talking. "Are you finished?" he asked.

354

She eyed him steadily. "Nobody gets that fast doing God's work."

"Maybe not."

"You planning to pull that trigger?"

"Haven't decided yet."

"Well, think fast, boy, 'cause I dropped my cigarette and it's burning my ass."

"Go ahead."

She dug the cigarette out from between her leg and the cushion. Stuck it in her mouth. "Do you mind?" She gestured at the ottoman. "My leg ain't what it was." Michael nudged the ottoman with his foot. She propped her leg, then leaned back and studied him like she didn't care if he pulled the trigger or not. "That flatland ball-licker send you up here to kill me?"

"Which flatland ball-licker are we talking about?"

"There ain't but one."

"What's his name?"

"Hell, boy, I don't remember his name. It's been nigh on fifteen years, and he put a gun in my face, too. A lady of my refinement don't think so clear under such circumstances."

Michael stepped closer and put the barrel against her forehead. "I'm not the kind to ask twice."

"Okay, okay. No need for that. I've got his name in here somewhere. Let me think, Let me think . . ."

"Tick tock, lady."

"I don't—"

Michael cocked the second hammer.

"Falls."

Michael backed the gun off an inch. "Jessup Falls?"

"That's the one. No patience for the suffering of regular folk. Black-souled and unforgiving. No value put on family."

"Family?"

A sly look came into her face. "You think you're the first one come up here asking after Salina Slaughter?"

"She's your family?"

Her mouth opened wide, eyes crinkling as she laughed in his face.

"You don't know fuck-all, do you, boy? There ain't no Salina Slaughter. Never has been and never was. Who you're really asking after is Abigail Jax."

"Abigail?"

"My daughter." She spun her cigarette through the open window. "How is the heartless, thieving, no-good ingrate?"

CHAPTER FORTY-SIX

Michael spent the next forty minutes with Arabella Jax, and it felt like an eternity. It was more than the sight of her, more than the smells or the slow, certain crumble of everything around him. There was black poetry to her unpleasantness, a rhythm of lies and pride and cunning that Michael had rarely seen, even on the street. She pushed when she could, drew back when she felt threatened and then pushed again. She wanted everything she could get, dollars and knowledge and insight, the key to Michael's soul if she could find a way to trick it out of him. She'd say horrible things, then preen like an insane teenager and look at him sideways. Michael couldn't tell how much was act and how much was real, but his skin crawled at the way she watched him, the way she sunk her barbs then opened her mouth and let smoke linger.

"You sleeping with my Abigail? She'd be pretty enough for a fine, young buck like you. That's a trait we share." Arabella smoothed limp hair behind her ear. "Is it hot where she's living?"

"I'm the one asking questions," Michael said.

"You have eyelashes like a girl. You like boys, maybe?"

"Let's talk about Abigail and Salina Slaughter."

"Bet that Jessup Falls is sleeping with her. She'd know how to work a man, all right. I think he may have been from Raleigh. You from Raleigh?"

"I'm not telling you where she is."

"I don't care where she is."

That was a lie; her eye twitched every time she brought up her

357

daughter. She wanted to know where Abigail was, what she was doing. She was hungry for it, and she was afraid. It went like that for a long time. Michael asked a question, and she tried to turn it around. She wanted to know who he was, why he was really there. She tried to find the angles, but Michael was holding the gun, and he knew all about angles. "Let's talk about Jessup Falls."

"What happened to your leg?" She sucked on a cigarette.

"Jessup Falls. Salina Slaughter."

"You want I should rub it?"

She played bold like that, but Michael played in a different league. He leaned forward, took her hand in his. She tried to pull it back, but Michael squeezed hard and let her see enough of his soul to know it could get worse. "Now . . ." He loosened his grip, patted her hand. "I'm going to ask you again . . ."

"You wouldn't."

"I'd rather not." He squeezed harder, pressure building.

"Oh, Jesus . . ."

The joints creaked.

"He sent you!" Her eyes flared wide, mouth suddenly slack. "Oh, sweet Lord. He really did." There was a new fear in her, a specific, urgent terror. She licked her lips, eyes darting frantically as her body locked rigid. The posturing fell away, the slyness and the rough edge. "There's no need to do like he done. I'll talk. Watch me. What do you want to know? I'll tell you. Watch, now. Just you watch me."

She was so eager that Michael understood. "You're talking about Jessup Falls."

She nodded fiercely, shut her eyes tight, and Michael released her hand. Whatever happened between her and Jessup Falls, it wasn't pretty. She was scared to death. "Let's talk about Abigail," he said.

And they did. She started weak and broken, but the spirit came back into her as minutes passed and Michael didn't touch her again. He watched it build, the slyness and calculation, the belief that maybe he wouldn't hurt her the way Falls had. In the end, though, Michael had what he needed. He understood some things, and none of them were very pretty. "If you're lying to me, I'll come back."

Her face crinkled as color returned. "Come or don't. I'll be dead in six months anyway."

She flicked a cigarette butt at his right eye.

Spit on the floor.

Michael took one last look at everything—the leg, the house and the loose, brown teeth—then left, and took the gun with him. There was a lot he didn't understand, and a lot that he did. Abigail was raised poor. Fine. Happens all the time. The most loathsome woman ever born brought her into the world, then did her best to screw her up. That happens, too. Life's a bitch.

But there was no one ever born named Salina Slaughter. Michael could still feel the hate in Arabella Jax when she'd laid it out for him.

"Dumb shit of a girl wanted to be rich so bad, she made it up. Didn't like that her momma scrubbed taters and washed dishes and did every other fucking thing just to put food in her face. Know how I heard about it? People down to the store were laughing at me! Said little Abigail was telling everybody her name was Salina Slaughter and she would own the mountain one day when her mother died. Not me, mind you, but that queen bitch Serena Slaughter, who was low and cruel and treated me worse than her dog. That's who Abigail wanted for her momma! That was the game she liked to play, and everybody in this hollow knew it! Salina Slaughter. Shit. Even after I beat that child bloody . . ."

That child had been ten years old at the time. Four years later, she stole every dollar her mother had, ran away in the middle of the night and hadn't been back since. But Jessup Falls had. He'd hurt Arabella Jax so badly that even now she was terrified of him. What had pushed Falls to such an extreme? Was it love of Abigail or some other thing? Just how hard was the man, and what did any of it have to do with Julian and the dead boys from Iron House? Pieces were still missing— big ones—and Michael felt them out there like spinning blades.

Money. Parties. Politicians . . .

The line twisted through Michael's thoughts like a bright, sudden banner.

Was the senator connected to Slaughter Mountain? When and where did he and Abigail meet? Did he know her humble roots, and where did he get his money? Michael kept coming back to that, but Arabella Jax knew nothing about her daughter's relationship with Randall Vane, knew nothing about her daughter at all.

The girl was fourteen when she ran away . . .

Michael had all these questions, and as much as they burned, he didn't need the answers to save Julian. He had the file, and it would be enough. Chatham County was a powder keg, and the file would be the torch to light it. He touched it briefly and ran through the steps he would take. He looked for flaws, found none, but had to make one stop first, and that was at the Iron Mountain Home for Boys.

He found Flint in the same bathrobe with a bottle of the same booze in front of him. He nodded once at the sight of Michael, then knocked back what was left in his glass. "Have you found revenge too sweet a song to ignore?"

"I beg your pardon."

Flint poured another glass, waved it in a vague circle. "Have you come to kill us after all?"

"I have no fight with you, Mr. Flint. In fact, I wish you both well. Where's Billy?"

"Doing the things that Billy does."

"I need to ask you a question."

"Then, sit, drink."

Michael sat, but no glass was offered. Flint was bleary and loose, the kitchen a mess around him. "Has anyone ever come here looking for me? Asking about me? It might have been a long time ago?"

Flint squinted, sipped. "So many boys, so many years."

"You would remember this person."

"Can you describe him?"

Michael described Stevan as best he could. "He would have asked about Julian, too. He would have either threatened you or tried to bribe you. He would have been very smooth or very unpleasant."

"I remember him, now, an unpleasant man with an expensive suit and an attitude. He came some years after Julian was adopted. Threw some money around *and* made threats. As I recall, he wasn't just interested in your brother. He wanted to know more about Senator Vane, too. Their relationship. The circumstances of the adoption."

"His name is Stevan Kaitlin. Is that familiar?"

"Vaguely, yes. Stevan. But I don't think he gave a last name. And the other one. What was it? Otto, I think."

"Otto Kaitlin?"

"No last name for him, either, but he was an older man, calmer, kind of in the background, but very intent. Just sat there and took it in."

Michael nodded because it made sense, then put a hundred thousand dollars on the table and ignored the way Flint choked on his liquor. "If anybody else comes up here asking the same question—cops, anybody—I want you to tell them the truth. Tell them his name was Stevan Kaitlin and that he wanted to know all about the senator. Feel free to mention Otto, too. Can you remember that?"

Flint's eyes stayed locked on the cash. "Yes."

"It will happen soon. In a week or two. Police or FBI."

"Week or two . . ."

"Just tell them the truth. Afterward, you should take Billy and leave. Find someplace new. Start fresh. No more gambling. No more drinking." Flint touched the money, and Michael stood. "Mr. Flint?"

Flint looked up from the cash. He was drunk and overwhelmed. Michael spread his hands on the table, money between them. "The compassion you've shown for Billy is a rare thing in this world." Flint's eyes drifted to the money, then snapped back up. "I almost killed you the last time I was here. I was angry, you understand? It was that close." Michael held his thumb and finger an inch apart, and Flint, either frightened or full of regret, tucked his hands in his lap as Michael leaned even closer. "Every day since then has been a gift. Every day from now forward is also a gift. Every minute. Every hour."

Michael straightened.

"You're a compassionate man, Mr. Flint, and I think you deserve a second chance." He slid the money across the table. "Ask yourself what happens to Billy if you drink yourself to death, then give yourself a break. This place messed up a lot of people, but it's just a place. You can move past it."

Flint looked up, eyes red and raw. "Is that what you tell yourself?"

"It's what I'm coming to believe."

Flint reached for the bottle. "Maybe it's not that simple."

"And maybe it is."

Flint poured another glass and put it on the table.

"Take the money, Mr. Flint. Start fresh."

"I'll tell the police what you said."

Michael sighed deeply. "Give Billy my regards."

Flint nodded, glass untouched. He stared at it for long seconds, then tucked his face into his hands, his whole body shaking as Michael turned on his heel and left.

CHAPTER FORTY-SEVEN

Michael hit the Chatham County line close to dusk, and found the road empty by the mailbox with blue reflectors. He parked on the grass shoulder a half-mile down and watched the dirt track that led to a house full of dead mobsters. No police. No movement. He checked the sky for aerial surveillance, and then craned his neck to check the gas station lot two hundred yards behind him.

It looked quiet, he thought, the air hushed and warm as the sun made its slow burn through the trees. But still, he was patient. He waited, watched; and when the last light grayed out, he drove in. Within seconds, he knew the site was undisturbed.

Ignoring the barn, Michael drove straight to the house, lifted the file and got out of the car. He stepped carefully, and made his way to Stevan's room. Nothing had changed there, either. At the bedside, he replaced the file where he'd found it. He took one last look around and then left, satisfied.

Forty minutes later, he had a room in a decent hotel. He showered, changed and found the senator's number in his phone's memory. The call was answered on the first ring. "I wondered if you might still like to meet?"

"Michael, I was just thinking of you."

"Would you like to have brunch tomorrow?"

"Are you back in town?"

"Just this moment. Do you still want to discuss Julian?"

"Of course, my boy. Of course. But why wait? My evening is free; I just poured a drink. Join me. I have the most wonderful study in which to drink, and the best selection of scotch this side of the highlands."

"All right."

"Shall we say, half an hour? Just give your name to the guard at the gate."

Michael squeezed the phone hard. He thought of the file, then of blackmail, betrayal and the price of a political career. "Half an hour."

Abigail was not a drinker. Drinkers lost control, made mistakes. Drinkers were weak. But tonight Abigail made an exception. It came in a clear glass bottle, and it burned going down. But, that was okay.

She was in mourning.

And she was appalled.

Jessup . . .

She dragged herself off the bed, sat at the dressing table and stared hard at the face she'd worn for so many years. She'd worked so hard to portray confidence and certainty of purpose, and yet the one person with whom she could be herself was Jessup. He'd seen her fail and seen her break. He knew truths about her, but had spent twenty-five years at her side, unfailing and true.

"How could I have been so wrong?"

The words slurred; her face fell into a blur. All those years of faithfulness to the senator, and she'd been so proud. Of what? Her *fortitude*? Her *moral character*? Always determined to do the right thing, to make the good choice. What a joke! What a sad, tired delusion!

Her reflection laughed a bitter laugh.

Jessup didn't want her anyway.

She picked up the gun he'd given her all those years ago. For two decades it had ridden with her in the Land Rover, and yet she'd never fired it. It was heavy, cool, and she thought of his face when he'd first pressed it into her palm: a hint of smile, but serious, first touch of white in his hair. *It's a dangerous world,* he'd told her. *You should keep this close.*

Had she been wrong even then?

Had he ever loved her?

She dropped the gun on the bed, stood and paced. She had brief thoughts of Julian and Michael, of the horrors she'd seen in the barn. But mostly she thought of her life, of choices made and opportunity missed. She thought of things she could not forget, and of failures she could not unmake.

To do and do and make oneself replete with change . . .

She wondered if she'd managed to change at all. All the tough decisions, all the sacrifices and lofty ideals. Had they made any difference? Or was she still the same person she'd been thirty-seven years ago? The same girl who swore she could do better? The very thought depressed her. The bottle emptied, and at some point she heard a light knock on the door.

"Abigail?"

She moved to the door and stood, silent.

"I can hear you breathing."

Pressure built behind her eyes, but no one could help her. "Go away, Jessup."

"Are you sure?"

His voice was soft; she touched the door and tried not to cry.

Michael left the guns in the hotel room. He wouldn't get them through security, and didn't need them anyway. That was the thing about knowledge.

It was full dark when he arrived at the estate. Reporters were still camped out: vans and gear and talent. They rustled when he slowed. Lights came on, then somebody yelled: "It's nobody."

Cameras went down; smokers lit up.

He gave his name at the gate, and a uniformed guard leaned in at his window. He wore a sidearm, carried a clipboard. Michael tried to read his face, but it was blank. "Identification, please."

"You know who I am."

The guard measured him with a stare that lasted fifteen seconds. "Any weapons in the car or on your person?"

"Is that a normal question?"

"We've received unspecified threats."

"No," Michael said. "No weapons."

"Straight up to the house. Someone is waiting to take you to the senator."

Michael drove through and the gate swung shut. Gas-burning streetlamps lit the drive; far in, the house glowed as if on fire. Michael rolled slowly, and saw two men waiting for him on the steps. One opened his door. The other was Richard Gale. "I'll need to pat you down," he said.

"Is that how the senator greets all his guests?"

"We've received—"

"Yes, I know. Unspecified threats."

Gale smiled tightly. "If you would?"

"Careful of the leg." Michael lifted his arms and let Gale pat him down. The talk of threats was just that, but they needed an excuse, and Michael let them have it.

"Will you follow me, please?"

The senator was right about one thing: his study was spectacular. Wood panels gleamed like honey; the rugs were handmade silk and at least a century old. Vane rose from a leather chair and opened his arms expansively. "Was I kidding?"

"It's very nice."

The senator wore a three-piece suit with French cuffs and a pink tie. He took big strides and offered a big hand. Behind him, French doors opened to formal gardens that were lit with colored lights. "What're you drinking?"

"I'll have what you're having. Thanks."

"What happened to your leg?"

"Nothing really. Not important."

"If you say so." Vane turned his back, selected a bottle and poured. When he turned, he looked like every politician Michael had ever seen, all smiles and twinkle and subtle dark. He handed over the glass, sipped his own, then pretended his question had not been ignored. "You've met Richard Gale."

Michael knew this could play two ways: long or short. Either way, the end would be the same. "Sure." Michael limped across the room and sat in one of the big leather chairs. He held up the glass, let light shine through the liquor, and decided to make it short. "He and a couple of his buddies smashed in my hotel door last night."

He sipped scotch in the dead silent room.

"I don't—"

Vane offered false confusion. Michael said, "You need better men."

The senator put his own glass down. "That's how it is?"

"I think we both know I'm not here to talk about Julian."

The moment held, then Vane nodded. "Very well." He looked at Gale, who opened the door and let three more men enter the room, probably the same three who'd been with him at the hotel. They fanned out, each of them discretely armed.

Michael held up his glass. "Can I get another one?"

The senator smiled and sat. "You're flip. I like that. It won't help you, but I like it. And I apologize for what has to happen tonight."

Michael put his glass on a table by the chair. "Let me save you some trouble."

"You're no trouble at all."

"And yet you plan to kill me." Michael looked at Gale. "That is the plan, isn't it?"

"Kidnap," the senator said. "Not kill. *Deliver* might be a better word."

"To Stevan Kaitlin."

His eyes hardened. "What do you know about Stevan Kaitlin?"

"He's blackmailing you—I know that much. He's been doing it for some time, too. Years, I should think, based on the numbers I've seen."

"Numbers?"

"More like a ledger, a record of what started a long time ago with Otto Kaitlin."

Michael pictured the file that Otto had given him for his seventeenth birthday. Information on Julian's new family. Pictures of the senator with various prostitutes. He'd assumed it was just for him, but realized now that Otto would have never let that kind of information go unused. "You paid a half-million dollars a year for five years, then three years at six hundred thousand. You've been at seven-fifty a year for a while, now. I'm guessing you've shelled out thirteen million dollars over the past sixteen years." Michael let that sink in, then smiled. "Give or take."

"Where did you see those numbers?"

"Same place I saw the pictures."

"Pictures?"

"I have the file."

Vane paled, suddenly still. "Get out." He waved a hand at Richard Gale.

"All of us?" Gale asked.

"Yes."

"Are you sure that's wise?"

"Get the hell out!"

"Very well." Gale and the other men left.

When the door closed, Senator Vane picked up Michael's glass, slopped in some scotch and handed it back. He poured one for himself and knocked it down, color coming back to his cheeks. "How do I know you're not lying to me?"

Michael pulled a photograph from his back pocket, unfolded it and handed it over. "I picked one of the good ones."

"Son of a bitch." The senator studied it for a long time. "Who are you? And don't give me that *Julian's brother* shit. What do you have to do with Kaitlin? How'd you get that damn file?"

He was furious, embarrassed; Michael understood. Like a lot of public figures, the senator had unfortunate tastes. Prostitutes. Pages. Cocaine. "Stevan offered you a trade," Michael said. "My life for the file."

"Actually, he wanted you alive. He was very specific."

"Whatever. The trade is off. I'll keep the file, and you keep your toy soldiers to yourself." Michael stood, put down his glass. "Thanks for the drink."

"What? You're leaving? Just like that?"

"I've said what I came to say. I plan to be here until I know Julian's okay. In the meantime, I don't want any more late-night visits."

"What about the file?"

"What about it?"

The senator struggled. "What are you going to do with it?"

368

Michael smiled darkly as he thought of the phone call he was about to make. "Whatever I please."

Michael was gone; the room was empty, door closed. Randall Vane stood in a raw, blind fury. Those Kaitlin fuckers had blackmailed him for sixteen years, the threat so personal and damning that he'd had no choice but to pay. Some of the worst pictures went back years, to a time when very few people knew about pinhole cameras and fiber optics. God, the shame! If the pictures came out, he would never survive it. Politically. Socially. Suicide was a real possibility.

He pulled the photograph from his pocket.

Shuddered.

Taken fifteen years ago, it showed him with a seventeen-year-old page named Ashley, a beach girl from Wilmington with blond hair and an all-over tan. They were naked in a Washington hotel room, the bed a puddle of wrecked sheets. She was laughing as he snorted cocaine off the smooth swell of her right breast.

"God . . ."

He burned it in the fireplace, stirred the ashes until they were dust. When he'd heard that Otto Kaitlin was dead, he'd dared to hope. But the son called a day later, Stevan Kaitlin, who wanted Michael dead. The senator didn't even know who this Michael guy was. He'd never heard of him. Didn't know. Didn't care.

But Stevan did. And Stevan still had the file.

He's coming to you. And when he does, you bring him to me.

Why?

That's none of your business.

And the file?

Yours, if you do as I say.

It should have been so simple. Bring in some hired guns, people he could trust. The guy was a dishwasher, for God's sake! But now . . .

The senator poured another drink, spilled it as his hands shook. In spite of what Michael had said, the photograph with Ashley was not nearly the worst. Otto Kaitlin had sent copies years ago: photos of him with prostitutes and attractive young lobbyists, some hard-core, graphic stuff. But the sex was not the worst of it—hell, he could survive

369

a good sex scandal. There were financial records, too, a paper trail of payoffs and sold votes. Not all of them, but a few. It would only take one, and he had few friends on the ethics committee. "What do I do, what do I do, what do I do . . ."

It would start over. The payoffs. The worry. The fear. He would be forced to yield, forced to bow. Another puppet master would take the strings, and the great Randall Vane would be made to dance.

Again!

Again, again, again!

The fire tool came alive in his hands. It smashed vases and crystal, tore great, white streaks in all his lovely wood.

"Shit!" He threw the heavy metal against the wall. "Shit, shit!"

"Senator?" The door opened a crack. "Are you okay?"

"Yes. No. Get in here." Richard Gale entered warily, eyes moving over the damage. "I want you to follow that motherfucker. Find out where he is, where he's staying. I need that file."

Gale kept his distance. "You told us to let him go. He's already through the gate. He's gone."

"Gone? You stupid idiot."

"That's uncalled for, Senator. The instructions were yours—"

"Get out. Just get the hell out. No, wait. Where's my wife?"

"Your wife?"

"Are you deaf?"

"No, but—"

The senator grabbed his lapels. *"Where's my fucking wife?"*

CHAPTER FORTY-EIGHT

Abigail sat in an antique chair before a Victorian dressing table. She felt disconnected from a day that was too big. From the past week. From her life as she'd made it. So, she sought comfort in the familiar. She applied makeup with a deft touch. She kept her shoulders square, but felt the shame of her weakness. She was drunk, and she was needful. Her heart was breaking as her lips moved in a low, fierce whisper.

Survival, strength, perseverance.

It had been her mantra since childhood. She closed her eyes, and said it again.

Normally, it centered her, gave her the balance to drive her life with the precision it required. But when she opened her eyes, she saw the face of a child, a small girl beaten bloody and trying hard not to cry as she dabbed and cleaned and wondered why her mother hated her with such passion. It was a terrible image, and terribly real: the bruises and torn skin, the raspberry dimple where pale, blond hair had been ripped out at the roots. She closed her eyes before the tears could find her, swayed in the narrow chair as the room faded to a bare, cold shack, and she heard a baby cry.

Survival, strength, perseverance.

Her hands spread on the table, eyes squeezed tight as her fingers touched a silver brush, a comb with ivory teeth. She tried to find herself, but could not. Julian would be arrested, and Jessup didn't love her. The past was rising up.

Survival, strength, perseverance.

Survival, strength—

No.

*T*he comb was pink plastic, tears hot on the girl's face as she tried to comb wisps of hair over a weeping, wet bald spot the size of her mother's fist. Her feet were cold and bare under a cheap print dress stained black from lack of soap. The mirror was cracked through, large streaks of silver gone so that in places it was like staring into nothing. But where there was silver, there was fear, raw and fresh and caught in wide, green eyes. She tried to blink the world away, but the room smelled of fatback and collards; she heard her mother's step in the door, the call of that precious child . . .

"What're you waiting for, you little shit monkey?"

The girl held herself very still. Her mother moved into the room, brought the smell of hairspray and sweet tobacco.

"No, Momma."

"Do it before I do the same to you."

"Please don't make me—"

"Do it!"

"No, Momma. Please."

"No-good ingrate." Fingers twined in her hair. "Worthless, selfish brat." Face slammed into the table. "Do it!" Slammed again, nose bloody.

"Please . . ." The girl saw broken teeth on checkered wood.

"Do it!" Face against wood. "Do it! Do it! Do it!"

Until another lump of hair came free and the world went black. The next thing she remembered was sitting wet on the bank of the creek, blue with cold and blinking in the flat, winter sun. The dress clung to her narrow chest, water in her nose. Her hands were shaking, and strange noises came from her throat. On the bank beside her, her mother was hard-faced and satisfied. "Now you're mine forever."

The girl looked down.

And saw the thing she'd done.

*A*bigail jumped when she heard the doorknob rattle. A small cry escaped, and she cast a worried, guilty look at her reflection. Her eyes were still wounded, but the mirror was flawless and the comb in her hand worth eighteen hundred dollars. She dabbed at her eyes, and smoothed herself.

"Yes?"

"It's me."

"Randall, what?"

"Open the door."

"Give me a moment."

The knob rattled harder, wood vibrating in the frame. Abigail crushed the past, as she had so many times, then opened the door for her husband. He stood large and winded, his hands so fisted that bone showed at the knuckles. He came into the room and shut the door.

Abigail stepped back, wary. Her husband had never been truly violent toward her, but there was something in his eyes like a hot, cherry glow. "What is it, Randall?"

"Where's Michael?"

"What do you mean?"

"Don't play with me, Abigail. I need to know where to find him."

"I'm sure I don't know."

"That's a lie. You two are thicker than thieves."

He stepped closer, and Abigail gauged the impatience and suppressed rage. She knew her husband's moods, and this was a bad one. "I've answered your question," she said carefully. "I don't know where he is. You should go."

"It's not that simple this time."

"I don't know——"

"Bitch!" He struck a table hard enough to crack wood. "I don't have time for games or lies or your misplaced, overprotective nature. This is important, so I'll ask again. Where is he staying? What hotel?"

"I don't know."

"He has something I need, Abigail, something very, very important. Do you understand? I need him. I need you to help me."

"Why?" She stepped back, got her hands on the desk chair.

"Because he wants to hurt me, so I have to hurt him first. Because if he hurts me, he hurts you. Because if I don't find him, it's over. Everything. You get it? Everything I've worked for. Everything I am."

But Abigail had stopped listening. "You want to hurt him?"

"He's a threat."

"You want to hurt Michael?"

"Where is he, Abigail?"

She was at the desk, one hand spread as her vision constricted and a low, dull thrumming rose in her skull. The room dimmed, but the senator was oblivious. Abigail's head tilted, and her neck creaked. The thrumming in her skull grew louder, a hive of bees that swarmed until her skin prickled. Her hand found a letter opener on the desk, a gift from Julian. The handle was bone, the blade sterling. "You want to hurt my Michael?"

"Hurt him. Kill him. Whatever."

She blinked and felt a swirl of dark current, a cold, wet blackness that rose up and roared into her skull.

Her eyelids closed, then opened.

Abigail went away.

Jessup made it outside and under the stars before he realized that walking away from Abigail would not be that easy. Something in her voice sounded broken, and she was not a woman to easily break. But she did not tolerate impertinence, either, and rarely appreciated help that came unasked for.

He stood for long seconds, then said, "Damn it all."

He walked briskly across the broad drive, then entered through one of the smaller doors in the back. He passed through the kitchen, the dining room, and was in the grand foyer when he saw Richard Gale and three of his men coming down the stairs. He'd met Gale once or twice over the years—brief stints when the senator traveled overseas or during random periods of heightened security—and had measured respect for the man's training and demeanor, both of which were professional. He was a mercenary, yes, but a good one. The man came, did his job and went. Jessup suspected that Gale found him provincial, but didn't care. "Have you seen Mrs. Vane?"

They met at the lowest step. Gale looked up the stairs, thought for a moment, then said, "She's in her suite. I believe the senator is with her."

"Thanks."

Jessup took the stairs two at a time, and when he was out of sight, one of Gale's men said, "Shouldn't we be doing something?"

"Like what?"

"Anything."

"You know what?" Gale looked after Jessup, then smoothed his lapels. "I believe our job here is done."

Abigail's suite of rooms was at the far end of a long wing on the north side of the mansion. She'd moved in seven years after her wedding day: clothing, furniture, everything. No one said a word about it; no one asked. The staff adjusted, and life went on with the senator and his wife living apart. Jessup rarely came onto this hall, not only because doing so would look improper—it would—but also because it was the safe place to which Abigail withdrew, her personal space in a house that was not really hers. He admired what she'd done with it: the colors, the light. She'd made the entire wing a reflection of her own impeccable taste.

He hit the hall at a fast walk. It was empty and still, his feet quiet on lush carpet. Abigail kept an entire suite of rooms: bedroom, sitting area, music room, library. Her bedroom door was the last in a row of six.

He heard the scream from twenty feet out, hit the door at a dead run, tore it open and stopped cold. The senator was on the floor, screaming. Abigail had one knee on his throat, the blade of a letter opener jammed into the soft spot beneath his collarbone. "You're going to hurt Michael?" She twisted the blade, made him scream louder. "I don't think so."

"Abigail, please . . ." He was begging, one hand on the floor, the other on her wrist. She twisted the blade again. "Ahh! Shit! What the fuck? Get off! Let go! Abigail!"

Jessup stepped inside. "Abigail . . ."

"Jessup. For God's sake . . ." The senator reached out a hand. "Get this crazy woman off me!" Jessup hesitated, torn. He knew exactly what was happening. Had no love for the senator. "For God's sake, man . . ."

Abigail leaned in close, pushed the blade deeper. "You touch Michael and I'll kill you. You understand?"

Jessup stepped closer, eyes full of knowing and dread. "Abigail?"

She laughed, flicked her head so that hair swung out of her face. "You know better than that."

"Oh, no."

She grinned. "Say it."

"No, no, no."

"Say it you poor, sad man."

"Salina."

"Louder," she said.

"Salina!"

She looked up, eyes bright over the same, sharp slit of smile. "You going to screw me this time?"

"Salina, don't."

"Salina? What the hell's going on?" Vane tried to force her wrist up, but she leaned on the blade. "Ahh! Damn!"

She said, "Do that again and I push it all the way to your heart. You understand me, fat boy?"

"Yes! Yes! Stop!"

She looked at Jessup. "Tell you what, handsome. You screw me good and I'll let him live."

"You know I can't—"

"I know that, you dick-less wonder. You don't think I've figured that out by now? Though, the times we had . . ." Her smile spread in a knowing way.

"Salina, listen." Jessup held up his hands, fingers spread. "This won't be good for anybody. You can't kill a United States senator."

"I won't take the rap. *She* will."

"You'll both go away. You *and* Abigail. You can't kill a senator and wish it all away. There are *consequences*."

"He's going after Michael." She put more pressure on the blade. "Tell him, fat boy."

"Yes. Yes."

"I can't allow that." She looked at Jessup. "This would be a good time for you to leave."

"You know I won't."

"Yeah, I know." She laughed a crazy laugh, and the senator found strength in the sound of it. He yelled and rose up beneath her, bucked his entire body, then caught her waist and flung her off. She struck the bed and he fought to his knees, bone handle protruding. He tried for his feet, but Salina was fast and sure. Even as Vane struggled, as Jessup hesitated and then tried to stop her, she reached for the thirty-eight on the bed, got her hand on the grip and spun.

Jessup froze.

The senator tore out the blade.

"This is my kind of party." Salina held the gun steady. The men were five feet apart.

Only Jessup truly knew how close to death they were. "Salina, don't . . ."

But Salina did.

The shot was a bright, hard crack, gray smoke and a lick of fire. The bullet struck high on the senator's forehead, lifted the top of his skull and dropped him on his back. Jessup looked from the body to the face of the woman he loved. It was exactly the same, and terribly different. The eyes were too hard, the smile too grim. He felt his way to the bed and sat. "Why did you do that?"

"Nobody touches Michael."

"But—"

"I did what I had to do," she said. "Now it's your turn."

Jessup was in shock. His head felt heavy in his hands. "My turn?"

"That's right."

She sat on the bed beside him. He looked up, distraught. "To do what?"

"Fix it."

He stared at her and felt such hatred. "I should let you fry."

She traced three fingers along his thigh. "We both know you won't do that."

"You are an evil woman, Salina Slaughter."

"What're you waiting for, you little shit monkey?"

CHAPTER FORTY-NINE

Michael found a small bar on the outskirts of town. It was quiet inside, largely empty with the only real noise coming from a jukebox in the back. He ordered a beer from the bartender and took a booth in the corner. The beer was cold and he sipped as he dug the cell phone out of his pocket and put it on the table. It was prepaid, untraceable; for a moment he pondered the power of technology.

Then he thought of bodies.

And his brother.

Michael could have grilled the senator for details about anything he wanted—Slaughter Mountain, Abigail Vane, Iron House—but it would have taken time, become confrontational, and in the end there was no point. He didn't care who killed those Iron House pricks as long as Julian was safe from criminal prosecution; the blackmail file gave him that certainty. Had he pushed for information, the senator could have balked, delayed or demanded further proof. Getting to truth could take time—if Vane even knew the truth—and Michael was not so worried about niceties. He could fix it now, make it go away before the cops dragged Julian kicking and screaming from whatever hole he'd found.

He spun the phone on the slick, black table.

Checked his math one last time.

Bodies had been pulled from the lake, men who had once been boys at Iron House, men who knew Julian. The cops would make the connection because cops were plenty smart and the math was not that hard. Why Julian might have killed them wouldn't matter in such a large case. The finer points of motive would fall beneath the weight of speculation and circumstance. The victims knew the killer. They had been enemies once, lured with cash to the estate, and then sunk in the same lake where a girl well known to Julian had died eighteen years ago. All things being equal, Julian would go down for the murders.

But circumstance, thankfully, was not a one-trick pony. Four miles away was a farm piled high with dead gangsters who for years had been blackmailing Senator Vane. The file would speak for itself. Photographs, ledgers, records of bribes taken and payments made. Michael's plan was elegant in its simplicity. Send the cops to the farm; let them find the bodies; let them find the file. Two things would happen immediately.

First, the bodies in the lake would pale beside the carnage at the farm. The dead gangsters would be traced back to Otto Kaitlin, and from there to the violence in New York: the explosion at the restaurant, the killings at Sutton Place, the escalating body count since the old man's death. The feds would get involved. FBI. ATF. It would be a massive response.

Second—and very quickly—they would connect all this organized activity to Senator Randall Vane. When that happened, the tone of the investigation would tilt away from Julian. With this much death and this many mobsters, entirely different avenues of investigation would open up. Eventually, someone would make a trip to the Iron Mountain Home for Boys, and there that person would meet Andrew Flint.

And Flint had things to say about the Kaitlins.

They'd come to Iron House asking about the senator. Julian had been a mere child at the time, and Flint would tell the cops as much. That would add one more link to the chain of evidence connecting Senator Vane to organized crime. The case, then, would no longer be about a few bodies in the lake. It would be about mobsters and crooked politicians, about payoffs and killers and lots and lots of bodies. Michael liked it because it was messy and powerful and could be read in ways that had nothing to do with a troubled children's author named Julian Vane. Maybe the mob killed the Iron House boys to implicate the senator. Maybe the senator retaliated. Maybe there were other connections, other players. Cops could only speculate at the extent.

Whatever the case, it was too big to be about Julian.

Way too big.

Michael was about to dial when his legitimate phone rang. For a second his heart skipped, but it was not Elena. It was Abigail's number, and he answered on the second ring. "Hello."

"Michael? Thank God."

It was Jessup Falls.

They met on the edge of an empty field three miles south of the east gate, far from reporters or other prying eyes. Jessup looked washed-out and old; even in the dim light, Michael recognized the look of a good man dealing with a bad thing. "The body is in Abigail's room. I can't move it by myself, and there's no one else I can ask. Everyone in the house is loyal to the senator. She'll go down for this if I don't fix it. You have to help me. Please."

That part hurt. The begging.

Michael looked out at the field. The cars were parked head-to-head, parking lights burning. He thought about what Jessup had told him, and found it thin. "Tell me again what happened."

"There's no time! Someone may have heard the shot. He could be found any second!"

Except for the fact that the senator was dead and that Abigail had pulled the trigger, Michael doubted everything Jessup had said. "It doesn't make sense the way you described it. She wouldn't kill him without good reason. Certainly not over some stupid argument. She's too controlled for that. Too smart."

"What does it matter? Please!"

"Where is she now?"

"In my room. Safe, for now."

"And the gun?"

"It's here. I have it."

"It's untraceable?"

"I bought it clean twenty years ago. It won't come back to us."

Michael searched Jessup's face. If he'd ever doubted the man's feelings for Abigail Vane, he no longer did. Jessup Falls was coming apart at the seams. Worry. Fear. Desperation. Michael understood. He knew the same feelings, but for Elena. He considered all that had happened, all that he knew and had learned. Then he decided to push. "Tell me about Salina Slaughter."

"Oh, God."

"I've been to Slaughter Mountain. I know you were there, too."

Jessup looked desperate to the point of collapse. He looked over his shoulder, toward the far, invisible house, then begged with every angle in his face. "There's no time. Don't you see? This will ruin her. Please, Michael. Help me. Please. I can't let this destroy her."

"If I help you—"

"Yes, yes. I'll do anything."

"—I want to know everything."

"Yes."

"Slaughter Mountain. Salina Slaughter. Everything."

"I swear."

Jessup nodded, but looked tortured, so Michael showed him a small mercy. "I won't do anything to hurt Abigail. She's a good woman; she's Julian's mother." He actually smiled. "I don't think less of her for killing a man like Randall Vane."

A shaky breath escaped. "Okay. Thank you."

"But after I do this, we talk."

Jessup nodded, grateful, and Michael said, "Let me have the gun."

Jessup retrieved it from the car, then hesitated. It was the murder weapon. It carried Abigail's prints, his prints. Their eyes met, and Michael held out his hand. "You have my word."

Jessup handed over the gun, and Michael took it. He wiped it down with a handkerchief, then withdrew the shells and wiped them down, too. He reloaded the pistol, wrapped it in cloth and tucked it under his belt. "I'll call you when it's done."

"What about the body?"

"Don't worry about the body. Leave it."

"But—"

"A little faith, Jessup."

Michael turned for the car, but Jessup stopped him. "I need more than that. The body is in her room. The implications . . ."

"Keep Abigail clear of the room; let the body be found. All hell will break loose in the next few hours, by dawn at the latest. Deny everything. Give her an alibi. It will look dicey for a day or two, but I promise you, this will not come back on her."

Jessup put a hand on Michael's arm. "This is hard for me. Trusting you."

"I could say the same thing."

Understanding flashed across Jessup's face. Michael had the murder weapon under his belt; he was a killer with mob ties. If Jessup wanted to take pressure off Abigail, all he had to do was call the cops on Michael. One call, and it would all go away. Michael arrested, Abigail free and clear. He looked at Michael differently. Something fundamental shifted, and Michael noticed.

"A little trust can be a dangerous thing, Jessup." He nodded from the car door. "But it doesn't have to be."

"You'll call me?"

"Keep the phone close."

Michael made his third trip to the farm in the dark of night. He eased down the long, twisted drive, found a likely spot in the house and left the gun where no cop could miss it. Abigail would be pushed hard in the first few days—cops usually looked first at the spouse—but ballistics would eventually come back to the thirty-eight on Stevan's bedside table. The timing wouldn't fit, as everyone at the farm had been long dead when a fatal bullet hit one of the nation's most politically divisive senators. But that wouldn't matter in the long run. All Abigail required was reasonable doubt, and in the end there would be too many other possibilities out there, too much connection between the senator and Otto Kaitlin's criminal empire, too much money and too much bile. After all, *someone* killed all the gangsters at the farm. *Someone* left the gun there. Would the cops really think that someone was Abigail Vane? Of course not. People were dead in New York, dead at the farm, dead in the lake.

And the senator was connected to all of them.

Michael left the farm. He turned right onto the blacktop and drove a half-mile to the Exxon station where he parked out of easy sight. He pulled out the disposable cell phone and thought how close Jessup Falls had come to the precipice of one-minute-too-late. Had he called even a minute later than he did, Michael would have been helpless to assist. He'd have already made the call.

But that's how thin the margin often was.

Seconds.

Michael powered up the phone, called the police department and told the desk sergeant he had a message for Detective Jacobsen. He didn't want to talk to the detective, just a message. "That's right," Michael said. "Half-mile past the Exxon. The mailbox with three blue reflectors."

The sergeant wanted more, but Michael wouldn't stay on the line. No name, no particulars, no explanation. Bodies at the farm. Dead guys and guns. People cut to pieces. Maybe the sergeant thought he was crazy; maybe he'd get promoted.

Michael looked at his watch. He'd been ready to scapegoat Senator Vane even before the man was dead. Why? Two reasons. He'd planned to turn Michael over to Stevan, so screw him. Most important, though, was Abigail. Whether she knew it or not, he'd given her the chance to call it off. *I love someone else,* she'd said, and that was good enough for Michael.

He looked at his watch again, and wondered if Jessup knew how she felt.

The cops came eighteen minutes later.

CHAPTER FIFTY

Abigail woke from the same dream that had haunted her every night for thirty-seven years. She kept her eyes squeezed tight, breaking softly as the images flickered, faded, refused to die. She was ten years old and half-frozen on the bank of her mother's creek. Her teeth chattered, and her mind ached with a terrible emptiness. She didn't know what had happened, only that she'd done bad. She saw it in her mother's face, in the leveled eyes and the sly, contented smile.

Now you're mine forever.

And Abigail looked down at what she'd done. She saw the face of that baby boy, water in his mouth, eyes half-open. She tried to wake him but he wouldn't wake. He was still as a doll, all powder blue and lifeless in her hands.

Now you're mine forever.

"No, Momma."

Forever and ever and ever . . .

"No!"

"Abigail."

"No!"

"Abigail. It's okay. You're okay. Just a dream." The voice was real, familiar. Abigail opened her eyes, confused. Something warm rested in her hand. She squeezed and felt Jessup's fingers. Faint blue light shone through a high, small window. It seemed to wink. She sat up, brushed hair from her face.

"Jessup?"

"Yes."

"Did I say anything in my sleep?"

"Not really," he said. "Just at the end when you said, 'no.'"

Some of the tension bled out. "Where am I? What time is it?"

"You're in my room. It's late. You're fine."

She shuddered from the dream, and he touched her shoulder. "What am I doing here? Oh, God. I blacked out again, didn't I?"

"Just for a bit."

"Did I do anything . . . you know."

"Nothing bad. No."

"I don't remember anything."

"Do you remember the senator in your room?"

"Vaguely. An argument."

Jessup nodded. "I came in in the middle of it. Your husband didn't like it. We left and came here. You zoned out after that."

"God, it feels like they're getting worse."

"It's nothing to worry about. You got a little fuzzy. I brought you here to sleep it off."

"My head hurts."

Jessup offered a weak smile. "I think you were drunk."

"I suppose I should feel relieved."

She started to rise, but Jessup pulled her down. "I want you to listen to me very carefully, Abigail."

"What?"

"It's important. Something bad *did* happen, but you had nothing to do with it."

"Oh, God." She tried to rise again, but Jessup stopped her.

"Listen. You and the senator argued. I came in and the argument stopped. We left and came here. This is very important. We talked about Julian. We talked about what's been happening the past few days. We talked about what to get your husband for Christmas this year. We thought maybe some art. An oil painting from that gallery he likes in Washington. Do you remember this?" She shook her head, fear spreading. "This is what happened: You and the senator argued. I came in and the argument stopped."

She looked at the small window. Blue light thumping.

"We left and came here," Jessup continued. "Listen to me. We talked about Julian—"

"What's happening, Jessup?"

"We talked about art for your husband."

But she wasn't listening. She pulled herself free and went to the window. The room was partially underground, so the window was high. She stood on a stool, looked out.

Cops were in the drive.

"It's okay," Jessup said. "Abigail. Trust me."

"Jessup." The voice was tiny and scared.

"You did nothing wrong. You and the senator argued—"

"Jessup?"

A lot of cops were in the drive.

CHAPTER FIFTY-ONE

Michael went to ground at a hotel in Chapel Hill, and it played more or less how he thought it would. A night maid found the dead senator shortly after the cops found the bodies at the farm. The police kept quiet about the farm. It was too explosive, too much to get their heads around in the space of a day. But the murdered senator was a different story. They came respectfully at first; they did their preliminary workup, and then went after Abigail with a vengeance. Randall Vane was a billionaire, and he'd been shot dead in her room. Her alibi was the man who for twenty-five years had been her bodyguard and driver. The cops saw the same tired motives they'd seen a hundred times before, but Jessup circled the lawyers like a seasoned professional. He kept her out of custody for a full day, then the cops came with a warrant. They hit her hard for six hours of custodial interrogation, but Jessup had her prepped by then, and the cops eventually had to let her go. Michael got the call an hour later. The man was distraught.

"She's breaking. She thinks she did it."

"What do you mean, she *thinks* she did it. She did it. You told me as much."

"Oh, Jesus." Jessup sighed deeply. "It's complicated."

"I can handle complicated."

"This is killing her."

Michael weighed his options. "I think it's time we talked."

"I can't leave her right now. Julian is still missing. You've seen the news. Even the staff is avoiding her."

"Okay, okay. Tomorrow, then. Or the next day."

"Michael, listen. Nothing's happening the way you said. They're all over her. You understand? They're eating her alive. Cops. Media. You've seen the things they're saying?"

"I've seen."

And he had. They were saying she'd killed him for the money. They showed pictures of her and Jessup, and speculated on the nature of their relationship. It was a perfect story: bodies in the lake and the senator dead, sex and money and hired help. The woman was beautiful, her driver handsome, and they chose the pictures carefully: Abigail with her fine, pale skin and arched brows; Jessup holding her arm; a diamond the size of a quail's egg on her finger. With a phalanx of lawyers around her, she came off like a black widow, came off guilty.

"I don't know how much longer I can keep her together."

"Give it a day," Michael said.

"She might not make it that long. She's undone."

"A day," Michael said.

It took less than that. Someone in the police department leaked the farm, and the story exploded to a whole new level. Organized crime and a crooked politician. Blackmail and torture. Links to the violence in New York. The media went ballistic; lead story in every outlet. When the body bags rolled off the farm, camera crews caught it; they caught the feds, too. There was a small army of them: panel vans and black Suburbans, serious people in dark suits and stenciled Windbreakers. Abigail's real break, though, came unexpectedly from a quiet, diminutive lawyer that no one had yet thought to question.

His name was Wendell James Winthrop, an estate attorney who very quietly put the senator's will into probate. A junior detective took the time to check it out, and discovered that Abigail was not even in it, not for a dollar or a dime. She could spend a year in the house, and then leave with clothing, jewelry and personal effects. Even Julian was excluded. A billion dollars, and they got none of it.

Yet, it did this wonderful thing.

When the police learned there was no financial motive for murder, their case against Abigail evaporated. They had combed through the file a hundred times by then, and knew more about the dead senator than they would ever need to know.

He'd been blackmailed for years; he was dead.

Most or all of his blackmailers were dead.

The murder weapon was found with all the dead blackmailers.

In the highest circles of law enforcement, there was talk of another hitter, a cleaner who came in and took out everybody involved. Some of the organized crime people at the FBI whispered about Otto Kaitlin and the enforcer whose identity he'd worked so hard to keep secret, but even the whispers were quieter than most. No one had ever established the existence of such an enforcer. They had no name, no photographs, no description. To some, he was a myth fabricated by a very clever gangster, a bogeyman to scare grown men. In the end it was decided, very quietly, that the full truth might never come out.

While this was happening, Michael watched the news in his hotel room. He took long walks in Chapel Hill, ate dinner out and thought constantly of Elena. He wondered where she was, and if she would call or not. He fretted over her injuries, worried about the baby. He waited to hear from Julian, but that didn't happen, either. Two days after the farm story broke, Jessup finally called. "She's sleeping for the first time," he said.

"Is she okay?"

"Like a weight's been lifted. Like she finally believes she didn't do it."

Michael was silent, then said, "That's the second time you've made a reference like that."

"I know. It was intentional."

"Perhaps it's time you explained some things," Michael said.

"Perhaps it is."

They met in Raleigh because it was big and anonymous, and because old habits died hard. Michael watched him roll in and waited a full thirty minutes to make sure he was alone.

He was.

The restaurant sold ribs and beer and was empty at three o'clock in the afternoon. They took a table in a small back room; ordered a pitcher of beer and asked to be left alone. When the beer came, Michael poured two glasses and waited for Jessup to meet his eyes. When the wait got long, he decided to start easy. "Any word from Julian?"

Jessup dipped his head, relieved. "He came home yesterday. The medicine finally leveled him out. He's thinking straight." Jessup sipped, got foam on his lip and wiped it off. "Apparently, he's taken up with Victorine Gautreaux. She was watching after him."

"Where?"

"Holed up in the woods and scared to death."

"How is he?"

"Confused. Fragile. The usual. I'm still not sure he understands exactly what's happened. He wants to see you, though. He thought maybe he'd dreamed it, seeing you. He's like a kid with anticipation."

Michael spun the glass, watching Jessup. The man was clearly afraid of the conversation that was coming, and Michael had theories on that. Julian, he decided, might be a soft approach to the place they needed to go. "He saw Abigail kill Ronnie Saints, didn't he?"

Jessup drained his beer, poured another. "Oh, man . . ."

"In the boathouse. That's why he broke down," Michael said. "That's why he ran away. He saw her kill Ronnie Saints and couldn't process it."

"She had the best intentions." Jessup's head moved, eyes on the cold glass. "She just wanted them to apologize to Julian. She tracked them down, paid them—"

"And then killed them."

His eyes snapped up, then. "It wasn't like that. Abigail doesn't have a mean bone in her body. She's tough and honest and fair, but she's sweet as the day is long. She would never hurt anybody. Even the thought that she might hurt somebody—"

"It's just that she's schizophrenic."

Jessup licked his lips, eyes nailed to the table.

Michael leaned in on his elbows. "She told me how it works, you see. On our drive to the mountains, she told me how it runs in families."

"This is a mistake. I shouldn't be here."

But he didn't move, and Michael knew why. Secrets are hard; they weigh a man down. "See, Andrew Flint said something interesting when I was at Iron House. He was quite taken with Abigail on the day she came to adopt us. She was beautiful, rich. But that's not what stuck with him. She told him a story about why she cared about us, about Julian and me. She told Mr. Flint that she'd grown up in an orphanage herself, that she'd had a sister, that she had certain sympathies for older siblings left to linger in a place like Iron House. She told it with some conviction, apparently. That's what Flint said. She told it with feeling. Did you know she told him that?"

"I knew."

"And yet I met her mother in a dump house at the base of Slaughter Mountain. Arabella Jax. A charming lady. You met her, too."

"Oh, man."

He shook his head; Michael ignored his worry and sudden distress. "She says Abigail ran away from home when she was fourteen years old, which leaves me with the question, why did she lie to Andrew Flint? Most importantly, why did she care about us at all?"

Jessup leaned back in his chair. Pushed the glass away. "Why don't you tell me, smart guy?"

Michael swallowed in a throat that was suddenly dry. He thought of the love Abigail so clearly felt for Julian, and how she'd been willing to go to the farm and face down Jimmy on the chance of saving Michael's life. Ten million dollars. Thirty. She didn't care about the money or her own safety. And yet she'd been so very afraid. Then things went south in the barn, and her fear vanished. He saw the way she'd come off the floor to take Jimmy's hand at the wrist. She'd been a different woman, then, cold and smooth and violent. Michael had rarely seen such perfect timing and physical control; but she didn't even remember this thing she'd done.

Schizophrenia runs in families, she'd said.

Siblings.

Parents.

Michael's fingers felt uncertain on the glass, but he made his face a stone. "Is Abigail my mother?"

"You ask because she and Julian share the same affliction?"

"Because she cares more than she should. Because she had no reason to come for us in the first place."

Jessup poured another beer, and took his time doing it. He drank deeply, looked up and left, as if for God to give him a sign. "You asked once about Salina Slaughter." His eyes came back, red and heavy. "Let me tell you first about Arabella Jax. You saw the way she is?"

"I did."

"She was worse when Abigail was young, vile and selfish and rotten to the core. I swear . . ." Emotion rose in his eyes. "I've never worked so hard to keep from killing a woman."

"You went there to ask about Salina Slaughter?"

"Years ago. She didn't want to talk about it. Not about Abigail. Not about Salina." He nodded, lips tight. "We got there in the end."

"You hurt her."

"I'm not proud of it."

"She's still scared of you. She tried to blow my head off the second I mentioned Salina Slaughter. She thought you'd sent me."

"She's a ferocious bitch of a liar. I did what I did to get the truth."

"Because you love Abigail."

"Because I needed to know. Because I had to understand . . ." He rubbed both hands across his face. "Ah, shit."

"Just tell me."

It took a minute, then he said, "Arabella Jax had looks, once. I saw old photos in her house. She had looks and she had men. She worked for Serena Slaughter up on the mountain."

"I saw the ruins."

"A mansion," Jessup said. "Huge wealth, big parties, some that lasted days. People would come in from out of state. Politicians. Celebrities. Rich folks in limousines. Arabella Jax washed dishes, did laundry, cleaned up. It was not much of a life. She had no money, hated her boss but had nowhere else to go. When she was young, she had affairs with guests of the Slaughters. *Nasty, fancy men with pretty words and shiny watches.* That's how she described it to me. There were a number of them, apparently, wealthy men who liked to bang the help." Jessup met Michael's gaze, shrugged. "It fell off as she aged and her looks went. She wasn't sleeping with the pretty-boys anymore, but with gardeners and the stable hands and the local drunks. The only thing unusual about the story is the sheer magnitude of that woman's anger. Far as I can tell, resentment just ate her alive, and Abigail was there to see it happen. She'd go to the house some, too; play while her mother polished and scrubbed and whored around. Can you imagine how it must have been for Abigail at that tender age? Living as she did, and then seeing that mansion up close, the crystal and silver, servants and fancy parties. Watching envy break her mother down, then going home to all the dirt and nothing in that cracker-box house."

"She would pretend to be a girl named Salina Slaughter."

Jessup shook his head, voice cracking. "It wasn't pretend."

"She really was Serena's daughter?"

"No, that's not it. She had . . ." Jessup wiped at his eyes, then suddenly stood. "Give me a second." He moved to the window, turned his back and dipped his head. Michael looked away because it was hard to watch a grown man cry.

Jessup looked uncomfortable when he finally sat. "I'm sorry." He sniffed, wiped his nose on a napkin. "It's hard to love a wounded soul."

"Take your time," Michael said, and meant it. In spite of his violent nature, he had a deep respect for powerful emotions.

"Abigail had a brother," Jessup finally said. "A baby boy just a few months old. She was only ten, but she loved him like he was her own. She fed him, took care of him. Arabella Jax didn't much care for boys. She thought boys would grow up and run off like all men do; they would treat her badly, use her up. But daughters, she believed, would stay home. They would stay home and keep her as she got old."

"She wanted her own servants."

"Servants. Slaves. Somebody to hurt." Jessup drank beer and his hands shook.

"She had a brother," Michael prompted.

"The brother. Ah, God." Jessup scrubbed large, worn hands across his face, pulled the skin tight, then let the hands drop. "She made Abigail drown him in the creek." Michael rocked back; Jessup nodded bleakly. "She beat Abigail half to death, and then made her kill the one thing she loved. I think that's when her mind broke."

"And Salina Slaughter was born."

"She has no idea, Michael. Don't you see? Abigail . . ." He choked up. "That sweet, perfect soul. She doesn't even know Salina exists. She has blackouts, memory losses."

"But she suspects."

"She fears some version of the truth, yes. She invited George Nichols and Ronnie Saints here; then they turned up dead after she blacked out. Chase Johnson, too."

"That's the third body in the lake?"

Jessup nodded. "Then the senator was killed. Abigail's been terrified that she might have had something to do with it. But you fixed all that. The police think gangsters killed the senator; they think the boys from Iron House were somehow wrapped up in that. Maybe they were dropped in the lake to pressure the senator. Or maybe they were wrapped up with Stevan Kaitlin in some other way. The cops believe it's all connected, and Abigail is trying to do the same. She's like a new person."

"And yet you haven't answered my question."

Jessup sighed, unhappy. "Truth can be a tricky business."

"Is Abigail my mother?"

"All right, Michael. All right." Jessup sighed deeply, gathered himself. "Abigail didn't run away until she was fourteen. That's four more years she spent with Arabella Jax. Four years of abuse and deprivation. Four years for Salina Slaughter to take hold. Four years of hell . . ."

"Go on."

"Arabella Jax wanted daughters, but God had his own ideas, I guess, and gave her two boys, one strong and the other sickly. They were born in the back bedroom of the house you saw. They'd have probably died without Abigail. They slept in her bed. She kept them warm, kept them fed. Protected them." Jessup shook his head, then pushed on. "Arabella held off for a while, but the day came when she told Abigail to drown them, too. She wouldn't do it, though, no matter how much Arabella beat her. It went on for two weeks, the beatings and bleeding and denial."

Michael felt a sharp pain in his heart. "What are you saying?"

Jessup nodded at the hurt that was coming. "I'm saying she ran off rather than kill you boys."

Michael had to walk away from that. Jessup gave him twenty minutes, then paid the check and found him in the parking lot, hands in his pockets as traffic blew past.

"Abigail is my sister."

"Yes."

"Does she know you're telling me this?"

"No."

"Why not?"

Michael turned, and in his features Jessup saw a road map of grief. "She's not that poor, broken little girl anymore. She won't be. She can't be. This is where she's strong. This life."

"And yet she left us there to die."

"A child can only take so much, Michael. You, of all people, know that's true."

"I never abandoned Julian."

"Didn't you?"

"That's not how it was."

"And yet Julian was left alone until Abigail gathered him up."

Michael looked away.

"For what it's worth," Jessup said, "she has nightmares about it, crucifies herself with guilt. And don't forget that she came after you as soon as she possibly could. She found you at Iron House. She tried to give you a life."

"This is difficult."

"Yeah, no shit."

"I'm supposed to keep it to myself?"

Jessup understood. Telling Michael in the first place had not been an easy decision, but he'd sold his soul on the day he made Arabella Jax scream and beg and spill her guts. It would be nice for something good to come of it.

"I guess that's up to you," Jessup said. "I'm not sure how Julian would take it. He's half-convinced that what he saw in the boathouse was delusion, but only half-convinced. As a man, he needs structure. He needs to know the people around him are strong enough to watch his back and make a difference. I don't know that he could handle having a woman like Arabella Jax as his mother. It would be a brutal truth after all the love he's known."

Michael thought about that and decided Jessup was right. Not all cruelties were physical, and his brother would not easily endure such a revelation. "So, Julian doesn't know the truth, and Abigail doesn't know that I know?"

"Yes."

"You're asking an awful lot, Jessup. She's my sister. We're family. Do you understand how important that is to me? To Julian?"

"She can't know that you know. Facing that past would kill her. Knowing you're aware of what she did, knowing Julian is aware . . . She barely lives with herself now."

"Jesus."

"I'm sorry, Michael. I truly am."

Long moments passed, then Michael said, "How did Abigail get here?"

"What do you mean?"

"I saw the place she was raised. I met her mother . . ." He stalled at the thought of Arabella Jax being his mother, then shook off the anger and disgust. "How did she go from Slaughter Mountain to the place she is now?"

"Strength and will and character. I don't know what happened after she ran away, but she was only twenty-two when the senator met her. By that time, she'd put herself through college and spoke three languages fluently. She was working in an art gallery in Charlotte, and, I swear to God, Michael, you'd think she was fresh out of some European finishing school. She was that polished; that perfect. The senator fell for her overnight."

"Did she love him?"

"Does it matter?"

The sun slipped low, and Michael felt flush with emotion. Like he was drowning. Like his skin was too tight. "Abigail will always have doubts, you know. The senator died in her room. Julian thinks he saw her in the boathouse."

"We can live with doubts," Jessup said. "It's the knowing that breaks us."

"What about Salina Slaughter?"

"I can manage Salina."

"Yet three people are dead."

"Only one thing makes her violent."

"What's that?"

"A threat against you or Julian. The boys from Iron House. The senator." Jessup shrugged. "Salina considered them a risk. She's very protective of you."

"You put George Nichols in the lake? Chase Johnson?"

"To protect Abigail from what Salina had done."

"Why did you leave Ronnie Saints in the boathouse?"

"I didn't know about Ronnie," Jessup said. "Didn't know they were meeting. Didn't know she'd killed him until Caravel Gautreaux saw you put him in the lake."

"Caravel?" That was news.

"Creeping around in the dark, looking for her daughter, I suspect. She's too smart to come near the main house, what with the dogs and all; but she saw the body from a distance and called the police. Thought she had a chance to screw Abigail good, like twenty years of hate finally found a chance to let loose."

"What is it with those two?"

"Jealousy. Resentment." Jessup rolled his shoulders. "Who the hell knows?"

Michael pushed thoughts of Caravel Gautreaux from his head, felt all the things he'd learned. He had a sister he could never acknowledge, and a long-dead brother he would never have the chance to meet. He had choices to make, and a mother he might very well kill. "How did you learn about Salina Slaughter?"

"What do you mean?"

"You tracked down Arabella Jax; you learned all this."

"Yes."

"How did you know about Salina Slaughter in the first place?"

"Ah . . ."

"It's a simple question."

"Oh, shit." Jessup walked away, shaking his head. He stopped a few feet away, stuffed his hands in his pockets and looked at the sky.

"Jessup . . ."

"She torments me. It amuses her."

"I don't understand."

"Salina comes to me at night. I slept with her twice before I knew it was her. I thought it was Abigail. I told her I loved her. I thought . . . you know."

"But it was Salina?"

Jessup sighed, unhappy. "My life's been hell ever since."

CHAPTER FIFTY-TWO

Cool mist hung in the gorge as Michael turned the Rover onto the steep, muddy track that led to the creek where his brother had been drowned. The sun was below the ridge but rising, the morning still and gray as he rolled in, quiet. There were no license plates on the car, nothing to identify him. A few dogs lifted their heads, but they seemed as worn and uncaring as everything else.

Michael touched the gun beside him. He'd killed a lot of people over the years, but had never done so in anger or hate.

That was about to change.

He'd tried to move on after meeting with Falls, tried to sleep, but every time he closed his eyes he saw a dead brother and Julian broken; saw Abigail as a child in that cold and filthy house of horrors. He saw them as they could have been, then as they were, and it was like a wall of spinning mist, like he could stretch out a hand and touch a storm of ruined lives. Even now, the scope of her depravity confounded him. In a lifetime defined by violence and the code of violent men, Michael had never seen a soul as poisoned as his mother's. There was no restraint to her selfishness, no boundary. She'd made one child kill another, laughed about it.

And now the bitch was going to pay.

He moved deeper into the gorge, found Arabella Jax in bed and put the muzzle against her forehead. She woke clear-eyed and nasty. No confusion. No doubt about the gun in her face. "I told you no lies," she said.

"Do you know who I am?"

Her eyes rolled left, but Michael had already moved the shotgun. The room smelled of mildew, festering leg. Michael felt cold, quiet rage as he looked down on the woman who'd brought him into the world, then left him in the woods to die.

"Give me a cigarette," she said.

Michael pushed the barrel hard against her forehead, and the fear came out in her. Her mouth opened wide, fingers hooked in the sheets. "You drowned a baby in that creek," Michael said. "I want to know where he's buried."

A sly look spread on her face, wheels turning. "What's it to you?"

Two seconds passed. "He was my brother."

She processed that fast, eyes moving up him and then down. "Am I supposed to get all weepy, now?"

"You should probably get ready to die." Michael thumbed the hammer, but she shrugged off the threat.

"I heard somebody found you boys. They wrote about it in the paper."

"You could have just drowned us."

She laughed a bitter laugh. "There may not be a hell, but I don't plan on taking chances. That's Abigail's job." She pushed up in bed, as if daring him to pull the trigger. "I guess you know her after all, or you wouldn't be here."

Michael stepped back. "Get out of bed."

"Get me a cigarette."

Michael dragged her out of bed. She hit the ground with a thump, then stood, shaking and angry. There may have been fear left somewhere, but Michael couldn't see it. He snatched a robe off a chair, flung it at her. "Put it on."

"You ain't gonna shoot your own momma."

"Put it on."

"Outside of that cocksucker Jessup Falls, I ain't met a man yet with the strength to squeeze a grapefruit, let alone a trigger. If you were that kind of man, I'd be bleeding already. I'd be——"

Michael made her bleed. He whipped the gun and hit her hard enough to knock her down on the bed. A red line oozed on her cheek;

after that, she cooperated. The robe went on, fuzzy slippers that used to be pink. She took a cane off the back of a chair and limped outside, slow and stunned and wary. Light was beginning to filter down, and the hollow yellowed out as they followed a narrow footpath around the shack and then into the woods. She looked back twice, then said, "You going to kill me?"

"Maybe I'll break your legs and leave you out here to die."

"You wouldn't."

"Thinking about it."

They walked for five minutes, forest pushing in. She stumbled once, and caught herself. "Where's the other one?"

"Other what?"

"Where's your brother?"

"Just keep walking."

They came to a place where a beech tree rose up, ancient and gray-skinned and proud. On its bark, someone had long ago carved a cross above the initials RJ. The carvings had stretched as the tree grew; now they were wide and rough, barely legible above a patch of smooth ground. "Well, there you go." She waved a spotty hand. "Satisfied?"

The markings had been carved deep, and when Michael touched them he knew that Abigail had been the one to put them there. He tried to see her as she must have been, ten years old and bone thin, straining hard to make the lines of the cross so straight and true. "What was his name?"

"Give me a hundred dollars and I'll tell you."

"Tell me or I put a bullet in your head."

Her lips pursed, and she said, "Robert."

"Robert." He touched the markings again and looked at his mother. "What did he look like?"

"Trouble with a big damn T." She waved a hand. "All you boys did."

Michael felt new rage. "You should have gone away for this. You should have fried."

"And if there was justice in the world, I'd be living rich or holding that gun. But that ain't the world God made. Now . . ." She thumped the tree with her cane. "You seen it. You said your piece. Now, give an old lady a few dollars or go on and get the hell out."

"Did you say justice?"

"You heard me."

Michael felt the gun in his hand and it felt like the hand of God, like the universe rolled back to show the meaning of poetry and purpose. This woman had made him a killer so that he might one day kill this woman. It was a circle so perfect it smelled of providence. The gun came up and it was light in his hand. Mountain air tasted fresh in his throat. He could kill her now and bring closure to what remained of his family. Abigail would be free, Robert's death avenged. Justice for the boys he and Julian had been.

"Do it," she said.

He stared into her eyes, and saw nothing.

"Fucking do it!"

But even as the trigger creaked under his finger, Michael pictured Otto Kaitlin, who'd raised him to be better than the things he did. He thought of Elena, and the man she wished him to be, then of his own child and the father it deserved. He thought of the future he wanted.

The gun came down.

"I knew it, you pussy." She spit on the dirt. "You limp-dick, red-assed cocksucker."

Michael looked at the ravaged leg and unrepentant eyes, the cracked lips and bitterness. "I hope you live a very long time," he said, and walked away.

He made it fifteen feet before she called after him. "Did Abigail tell you your real name?"

Michael looked back, momentarily undone as spite spread on his mother's face. It was an orphan's ultimate question. Who are my parents? What is my name?

"She didn't tell you Robert's name, so I'm guessing she didn't tell you yours, either. She didn't, did she? Selfish little brat."

"We're done here." Michael started walking. She raised her voice.

"Whatever they named you at that orphanage ain't the name God will know you by! That name comes from me!"

Leaves slapped at his face. The ground was smooth and damp.

"A momma leaves a mark when she names a child!"

402

Michael turned. "I want nothing from you."

"What about your father's name? You want that?" Michael raised the gun, pointed it at the soft place beneath her chin. "We already know you don't have the guts."

Michael put a shot past both sides of her head, the bullets so close and fast they lifted hair.

She froze, mouth open and dead silent. Michael said, "Next one goes in your right eye." She risked a step back, and Michael matched her movement, the forest very green around them. "No one would miss you. No one out here would even care."

Arabella held perfectly still, a cigarette smoldering between two fingers. Behind her, the gulley dropped off forty feet, water creaming white at the bottom. "You want your real name or not?"

"Not."

"Then you're nothing."

"I disagree."

"You have nothing."

"I have eighty million dollars," Michael said. "I have a brother and a sister, a family of my own." He dropped the hammer on the gun, slipped it under his belt. "What do *you* have?"

CHAPTER FIFTY-THREE

Two days later, the last reporters left Chatham County. The police were finished with Abigail and Julian; the feds were gone, headlines fading as bodies were buried and the investigation moved north. Late-morning sun slanted through Julian's window as he stood before the tall mirror and finished knotting a silk tie. His suit was pressed and dark; he was anxious.

"May I come in?"

Abigail stood in the open door, a half-smile on her face.

"Sure."

She crossed the room and stood beside him, peering into the mirror. "So serious," she said.

"Don't."

"So thin."

"Please."

"I'm sorry." She moved in front of him, adjusted his tie and then ran fingers down his lapels. "You're right. It's just that the world has been so serious. We should be the opposite. You're safe. You're well."

"I don't feel well."

He was pale and terribly thin. The suit hung from his frame. "You'll be okay, sweetheart."

"I don't know." Julian held very still, eyes large and wounded as he studied his image in the mirror. "I feel . . . divided."

"You don't mean . . . ?"

She was thinking of his schizophrenia, so Julian shook his head. "Not like that, no. It's just . . ."

"What?"

She peered up, worried for him, frightened of a world that, to her, looked so thin beneath his feet. It had always been like that, soft words and troubled looks, the conviction he would melt as slow and sure as newsprint dropped on an empty sea. He shook his head, unwilling to talk about it. "I'm nervous, I guess."

"Your name is known in forty countries," Abigail said. "You've sold millions of books. I've seen you speak to a room of thousands . . ."

"This is different."

"Why?"

Urgency gave weight to her question. The moment stretched, and Julian felt a connection between them, a bond that was real and strong and dark with things unsaid.

"It just is."

It was a child's answer, and he knew it. Yet, how could he explain that this was not about knowledge or strength or the man he'd set out to be? No matter what he accomplished, he would always be the boy from Iron House. He would always feel hunted and exposed, a half step too close to shadowed corners. He could bury such feelings for a while, but there was only so much dirt in the world. And that was the problem. For as wonderful as Michael's presence was, it reminded Julian of secrets and shadows, of roots in loose soil and the unforgivable thing he'd done. He was everything his mother said, yet had stabbed a boy in the throat and let his brother take the blame.

"Suppose he doesn't care for the man I've become?"

Abigail smiled and pressed her palms on his chest.

"You're an artist and exceptionally kind. You're a wonderful son. A fine man."

"Does he know I take medicine? That I'm, you know . . ."

"He knows." She nodded, her fingers again on his tie. "He understands."

Julian caught her hands, and felt words tunnel from some deep place. "What if he hates me?"

His fingers tightened on hers, but she laughed the question off. "He's your brother, and he loves you. He's family."

Julian nodded, though she had to be wrong. "You're probably right."

405

"I know I am."

He stepped away, looked in the mirror and saw eyes that were too naked for the world outside. Michael would look into them and see all the way down. "Does this suit look okay? I could wear the navy with chalk stripes." She studied him, pensive, and he said, "What do you think?"

"I think you shouldn't try so hard. The suit. The expensive shoes." She cupped his face, kissed him on the forehead. "He's your brother, Julian. Be yourself, and don't worry so much."

"I'll try," he said.

"Smile for me, now." She waited for the smile, then wiped an imaginary smudge from his cheek. "Ten minutes. I'll meet you out front."

She left, and Julian watched his smile fall apart. In the mirror, he was tall and thin and perfectly dressed; but that's not what he saw. He saw the boy who'd put a knife in Hennessey's throat and let his brother take the blame, the same boy Michael would see, the weakling and the failure, the child he'd been. He swallowed past a lump in his throat, then took off the suit and hung it in the closet. His arms were thin, his chest bony. He felt guilt for all the wonderful things in his room, for the mother and the money and all the other things Michael had lost when he took the knife and ran into the snow. He felt guilt for his life, then sat on the bed and hugged himself as small certainties crumbled like sand. "Make me like Michael," he said. "Make me strong."

But in the mirror he was pale and weak and small.

"Please don't let him hate me . . ."

He listened for an echo in his mind, but heard only silence.

"Please, God . . ."

He put on jeans and tucked in a shirt.

"Please don't let him hate me."

Jessup drove them to a small park forty miles from the estate. It was anonymous, he said, a good place to meet far from prying eyes. "You guys okay back there?"

"We're fine," Abigail said.

But Julian's mouth was dry; his hands itched. "Are we late?"

"Right on time." Jessup turned into the park, and followed a narrow lane to a shady place with benches and tables and views of a lake. Julian saw a car parked by itself, a man alone by the hood.

"Is that him?"

"It is," Abigail said.

They drew close, and Michael stepped out to meet them. Julian took his mother's hand. "Will you come with me?"

"This is for you and Michael."

Julian peered out. "He looks stern."

She smiled and said, "He always looks like that."

Julian hesitated, terrified. "I'm frightened," he said.

"Don't be."

"But what if . . . ?" The words trailed off, and he heard the rest in silence.

What if he hates me?

What if he looks into my soul and simply leaves?

"Have faith." She squeezed his hand. "Be strong."

Julian took a deep breath, then opened the door and stepped out as if onto another planet. Colors were too bright, the sun like a palm on his cheek. Michael looked tall and broad, and Julian studied the lines on his face as they walked toward each other. He looked for reason to hope, for something to take the great, giant weight off his chest. When they were two feet away, Michael said, "Hello, Julian."

A vacuum opened in Julian's head and sucked away every clear thought he had. Michael looked the same, but different. Slight stubble covered his cheeks and his eyes were very bright. His hands were large and twitched once as Julian looked for words and failed.

"I . . ."

His voice was a bare whisper, but Michael nodded, the clean lines of his brow coming down, eyes softening. Julian saw then how he would draw him, a square-shouldered man with one hand rising up, head tilted slightly down as he said, "It's okay."

Michael stepped closer.

"I'm sorry," Julian said.

Michael's hand settled on the back of Julian's neck. He was shaking his head, but smiling. "For what?"

"I'm so sorry . . ."

Then the arms wrapped Julian up. He felt heat and strength—his brother—and there was no anger in him. His cheek was rough on Julian's, something warm and wet. "It's okay," Michael said.

He was crying.

"We're okay."

They met again the next day, and the day after that. They sat in the sun and talked, and it was a strange thing for both of them. So many years had passed; so many things had changed. But they were brothers, so they found their path. They talked and they grew and their time apart seemed less monumental. Michael didn't tell Julian everything about his life—not the killing, not yet—but he opened up about Elena and the baby, spoke with great truth about the things that truly mattered.

"You still haven't heard from her?"

"Not yet, no."

There was pain there, raw and deep. "I might be in love, too," Julian said.

Michael looked across the park to where Abigail sat at a picnic table with Victorine Gautreaux. They, too, were trying, but the struggle was hard to watch. A gulf still existed between them, but occasionally they laughed. "Tell me about her," Michael said.

They were sitting on a bench in the same park. Shade made the place cool, and children played across the lawn. Julian watched a small boy kick a ball, then said, "She's a lot like us."

"Screwed up?"

Julian laughed awkwardly. "Yeah."

Michael nudged him with a shoulder, smiled. "The poor girl."

"Are you serious?"

Julian looked worried, so Michael shook his head. "She's beautiful and strong. She knows what she wants."

"I'd like to marry her, I think."

Michael looked at the girl, saw cold blue eyes and the careful mask that hid her fear. He thought of her childhood, and what he knew of Abigail's. "You should do that," he said.

"Yeah?"

He nodded, certain. "You should do that soon."

Those times in the park were the best parts of Michael's day. Afterward, he would return to the hotel and stare for long hours at his silent phone. Abigail had asked him twice to stay at the house, but he'd declined, pleading the need for discretion. But that was only part of it. He needed time to be alone, time to miss his woman and mourn.

Jessup called once, and asked to meet. "Abigail doesn't know," he said. "This is just me talking."

"Where?" Michael asked.

They met in a parking lot halfway between the estate and Chapel Hill. Jessup was in the Land Rover; Michael slid into the front seat beside him. "How's Julian?" he asked.

"Better, I think. You've seen him."

"He puts on a strong face."

"You should see him with Victorine, though. She's hard and opinionated and ignorant about a million things—but she's smart and fierce and unbelievably talented. She's good for him. They fit in a way that's satisfying to watch."

Michael nodded because that was his read, too. One was strong, the other less so. Both damaged, both artists. "How about you and Abigail?"

"There's a wall between us," Jessup said.

"You should tear it down."

"I don't know . . ."

"Tear it down," Michael said. "Don't wait. Just do it. Talk to her. Tell her."

"Look, this is not really why I called you."

"I'm sure it's not."

"Abigail asked me to go through some of the senator's effects. Papers, files she lacked the heart for. I found some things you might be interested in."

"For instance?"

"The senator had the autopsy report on the girl that drowned all those years ago."

"Christina?"

"Christina Carpenter, yes. He had the report in his private safe. It turns out she'd had an abortion the day before she died. The cops kept it quiet, but the senator knew."

"And didn't tell Abigail."

"For whatever reason."

Michael thought about that: a teenage girl dies the day after an abortion. There was a lot of emotion wrapped up in that simple scenario, a lot of tension, too. "Was Julian the father?"

"Blood type was inconsistent. I don't know. Maybe she drowned herself on purpose. She was a kid with religious parents and an unplanned pregnancy. Maybe Julian tried to save her but couldn't."

"It would explain the skin under his nails, why he was wet . . ."

"And why he couldn't remember anything. It would have been traumatic."

"Maybe the senator was the father."

"That could explain why he kept the autopsy records. Hell, maybe the senator killed her."

Michael lingered over another possibility. "Maybe Salina did."

"Don't even joke about that."

But both men were thinking.

"You said you had a few things to talk about. What else?"

"This is just for you, okay?"

"Okay."

Jessup glanced away, lips thin and tight.

"What?" Michael asked.

"Fuck it." Jessup pulled a thin file from beside his seat. "This was in the senator's safe, too."

He handed the file over, and Michael opened it. "These are medical records."

"Abigail's."

Michael flipped pages, and Jessup said, "I thought you should know how badly she wanted to bring you boys home."

The comment made little sense, but then it did. "She had a tubal ligation."

"Shortly after she married. She never told the senator."

"But he found out," Michael said.

"He had the file, yes. I suspect he figured it out right before they moved into separate bedrooms. Whether he confronted her, I don't know."

"She told me they were unable to conceive."

"That's what she told the world. It's how she convinced him to adopt."

Michael closed the file, and Jessup took it from numb fingers.

"She wanted to bring you boys home, Michael. She wanted to make you safe and whole and loved."

The next time they met, it was just the three of them—Michael and Julian and Abigail—and it was strange how much that corner of shade and grass felt like their special place in the world. They sat at the same table under the same tree, and saw children that looked familiar. Words came easier; responses were less guarded. Yet, a subtle unease persisted, and Michael wondered if the problem was his alone. He glanced at Abigail, who looked rested but not quite at peace. He wanted to tell her that he knew the truth, to offer forgiveness for the way she'd left them and thank her for the things she'd done. Maybe that would afford her a measure of respite, a path to clearer skies. But Abigail made a good mother to Julian, and Julian made a good son. Michael saw respect and love and comfort. Dragging out the truth would help nobody, so he let the truth lie. He enjoyed this moment in the sun, and left Arabella Jax where she belonged, unspoken of and unloved, quietly rotting in the small shack the three of them had once known as children.

They took a brief walk along the shore, and Michael felt healing in his leg. As the day wore on, they returned to the table and had white wine in plastic cups, though a sign at the entrance declared it against the rules. Julian fretted and fussed and worried about cops, all of which made Abigail laugh and Michael smile. When the bottle was nearly empty, Michael caught Abigail's eye, and said, "I heard about the senator's will." She tried to interrupt, but Michael held up a hand. "I have plenty of money. It's yours."

She took his hand and smiled. "That's kind of you, but unnecessary."

"But the paper said you could only take jewelry and personal effects . . ."

Abigail laughed, and the sound was pure joy. "Oh, Michael. My jewelry alone appraises at twelve million dollars, and the art Randall gave me is worth twice that. The house in Charlotte is in my name, the house in Aspen." She shook her head. "Randall was not as bad as the papers made him sound. We were in love once, and that mattered to both of us. He indulged me, made investments in my name. That reminds me. I have something for you boys."

She fished in the wine basket and came out with two small boxes that were elegantly wrapped. She handed one to Michael, the other to Julian. "Open."

Michael thumbed off the ribbon and tore the paper. Inside the box was a cigarette lighter made of gold and platinum. His name was engraved on the side. Julian had a similar one. "I don't understand."

"It's a keepsake," Abigail said. "A reminder."

"Of what?"

"New beginnings."

Michael looked at Julian, and she smiled because no one understood.

"Randall gave me another gift," she said. "When the orphanage closed, he bought it for me. The buildings, the grounds. All of it."

"But why?" Michael asked.

"Partly because I wanted to keep Andrew Flint close. Mostly, I wanted to own it in case this day ever came."

"I still don't understand."

She gestured at the lighter Michael held. "Turn it over."

He did as she asked. The other side was engraved, too.

Iron House

"Burn it." She reached across the table, took both their hands. "Burn it to the ground, and then let it go."

CHAPTER FIFTY-FOUR

Andrew Flint was gone when they got to Iron House. The gate stood wide, the old house empty. When Michael told Julian about Billy Walker, he found his brother strangely silent. He stood by the patched door and gazed up at the third-floor corner room in which they'd lived. "Flint had all your books," Michael said. "I think he read them to Billy."

"It's not why I wrote them."

"I know it's not."

"I wrote them to teach children about evil, not for evil children to read them."

"I don't think Billy's evil anymore."

A light breeze ruffled the grass, and Julian closed his eyes as dusk gathered in the valley. It was very silent where they stood, just wind and the slow churn of memory. "They're really dead."

He meant Ronnie Saints, George Nichols and Chase Johnson. Michael stripped a tall weed from the ground. "Dead and gone."

Julian opened his eyes and they caught a glint of red sun. "Do you know how they died, Michael?"

Julian was thinking about the boathouse, about the memory fragments still buried in his mind. He saw Abigail kill Ronnie Saints. But was it real or delusion? That's what he really wanted to know. Michael thought for less than half a second, then rolled his shoulders and said, "I don't think it really matters."

And he believed that. Because Michael's job was still to protect his brother; because what Jessup had said was right.

We can all live with doubts.

It's the knowing that breaks us.

"I'm sorry I killed Hennessey."

Michael put his arm around Julian's neck and said, "Fuck that kid. He was a dick."

"Yeah?"

Michael squeezed tight and said, "Julian, my brother, I think it's time to build a very large fire."

They made their way to the front door. Michael used the key Abigail had given him. "Do you want to see anything first? Our room? Anything?"

"Why?"

Michael liked that answer, because it was damn good. Because it fit the man Julian needed to be. They went to the subbasement so the place would burn from the bottom up. They piled boxes and busted furniture and bundles of rotted cloth. They put on everything they could find, until the pile was so tall they had to throw stuff to get it on top. "That's what I'm talking about," Michael said.

The mound rose eight feet and was another ten feet wide at the base. Stepping back, breath short, Julian stared for a long time, then asked, "Do you remember what old man Dredge told me?"

"Sunlight and silver stairs?" Michael asked.

"Doors to better places."

"I remember."

Julian struggled for a moment, then asked, "Do you think there are such things?"

"Doors to better places?" Michael flattened his palm and showed the lighter. "I think we're going to make one right now. Do you have your lighter?"

Julian pulled it warm from his pocket, a scared, delighted grin on his face. "We're really doing this."

"You want to go first?" Michael asked.

"Together."

Michael bent, Julian three feet away. "Wouldn't it be funny if she forgot to put in lighter fluid?"

Julian laughed, and they lit the fire that would bring Iron House down. Flames licked up piled boxes and they moved for the door as it reached the ceiling. They stood for a full minute, watching as Julian turned the lighter in his fingers, then slipped it into his pocket. "Do you feel anything?" Michael asked.

"I feel warm."

"Are you being funny?"

"All kinds of warm."

They watched until it was too hot to stay, then made their way up and out, drove to the high, metal gate, then got out of the car to watch yellow fingers stroke the basement glass. "Soon," Michael said, and Julian touched the place above his heart.

"Mom should have come."

But Michael shook his head. "This is for us."

"Are you happy?" Julian nodded toward Iron House.

"Shhh." Michael said it gently. "Just watch."

So they watched as night fell and cool air spilled from the face of the mountain. Michael draped an arm across his brother's shoulders, and they stood in silence as glass shattered from the heat, as smoke poured out and Iron House burned.

CHAPTER FIFTY-FIVE

The next days were bittersweet for Michael as Julian's step grew light and Abigail found increasing joy in the sight of this long-troubled man moving with slow but steady grace into a better life. He would never be a strong man, but the destruction of Iron House gave him a confidence she'd never seen. She and Michael discussed it once over drinks on the terrace.

"Maybe it was the death of those boys," Michael said.

"Or Victorine Gautreaux."

Michael watched a boat move on the water. It was far away, but he thought he saw Victorine laugh. "She's good for him, isn't she?"

Abigail nodded, but her eyes were cloudy. "I keep looking for signs of her mother," she said. Michael understood. Family was a powerful force—it could shape you, build you up or ruin you—and it was that force that made Michael's days so unexpectedly difficult to endure. Abigail and Julian shared a connection built over years, and there was so much history there, so much understanding that Michael felt apart. They were mother and son, for better or worse, and it was hard to watch an intimacy he would never share, hard to know the truth and feel such love in secret.

She was his sister, but only in blood.

They were brothers, but so very far apart.

They all tried, of course, but Michael found, as two days grew to five, that he thought often of Otto Kaitlin. Like Abigail and Julian, they'd walked a bridge built on decades of trust and time and mutual sacrifice. And bridges like that were strong; they felt good under one's feet. So while Michael would always be welcome, while Abigail and Julian worked day and night to make him *know* that fact, he kept his phone in his pocket at all times. He waited for Elena to call and slept at night dreaming of his own family—a wife and child—the dream that started all this in the first place. Until the day came when he could no longer sit still.

"Where will you go?" Abigail asked.

"I'm not exactly sure."

"Will we see you again?" Julian's voice broke when he said it, and every ounce of new confidence melted as he tried very hard not to beg. "We're just getting started . . . We're just . . ." He looked from Abigail to Michael. "Come on, man. You can't just leave."

"It won't be like it was. We'll see each other before you know it."

"Do you promise?"

"I do."

The boy came out in Julian's face, all the fear and need. "Do you swear?"

Michael hugged him fiercely. "I swear."

They said their good-byes at the house, in private, then Jessup drove Michael to airport in Raleigh. They spoke little, but that was okay. "Where do you want me to drop you?" Jessup asked.

"American Airlines."

"Abigail said you don't know where you're going."

"I don't."

"Okay." Jessup followed signs to American Airlines, then pulled to the curb and stopped. Through big glass walls they saw a crush of normal people doing normal things. "Here you go," he said, but Michael made no move to get out.

"Victorine and Julian may get serious," he said.

"Yeah, maybe."

"The senator's dead. I'm leaving."

"What's your point?"

Michael turned in his seat. "She may find herself very alone."

"You mean Abigail."

"You know exactly what I mean."

"She'll think I'm after her money." He shook his head sadly. "It's been twenty-five years . . ."

"She needs you."

The line of Jessup's jaw grew firm. "I'll always take care of her."

"It's not the same and you know it." Michael opened his door. "You should speak your mind."

"And you should leave a man to tend his own business."

Michael stared long enough to see Jessup swallow once, then climbed out and leaned back in to study the older man's face. He saw strong lines etched by sacrifice and worry; saw want and need and deep, abiding fear. He dug for words of encouragement, but in the end said nothing. Because Jessup was right: a man should tend his own business, especially when it involved the heart. He would find the strength or not; live alone or take her hand. "Thanks for the ride," Michael said.

"Anytime."

Michael closed the door and thumped the roof. He went inside—no luggage or ticket—then turned before the crowd could swallow him. He saw Jessup through the glass. Pale and still, he stared a thousand yards into nothing. Michael watched for several minutes, then the man dipped his head once and the car pulled slowly away.

It took Michael another ten minutes to find the man he was looking for. Same clothes, same hat. "Do you remember me?" Michael asked.

"Hey, thousand-dollar man!"

The skycap's face lit up, teeth big and white. Michael eased a thick wad of cash from his pocket. "How'd you like to make another five?"

"Thousand?"

"Thousand," Michael said, and started peeling off bills.

CHAPTER FIFTY-SIX

FIVE MONTHS LATER

Michael sat in a crowded café in the heart of Barcelona. His table was by the window, and he looked up often to watch people pass. A pretty girl brought him more coffee, and smiled as he tried new Catalan words and got them wrong. She corrected him, then flashed a bright smile and laughed as she moved on to another table.

Michael made a note in the margins of a thick, battered book. This was his regular place, and though everyone knew his name, that was about all they knew. He was a quiet American who kept to himself and tipped well. He lived on a narrow, cobbled street around the corner, in an apartment with a red door. He was always polite, but some of the waitresses found him sad, and worried at the cause. More than one had tried to take him home at the end of a long night, but he always gave the same answer.

Estic esperant a algú.

I'm waiting for someone.

And that's how Michael saw it, as a wait. He told himself the same thing every day.

She will call.

Yet, five months had passed. The skycap could tell Michael only that Elena had caught the flight to Madrid; after that, he had no idea. Not much for five thousand dollars, but Michael considered it a bargain just to know. So, he'd flown to Madrid, and from there to Barcelona, which was the beating heart of Catalonia. He didn't expect to find her here—the city had millions of residents—but that was okay, too. He just wanted to be close.

To be near.

So, he found an apartment on a narrow, crooked street. He ate local food and studied Catalan because that was the language Elena's father spoke, and because his child would one day speak that language. What surprised Michael was how much he enjoyed learning it. How much he enjoyed life in a strange country. How much he enjoyed life. It was only at night that he doubted, and the hours before dawn were often long with worry and regret. But the sun always rose, and each day began with the same thought.

She will call.

Michael sipped his coffee and touched the window with a finger. It was cold outside, winter. He took a last sip and paid his bill. As he stepped outside, he thought of all the villages high in the Pyrenees and wondered which was hers.

He rounded onto his street and ducked his head as cold wind hit. It whistled over cobblestones and through shutters, keened so high that Michael didn't hear his phone ringing until he was through the door and inside. For a second he was confused, but only for that second. He ripped his coat open and dug inside for the phone. It rang a third time before he got a hand on it. He pulled it out, didn't recognize the number. "Hello, hello."

He heard static and background noise. Voices. Metal on metal. "Michael?"

"Elena. Baby."

Static scratched, and her voice faded. "Oh, God. I'm so sorry . . ."

"Elena, what? I can barely hear you."

"The baby's coming."

She faded. "Elena!"

". . . don't know what to say. I thought I had time, but the baby's coming early. I'm sorry, Michael. I'm so sorry. I wanted you to be here. I was going to call. Oh. God . . ."

She made a loud, terrible noise and Michael heard voices in Catalan. Intercom sounds. "Where are you? Tell me where you are."

It took long seconds, and Michael recognized hospital noises. She was on a gurney, he thought. Stern voices that had to be doctors.

"What hospital? What town?"

"Ahhh . . ."

"Baby. What hospital?"

She told him between heavy breaths—a hospital, a town. For an instant, the static faded and he heard her perfectly. "It's coming. It's coming."

Then someone took the phone and hung it up.

Michael tried to call back, but the phone was dead. He stared at the wall for long seconds, utterly frozen for the first time in his life. She'd called; the baby was coming. His mind was locked tight. But then the paralysis broke. He tore through the apartment until he found a map and his keys. "What else do I need? Think! Think!"

But, he needed nothing else. Wallet. Keys. Map.

He squeezed into the tiny car in the tiny garage; his hands shook as he opened the map and found the road that would take him to Elena. He started the car, pulled out onto crowded, icy streets and fought his way to the open roads that ran fast and true to the north. He pushed it until the little car shook.

The baby is coming, he thought.

The baby is coming.

But that was not entirely true. Elena labored for three and a half hours.

He made it with eight minutes to spare.

ACKNOWLEDGMENTS

A time came in the writing of this book where I almost walked away from it. It was just one of those things, a prolonged moment of doubt and discouragement. Nothing was working as I hoped; the pages fought me. I might have done it, too—let it fall, started something else—if not for my editor, Pete Wolverton, and my publisher, Matthew Shear, who read the first big piece of the manuscript, saw the potential, and assured me that I could pull it off. Their confidence saw me through a few long months, and I would like to thank them first and above all. Matthew, Pete . . . this book would never have happened without you. Thanks for the faith, and for keeping my feet on the trail.

I would also like to thank the other members of my editorial team, Anne Bensson and Katie Gilligan. Your keen insights made the book better every time you looked at it. Thanks for that! And thanks again to you, Pete. Every trip south is worth it.

For the fire being built under *Iron House,* my publishers deserve tremendous appreciation. Sally Richardson, Matthew Shear, Tom Dunne . . . I know you oversee a lot of books, but always felt your eye on this one. Few great things happen without you firmly behind a novel, and I thank you for having faith in what I do.

In the marketing of this book, Matt Baldacci, as always, does a fabulous job, as does his team, Nancy Trypuc and Kim Ludlam. My publicists, Stephen Lee and Dori Weintraub, are spectacular. Thank you both for all you've done. I truly appreciate it. Thanks as well to Kenneth J. Silver, the production editor, Cathy Turiano, the production manager, and Jonathan Bennett who did the interior design. You guys make a beautiful book, and I do love a beautiful book! I would also like to thank my copy editor, Steven A. Roman, who tries very hard to keep me from embarrassing myself. Any errors in the book are mine, not his. I also need to thank the many people in the Art Department who worked diligently to create the right jacket. Never an easy job. As always, I'd like to give an especially loud shout-out to the hardworking sales force at St. Martins Press and Griffin Books. Mickey Choate deserves my gratitude, as does Esther Newberg. You are both wonderful, wonderful agents.

I also need to thank my great friend, Neal Sansovich, whose pure heart and perpetual optimism lifted me from some dark troughs when the days got especially long. Your friendship means a lot to me, Neal. Thanks for deep talks and good soil.

I come at last to the most important people of all. Only the family of working writers understands the unique challenge of living with a novelist. The process takes a while; we tend to get distracted and work strange hours. The process is not always pretty, and no one deserves a deeper bow of appreciation than my wife, Katie and my girls, Saylor and Sophie. I'd be nothing without you.